THE
REINCARNATION
LIBRARY

Seven Journeys

BY

DOROTA FLATAU

(*Author of "Yellow English" and "Bait."*

Æ

AEON PUBLISHING COMPANY

MAMARONECK   NEW YORK

2000

First Published 1920

© 1999 by Aeon Publishing Company, LLC
All rights reserved.

ISBN: 1-893766-02-0

Library of Congress Card Catalog Number: 98-76190

Æ, Aeon, Aeon Books and The Reincarnation Library
are trademarks and service marks of
Aeon Publishing Company, LLC.

Printed and bound in The United States of America.

CONTENTS

THE BIRTH 1

FIRST JOURNEY 3

SECOND JOURNEY 39

THIRD JOURNEY 93

FOURTH JOURNEY 141

FIFTH JOURNEY 203

SIXTH JOURNEY 261

SEVENTH JOURNEY 285

FIRST JOURNEY: PRIMEVAL	SECOND JOURNEY: CRETE	THIRD JOURNEY: INDIA	FOURTH JOURNEY: CHINA
Anus → Dimidia's widowed mother	*Lucarius* → Head Ephor of Crete; Rhoea's father	→	*Yu-Cho* → Wealthy ship owner; father of Yu-Chi-So
Dimidia → Rhoea's jealous rival	*Dimidia* → Rhoea's devoted slave	*Dimidia* → Young friend of Ugisa	*Me-Dyah* → Arranged wife of Yu-Chi-So; jealous of Aré-yah
Rhoea → Huntress; captive mate of Ugiso	*Rhoea* → Patrician; aspirant to throne as Queen; daughter of Lucarius and Deseré	*Rhea* → Haughty Maharajah of Martand; squanders kingdom to win Ugisa	*Aré-yah* → Tea-house courtesan; mistress and friend of Yu-Chi-Soh
Ugiso → Hunter/Warrior	*Ugiso* → Syrian slave; Dimidia's fiancé; Rhoea's lover	*Ugisa* → Rhea's unwilling mistress, corrupted by his excesses	*Yu-Chi-Soh* → Husband to Me-Dyah; dissipated merchant
Ruipi → Chief; Rhea's unwanted suitor; Deseré's mate	*Ruipi* → Cruel King of Crete	*Ruipi* → Former Prince of Avantipur; woodcutter	*Lui-Peh* → Temple Monk or "Lordly One"; friend to young Aré-yah
Deseré → Wife of Ruipi	*Deseré* → Former wife of Lucarius; forced mistress of Ruipi	*Deseré* → Flees to forest to avoid Ruipi	*Deseré* → Matron of Venice forced to marry for money
	Ito → Philosopher, Drunkard, Gossip	*Yogi* → Ascetic, wise-one	→
			Wong-Chu → Aré-ya's rich young lover

Journeys

FIFTH JOURNEY:
FRANCE

Monsieur Denys ➤
Blind fan-maker;
grandpapa of Rhoea
& Dimidia

Dimidia Denys ➤
Mean spirited half-
sister of Rhoea

Rhoea Denys ➤
Hard-working
Parisian fan-maker

Ugiso d'Elbrai ➤
Drug abusing
aristocrat; friend
to Rhoea

Ruipi du Buisson ➤
Virtuous Marquis;
friend to Rhoea

Madame Valeron ➤
Widow desirous of
entering aristocratic
society via marriage

Monsignor Tullia di Masino
Falsely accused prisoner;
at peace with himself

Count Filippe de ➤
Maureaux
Court dandy;
Dimidia's husband

SIXTH JOURNEY:
SICILY

Marietta ➤
"The Witch"; aids
Dimidia when
no one else would

Dimidia Torretta ➤
Brings shame to
House of Torretta;
younger sister to Ruipi

Rhoea Serrafia ➤
Kind friend to Ugiso;
charitable signorina

Ugiso Torretta ➤
Young cripple
condemned to work
in sulphur mines

Ruipi Torretta ➤
Remorseful Baron of
House of Torretta

Contessa di Racalmuto ➤ *Deseré*
Greedy Contessa
turned charitable matron

Piedro Ludovico
Dimidia's husband;
Ugiso's tormentor

SEVENTH JOURNEY:
ENGLAND

Sir Peter MacLaughton
Baronet husband of Lillian

Lillian Amersham
Rhoea's elder sister

Rhoea Amersham
Lillian's much loved younger
sister; Ugiso's dream-friend

Ugiso Lynruth
Artist; Rhoea's dream-friend

Ruipi Peal
Carpenter

Deseré
Wife of Ruipi

Seven Journeys

THE BIRTH

Now oh soul, formed but not finished, fashioned but not complete, fare ye forth, so that ye may gain that wisdom which will make ye worthy to rest in peace, and become part of the Great Whole.

At this thy birth thou art fated yet free. To become perfect, thou must gather attributes and dispense that which thou gatherest, whether for good or evil rests with thee alone.

Alone and yet not alone, for joined to thee is thy mate, ye twain share one soul.

Thou art greater than those worlds which glitter and ever move restlessly there below, thou art less than the smallest dewdrop which trembleth on a blade of meadow grass.

That spark of Me, thy Maker, with which thou art imbued will ever live. Cling to It, nor loose thy hold, for It shall bring thee everlasting happiness, eternal life.

That for which thou must seek is truth. Return not to Me till, like a tired child seeking its mother's arms at close of day, thou art weary and must rest, then, and not till then, wilt thou find Me, but unless thou hast found that for which I bid ye seek, thy rest will be brief and again ye must journey forth.

Wonderingly questioned the Soul. . . .

"How is that which thou termest good to be recognized from that called evil?"

"Thou newly born and pure one, for thy guidance I have endowed thee with an intuition which will ever warn thee when thou art right and when thou art wrong."

"Divine Maker, Thou Who art noble and wondrous wise, how cometh evil into this Thy sphere?"

"Evil was born from sinful thought, from wicked deeds. Those who give birth to wrong must by their own effort exterminate it. Souls who create evil can know no rest until they have made reparation."

"Then Thou makest souls to suffer . . . ?"

"Not so. Each soul maketh its own suffering, and as all of ye are part of Me, thy suffering is also mine. Until Evil is no more, perfect happiness cannot be. To this end I create souls and send them forth to battle against the crucible of sin through which they must pass, so that they may learn. In time all Evil will be conquered and become submerged in Good. Then, and not until then, shall Peace return , and everlasting life reign triumphant. Remember, Good must conquer Evil. To this end shall ye labour."

"And how . . . ?"

"Conquer self!"

First Journey

CHAPTER I

"Hooeeee-ah! Hooeeee-ah!"

Hark! there was the cry again.

Rhoea sprang from her couch of bracken, naked except for the skin of a young wolf with which she had girded her loins, her straight supple body shining like polished gold taking its colour from the sun.

She shook back the tangle of red hair which hung far below her waist, the dark blue of her large, almond-shaped eyes became black from the tensity of her gaze.

The blood from the young eagle which she had been devouring dripped red from her scarlet lips on to her broad strong chest, and ran in a little rivulet between her twin breasts, which stood out firm and perfect as autumn apples.

"Hooeeeah!"

Again that long-drawn, whistling cry.

Dropping the half-devoured eaglet, Rhoea stooped, picked up a rough-hewn stone axe, gripped it, and crouching low, waited.

She knew it was her dread enemy "man" who emitted this cry, he was the only animal she feared, the only one with which she preferred not to do battle. She was as cunning as the lynx, as savage as the wolves with which she fought; she knew herself to be these beasts' master, but man! He was like her, only stronger, wilier, she had heard of him from her mother.

Rhoea remembered the only cave life she had ever known, when she was nothing more than a cub and dwelt with the cave folk on the side of a hill; that was before the tribe from over yonder near the great sea, came hunting in the forest and creeping down took the hill-dwellers by surprise.

Her father was killed, and her mother carried off by the slayer as his lawful prey.

At the first onslaught Rhoea, who was then quite a big cub, had rushed to the forest and climbing a tree for safety, had crouched, watching from among the branches until the raiders had departed.

From then on she had lived as best she could, trapping the smaller animals and birds until she grew bigger and lustier and able to do combat with the larger brutes, but man! ah! he was a dangerous foe. She had always carefully avoided his haunts, or only stealthily approached when the terrible loneliness which assailed her became too strong to be shaken off, and then she was always careful to go softly and to avoid being seen or heard.

She learned much from these surreptitious visits. They were clever these people who dwelt together, building their abodes by digging deep down, that would keep them warm, and the stones placed round three sides to protect them from the cold wind. Then the stamping on certain tree-barks in order to squeeze them dry and make them strong to trap birds, or bind wood and stone together to form weapons, these were useful things to imitate.

This wolf-skin garment which she wore. Rhoea had never thought of such a thing until she saw these other women wearing skins. One woman in particular fascinated her. She was paler, thinner, weaker than the others, her hair, too, was red, not with the rich bronze ruddiness of Rhoea's own locks, neither did she have great quantities of it, but straggly wisps that fell to her chin and shoulders, through which, the sharp eyes of the young savage noted, pale blue orbs peered. Rhoea had named this creature Dimidia, and ever when it was safe to do so, she crept close to the camp to search for, and watch Dimidia's every movement; she judged that they were of an equal age. None of the men of the tribe attracted her as did this woman, she noted that Dimidia had not yet been given to a man and she wondered why.

Many of the women had cubs and the fact filled her with a fierce longing to possess a like plaything, but how to procure one baffled her, perhaps the tiny mortals had fallen from the skies, or been dug up out of the earth. Her search for a cub was insistent but fruitless.

"Hooeeeah! hooeeeah!"

Ah, that was consoling, the cry was further away, no doubt they were hunting boar, that would take them north, far from where she stood, for the fire in the heaven was finishing its round journey, softly kissing the tree-tops and mountain peaks good-night, before closing its eye that gave golden light to the world; now was the time all the beasts in the forest would be stealing down to the great pool to drink, and that was where these disturbers of her peace were doubtless bound for.

The stone axe dropped from her hand, her limbs relaxed, and she fell with a sigh half weary, half regretful, in that the danger had passed, on to her couch of bracken, and there lay flat on her back while the great grey arch of dusk covered the blue of the heavens, turning it into a purple cloister for little holy stars. Rhoea wondered what it was that had come to her, for water fell from her eyes, stinging the lids, and falling salt and bitter to her lips.

What was this?

Perhaps that cry had cast an evil spell on her, and before the warmth came back with its lamp of crimson and gold, she would be lying stiff and cold, like the hind she had slain that morning. Tossing her two great arms above her head, she moaned aloud, wide-eyed and afraid.

Not fearful of anything concrete, but of herself, for ever since the mournful howl of the cold winds had turned to soft crooning, calling forth the tender curling leaf and creamy flower buds, making the birds sing and the earth warm, the loneliness that was always with her had taken a fast hold, that bit and gnawed at her very vitals.

She feared yet longed to creep in among the cave dwellers, to be one of them, to live near Dimidia whom she loved yet hated, would serve, yet knew it would be a joy to strangle.

She seldom saw the men of the tribe, for her stealthy visits were paid when she knew the hunters were away seeking their quarry; therefore, she had caught only momentary glimpses of them.

There was the tall, straight, smooth-faced one with long strong limbs and eyes like a hawk. He moved with great easy strides, and Rhoea felt she knew what it would be like to belong to him. That was it, she did belong to him, he was hers.

Lying there gazing up at the glittering stars, her thoughts dwelt on the life she had lived, the time when this tearing loneliness had not beset her, when she was always with her mate. Then what had happened! And when?

She could not remember what had surrounded her, no recollection of the forest or beasts, of her body, limbs, hunger or thirst; still, she must have had them. All she was sure of was, that a warning to beware of evil had been given her, a long period of peace and content which ended when a dark shape, surely another man, perhaps from some strange tribe, had torn himself from his woman . . . a— yes, a great sound crying out: "Never a man shall forsake . . ." and surely the word she never could hear must have been "woman."

"Never a man shall forsake his woman."

Yet for her sake some man had forsaken his woman, and she recalled wrenching herself from her mate to join this other; then a divided feeling of desire to remain with this stranger, and in a longing to return to her man, a part of her had torn away, and this that now remained, fell, fell, and falling, went whither? Had she been killed? If so, was she now dead?

The problem that vexed her remained as ever unanswered.

She tossed and turned restlessly, calling aloud to the stars that hung so low she verily believed she could gather them from their vault were she to climb the high hill that gloomed behind her; one day she would mount the summit and take a handful.

Her sense of loneliness grew until at last she could bear it no longer. Rising, she went to where her friends the Scarlet Poppies grew.

"I am seized with a strange unhappiness," she said seriously, kneeling beside the scarlet opium-laden flowers. "When I rest near you my eyes close tight and the dark passes swiftly, pushed aside by the red fire, so that I may see to hunt. I have come to be here among you, so that you will be kind and shut my eyes, and then I will forget this pain that tears me from within."

Her body sank to the earth and Rhoea slept.

CHAPTER II

A little new day came peeping shyly, laughingly, over the horizon, wiping the black smudge of night off the mountains and fields, using the caressing soft winds as dainty serving-maids, to dry the dew tears from the scented flower-cups nodding happily on their stalks of green.

Bare-limbed, Rhoea lay still asleep among the poppies, her strong body as beautiful as God had ever meant flesh to be, her masses of copper-red hair covering the pale gold of her bosom. For long the man stood gazing, filled with amazement at her loveliness, and a wonderment as to who this radiant young being could be. Closer and closer he crept.

It may have been a bell-note bird-uttered, or a dry leaf that broke beneath his feet, or perhaps the tensity of his gaze it was, that wakened the sleeper. Rhoea opened her eyes to gaze straight into two others, as deeply blue as her own, close bending over her.

For one heart-throb she thought she was still sleeping. Then the man moved and the instinct of a trapped animal animated her, a low growl issued from her throat; she sprang swiftly to her feet and stood half crouched, not sure whether to run or to stand and fight for her liberty.

Then as she looked a strange thing happened; she felt her limbs weaken, her heart turned to water within her, the veins in her neck and wrists beat, turning her head dizzy; her impulse to escape weakened.

This was her man!

Still the female instinct made it imperative that she should not be caught and made captive without a struggle.

She would fight, he would easily overpower her, or she would run; surely he could overtake her.

For a long moment these two stood gazing into one another's eyes, then—"Who are you?" he queried.

"Rhoea." The music of his voice had startled the answer to his question. "I am free," she added quickly.

"You are mine." There was no threat in the words, he was merely stating a fact.

"Not so; I am free," fell fiercely from her lips.

"You are mine," he repeated. A tiny shade of menace had crept into his tone. Her relaxed limbs tensed, with an effort she withdrew her gaze, then swift as a motherhawk homing to her young, she turned and fled. Within a dozen yards he had captured her, and, strong young savage though she was, struggling availed her nothing.

Panting and beaten, she knelt on the soft earth to where he had forced her, holding her two wrists strongly and lightly as he gazed down at his prey.

Even while she fought to free herself, the whole of her woman's soul exulted at being taken captive by this man.

Yet fear of the unknown, as to where he would take her, what do with her, shook her whole being.

With a swift movement he clasped her two hands in his one massive palm, and seizing a long thong of beaten bark from round his hips, he bound her wrists and arms together, her legs he treated in like fashion; then he sat down beside her.

"Now you are mine."

"What will you do with me?"

"Take you to my home."

"I shall not go."

"I will carry you."

"Then I shall run away."

He laughed, and, rising, picked her up despite her wild struggling, and threw her across his great shoulder as though she were the smallest hind slain in an easy day's kill.

Her heart leapt with pride at his massive strength, even while she set her sharp teeth and bit deep in his shoulder, screaming exultantly as she drew blood.

Thus Ugiso carried Rhoea to his home.

Once during the long march he laid her down whilst he

killed a great boar, that with lowered head came rushing at him, squealing with rage.

Rhoea took no interest in the fight between man and beast, she was too busy biting savagely at the thongs that fettered her.

Leaving the carcase of the slain boar lying where he had killed it, Ugiso picked up his newly-acquired woman and never paused until he reached the camp. Swarms of wolf-like dogs bayed out their antagonism to the stranger Ugiso carried; shrieking man-cubs clamoured round with shrill cries and elfish laughter; men and women clambered out of their earthen holes and cried questions to which Ugiso deigned no answer.

The commotion which her entry caused did not disturb Rhoea in the least; she felt perfect confidence in her strong man to protect her if need be. Here she was being carried into Dimidia's very camp! Through the tangle of her thick hair she peered, searching for a glimpse of the woman who so strongly attracted her.

Kicking the dogs on one side and carefully stepping over the heads of the tiny man-cubs that clustered round him, Ugiso strode up the hillside, over to the furthest left-hand corner, near the running pool, and there in a deep-dug square, surrounded on three sides by a rough stone wall, the whole roofed over with great stones, the interstices filled in with oak logs, bracken, moss and clay, making all water-tight, he lifted Rhoea from his shoulder, and holding her in his two arms as a mother might her babe, smiled into her eyes.

Rhoea snarled at him like a wild cat.

Gently placing her on the earth, Ugiso remained stooping beside her.

"You are my woman," he said.

Her lips so long unaccustomed to speech remained closed;

had she spoken it would have been to revile him, although her whole heart cried aloud in response . . .

"And you are my man," from her throat, through her teeth, came a savage snarl.

"Will you remain quietly with me if I unbind your limbs?" he asked.

"Never," she spat back.

"But why? you are mine." He was plainly puzzled; his smile died. "I cannot leave you bound, and if you try to run away, it will only give me the task of fetching you back and beating you," he remarked perplexedly.

"I will break your skull open," she promised.

His quick kind smile flashed back. For a further few moments he regarded her, then raising her, went to the corner and, bringing back the carcase of a young rabbit, held it to her lips, which she pressed firmly together; but she was hungry and soon was eating heartily of that which he fed to her, then scooping water into an earthen bowl, he put it to her mouth. She drank greedily, and watched him silently as he too ate, and, lying on his stomach, drank from the running brook.

"To what tribe do you belong?" he questioned.

"None."

"To what man did you belong?"

"None."

"Then why will you not stay with me? I will give you plenty to eat, and, if you are good, I will not beat you."

No answer being vouchsafed to this, again silence fell. Ugiso was thinking.

Suddenly he left the cave.

Quickly Rhoea struggled to a sitting position, wrenching and biting at the thongs that bound her. Finding her efforts of no avail she lay quite still; her eyes roamed round the abode, taking stock of its contents. That medley of skins no doubt he slept on, those finely ground stone weapons, some of them grandly formed with stout oaken handles, were used in hunting or digging; those long strings of divers shaped teeth, which hung suspended from a rough peg, driven between the stones that formed the walls, were trophies of his kill; he must be a great hunter.

Her solitude was cut short, a shadow fell across the floor; Rhoea looked up and her eyes encountered those of Dimidia.

For sixty seconds the two women took stock of one another, then:

"Who are you?" asked the new-comer.

"I am Rhoea; you are Dimidia."

"That is how I am called."

"Yes, I knew." Rhoea felt no surprise in learning that this was really the name of she who had always attracted her so; neither did the other express any surprise.

"Where do you come from?"

"The forest."

"Why are you here in Ugiso's cave?"

"Ugiso brought me."

"You must go."

"I am bound."

"I will release you."

Instead of gratitude, Rhoea experienced a feeling of keen resentment at this offer. This was a fight between her and Ugiso alone, no one else had any right to interfere.

"Do you belong to Ugiso?" she demanded.

"I am going to." Dimidia took from the belt of calf-skin, which held in place the one garment of sheep-skin she wore round her waist, a sharp-ground stone knife. As she advanced, Rhoea hated with all her heart this white, flat-chested, scanty-locked weakling, who with the aid of her stone knife proceeded to hack apart the thongs that bound the great bronze limbs. Intermingled with her feeling of hate for Dimidia was one of gentleness and understanding; of course, this weak thing loved Ugiso and was jealous of any interloper. Yes, she sympathized and understood, but strongest of all was the wild excitement that possessed her as she wondered what Ugiso would do when he found her gone.

"Ugiso will kill you," she warned her liberator.

"No." Dimidia was too intent on severing the tough thongs to waste time in speech.

"He will beat you," warned Rhoea.

"Ugiso says he is too strong to beat women." There was a touch of scorn in Dimidia's voice.

Now her legs were free, but the unaccustomed confinement left them numbed. Rhoea beat them on the earth while Dimidia proceeded to loosen her arms. At last they too were unbound.

"Ah!" Rhoea stretched them far above her head.

"Now go swiftly, not down through the camp, but up over the hills. Go!"

The stronger woman looked down at the puny one, and the desire to kill was strong within her; but she knew that wherever she met Dimidia, whatever might happen, she would always feel this same sense of inferiority, this same protecting sense, and still she hated her with a deadly hate.

Without a word Rhoea turned and fled up the mountain side. It was not until she was well over the crest, that Ugiso overtook and brought her back, exhibiting no trace of annoyance or impatience as he placed her on the skins in the corner, while he proceeded to plant a strong post deep in the centre of the cave, then winding a long thong many times round her waist, while she bit and struck at him like the savage she was, he attached her firmly to the stake.

"What is this, Ugiso?" Dimidia had returned.

"A forest bird I am taming."

"She has an evil eye, far better let her go."

"No, she has escaped once. Did you help her?" And now, for the first time in her life Rhoea blushed, the red blood dyed her very neck and chest with shame for another.

"I have never seen her before; how then could I assist her to escape?" Dimidia lied calmly, looking full in the man's eyes as she spoke.

"What manner of woman was this?" the captured savage wondered, who could say that which was not. A little of her reverence for Dimidia died.

"What will you do with her?"

"She is to be my woman."

"Take care, she will bring evil luck."

Ah, this word "evil." It moved a train of thought in Rhoea's brain. She had been warned to guard against evil, but at that time she was joined to these two, they were part of her, she and this woman together were mated to this man. Now perhaps she would learn what "evil" was. With quickened interest she listened.

"To-morrow I will make a great sacrifice and the evil will go from her," stated Ugiso grandly, giving an added twist to the green thong round the stake.

"It would be well to make a sacrifice of her," advised Dimidia.

"My daughter speaks wisely, sacrifice the witch." It was Anus, an old blear-eyed crone, flat-chested as her daughter, with withered limbs and toothless gums, who spoke.

"Those are not good words," Ugiso reproved.

"They are wise words, my son. Sacrifice this stranger, so that your killing may be good, your hunting fair."

"That will I never do."

"Then what will you do with her?"

"She shall dwell with me as my woman."

"And what of my daughter?" squealed Anus.

Ugiso fell silent, for before he had seen Rhoea there had been great talk in the camp of his mating with Dimidia. He could not deny that a something in her had attracted him, and no doubt in time he would have taken her to live with him, she being the only woman to whom he had given a thought until now.

Ever since that cold hungry season, when Anus's man had been set on by a band of wolves, made daring by hungry maws, and torn to pieces, Ugiso, having no parents of his own to support, had willingly provided Anus and her daughter with food. Now if he took this stranger to dwell with him, who would hunt and kill for them? Aloud Anus voiced this question.

"I shall continue as ever to bring you meat," he promised.

"And what of her?" indicating Rhoea.

"Oh," Ugiso laughed, "I am a hunter, I kill. How long is it, Anus, since you have doubted my power and skill to bring double what any other man in this tribe can do? Even Ruipi, I am willing to wager, could not equal my day's kill," boasted Ugiso.

"Then if you keep this witch, you lose my daughter," shrilled Anus.

This did not please Ugiso. Of the two he preferred Rhoea, but something in the weak Dimidia appealed to him; he did not relish the thought of losing her altogether.

With keen intuition not yet blunted by flesh and many births, Rhoea divined his thoughts. She knew better than the man himself the problem that vexed his soul.

A fierce jealousy of this other woman who had been part of herself stirred her. Much as she desired to belong to Ugiso, she would permit of no half allegiance. Pride and scorn moved her to brag.

"I need no man to kill for me," she spoke slowly, contemptuously. "I, Rhoea, have ever lived alone, fearing neither scream of wild cat nor howl of wolves. The trumpeting of elephants or roar of mammoth and lion soothe me to sleep. Alone have I done battle with great death-dealing rhinoceros. Then what need have I of one to kill for me? I, who have the strength of an elk, combined with the cunning of ape and sly hyena. O strong and boastful hunter, release me, so that you may be free to take yonder weak-armed one who cries for you, and do that for her which she would fear to do for herself. . . . I, Rhoea . . ."

Suddenly her tongue stayed its speech; she realized that she, too, was just about to utter that which was not so, even as Dimidia had done a short time ago. Rhoea had been on the point of declaring her longing to go hence and never see the face of this man again, this man for whom all her savage heart longed. She hung her head and was silent.

"She is a witch, I tell you," Anus insisted; "for if it is true that she has slain so great and savage a beast as a rhinoceros, then it must have been with the aid of her evil eye, for never had woman strength to perform such a deed unaided."

"If you keep her one day, she will surely slay you, Ugiso," sighed Dimidia.

Rhoea felt abased before this soft, weak, crafty being, who possessed the very qualities she lacked. Surely any man would glory in a strength that would help him protect this helpless, useless being.

But Dimidia's words had the exact contrary effect for which they had been uttered. They roused in Ugiso the thrill of future battle.

"Ha! ha! so this find of his would try to kill him." His sense of mastery was thrilled. He would keep and tame this forest thing, as he had kept and tamed the beautiful striped horse, which at first had bitten and lashed with her heels at him, and now whinnied and came nuzzling into his hand for the young green grasses he brought her.

It was sad if he must lose Dimidia, but sooner that than relinquish his captive.

"I shall keep her here," he stated firmly.

Rhoea's heart rejoiced, but outwardly she gave no sign.

Anus scowled and shook her bony fist in Rhoea's face.

"As she has said, she is of the hyena breed, she will bite your throat while you sleep and suck your life's blood. Woe, woe, to the tribe, for she will bring evil on us all," she wailed spitefully.

From Dimidia's eyes dropped water, as she turned and followed her mother down the hill-side.

Then as night crept softly down, like a great purple flower out of which grew glittering blue stars to trim the violet cloak of darkness, a soft sea breeze caressed the hillside, lulling little man-cubs, mighty hunters and chattering women to sleep, first making them drowsy with the perfume of scented scarlet lilies, white-eyed jasmine and soft sweet smell of earth.

High in the air came the startled cry of some frightened skyling, its excited twittering as it regained the lost nest, the mournful hooting of green-eyed owls, then stillness, broken only by the ever restless forest sounds, a tired leaf dropped, a branch creaked, startling the prowling beasts who roared and howled for their prey and gave voice to the agony of being that filled their brutish forms.

And over there in the far corner Ugiso slept.

Rhoea, sitting huddled on the soft skins, her arms locked

round her knees, with unclosed eyes gazed and wondered. Towards the birth of a new day her eyes closed wearily, a dreamless sleep claimed her.

CHAPTER III

Rhoea was left severely alone by the other tribesmen. She belonged to Ugiso the strong. His sunny temper would avail a marauder nothing, for he was well known to be relentless if there was reason for making him so.

On sallying forth to hunt he would leave his captive securely bound and tethered to the stake, never returning without bringing her some delicacy, such as a handful of wild berries, a wet river fish, or the toothsome liver of a young boar.

Occasionally he would attempt a rough caress, but finding himself savagely repulsed, he would not force her to accept his attentions. Instead he would seat himself at the opening of the cave and with great cunning and skill fashion new weapons out of flint, bone or wood, or clean and sharpen those already in use, chatting meanwhile with any of the tribesmen who approached.

The appearance of Ruipi marked an epoch in Rhoea's life. He came suddenly one evening, when for a few moments Ugiso was absent, and as she looked up to meet the concentrated gaze of the black-bearded giant, whose hairy massive frame stood clearly outlined against the crimsoning sky, Rhoea knew him again and trembled.

Here was the black shape that she had at some dim far-back time deserted her mate for; as her clear blue eyes looked into his black smouldering ones, she feared and disliked him.

He did not speak to her, nor, on the return of Ugiso, when the two men squatted in the cave's opening, did he speak of her; but sitting where he could see her, his eyes never left Rhoea, who correctly divined his lascivious thoughts.

Then when his woman Deseré, a clumsy-limbed slit-eyed creature, came stealthily up to rest near her man, she too gazed steadily at Ugiso's captive, nor did she fail to notice where her man's eyes dwelt.

Rhoea knew that in Deseré she had a bitter enemy.

Dimly remembering the events that had preceded her meeting with these people, she never thought to wonder how she knew, nor whether they were equally aware of all that somewhere, at some time, had occurred.

During Ugiso's absences Rhoea had come to expect visits from Dimidia, sometimes she came alone, sometimes accompanied by Anus. At first their cruelty had been confined to bitter cutting speeches, to which Rhoea listened in silence; then as they discovered that Ugiso remained in ignorance of their words, or indeed of their visits, they ventured on tortuous physical savagery.

It was Dimidia who heated the flat piece of flint. Then, holding the tied creature's long masses of almost poppy-red hair aside, suggested to Anus the placing of the heated metal on Rhoea's back. It was Dimidia, too, who seared the soles of the captive's feet, and drove sharp thorns in the firm flesh, leaving them there to bite and fester.

Rhoea bore all these things with stoic fortitude, scorning to complain to Ugiso. Remembering her bragging words of how alone she had fought with, and conquered great forest beasts, how now could she cry out and complain of the treatment these weak women inflicted on her?

Through it all she never lost her feeling of almost reverence for Dimidia; hate and jealousy only entered when Ugiso was in question.

No such feeling of tenderness moved her towards Anus; the hideous old hag Rhoea determined to strangle by squeezing the skinny throat, till her tongue protruded and her face went black, and she ceased to struggle or breathe.

Deseré took to accompanying the crone and her daughter on their visits to Rhoea. She, too, joined in the cruel sport of torture. Ever since that evening when she had sat silently watching Ruipi eyeing Ugiso's woman, she felt the dangerous attraction this great glorious young thing would have for any man. Perhaps she, too, dimly remembered the tragic happening of long ago, when her mate had torn himself from her side to follow an alien soul.

As they jeered at and tortured her, Rhoea never uttered a word. Within her heart she pictured herself free and these women belonging to her. She would not be unkind to Dimidia or even really harsh to Deseré, but she would master them; they should cringe before her. It was a sweet thought, and she often dwelt on it.

One day her animal instinct was awakened when Deseré appeared alone, and contrary to her usual tactics, used smooth words and behaved gently.

"You would be free, Rhoea?"

Her eyes narrowed. She watched Deseré suspiciously.

"Come, tell me, Rhoea, I am sorry for having played so cruelly with you," pleaded Deseré.

Then. . . . "My man is head of the tribe. For the first time the ever-burning fire on our hearth went out last night, leaving a great blackness. He knows it is your evil eye that caused it. He called a meeting of the men. They have spoken the word. Either you are to be offered up as a sacrifice, or Ugiso must die."

"Why must Ugiso die?"

"Ah." Deseré's slit eyes snapped triumphantly. She had moved this dumb thing to speech. "Because he brought you here," she answered.

"That must not be. It is better I should be sacrificed," Rhoea decided.

"But Ugiso is stubborn, he may not allow it."

"And then. . . ."

"Ugiso must die."

"No, no."

"But if you went away, all would be well."

"How can I go. I, who am bound to this stake?" asked Rhoea, her heart in her eyes as she watched Deseré.

"I could loosen the thongs and you could escape."

"Yes, quick," commanded Rhoea.

"You would go far away and never return?" questioned Deseré.

For a moment Rhoea closed her eyes; to go far from her man, to never see him again, to never have let him know how she loved him. Could she do it?

"Otherwise Ugiso must die." Deseré was desperate, for had not Ruipi taken to spending much time here in this cave talking to Ugiso, whilst his eyes gloated on the straight great limbs and rounded breasts of this forest thing?

"Loosen these thongs," Rhoea ordered.

In a few moments she stood up free and unshackled, then swift as a young antelope, with long, steady strides, she fled up the hillside and over the mountain top.

Whilst Deseré with an evil chuckle slid quietly back and communicated the good news to Dimidia and Anus.

All that night and the next day Ugiso searched vainly for his missing woman, and late into the second night. Then he dropped wearily to the earth, preferring to risk the dangers of the forest to returning to his far off camp. Heavily the lids dropped over his eyes. He never knew whether he slept, all he was sure of was that Rhoea lay somewhere in pain or danger.

Never opening his eyes, he stumbled to his feet and rushed

blindly ahead. A mammoth bellowed at his approach, then turning, lumbered heavily away. Crash, crash, through the dry forest. A wild cat spat and clawed at him, a gigantic elk lowered its head and pawed the ground preparatory to giving battle. Ugiso passed them by unconsciously. A pack of snarling wolves dared near, but turned and fled as he swept down on them. The whole forest feared this courageous mortal.

On, on, like a man demented, but one with a set purpose, never pausing for an instant, neither did he open his eyes until he knew he had reached her.

There she lay with one leg crumpled clumsily beneath her, in her wild flight she had fallen heavily and broken the limb.

All the silent antagonistic past was forgotten. Stooping, he straightened the injured member, then sitting beside her he took her in his two arms, murmuring little love words and touching her face with his lips.

Still as death she lay, her head on his shoulder, her hair covering his naked breast, then with a sob she threw her arms round him, holding him tight to her. Her man!

Softly she caressed the still red, oblong mark on his left shoulder, just above the blade, where her teeth had once drawn blood.

"I knew you would come. I sent for you," she murmured.

"Yes, I heard," he answered simply. Neither thought to wonder how the wordless message had been sent or received.

Then her heart was drawn to him through her lips.

And so they slept a magic sleep, only awakened by the pearl and silver of another day. Neither moved until the sun-god planted high his scarf of gold. Fate had given them the heart of joy, and they lived their hour.

As the shadows grew big, Ugiso bound the broken limb in a rough-formed support of oak-wood, and lifting her, carried his woman back by easy stages to the camp. They did not speak much these two, their hearts were too full for words.

She clung close to him, as they went past where the trees are tallest and shadows deepest. The sun sifting through the branches, touched the green bracken and tiny wild flowers. Past the deep pool edged with cardinal flowers, and brown jewel-spikes to guard the queen water lilies that floated regally on the blue surface. Sprays of scarlet berries caught Rhoea's hair as though they claimed it for their own.

Beneath an arch of honeysuckle and sweet briar rose, past great swelling lilies, until the rinkle, rinkle, rinkle of the little river that curled shyly and looped and doubled on itself, made them pause to rest and drink deep, before setting off once more.

Reaching the camp Ugiso strode as once before up the hillside, carrying his burden and laying her gently on the skins, he laughed down into her eyes and his face flushed and his limbs trembled as she smiled back.

Turning he wrenched the stake from its place, snapping it in two and casting it far from him.

And now began a space of perfect happiness for Ugiso and Rhoea.

At first she had feared for his life on account of what Deseré had told her, not daring to question him, for had she done so it would have necessitated the telling of Deseré's connivance at her escape.

Gradually she realized that the whole story was untrue, she puzzled over this. Not that Deseré should wish for her disappearance, but this saying of things that were not, confused her.

When her limb mended she joined him in his hunting. Her skill and knowledge of the denizens of the forest proved to be greater than his own. This fact was soon known in the camp and gained for Rhoea and Ugiso (because he owned her) admiration and fame, not unmixed with jealousy, which led to many a fight between those other men, who desired Rhoea, and Ugiso.

Among the women Rhoea commanded respect, but envy prevented any of them from loving her. They feared her strength and cringed before her disdainful contempt of them. The three conspirators who had tortured her trembled, when they saw that peace and affection existed between Ugiso and his woman, afraid of the man's wrath if he learned of their cruelty. As time passed and they realized their victim must have remained silent, they marvelled and recovered their courage to a certain extent, but not sufficiently to allow them to approach Rhoea, Rhoea who seemed in some uncanny way to know so much, to read their innermost thoughts.

At first Anus fretted in case Ugiso should forego his promise and cease to provide food for her daughter and herself, but he had not forgotten, nor had Rhoea. It was she who killed for these two women, taking a savage pleasure in knowing herself to be their provider. It may have been that Ugiso noticed this, but he made no mention of it.

"Ho, Anus," called Rhoea standing outside the old woman's cave, with a young buck freshly killed slung across her back, and a couple of fat lion cubs hanging in her hand. "Come, take what I have brought you."

"Ah! Give thanks to Ugiso for his thought of us," mumbled Anus, greedily snatching the carcases.

"Ugiso kills for me alone, it is I who hunt for you," Rhoea spoke proudly.

Anus smothered an angry snort, it would not do to quarrel with her meat-bringer.

"Yes, your skill and strength are talked much of among the men who at one time admired Ugiso." It was pale-eyed Dimidia who spoke.

"Do they not admire him now?" demanded Rhoea.

"How can they when it is known that he lets you share his killing. True our women sometimes may go with their men, but only to carry weapons; killing is man's work."

Dimidia's softly uttered words bit deep into Rhoea's heart. As always, she felt humbled before the weaker woman. Still, rather the sneers of the tribe than that Ugiso should work for these two. But it was not good that her man should be held lightly because of her.

With lowered head Rhoea departed.

Dimidia wearing a malicious smile and a heart full of envy and hate, re-entered the cave and ground fine some brittle white stone she had found, rubbing it on her body and face, until her skin was white as a newly peeled silver birch. Then sauntering forth she joined Deseré, who was toiling upwards towards the cave where "Ruipi spends much time gazing, ever gazing, at that evil-eyed foreign witch," Deseré confided bitterly to Dimidia.

Now in the soft glow of evening light, the thin Dimidia, with her thick coating of ground white stuff, looked ethereal. The contrast between her and Rhoea, beside whom she seated herself on arriving at the cave, was marked and Rhoea was strongly conscious of the admiring wonder in Ugiso's eyes as they continually turned towards the centre of the cave where the three women sat.

Deseré, squat and black with a cow-hide round her haunches, Rhoea, strong-limbed and golden-bronze, wearing the rich red pelt of a deer round her hips, and Dimidia, thin and white, the spotted coat of a wild cat tied with a green hide round her waist.

Ruipi, squatting on his haunches, never moved his dark smouldering gaze from Rhoea.

Then Anus died.

When Rhoea heard of it, there came before her a vivid picture of the crone stumbling along a lone straight path towards Someone somewhere who would deal her out a fresh destiny; idly the living woman wondered if ever they would meet again. She knew she must look after Dimidia. There was no question as to that. Someone must fend for this weakling. Rhoea did not doubt for one instant but that this must be her task.

Limply Dimidia accepted the situation, lazily lolling in her cave, taking Rhoea's attention as her right, becoming fretful and complaining if her self-appointed slave was not sufficiently industrious. The only tasks she interested herself in was the grinding of the brittle white stone, with which to smear her body, and coming forth to display herself thus bedecked, before the eyes of Ugiso. The attraction he had always felt for her did not grow less, neither did it increase. Rhoea was his woman, his affection for her predominated.

Still he liked to see Dimidia, to have her near at hand.

Rhoea knew, and the knowledge was bitter. If she could only become possessed of the attributes which Dimidia had and she lacked. Then Ugiso would think no more of any other. She alone would reign in his heart.

Long hours she lay prone in the forest turning the problem over in her mind. The only solution seemed to be to kill and eat Dimidia and so assimilate the lacking qualities, but the thought revolted her, more especially as she did not feel that even this drastic measure would fetch her any closer to her desire.

CHAPTER IV

It was when hot Summer stretched her limbs and, finding them grown tired and old, sighed and, kissing the earth a fond farewell, bowed to the coming radiant Autumn, halting once, twice, thrice, to whisper overlooked messages before hurrying away to another quarter of the world where she was awaited as a long overdue guest, leaving brilliant, breezy Autumn in her robe of scarlet and yellow to mount guard over forest and pool. The hoydenish winds that came in her train brought a clutter of leaves to the ground, soak-swilled from the rain that tore, shouting, adown the mountain side, sweeping along great boulders and branches with gurgling, rumbling laughter, leaving them wrathful and offended in a swirling river that frothed like yeast.

Rhoea, sitting close curled near the fire that burned in the cave, saw a thing that turned her whole being to a living flame of jealousy.

Ugiso, seated near her, was intently working with a sharp, broad, flint-blade, on the pelt of a long-haired red fox.

Rhoea gasped and for many heart-beats she forgot to breathe. This pelt was for Dimidia. She knew it as surely as she knew she loved Ugiso. Her own fur covering she won herself from the beasts on which they grew.

Her man had never given her a pelt, yet for this thin, puling, miserable creature, he worked carefully, painstakingly. Dimidia must have waylaid him and asked for the gift, warning him, no doubt, to say nothing of the request.

"That is a good skin," she remarked.

"Yes." Ugiso did not raise his head from the work which engrossed him.

"It will be warm for the cold season."

"Yes."

Rising, Rhoea left the cave and going swiftly up the mountain side, gained the forest, where she threw herself face downward on the soft moist earth, snarling and moaning like an animal in pain, biting her hands and clawing the ground.

Dimly she realized that her punishment was deserved. A

faint memory of having broken away from this man who had been given her for mate stirred her.

With grim set lips she rose and retraced her steps, a long spray of red berries slashed her face. Impatiently she plucked it and, carrying it in her hand, approached the cave, where Ruipi, who, as usual, had come to sit with Ugiso, moved aside for her to enter.

"What, can you never keep away from your hunting?" drawled Dimidia jeeringly.

"Hunting is good, it teaches much," answered Rhoea slowly.

"To catch and to kill?" The malign-faced Deseré, hunched in the far corner, laughed in concert with Dimidia as the latter put her question.

"To kill fairly and to hunt only in the open that which belongs to no other."

Dimidia understood. Her laugh broke off discordantly. Ugiso looked up, not understanding, but hearing a foreign note in Rhoea's voice. Then he glanced smilingly at Dimidia who lay alongside him, her bent elbow almost resting on his knee.

The smile ran like fire through Rhoea. Hardly conscious of what she was doing, she twisted the branch of scarlet berries round her damp red locks and, catching Ruipi's bold, admiring glance, for the first time she smiled back at him.

Ugiso caught the smile and frowned blackly, whereat Rhoea's heart rejoiced exceedingly and Deseré's evil grunt passed unnoticed.

Of course, here was the way to wean Ugiso from the thought of Dimidia. Rhoea recalled the time when the tribesmen sighed round her door and challenged Ugiso to battle. Then he had feared to leave her, never easy if she was out of his sight.

As he had proven his prowess and beaten her admirers off one by one, Rhoea had been content. But now . . . none dared venture near, excepting the black Ruipi, Chief of the Tribe. That being so, he must be sacrificed to aid her in bringing Ugiso's heart completely into her keeping again.

Great crimson patches dyed her cheeks, her blue eyes under the drooped lids glinted sideways at Ruipi, a little smile of meaning mystery played about her lips.

Here in this cave was being fought out a tragedy æons old, yet ever new. Souls were building their own hells, hearts were making their own sorrows, and outside the wet wind screamed and sobbed, the black branches creaked and moaned a dirge, and the rain dropped rivers of tears, which the very ground-larks and tree nestlings quivered to hear.

That night, while Ugiso slept, Rhoea lay tossing restlessly and it seemed as though a brazen bell in a rockbound cave was moved by the ever restless sea to ceaseless chanting. . . .

"Never a man shall forsake his woman."

"Never a man shall forsake his woman."

Rhoea shuddered and covered her face with her hands. But she could not shut out the booming dirge.

Day danced in with care-free feet, the rain had ceased, leaving the world sweet and fresh as a new-bathed nymph, little white wind clouds ran races across a blue sky, and a soft wind laughed at the jokes his stronger brethren had indulged in during the night.

Ugiso had taken his weapons and stood waiting at the cave entrance. He looked back at Rhoea, who had made no move to accompany him. Then . . . "Come," he said softly.

Exultant, but silent, she strode off alongside him.

This then was the solution to her problem. This was the way to keep her man hers; to make him jealous, to let him see that others wanted her. What mattered it that Deseré suffered, or Ruipi be played with?

Her man! That was all with which she was concerned. He must belong to her, body and soul, heart and mind; this queer small voice whispering, ever whispering of the wrong she was doing, telling her that this was some of the evil of which she had been warned, counted as nothing, for Rhoea was a woman in love and she, and such as she, would willingly tear the sun from the heavens to burn the three worlds, would sacrifice honour, life, friends and kin, to hold the beloved man.

Now there was an oft-told tale among these people, of the terrible time when evil had lived among them, when it had walked like a wide-mouthed, slavering beast of prey, leaving a trail of misery wherever it stalked. Strong men, their women and little cubs, grew hot and burned, writhing and twisting, screaming out strange words, then lay still and would not breathe, turning to stiff, icy coldness.

Sacrifices that were made availed nothing, and when Validus, the greatest Chieftain the tribe had ever known, was seized and shaken to stark clay by this fiend, his woman was murmured against, for round her neck hung a great glittering eye of a palish colour, like a star at dawn, and in its depth there glowed and winked sparks of wicked red fire that must surely have been stolen from the sun, intermingled with the blue of the sky, and faint greens thieved from fresh morning breezes. Who could doubt but that the elements thus captured by a mortal, would not hold immense power for good or evil?

A mighty consultation took place, where it was unanimously decided to burn the woman and destroy this evil thing. The listening women seated round the edge of this conclave shrieked acclamation, for the woman of Validus was young and beautiful and had drawn many of their men's hearts to her feet. Now they knew she had derived her power from the malicious multi-coloured orb.

In solemn state they marched to the cave of their late great Chief, and finding his woman had followed her lord, lying cold and stiff beside him, they tore the evil eye from round her neck and, with great beating on skins stretched tight between oaken sticks and blowing loud noises through hollow shells, they carried it and cast it into a deep pool, where to their horror, it rolled mockingly, sending up shoots of spiteful fire, brighter, more vivid, than ever.

Fearing greatly, they tore it from the clear lagoon and, taking it far into the forest, they dug such a hole as never before had been known and, casting the malicious spirit into the bottom of the pit, piled back the earth, stamping it firmly down, setting huge stones over the spot in order to prevent a return of this thief who had been guilty of stealing portions of the elements.

Thus was evil buried.

Ever after, this spot was avoided by the people of the tribe, but hunters who had accidentally approached it, brought back strange tales of wonderful glowing flowers that had sprung up round the cairn, prophesying dire happenings for anyone reckless enough to cull such blossoms.

Rhoea knew the history of evil. It recurred to her mind, and now, stepping softly through the forest, there went three. The man, the woman and a tempting Devil. What evil could harm her so long as she kept Ugiso for her own, she was strong and could bear anything excepting the loss of his love.

One little blossom could not do any great harm, and while Ugiso stalked a lion to its lair, Rhoea turned and fled swiftly towards the cairn. Suddenly she paused in her flight, for the terrible thought came, "What if this evil in some subtle way attacked Ugiso?"

She had outrun the Devil.

Panting and trembling, she regained the spot and waited

Ugiso's return. He came laughing up to her, the body of the yellow lion lying across his back.

That night Dimidia wore the pelt of the long-haired red fox that Ugiso had prepared for her. It well became the powdered whiteness of her skin and the man grunted approval. Even Ruipi's eyes wandered from Rhoea to gaze at the languorous fragile form.

Deseré blinked watchfully at the whole scene. And that night, while Ugiso slept, Rhoea crept from beside him and, never pausing, made straight for the cairn.

"Even if my man wakens he will not wonder," she told herself as she hurried along through the forest she knew so well, "for he will think I have some moon-madness."

For whenever the moon was full in the heavens, Rhoea would be seized with a strange restlessness, caused, so she explained, from the fact, that while she dwelt alone, she had hunted well on these bright nights, taking advantage the light gave her over wild beasts. On dark nights she lay still and hidden, for then the other animals in the forest saw with quicker eyes than she did.

Even since she had become a member of a tribe, this restlessness on moonlight nights never left her.

Soon she reached her goal, and pausing a few yards off she stood peering forward to where the flowers grew.

By the light of the moon, she scanned the many-tinted waxen blossoms, which shone like opal jewels aglitter, on high thick fleshy stems, dark green and spotted; the corolla, trumpet-shaped and translucent, shaded from rich scarlet to wine-purple, set firmly in a blue-green calyx.

Wide-eyed and motionless Rhoea looked and looked at the living sensuous things, which seemed to mock and dare her. With hands tight clutched over her bosom, she stood fascinated, drinking in the stories of wild beast orgies, of bartered bodies, and women's shame, of men's black torture, of tiny cubs' sobs, which they seemed to tell gloatingly.

Fearful, but desperate, she slowly approached, stretched up a hand, grasped the fleshy stem, drew it towards her, and snapped off a great fiery blossom, which groaned and screamed angrily.

Its malicious noise disturbed a bat, black as night, which fluttered against Rhoea's face. Her startled cry roused all the furred and feathered things, who in turn carried terror throughout the forest.

A dull sickly dawn was rubbing the sleep from its eyes with a smudgy finger, ere Rhoea sank weary but jubilant, her terrors forgotten, on to the couch of skins beside Ugiso, the trumpet-shaped wicked bloom hidden safely away.

For the first time since her coming to him, Ugiso went hunting alone, making no suggestion that she should accompany him, neither did she offer to do so.

Late in the day she rose and taking the Evil Blossom, sallied forth to a sedge-fringed mere, then binding a bright green thong round her brow she lay flat on her stomach, gazing into a deep clear pool, while she fixed the thing on the centre of her forehead, smiling at the satisfactory effect the richly coloured flower produced.

It was thus Ruipi found her.

With a grunt of satisfaction he squatted on his haunches close to the recumbent form.

Startled, her eyes met his black smouldering ones, in which there shone the gleam of a hunter, whose prey is in sight.

Silently they rested, watching one another cautiously.

Then Ruipi stretched a hairy arm towards her, she snarled like a wild cat.

"I shall take you from Ugiso," he said.

The spoken word broke the spell, and removed the numbness that had bound Rhoea's limbs; springing to her feet, she would have fled.

Hawk-swift Ruipi barred her way.

Strong as she was, she knew his strength outmatched hers; with all her soul she sent out a wordless message, calling Ugiso to her aid, she knew he would come, but to keep from Ruipi's arms in the meantime would be difficult.

Force would not avail, then she must try cunning; even as she decided this, a wild fear struck at her, and she tried to shut off the invisible communication she had set afloat. Her limbs drooped, and she trembled, for if Ugiso came she knew either his or Ruipi's life would pay forfeit; her man was strong, but this black giant might prove stronger.

She must get away before Ugiso appeared.

Ruipi watching her narrowly, realized that some decision was exercising her mind. Her relaxed limbs, and drooping head, he interpreted as signs favourable to his desire; he took a step towards her, his arms outstretched.

"What of Deseré?" the first words that occurred to her tumbled from Rhoea's scarlet lips, made more vivid by their colour counterpart glistening and curling on her forehead.

"She can go," announced Ruipi cold-bloodedly.

"The tribe . . ." anything, anything, she was fighting desperately, both for time, and for this body which belonged to Ugiso.

"I am strong, they must obey me."

Paler than she had ever been in her short young life, Rhoea forced a smile. . . . "I am afraid," she whispered.

But Ruipi was tired of words, with a growl like the purr of a wild beast, he sprang forward, his arms encircled her, making her fierce struggles futile.

Then through the reeds crashed Ugiso, straight at them he came like a mad young bull.

So suddenly was Rhoea released that she staggered, breathing in hard short gasps from her throat, back, back, down the sloping bank of the pool. By that time the two men had met, this was a matter of hot life or cold death.

There was an instant's flash. Ugiso had struck with a stone axe, sharpened to a wicked keenness. Ruipi swayed sideways, and so saved his head, catching the swinging blow on his side; his ribs crashed as he let fall his heavy club, breaking Ugiso's shoulder as though it had been rotten timber. The bone stuck out through the battered flesh, and with his uninjured arm, he hurled his axe straight and sure. With incredible swiftness Ruipi swerved, but not too soon to save a deep chip on the scalp; blood gushed from his mouth and ears in a torrent.

Roaring like beasts, they grappled fiercely, a writhing mass of mangled flesh.

Then Ugiso got his legs twisted round his rival, his hand tore at Ruipi's windpipe.

It was only now Rhoea succeeded in loosening the giant boulder at her feet; with hands torn and gaping, she raised the murderous rock far above her head, and hurled it straight at Ruipi, at the very instant that he fell gasping and twitching his last, a sprawling mass of slaughtered flesh.

The stone fell in front of Ugiso, who blinded with blood, and faint from his wounds, staggered back, falling down the bank, his whole weight propelled against Rhoea.

Down, down, to the furthermost depths of the pool they went, his helpless carcase bearing her down, ever downward.

An inky blackness, her eyes started from their sockets, a roaring, a bursting in her head. . . .

There were still bubbles on the pool, and wide rings making

angry circles at the unwonted disturbance, when Rhoea and Ugiso, feeling singularly free and untired, looked back, and saw two human forms rise, and float on the water; a pitying smile for the poor discarded flesh, a momentary regret for the covering that so long had hampered them, so sorely smitten, so strangely still.

Swiftly they were borne away.

Only the three silent forms, and a floating scarlet flower, bubbling joyously round the lifeless bodies, remained to tell the tribesmen of what had befallen Ugiso, Rhoea, and their Chief.

A RESPITE

Along the straight path they journeyed, with other returning souls, each showing plainly the marks of flesh.

Knowledge weighted their backs and bowed their heads, as they hurried to the feet of their Maker, not in fear and trembling, but desirous of reaching the Divine Presence, to feel His love, to hear His voice, like tired babes, seeking refuge at the close of a weary day.

As cooling rain on a desert road came the Voice.

"Ah, my children, well do I know thy sore struggles, and great temptations. Know that I was ever with thee, and ever shall be. Know also, that thy smallest conquest over evil is counted as a great triumphant victory, which peals and resounds through the Heavens, and is told and retold to hearten weaker ones on to fight ever for God."

And now the voice grew sad and stern.

"Know also that thy every sin, whether great or small, of deed or thought thou must atone for. But I bid ye be not faint of heart, for that evil which is done by man can be wiped out by man. Gird ye then, for thy great battles, take courage, and remember that my Spirit is ever with thee, rejoicing with thee when thou doest right and conquer self, overcome evil. Sorrowing with those who are weak and who let their thoughts stray, their deeds be guided by that evil which is strong and of great craftiness.

"Rest ye here, till thou art no longer weary, then return to that flesh which thine own actions, thine own thoughts have prepared for thy souls, and weep not at going, for I tell ye that but a short span of time shall pass, before ye again shall stand here before Me.

"I, thy Maker, who love ye, have spoken."

Second Journey

CHAPTER V

Lucarius, the most powerful of the five Ephors in Crete, under the reigning monarch Ruipi, was troubled.

With closed eyes, he lay naked on the black marble slab which so well outlined his well-formed body, and gave himself up to thought.

A thrill of wonder passed through the dozen or so hand-maidens who were bathing the white limbs with cooling perfume, for their master had failed to observe and punish the slave who had inadvertently let fall on the marble floor a crystal stopper belonging to the slender perfume-flask.

The task was finished, even to the curling of the golden beard, and the arranging of linen sheets over the recumbent form, round whom they now knelt, slowly moving great fans of peacock feathers.

A slave of Ethiopian blackness entered to announce the arrival of one Ito, the lover of wine, and a philosopher who was everyone's friend excepting his own.

"Admit him," commanded Lucarius.

Although he was pleased at the prospect of speaking with Ito, his eyes remained closed, he never ceased stroking the tiny ape that sat gibbering on his chest, and no muscle of his face moved, for emotion aged, and that which Lucarius treasured most was Lucarius, therefore nothing which would mar his beauty, or trouble his mind, was to be tolerated.

Ito was a useful fellow, his quick perception and fertile brain were ever at the service of his friends, his utter lack of principles combined with a perennial cheerfulness were soothing, and moreover his besetting sin (or as Lucarius and others in Crete put it—virtue), a loyal adherence to wine, purple, crimson, or amber, obviated any danger of his becoming a rival for power.

It was good that Ito was here.

Lucarius permitted his full red lips to relax in a smile, as he remembered the fat, swaying Ito's leer and scarlet face, four years ago, when he, Lucarius, then a minor Ephor, had confided in his tipsy friend, that King Ruipi having become enamoured of the beautiful Deseré, the Delphian lady whom Lucarius had loved well enough to make his wife, had intimated that he, the mighty monarch, would so far honour the choice of Lucarius as to make it his own.

"Deseré! my wife," stammered Lucarius.

Ruipi was famed for the passion and brevity of his many amours.

"It is but seldom a wife attracts me," Ruipi chuckled coarsely, "but since I have seen thine, I am seized with a longing that is not to be denied, for her."

"But my wife," was all the bewildered Lucarius could move his tongue to repeat, then . . . "my little daughter, surely thou wouldst not deprive her of a mother's care?" he pleaded.

"Thy daughter, I am informed, is already a maiden of thirteen; soon she will be ripe for the plucking, and I myself will see to it that she weds one fitting the rank her father will have, if he prove worthy," with which significantly uttered words Ruipi had dismissed the trembling Ephor, leaving him to think the matter over.

Even as he left the Royal presence, with a seemingly over-whelming proposition troubling him, Lucarius, true to his creed, refrained from frowning, or permitting any agitation to trace its mark on his countenance.

It was of this time he now thought, and a gentle smile played round his full sensuous red lips, as he recalled his en-counter with Ito at that crucial moment.

"But what ails thee, my good friend?" hiccuped Ito, after lis-tening to the distressful confidences poured into his ear.

"Thou dost not understand, the King has demanded of me my wife," Lucarius repeated.

"Then am I to condole with, or congratulate thee?" enquired Ito.

"There are many women in Crete, why should he choose mine?" wailed Lucarius.

"Thou has spoken, there are many women in Crete, and thou hast only one life; all the King's for the taking."

Lucarius groaned.

"Look thee, Lucarius," Ito counselled, "thy master is ambi-tion, as mine is wine; to those who serve either it is well to ig-nore one Cretan motto, namely 'No excess,' for our masters are jealous and brook no limitations; then, like good citizens, we must study the second motto . . . 'Know thyself.' Thou, Lucarius, would still be Lucarius if bereft of the noble Deseré, but deprived of thine ambition thou wouldst be even as I without my beloved wine, a thing of naught, a pricked wine-skin, cast aside and left to shrivel and moulder in the heat of the noonday sun."

"But if I gratify Ruipi's whim, it would ruin Deseré's life," moaned Lucarius.

"To learn life one must ruin lives. Never has ode been writ-ten without the waste of much ink. Nature herself gives us many crude sunsets, ugly mooded days, and warped formations in learning to create perfection."

"True," agreed Lucarius.

"Ambition is a wild horse with no heart, all fire and determination, and a mouth that calls for gentle handling. Once mounted on such a steed it is wise to forget everything else, and so enjoy the ride, directing thy horse where thou wilt; a moment's carelessness is apt to leave thee roughly dislodged, suffering from a broken skull or, worse still, a cracked reputation; the former is to be pitied, the latter a matter for the jeers of thy friends. Pity is to be borne, jeers kill."

"I shall proclaim this tyrant's iniquitous proposition, I shall demand protection," stormed Lucarius, then as Ito remained silent, he added weakly . . . "Besides, Deseré would never consent."

Ito chuckled.

"And pray for what reason art thou mirthful?" demanded Lucarius irritably.

"To watch thoughts mature ever amuses me. Now come, Lucarius . . . 'Know thyself,' and that being rightly interpreted means to know what thou wantest and get it, and so come to fame."

"What is fame?" Lucarius attempted to instill contempt into his question.

"The nettle-encircled handle at which thou clutcheth, which ends in a gold plate on thy coffin-lid my friend. Now, have done with sentimentality, which bespeaks a sensualism of the mind that wearies me. Some wine, that we may drink to the happiness of the adorable Deseré in her new life."

As Ito well knew, Lucarius sacrificed Deseré, letting himself be persuaded in this course by the bibulous philosopher, who pointed out that Deseré, though still charming, was no longer young, and moreover there were many beauteous maidens left, whom Lucarius could put in her place.

So it was arranged, and the Lady Deseré had gone, at her husband's request, on a visit to the Royal Palace, from whence she never returned, for she was not permitted to leave the carefully barred and guarded apartment, into which no male, other than Ruipi himself, entered.

That was four years ago, and Lucarius had never heard of, or seen her since. Each time he passed through the Lion Gate, and climbed the long flight of steps leading to the Palace, he experienced a twinge of fear in case he should encounter Deseré, for she would surely have heard from the King that he possessed her with her husband's connivance, nor did he dare marry again. However, all had gone smoothly, his story that Deseré, having returned to visit her parents in Delphi, had unfortunately contracted an illness and died, was accepted without question, and he had greatly prospered through the barter of his wife, as witness his position of to-day, chief of the five great Ephors of Crete, an enviable position and a powerful one.

His daughter Rhoea firmly believed that her mother was dead.

Gently Lucarius caressed the small furry beast with its wrinkled evil face, and smiled.

As Ito entered, though it was yet some hours before noon, there were evidences pointing to the fact that already he had been pouring frequent libations to the God Dionysus.

"Greetings, oh Lucarius," he cried.

"Greetings, Ito, thou comest in answer to my desire to speak with thee," murmured Lucarius.

"Ah, then thou art in trouble." Ito nodded like a dissipated owl.

This statement was so true that it caused Lucarius to languidly open his eyes and scan the bloated face of his visitor. . . . "True, but how dost thou know?" he queried.

"It is the easiest thing in all Greece to fall into trouble. It is the hardest thing in all the world to get out of it; for the former, one need only be foolish, the latter requires unique wisdom such as mine, that is the reason I have so many friends."

"True I am in trouble." The great Ephor closed his eyes again.

"Women?"

"No."

"No, it is never women, but only a woman, who troubles man," chuckled Ito.

"It is money," sighed Lucarius.

"Ho, ho," roared Ito, "the greatest Ephor of Crete, who taxes and browbeats we poor citizens, making us to go without the very necessities of life in order to provide his own, which would be our luxuries, talks to me of money; by my gods, thou makest me thirsty."

"Wine," ordered Lucarius languidly.

"To the kindest of mistresses, the older she is the better I love her." Ito bowed gravely, holding up the slender stemmed glass by its two curved handles, in the direction of the beautifully formed slim amphoras carried by a slave, which contained rich wine from Malavesi.

"True it is that in the midst of life we are in debt. What has happened, mighty Ephor, that thou lackest money?" asked Ito, who had drunk deeply, after pouring a little of the wine on the floor.

"The great Ruipi has become nervous," Lucarius sneered; "his excesses are being murmured against by the citizens; by the very soldiers; therefore, to protect his own trembling carcase, he has issued an edict, that restricts we aristocrats from exacting our just dues."

"Then thou must determine on some other way of replenishing thy purse."

"How?"

"Reforms change methods, not morals, and thou, sweet Lucarius, art too clever to be honest."

"Ruipi has been stern on the point, and he has many spies."

Lucarius did not resent the impugning of his honesty.

"At our sports yesterday, I noted it was not always the best horses that won, but handling poor ones well, that brought the chariots first."

Lucarius waited, Ito had never yet failed to extricate him from a difficulty.

"I saw the adorable maiden, thy daughter, at the sports held in honour of the funeral of the patrician Eumelus."

Still Lucarius held his peace.

"I was not alone," continued Ito, signing to the slaves, cup-bearer and glass holder to approach, then after again moistening the floor with a little of the wine, repeating his toast, and drinking, he resumed . . . "There was one with me, who fell suddenly into a great deep pool of many glamours."

"And pray what has his stumbling to do with me, or for the matter of that with thee?"

"It is thy bait that has caught the big fish. I am the grappling hook he calls on to save him, he is not accustomed to this particular pool, and will likely die of cramp or fever, if he be not rescued."

"Thy story hath a meaning," yawned Lucarius.

"How wonderful to possess that wisdom which is our only excuse for being alive," scoffed Ito, then . . . "Tell me, Lucarius, why is it thou art so pressingly in need of money?"

"Thalia's seed-pearl sandals are not uncostly trifles; my home,

my needs, my daughter, all cost money. Money can do anything."

"The man who thinks that money can do anything will generally do anything for money," commented Ito. "So the beauteous Rhoea is proving a costly burden, you say."

"Rhoea is a true child of her two parents, she hath a form as
graceful as my ever lamented Deseré, a love of fine things such
as mine own, with my disregard of money for money's sake.
Her red gold hair and dark eyes are her own."

"And these two last named, combined with the other attributes thou speakest of as inheritances from her mother, are the
baits that caused my friend's fall."

"Thou meanest ———?"

"I mean that the small god with the flowery bow used thy
daughter to ensnare the heart of one Barbatus, a merchant from
Malavesi, who grows the grape that has made Malavesi wine,
the beverage to tempt Dionysus, the son of Zeus himself, to
honour Greece as his birthplace."

Lucarius sat upright, he almost forgot his beauty so far as to
permit his expression to denote anger.

"Take care, Ito; do not too far presume on our long friendship; wouldst thou dare mention a plebeian rogue as suitor for
the hand of my daughter?"

"He is a wealthy one, this Barbatus. It is said he does not
know the length of his vineyards, nor the extent of his olive
mountains, neither could he count his sheep, nor his slaves.
Ships, too, does this Malavesi own; oh ho, yes, a wealthy man."

"That counts as naught in my eyes," haughtily spoke Lucarius.

"Consistency ever bored me; thy lack of it is one of thy many
virtues, Lucarius, for but now thou didst vow money could do
anything."

"It, alone, cannot purchase my daughter;" the incensed tone

caused a trembling amongst the kneeling slaves, who, having ears, must only hear their master's orders, and naught else; to learn secrets meant chastisement or worse; to repeat them, death.

"But, if allied to a straight strong arm, and a loving heart ——"

"Pah!"

"Take care, Lucarius; I noted, as also did Barbatus, that he was not the fair Rhoea's only victim."

"Who else would dare ——?" questioned Lucarius sharply.

"One whose daring lost you Deseré."

"Ruipi ——?"

"Himself!"

"By all the gods he shall not have her."

"There are many gods, but even they, it is said, cannot save a man's life, when he has but one throat, and that is slit." Ito chuckled.

"I shall see to it that Rhoea is given in marriage to an aristocrat of my own choosing, and that without delay," decided Lucarius.

"And to whom?" queried Ito interestedly; continuing musingly, as Lucarius fell into deep thought, "it is pretty to hear tales that are told of cargoes the ships of Barbatus bring, cargoes of ivory and golden bars, cedar wood, and the scented sandal, precious stones, and apes and fans, fine silken pieces. Oh yes, Barbatus is a rich man, and generous with his wealth; counted among the aristocrats, too, in his own country-side."

"Ruipi!" Lucarius breathed the hated name through set lips, "Ruipi, by Zeus!"

"One more glass of wine, and I will leave thee in peace," promised Ito. "To the most adorable mistress ——"

"Where is this—Barbatus to be seen?" interrupted Lucarius.

"Lucarius, the delight of thy society hath caused me to forget that the poor rich Barbatus is waiting in the outer hall for me, while I stay gossiping with thee. I must hasten to him."

"Bring him here."

With a satisfied grin, Ito lurched unsteadily to the door.

"Those fat ingots shall soon be mine, friend Barbatus," he hiccuped joyfully, as he joined the heavily-built young wine-grower, who was patiently waiting in the outer hall of Ephor Lucarius's palace.

CHAPTER VI

"I am worthy of a greater price than this wine-merchant can pay," Rhoea decided aloud, speaking more to the reflection that gazed back at her from the polished bronze mirror, held motionless by Dimidia, then—"Plague take marriage," she anathematized pettishly, throwing herself back on the long low lounge, before which the pale, oval-faced young slave from Syria knelt with the mirror.

"The Lord thy father hath decided," Dimidia's low voice soothed.

"In truth he may have done so, but never yet have I done that which displeased me, neither is it my intention to break from that rule. My noble father should be well bitten on the back of his hand, for permitting so ignominious an alliance for his only child, to come under consideration."

"Thou wilt not marry this citizen from Malavesi?" asked Dimidia.

"Not I, for all his vineyards, olive-groves, vessels and wealth," the young patrician asserted scornfully, then rising to lean on her elbow, she looked at her slave with a faint gleam of curiosity in the deep blue eyes of almond shape, that appeared almost black, set as they were in a face of rose-petal whiteness, a skin of satiny softness that had never been bathed in anything harsher than the milk of wild asses, the arched brows, and curling lashes, many shades darker than the crown of red gold hair, fine and shining as shavings from new minted gold, made her good to look upon.

"Tell me, Dimidia, what thoughts hast thou on marriage?" she commanded.

"For thee, Mistress, I think no one worthy."

Rhoea laughed, well pleased both at the words, and the sincerity that underlay them.

"And for thyself?"

A faint colour crept into the olive cheeks. "I could hope that my beloved mistress would not choose a husband for me," she said slowly.

For a moment Rhoea thought this over. "Wouldst thou never marry, or only a man of thine own choosing?" she questioned.

Dimidia's breath came a little quicker, the lids covered her great speaking eyes.

"I would never marry if it displeased my mistress?" she countered.

"Answer my question." Rhoea's voice was sharp.

"Only he whom I would choose." Dimidia trembled as she spoke. She knew the Lady Rhoea.

"There is such a one?"

"Yes." The monosyllable was scarcely audible, she could even now feel the sharp pain of the cane on her back.

"Who is the rascal who hath dared approach one of my slaves?"

"A native of my own land."

"It is three years since my father bought thee; hast thou then so much faith in man's constancy, foolish one, as to believe he will have remained faithful and unwed for thy sake?"

"I know he has, Mistress."

"How know ye this; hast thou dared speak with strangers from Syria?"

"No!"

"Then ———?"

"He is here," and now not a vestige of colour remained in the delicate face, even her lips were blanched and deathly white; she knew what she was risking by answering truthfully, not only her own skin, but that of the man she loved, perhaps even his very life.

In the midst of her anger, that this chattel should dare confess to a heart, Rhoea wondered at this strange slave, whose back still showed scarce healed stripes where the cane had fallen; each time, she reflected, Dimidia could have avoided these punishments, as did the other slaves, by a little subterfuge, by diplomatically evading the truth, yet she had never done so.

"Thou knowest I shall beat thee?"

"Yes."

"And have this knave of thine lashed?"

Dimidia's body sank, she was near fainting, a world of entreaty shone in the mournful brown eyes.

"Why dost thou tell me this?" Rhoea's curiosity was strong, she had never done marvelling at this singular slave.

"Thou asked me, Mistress."

"Hadst thou answered me differently I would have believed thee."

"I could not have answered thee otherwise, and still spoken the truth."

"By the god of gods I do not understand thee. It is not fear of chastisement that leads thee to ever say that which is so, neither is it possible to flog a liar into telling the truth. Hast thou some strange god who demands rigid veracity?"

"It may be so. I do not know."

"Wert thou always truthful? Speak, tell me."

"No, for when I was a child, I would often say that which was not so, and though none discovered I had done so, I would weep, and fear—I knew not what, still it seemed to me as though at some time I had suffered, or caused great suffering through my lying and cruelty. As I grew older my determination to only speak truth and never inflict cruelty became stronger."

"Is that all?"

"These things, and to be strong and brave and never complain," added Dimidia.

For the moment Rhoea's wrath was forgotten in the interest this chattel always succeeded in arousing within her.

"It must be that some Spartan blood runs in thy veins," she suggested.

"It may be so, Mistress."

"That mass of wine-soaked flesh, Ito, the philosopher, is of the opinion that some part he terms 'the soul' hath lived in previous times, and will ever exist; hast thou any recollection of a former state?"

"Not clearly, and yet ——"

"Yes, yes." Rhoea sat up eagerly.

"I crave thy pardon, beautiful Mistress, but it seems as though thou and I had met before."

"I, too, have experienced that feeling, and that then would explain the interest I have ever felt in thee."

"Thou hast always been the kindest of mistresses. I rejoiced when thou demanded me of thine honoured father."

"And even while so doing I was conscious of a strange resentment against thee such as I ever felt towards my mother, a seemingly unnatural sense, that caused me to rejoice on hearing she had left Crete for Delphi, without bidding me farewell, which fact did not distress, or amaze me, for she had no more love for me than I possessed for her. But with thee, a slave, unless Ito is correct, it is monstrous that I, a patrician, should suffer any such emotion." Slowly Rhoea rose, and seating herself, bade Dimidia dress her hair.

In silence this duty was performed, the thoughts of both maidens (who were of an equal age, verging on seventeen) were occupied.

Rhoea recalled the day she had gone with her attendants to visit the slave market, and meeting her father, who was inspecting a group of newly-acquired human chattels, had joined him. Among the fifty or so females, her eyes had lighted on Dimidia's frightened, crouching figure.

Fascinated, she watched her, all unwittingly a strongly protective feeling sprang into being, and Lucarius had carelessly consented to the young Syrian maiden becoming his daughter's property, whom the little aristocrat chose as her constant attendant, tyrannizing over, and petting her adoring slave as moods moved her, allowing no one else to order or punish; Dimidia belonged to her, and to her alone.

Now as the hairdressing proceeded, in the fashion which this spoilt child of the Ephor demanded, in the shape of a conical shell such as only the matrons of Crete were supposed to wear it, instead of twisted modestly on the nape of the neck, which was the approved method for young maidens, Rhoea felt a rising anger and resentment of the Syrian who had enamoured her slave.

Then as her handmaiden delicately tinted the fair cheek with rose, painting the lips scarlet, and brushing the whole with fine rice powder by means of a soft ball of swansdown, all of which Rhoea well knew would add to the disapproving shakes of Cretan ladies' heads, and the whispered wonder of what maidens were coming to, to thus ape matron fashions, she suddenly determined to inspect this villain, and learn for herself what manner of man it was whom her favourite slave wished to marry.

As the soft white garment for outdoor wear was being gracefully draped on her slim young form she asked:

"On what task is this Syrian knave employed?"

"He tends the garden within the amber wall," Dimidia answered simply, making no pretence of not knowing whom her mistress meant by "Syrian knave."

The little maid looked adoringly after her beloved mistress, who had refrained from punishing her, although her slave well knew many of her utterances had displeased the noble lady, who departed silently, to accompany her father to the Agora, where a new play by the witty Bas of Priam, interpolated with music especially composed for it by no less a person than Terpander, was to be performed, and Dædalus had promised to introduce a new dance of his own invention. The whole of aristocratic Crete, with slaves and followers, flocked to see and be seen.

Walking by her father's side, with demurely lowered lids and prim pressed lips, Rhoea was quite conscious of the admiration her appearance excited, as she joined the gay throng.

Not a murmur escaped her ear, nor a glance went unnoticed, nor was this laudation of lip and eye meant to be secret; the beauties of Crete approved of this public method of doing homage to their charms, and husbands and lovers who were wise concealed any jealousy they might feel, for if the gay young noblemen found one of their set who objected to his lady, or ladies, being subjected to loudly expressed admiration, then the poor foolish objector immediately became the butt of every irrepressible youth in Crete.

Lucarius and his daughter were quickly surrounded by a

host of friends, through which the bibulous Ito, followed by the stolid Barbatus, soon pushed a way.

Rhoea greeted Barbatus civilly but coldly, turning to Ito, whom she addressed banteringly.

"How now, wicked Ito, thou hast sinned deeply," she laughed. "I am happy to learn that I am losing my besetting weakness of slothfulness then, for to do anything deeply requires irksome energy," he replied in the same strain. "Tell me, adored one, in what way have I met with this unlooked for success?"

"By not visiting me."

"That was penance, not sin, modest one."

"Scandal has it that thou hast been fully occupied."

"Ah, scandal, were it not for she, and her twin, gossip, we would needs turn all our merchants into civil soldiers to help guard our homes; but what have those shells thou stole from the seashore, for ears, heard of me?"

"That Ito, who is so contemptuous of my sex, hath been busy forming fair friendships."

"For once the twins speak truth, but they are merely friendships formed on the teachings of the wise Plato."

"And what may those be?" queried Rhoea.

"A follower of Plato learns to make friendships with the opposite sex without incurring debts."

"If thou only wouldst thou couldst rival Plato," laughingly jeered Lucarius, who had been a silent listener.

"I am too busy composing odes to sing them," sighed Ito.

"Still, wouldst thou not sacrifice thy besetting weakness in order to reach the top?" inquired Lucarius.

"I know of nothing worth having for which sacrifice is worthy, and moreover why should I strive to climb a lonely height, when all my friends are here at the bottom."

Barbatus, after several tentative attempts to engage Rhoea in conversation, which she greeted with icy politeness, had abandoned the task, and stood back leaning against a huge fluted pillar, never removing his eyes from the object of his adoration.

Now a diversion was made, in an interval between the acts, by a young Cretan nobleman who, leaping into the circle reserved for the players, improvised a passionate and flowery oration in praise of the most beauteous maiden of all Greece, Rhoea, daughter of the mighty Ephor Lucarius.

Flushed with pride Rhoea gloried in so public an acclamation; never before had so young a maiden achieved this success, no Queen had ever been so lauded. Rhoea's eyes shone, her heart beat exultantly, this indeed was sweet life; this adulation was the meat and drink for which she craved.

When the applause which greeted this peroration had abated, a still greater honour awaited her, one which caused her father considerable inward trepidation.

His Majesty King Ruipi presented himself to converse with the beauty of the day.

Concealing the intense loathing and innate fear she had of this gross monarch, Rhoea sacrificed her feelings to her pride, exerting herself to fascinate an already infatuated sensualist.

With unblinking eyes, the neglected wine-merchant drank in the whole scene.

"I wish to lay my tribute of adoration at the feet of our goddess of beauty," Ruipi's coarse voice rang out, as he bowed low over Rhoea's hand.

"One who is soon to remove her sway from Crete," Lucarius remarked, intervening with polished ease between his daughter and his king.

"What meanest thou, oh harbinger of evil tidings?" and

while the King's mouth smiled, the King's black eyes smouldered dangerously.

"Only that my daughter is about to bereave her unhappy father, by marrying and departing hence for Malavesi," sighed Lucarius.

The suddenness of such an announcement caused a quickening of varied emotions among his listeners.

Lucarius spoke thus, feeling that a situation so fraught with danger called for drastic measures, the fact that nothing definite had been settled with Barbatus was a minor matter in face of the peril with which Rhoea was threatened, when such a mighty and infamous personage as Ruipi publicly betrayed admiration for her.

This scoundrel, who had ruthlessly torn his beloved Deseré from his arms (or so Lucarius expressed the loss of his wife in his thoughts) was not going to snatch his daughter to make of her a plaything. Therefore he announced an engagement that had never existed, his autocratic position of parenthood caused him to disregard Rhoea's feelings, and the contempt with which he held the plebeian wine-maker, led him to speak thus without consulting either party to the projected alliance.

The massive face of Barbatus flushed a rusty red, his hands knotted themselves together, until the veins stood out like cords.

The light died from Rhoea's eyes, her scarlet stained mouth fell open, her head turned quickly, a white heat of anger and amazement was evident in every line of her face and body as she gazed wrathfully at her father; to be sure he had mentioned something of this prospective marriage to her, but she had paid small attention to it, as a thing for future discussion, when she depended (as she had ever done) on her power to coax and wheedle him into permitting her to make her own choice, but to suddenly have so undesirable an alliance, one which she refused even now seriously to contemplate, spoken of as a thing arranged, bereft her for the moment of power of speech.

Then some words the King was uttering in his peculiar thick tone reached her senses.

"It is not only her father, but a country and its unworthy King who would mourn such a disaster, were it ever permitted to occur."

Lucarius felt the underlying warning; he read the King's malignant meaning beneath the King's evil smile.

"A father must subdue his own feelings, where his one treasure's happiness is taken in hand by fate," he sighed.

"Fate is a bully, fear not to strike back and, like all bullies, she will cringe before the blow," Ito remarked merrily. He sensed the tensity of the situation, and spoke at random in an effort to relieve it.

"Well spoken, my philosopher," croaked the King, "and thou, maiden, is thy heart so set on this marriage that thou wouldst contract it even though it left many sad at its accomplishment?" he inquired of Rhoea.

"A daughter's heart is in a body that belongs to her father, sir," she answered cunningly.

"Thy words are wise, oh peerless one; as thou sayest, a daughter belongs to her father, just as a father belongs to his King, and as a child obeys her parent, so will that parent reward her; in like manner will a monarch reward his obedient subjects." As a mark of regal favour, he bent and imprinting a salute on her white forehead, bowing low, departed.

It needed great self-control on Rhoea's part to refrain from openly shuddering when the thick, voluptuous lips touched her skin; the fact that he was king, and so she would be envied by every other woman present, brought vanity uppermost to predominate over instinctive loathing.

The play was ended, the music silent, the dances over, with never a word to the humbly following Barbatus, Rhoea walked with high-held head beside her father, to their waiting chariot.

Here again Ruipi appeared, and taking her hand assisted her to enter the equipage, smiling, well pleased at the cries of admiration that greeted the young patrician maiden's appearance, the cry of:

"All hail, Queen of Beauty," evoked from him the thick whisper:

"The Queen of Beauty, should be Queen of Crete."

Those words rang in Rhoea's ears, bringing a return of radiant triumph to her eyes, as she drove off, pelted madly by the irrepressible noblemen who showered masses of exotic flowers on the brilliantly gilded chariot, that dashed away, leaving Barbatus unspoken to by the fair creature, with whom he had fallen deeply in love.

"I know not whether to weep, or to ask on account for a few of those merry ingots thou promised in the event of a certain happening, friend Barbatus," sighed Ito.

CHAPTER VII

That night Crete was even more gay than its brilliant wont. Every patrician was either on the road to, or already attending a feast. Garlands of flowers hung from balconies, or fell in great ropes down fluted pillars.

Endless rows of slaves, holding flares of scented wood, illuminated the street and the agora, where soldiers, sailors and plebeians sang, danced, and drank deeply, in good imitation of the aristocrats.

Great chariots, gorgeously decorated with gilt frescoes, drawn by spirited horses, came charging along the streets, preceded and followed by hosts of brass-throated slaves, who, as they ran, bellowed of the merits, riches and greatness of their separate masters, whose brand was burned on their black backs, and whose bronze swords and gilt-tipped spears they carried.

From the great palaces there issued the sound of citheras, harps, and even the high flute notes of the common syrinx were employed to make music, while the nobility of Crete ate and drank deeply.

Above the sea-girt city, like a pearl in a sapphire setting, the moon slowly rose, lingering, to softly caress the lofty mount Upsiloriti, birthplace of mighty Zeus, before pausing, high hung like a painted bubble, to look down on these scenes of revelry.

The coming of the moon was watched by three people. One a woman, seated alone, looking out through a tiny barred aperture in the wall of a room high up in the King's palace. The harshness of her expression marred the beauty that age had not yet deprived her of; the close-set, black eyes were hard, and betokened secret scheming; although they were fixed on Heaven's lantern, its beauty or even its very appearance passed almost unnoticed by her.

This was Deseré, mother of Rhoea, who, unseen by Lucarius, had often watched him and her Royal master's other guests in their going and coming, her heart filled with both envy and gloating.

Envy because she longed to take a place for which she never ceased to plot, that of lawful, wedded Queen; gloating because she had succeeded in gaining that which passed for love, from the man she adored, the swarthy Ruipi. The last fact would have considerably astonished the golden-bearded Lucarius, whom pitying nature had endowed with a colossal vanity, perhaps in compensation for his many shortcomings.

Deseré had been quite well aware of what was to be her fate from the day she obeyed Lucarius and entered the Palace, having previously arranged the whole matter with Ruipi; in this way she could join the man she loved, and save a scandal and outcry, so she chose it. Despite her gratified desire she cherished a brooding resentment against Lucarius in that he had so lightly abandoned her.

Wearing the robe of Royal purple which she ever affected, her dark hair encircled with a crown of golden leaves, Deseré watched the arrival of guests (among whom she recognized many of her former acquaintances, including Lucarius), her thoughts on all she had heard, through her slaves, of various happenings in Crete.

Ruipi's words to Rhoea had been overheard by twenty ears, and like wild-fire were poured into eagerly listening twenty thousand, each tongue that repeated the King's words adding a tittle.

That her own daughter, whom she had always disliked, should aspire to become Queen of Crete, wife to Ruipi, was something not to be tolerated. Protestations would be useless, then strategy must be employed.

Deseré's slaves moaned in their sleep that night; on their backs were raw red welts, her hand had fallen heavily.

The second watcher of the moon was Dimidia; strange thoughts came to her as she sat crouched on the lowest step that led to Ephor Lucarius's palace. Of her early life in Syria, where she had played beneath the date palms and watched the tragic-faced camels; of the first time she had seen death, that was when a camel had gone mad and crushed with his breast bone the cruel man Sardis; how his face had depicted hate of the beast, then fear, which turned to grim horror, the hideous shriek, which ended in a groan, then a rattle, as he lay still, and though the inexorable animal continued to crush him, Dimidia had watched, fascinated, wondering at the calm peacefulness that settled over the lifeless man's face.

Then death must be a good friend, to be loved, not feared.

Had she ever died?

She thought she must have at some time, and that death had come as a relief.

And the Syrian whom she loved, did he care for her?

At least he was not indifferent, whenever opportunity allowed he was kind and gentle to her.

These shadows that played about her feet, were they real, and the trees and shrubs that cast them mere phantasies of the imagination, or was it the other way about?

The night was hot and drowsy, Dimidia slept, and as she sat sleeping in the moonlight she seemed to pass through many adventures. Sometimes she smiled, at other times she moaned, or sighed, her pale face grew whiter, or was it the light of the moon that made it appear so?

And away by the lake in the garden, a Syrian, tall and strong, stood leaning against the high wall of amber that surrounded the square. His clear-cut features, of olive hue, stood out boldly, as he gazed upward at the moon. He held high his arms, and slowly moved his legs, which until this late eve had been shackled for many weary months, and now they were freed from the irksome chains, he smiled.

His thoughts were neither of the moon, nor of his hated chains, rather they dwelt on the apparition that had appeared to him, while he and his fellow slaves toiled late in the pleasure garden.

Intent on his work he had suddenly been inspired to look upwards, and there, prone on the top of the broad wall, lay a vision clothed in a fine silk garment, her chin cupped in the palms of her hands, her hair turning to flame in the setting sun, her eyes like blue waves over black rocks, rested full on him.

He forgot his work, forgot he was a slave. Nothing else existed but this wonderful being on the amber wall, her little pink heels and toes showing bare through their sandals.

The overseer's sharply-spoken words fell on deaf ears, the cruel lash descended on a back that did not feel, then "she" had raised a slender hand, and silence fell on the garden.

She called for her ivory ladder with rivets of turquoise and gold, her slaves hastened to spread an azure carpet, and knelt as she passed along.

He could not tear his eyes from her; she frowned, but he knew that was only her pride, that his palpable admiration was not really displeasing.

Then she spoke, and the sound of her voice brought a throb to his heart, it reminded him of the soft wind that sang over the Syrian desert at dawn.

He longed to bend and kiss the glint of her sandal-lace.

At her command his chains were loosened.

She drew near, the haughty little head set on a slender neck was turned upwards gazing at him, until he yearned to crush to his own the mocking scarlet mouth, like a flower half uncurled.

"Thou shouldst have a red blossom on thy brow," the words were forced from his lips against his own volition, they fell back on his ears as though some other voice than his own had uttered them. He started and trembled, not for fear of the punishment that would surely follow so great a daring as this, of a slave addressing a patrician lady, but from the much greater dread that she would be angry and depart.

Miracle of miracles, she answered him!

"Yes," he heard her say, "yes, I know," then she, too, faltered, a look of bewilderment passed across her face, and, turning abruptly, she mounted the ivory ladder, and vanished from his sight.

With her went the sun.

Cool night fell, it was time to cease work, his fellow slaves departed, he was roughly bidden to stay and guard the garden. Now, standing watching the moon's white breast slipping through her robe of velvet night, he waited.

What it was he waited for, he did not ask himself. All he knew was he must stand here and wait, all through the night if needs be, until dawn flung wide the gates in the East to make clear the way for the glittering chariot and fiery steeds of the great god Apollo.

Tall white lilies and crimson roses whispered together, while the perfume of star-eyed jasmine and creamy magnolia mingled with the heavier scent of twisting, swaying oleander.

Unobserved, a pure white rose nodded gently to the floating water lilies and purple iris.

So silently stood the Syrian slave, that a blue moth dared to carry openly a love message from the flaunting, scarlet pomegranate blossom, to the shy-eyed clematis that clung close to the amber wall.

Far in the distance a wood pigeon cooed softly to its mate, and a nightingale burst its heart in song.

And then, he hardly dared believe his eyes were not revealing to him only the vision his heart so fiercely longed for, she came!

There on the wall she appeared, a delicate white form.

"Oh slave," she called softly, peering down into the garden.

With trembling limbs he stepped out into the moonlight.

"I am here, lady."

Now she stood before him.

How long they stood thus gazing into one another's eyes neither knew.

"By what name art thou known?" she questioned.

"Ugiso."

"Oh."

A long pause, then slowly, as though searching a roving memory: "I—know—that—name," she said. "I am called Rhoea," she added.

"Rhoea," he repeated slowly.

"Thou hast not quite spoken it aright. I returned to see that thou wert protecting the garden," she lied.

A heavy-winged owl fluttered across the blue of the moon.

"Why didst thou say I should have a crimson blossom on my brow?" she demanded.

"It should be there," he spoke stumblingly.

"Yes, I know, but why?"

"I do not know."

Wrenching a scarlet hybiscus from amongst its dark leaves, he held it out to her, with a twist of green thong.

Slowly she accepted the proffered things, and hesitatingly bound the flower to her forehead, eyeing him curiously as she did so.

His eyes burned like living fires.

"If it were known that thou addressed me thou wouldst be put to death," she informed him.

"Yes." The indifference of his tone piqued her.

"Wouldst thou not be afraid?" she questioned.

"I could fear nothing except losing thee." His voice trembled as he spoke.

The thrill his words sent through her heart wakened some latent memory of wonderful nights in a cave, of strong arms round her, of a great forest, of strange beasts.

"I shall not come again." The voice she tried to make haughty only sounded a little shrill from excitement.

"Thou must," he breathed.

"No, no," but her eyes contradicted her words.

"Thou wilt come again and again; I cannot live without thee."

In vain she struggled to regain her habitual attitude of scornful disdain.

"And why should I care for the miserable life of any slave?" she queried.

"I do not know," he answered the words, not the tone.

"And why must I come again? It is a pretty thing if slaves are to issue orders," she jeered.

"Thou must come again, for I cannot come to thee," he repeated doggedly.

"For what purpose?" Rhoea had recovered some outward semblance of her old manner.

"So that I may speak with thee, look at thee, tell thee of my Syrian desert. Dream with thee of what might have been had I been free, and thou a maiden of my own country. Paint with poor words pictures of silken tents set in the midst of great wide deserts, rolling free beneath cool palm trees. Of burnished skies that leave night air warm and languorous, trembling with love songs that the very stars bend close to hear. To tell thee, oh Rose of all the world, that I would hold thee so close and kiss thee so tenderly, that not even death could tear thee from me. Ah, if thou wert mine, if thou wert mine ———"

His strong arms were round her, his hot young lips sought hers: "Thou art mine, thou art mine." His voice broke in his throat.

Then the tense stillness of the night was broken by a deep sobbing, contralto voice, sweet and low, filled with anguish. The words of the song beat down on these two hidden in the shadow of the amber wall.

"Oh thou, my moon, and thou, my star,
I yearn for thee in land afar,
I gaze on thee through prison's bar
Oh thou, my moon, and thou, my star.

"Thy kindly light, my star and moon,
Braves me to crave of thee a boon.
Oh pitying star, oh soft blue moon,
Guide tender Death to take me soon."

The last echo of the plaintive song had passed on its journey, only the chattering of an angry ape, and the cry of a nightjar disturbed the heavy air when Rhoea uttered a low, startled cry, as she stumbled over the sleeping form of Dimidia, for now it was very dark, the moon had hidden her face behind a threatening cloud.

"What art thou doing here?" Rhoea demanded sharply.

"Thy pardon, mistress. I—I had fallen asleep."

"Thou wert weeping," accused Rhoea, for she had heard the maiden sobbing, and was suspicious that her adventure had been spied upon.

"I had embarked on a long journey."

"What meanest thou?"

"I dreamed."

"Come," commanded Rhoea.

Softly the two young things crept through the great marble passages, going so quietly that none of the sleeping slaves wakened.

"What was this dream that caused thee to weep?" asked Rhoea, when she had softly gained her own apartment.

"I dreamed that I was the pure White Rose that grows within the amber wall, and two there were that loved me, one was he who tended and cared for me; I trembled, when he whom I called Master caressed my petals; the other was a tiny grey Singing Bird, who came every day to pour his passionate love into my heart, loud and clear he sang, telling of things deeper than prayer, and all who heard thrilled at the depth and glory of the song that was sung to me, making hope blossom, and the very mountains laugh out, and the glad hills shout with joy.

"Then there came one, whose beauty rivalled and outshone mine own. We trembled at her coming, and bowed our heads to make her obeisance. She was too lovely and scornful to notice me, her humble slave ——"

"In what form came this beauty?" Rhoea interrupted to ask, breathlessly intent on the dream that had come to her slave.

"In thine, mistress," answered Dimidia humbly.

"Continue," ordered Rhoea.

"The one I called Master, seeing her, forgot me. Therefore I was sad, but what could a mere White Rose do against such beauty as adorned this great lady. My Master loved her as he had never loved me, she scorned his poor words, and his humble birth, so he pined and was like to die.

"Then one morning he heard my Song Bird pouring out his very heart at my feet.

"With a great shout of joy my Master ran to where I rested; plucking me, he kissed my petals.

"'Go,' he cried, 'take this secret the Bird hath told thee, oh White Rose, and whisper it to my lady.'

"He sent me to her, she held me in a hand fairer than my own whiteness. Humbly I gave her his message."

"Yes, yes, and what said she?" cried Rhoea impatiently, as Dimidia paused.

"She listened, then with a cool, cruel smile cast me far from her. As I lay crushed and bruised, my Song Bird sought me out, and seeing me lying thus, broke his heart and fell lifeless beside me. Then came my Master, to ask of his lady her answer, he too saw me, and understood. With a grief-low cry, he sank to the earth close, close to me. I saw the Heavens open as together we died."

"It was a strange dream," mused Rhoea.

"Strange indeed, mistress, but now I do not know which is reality, that which happened when I slept, or these things I do now that I am awake?"

And even had Rhoea possessed all the wisdom of all ages, she could not have settled this question that puzzled her slave.

CHAPTER VIII

The morning following the day of such great events in Rhoea's life she wakened early.

Contrary to her usual custom, she did not immediately summon her slaves, but lay on her couch, many thoughts occupying her mind.

The olive-skinned Syrian slave in the moonlit garden, with his strong arms, and hot lips, his head of black silken hair. Rhoea smiled, and nestled further down in her soft nest, closing her eyes whilst living again the wonderful hour she had stolen from Fate.

If her father knew he would kill her; then her father must never know, and she would not repeat the escapade. Yet even while she formed this inward resolve, she wondered if she would just once more scale the amber wall, and taste again the fierce delight that outsoared the clogs of convention.

Draw from him those mad kisses, feel herself pressed close against his loudly-beating heart, his hot breath on her neck.

The recollection of it all made her tremble. She thought only of herself, her own desires, no reflection of the suffering she might inflict on these Syrians, on the maiden who loved him, or the hapless slave whose heart she had stormed for a moment's pleasure, leaving him to suffer one long regret, entered her mind.

As to this proposed union with the wine-grower Rhoea frowned, and dismissed the notion with angry disdain.

It had been very indiscreet of her father to have taken so drastic a step, publicly announcing a betrothal that never had, and never would exist.

She had always managed to wheedle her parent into doing what she wished, and although this time it might prove a difficult task, she did not doubt her ability to succeed.

"The Queen of Beauty should be Queen of Crete."

Ha! the King's significant words rang again in her ears, stirring vanity and ambition.

The mere thought of Ruipi, the man, made her shudder; it was the position she coveted, for that, she was willing to barter her body and soul.

Clapping her hands to call her slaves, she bathed, dressed and was ready to visit her father when he sent for her.

Lucarius had never ruled his daughter with the Cretan iron rod, excusing his indulgence on the plea that she was an only child, and motherless; this morning he awaited her coming with much inward trepidation.

On one point he was determined, this marriage with the wealthy Malavesian must take place at once.

Gravely and firmly he informed his daughter that this was to be so, amazed beyond measure when the expected tears and protests did not come.

Rhoea, seated on a cushion at his feet, looked up at him with the clear, limpid eyes of a child.

"Is it thy wish, my father?" she asked softly.

Thus was Lucarius disarmed. He bent lovingly over his obedient daughter, who, after all, was not going to ruffle his temper by making a scene.

"It is, sweet child."

"May I ask why?"

"It is time thou wert given in marriage, and this Barbatus is a worthy man, he will make thee happy."

"Most thoughtful of parents, is it of my happiness thou thinketh?" cooed Rhoea.

"Of nothing else," Lucarius lied gently.

"And think thou it will make me happy to leave so loving a parent, with a man whom I do not know?" she asked plaintively.

The cunning little witch. Lucarius grew wary.

"Dear one, I will be sad at losing thee, but a father of such a daughter must make sacrifice. This Barbatus is young, strong, deeply enamoured of thee, counted an aristocrat in Malavesi, and possessed of great wealth."

"Indeed, thou art a wise father, for all these attributes are great inducements to any maiden." Rhoea gently stroked her father's hand.

"And so sage a one as my Rhoea well knows that money is a needful commodity!"

"It would be great pleasure to help my father," she sighed.

"That thou canst do by marrying."

"I had hoped to do so," she murmured.

"This Barbatus seems like to be generous," mused Lucarius.

"Then indeed I may achieve my greatest wish, and prove the modest means of helping my dear father," said Rhoea.

"Dear child"; bending, Lucarius dropped a light caress on the red-gold hair.

"Though I had dreamed of bringing thee greater things than even wealth," she sighed.

"How so, best of daughters?"

"It has ever been a dream of mine to see my father take his rightful place as something even higher than chief Ephor; I would have him the great Tyrant for which his strength and talents are best fitted. Yesterday my dream seemed likely to be fulfilled."

"What meanest thou?" The voice of Lucarius had lost a little of its softness.

"Some words that were spoken to me by the highest in the land caused my heart to hope."

"The King?"

"The King."

"He is a vile black thing; it is because of his marked admiration of thee that I spoke loudly of thy forthcoming marriage."

"Wouldst thou not have thy daughter Queen of Crete?" asked Rhoea quickly.

"Ruipi will make no woman his lawful queen, and sooner than thou shouldst be seized upon, to pander to his evil pleasure before being cast aside, I would squeeze the life from thy body with mine own hands."

For the first time in her existence, Rhoea felt a spark of respect for her father.

"Fear not, such a thing as thou describeth I will never be." Strength and determination rang in the young voice.

"Then thou wilt marry this Barbatus?" he queried.

"I have ever obeyed my father," she countered skillfully, "but before this matter, which so closely affects our happiness, is settled may I be permitted a little time with which to become better acquainted with this aristocrat from Malavesi?"

Her request was granted, and on the best of terms father and daughter departed to witness the sports which were being held to celebrate the completion of a tomb the patrician Antiloclus had erected to hold the bones of his ancestors, and his own, when his time came.

Piloted by Ito, Barbatus came timidly to greet his liege lady, her reception of him threw him into perspiring confusion, while it filled him with overwhelming delight, for she was smilingly gracious.

"I fear me thou only approacheth through Ito's leading," she coquetted.

"I—I came because I wished," stammered Barbatus.

"It is full easy to lead a man the way he would go," declared Ito.

"But what if his heart and his head are at variance, each pulling strongly in opposite directions?" laughed Rhoea.

"Then he should ask himself which is likely to lead him into the greater temptation," declared Ito.

"So that he might spurn it?" asked Rhoea.

"No, grasp it, for the lesser desire can be strangled, sooner or later the stronger will conquer, then why dally? To play with temptation is mental immorality," Ito decided.

"What knowest thou of temptation, noble lady?" asked Barbatus timidly.

"All too little," pouted Rhoea. "I would dearly love to be greatly tempted."

"With what could any man gratify thy wish?" the Malavesian spoke eagerly.

"Great power," answered Rhoea promptly.

"That, thou must always have over any who have hearts." Barbatus bowed lowly.

"Not over hearts alone, but over lives and even kingdoms." Rhoea was well aware that the King had drawn near and was listening; she feigned ignorance of the Royal presence.

"Such desires are not conducive to virtue, my daughter," Lucarius chided gently.

"That which does not make for virtue, at least has the virtue of making for knowledge," Ito interpolated.

"Thou speaketh lightly of virtue," said Lucarius severely.

"Ito would have it despised," laughed Rhoea.

"Thou doest me wrong, lovely one. The unpopularity of virtue is due to the virtuous."

"In which case thou art entirely exonerated from my daughter's accusation," bantered Lucarius.

Ito turned a mock reproachful eye on the speaker. "Even thou, my Lucarius, have listened to malicious tales of me, it would seem. Ah, well," he sighed deeply, "I must take what poor consolation I can find in remembering that it is the famous who are most slandered."

"My poor Ito, I will not have thee suffer," condoled Rhoea.

"My humble thanks, gentle one; but when I suffer I thank the gods, for it is a sure proof that I am still alive," replied Ito smilingly.

"I am desolated to think that ambition is so infinite and human capacity so finite," sighed Rhoea.

"Not thine, surely maiden," Ruipi's coarse voice spoke in her ear.

With an affected start of surprise Rhoea bowed low.

"Oh, sir, my poor words did not include thee, for thou hast all I could desire," Rhoea murmured for the King alone to hear.

"And thou—my Paradise," he whispered.

"Then we might effect a barter." Rhoea screened the eagerness in her eyes with a roguish smile.

"No matter what I gave, I would be the gainer." His eyes wandered greedily over her youthful loveliness.

"Thou speakest thus because thou hast so much," she drew him on.

"Everything I have is as nothing to what thou couldst give in exchange." His voice had grown thicker.

"Thy palaces, thy jewels, thy wealth, thy ships," she recited.

"Willingly."

"And thou wouldst ask ———?" The blood drummed in Rhoea's ears as she put this pointed question, the answer to which meant so much.

"Thy lips," he whispered hoarsely.

Her heart died within her. Then her father had been right, but not all the wealth of Greece would induce her to become the plaything of this loathsome creature, from whom her whole soul shuddered, and yet she was ready and willing to become his wife in order to share his throne.

"The King is pleased to jest," she smiled coldly.

The entrance of Antiloclus, the giver of the sports, creating a diversion, she was enabled to turn her face from her Royal admirer.

Antiloclus had approached her side in order to plead that she, as the most beautiful lady of Crete, should present the winner of each event with his prize.

With her father's permission she consented.

The excitement of the chariot race failed to move her, nor was she interested in the loud discussion that arose when the winner was accused of dangerous driving.

With gracious ease, she took the hand of the beautiful woman of irreproachable character, who had been allotted as the first prize, and presented her to the winner.

Then followed javelin-throwing, wrestling, archery, dancing, foot races, boxing matches, more chariot races.

Competitors from Sparta, godlike youths, and maidens like

goddesses, naked but unashamed, proud of their perfect bodies, had journeyed hither to pit their strength and skill against these Cretans, whom they termed "barbarians," in that they clothed themselves for their sports.

With a burning rage consuming her, Rhoea forced a smile, and displaying great composure, presented the various prizes, which ranged from human slaves, black, white, or olive colour, to horses, oxen, mules, pots, pans, or rough masses of metal.

She soon recovered from her bitter disappointment, and with fresh zest employed every trick of which feminine coquetry is capable, to ensnare Ruipi. Deliberately ignoring him, then turning the witchery of her smiles softly towards her prey, pouring honeyed words of fulsome flattery into his greedy ears, raising him to an ecstasy of delight, in order that his fall into the abyss of despair should be the greater when she turned merrily to Barbatus, or one of the many young nobles who crowded round her, to become engrossed in their gay badinage, to the complete exclusion of the surly, enraged monarch.

Jealously watching her accepting the admiring homage all these men fought to shower at her feet, Ruipi ground his teeth, whilst silently vowing that she should be his.

"Ah, cruel one, thou takest all and giveth nothing," he whispered, as the sports ended and the mighty concourse rose to depart.

"Not so, sir, indeed, I am counted profligate, I would ever give meat to the hungry, but never drink to the drunkard." Rhoea smiled.

"And to me?" he questioned eagerly.

"Bread, not roses."

"But it is bread I crave," he protested.

"Yes, for thou hast too many roses." Rhoea knew she was

playing a daring game, but time pressed, and her father was set on this marriage with Barbatus.

Ruipi thoroughly understood her meaning. She would consent to be his, only as his wife, not as his mistress. Marriage was a dear price to pay, even for the possession of this tantalizing, fascinating maiden.

"The gods have endowed thee with great wisdom," he said gravely. "I would aspire to rise to thy height."

"Sir, thou art too modest, thou wouldst more like gain wisdom by stooping than by soaring."

"I would be beneath thy feet, and feel myself exalted in being so happily placed," he declared passionately.

"Thou art the King," she reminded him.

"Not thine, rather would I be thy slave and serve thee kneeling."

"And being a slave would evade the law which would hold me responsible for my slave's shortcomings. No, no, sir, far better keep thy throne."

"A question trembles on my lips."

"He who does not fear, pleases himself; thy question would surely be a command."

"I would not have it so."

Rhoea's heart beat fast, she felt the hand which the monarch held as he led her to her chariot, tremble in his grasp. Was she after all to succeed? In another moment her chance would have departed.

"I have always found it wise to tear off the curtain of doubt by question," she encouraged him. They had arrived at the chariot; she had no excuse to linger; already she felt the bitter tears of blighted hope stinging her lids, still she smiled bravely.

"Fairest beauty, I would make thee my Queen," he whispered.

"Sir, thou dost me great honour." With all her self-control her voice shook.

"My throne will only be bearable if thou wilt share it."

Her world swung dizzily round, her intense longing made her fearful that he had not meant the full purport of what his words conveyed.

"The King can always count on me as one of his most loyal subjects," she assured him.

"It is not as a subject, but as my wife I would have thee!"

Success! Her heart cried aloud in triumph; she laughed aloud, looking straight into his eyes.

"Sir, in all the long years which the gods may grant us, I humbly pray that all thy requests may be so truly to my liking."

And so Rhoea accepted King Ruipi as her affianced husband.

Before the whole of eagerly watching Crete, the monarch bent and pressed his thick lips to the white brow that so ardently yearned to wear a Queen's crown.

CHAPTER IX

Lucarius had witnessed the public kiss bestowed on his daughter with great irritation.

Rhoea could not understand her pleasure-loving, ambitious father's wrath on hearing her great news, and his repeated declaration that he would sooner have dedicated her to serve Hestia, than that such a fate as she looked forward to should be hers, greatly perplexed her, for she had expected him to be overwhelmed with gladness at the prospect of his daughter becoming Queen of Crete.

She disregarded all the reasons he assigned for his attitude, that Ruipi was an evil-living man, who had robbed maidens and matrons of their virtue, before abandoning them; that he was cruel, unscrupulous, greedy, all these things Rhoea knew without her father telling her. Had he been doubly the monster Lucarius painted, this maid of seventeen would still have schemed to become his wife; she was determined to reign as Queen of Crete.

Finding he could not force this unnatural daughter to obey his will, Lucarius went in fear and trembling, that only righteous anger bolstered for the ordeal, to voice his protest to the King.

Ruipi was prepared for his coming, and blandly overrode all the indignant father's objections.

"If thou persisteth in forming this alliance, what of —— Deseré?"

Lucarius had grown desperate enough to mention the name of his wife for the first time since he had bartered her to gratify his overweening ambitions.

"She must accept my will or ——" Ruipi paused significantly.

"Or what?" asked Lucarius.

The King sighed: "Or I fear me the fate which rumour credits her with having met must now be hers." He spoke quite sadly as though putting Deseré to death would grieve him.

In despair Lucarius eventually summoned Ito, whom he had not seen since the fateful day Rhoea had wrung the desired proposal from Ruipi, some weeks ago now.

"Ah, if I could but live again the past," wailed Lucarius, when the wine-soaked Ito had listened to the story he told him.

"Thine is the eternal cry to Nemesis of those climbing up, and no sooner have they succeeded in burying that which they term 'the past' than they hasten to form another one, which after all does not exist. What thou termest past is but an echo of 'now,'" nodded the philosopher.

"What am I to do in order to avert this tragedy?" begged Lucarius.

"Tell the divine Rhoea the truth."

"Never," declared Lucarius emphatically.

"Thou wouldst not have been true to thyself hadst thou done so," mused Ito. "I have always marvelled at the clever criminal who permits himself to be branded insane in order to gain his liberty; such loss of self-esteem wounds my æsthetic sense. Now thou, Lucarius, would do nothing that would cause thy vanity to suffer."

"Thou art heartless to talk thus, like an empty windbag, whilst I am in torture. It is well seen that thou hast never suffered." Lucarius spoke bitterly.

"I! Thou utterest such words to me. I, who am the greatest sufferer the world has ever known. See the tears that leap to my eyes, as they ever do when I dwell on my one great grief." And truly as he spoke his eyes filled and he gazed reproachfully at the Ephor.

"Indeed thou dost surprise me. What then is thy long hidden sorrow?" inquired Lucarius curiously.

"When I think on how much wine there is in the world and how small a cup there is to hold it, I weep, I weep," and Ito sobbed unrestrainedly.

With the aid of some of his beloved liquid, and many soothing apologies, Lucarius consoled his friend.

"Then, my sweet Lucarius, if thy daughter will not obey her parent, and that parent will not obey my wisdom which advises thee to tell her all, leave the matter in the lap of the gods, who willy nilly work their inscrutable way on us poor mortals, who, like ants on a hill, flee wildly from the terror of a shadow to place themselves beneath the very heel they sought to escape," a cheered and smiling Ito counselled.

With which piece of wisdom Lucarius was forced to be content, and Ito departed, leaving him gazing mournfully at his own reflection in a bronze mirror, searching for the wrinkles he greatly feared these troubles would trace on his smooth countenance.

Tidings of the King's betrothal flew apace, until all, to the lowliest slave, had heard of it.

The night of the day that the news came to Deseré's ears, she left the palace for the first time since she had entered it four years ago. On foot and alone she crept forth, of her going or where she went, none knew.

The slave who worked in the amber-walled garden heard of the King's prospective marriage and smiled. He knew it could not be true, and all day long amid the dust and toil, with sweat pouring from his brow; to the quiver of the lake, and the rustling of the grasses, his heart pulsed its measure of quick, deep beats, singing of happiness; for every night the King's sweetheart scaled the wall, to lie in his arms, to listen to the love that he tore from his heart; love like a crimson, passionate rose, scattering the petals with a lavish hand for her delicate feet to trample on.

Afar off sounded the croon of the sea, singing a song to soothe suffering hearts and lull little children to sleep, ever and anon moaning out a warning cry to too trusting lovers, falling back with a sob of despair that sent sea birds mewing affrightedly at the secrets they heard, but did not dare tell.

"It is the fault of the round moon that I come, for it ever makes me restless," Rhoea needlessly excused herself to the Syrian slave.

"Then I must always be her faithful friend, for bringing thee to my arms," he smiled.

"It pleases thee to hold me thus," she coquetted.

"Blossom of my heart, no joy of paradise could compare with this, just to hold thee in my arms, and keep thee there," murmured Ugiso.

And Rhoea lying happily on his breast, stroked his smooth cheek with cool finger tips of coral and pearl, smiling back at him with eyes that saw herself wearing the crown of a Queen.

"What of the time when I cease to come to thee, my Ugiso?" she asked.

"That time could never be, Little Heart; thou art too pure, too beautiful to be cruel; thou who hast given me the wine of thy lips, would not leave me to die of thirst for them. Thou wouldst not turn this scented garden into a pit of choking dust to blear my eyes and sear my heart. Ah no, ah no!" and he bent and kissed again and again her lips which were like twin sins.

"I am very beautiful, am I not?" she asked him.

"Many tongues and all eyes must have told thee that," he answered.

"But thou must tell me again," she commanded.

"What am I to tell thee that thou dost not know?" he asked softly; "that thy eyes are like the mystery of the great blue seas, thy hair bright and soft as a wild bird's wing, thy skin like the petal of a white flower, in thy lips lie sweet madness, and in thy laugh, sun-kissed magic of the desert palms. Oh, heart of me, no sadness or care can venture near while I have thee."

A late moon swung high, and shining on the white hand that lay on the slave's neck, caused the red sparks of wicked fire to shine evilly in the King's betrothal ring which Rhoea wore on her finger. The gleams in the depth of the milky stone moved mockingly, as her hand subconsciously sought for, and found a little mark behind Ugiso's shoulder, a curious scar that might have been made by sharp, cruel teeth.

Crouched in a corner of the amber wall, hidden by vine tangle, sat a figure clad in a cloak of sable hue.

Not a movement escaped those gloating, close-set eyes: with all her heart Deseré hated this daughter of hers.

So engrossed were the lovers, that they never heard her as she stole stealthily away, and gaining the palace, sent for the King.

Reluctantly Ruipi obeyed the summons of this woman who exercised a strange sway over him. He did not want to lose her, but rather that, than she should interfere with his pleasures.

He came, not knowing whether Deseré had heard of his approaching marriage, neither did she enlighten him.

Nature has endowed women with cunning to compensate them for their lack of physical strength; that is why women fear no rival but woman.

"Sir, thou findest me in great distress," she told her Royal master, when he stood uneasily before her.

"If it is a distress out of which I can reasonably assist thee, thou hast but to command," he promised courteously.

"Thy noble kindness encouraged me to hope for such an answer." Then with no further preamble she told him her story.

Of the great longing to see her daughter which had seized her until at last she could bear it no more; how she had left the palace that night and gone in search of her child, and of what she had seen in the dimly-lighted garden. All, all, she poured forth, telling it as though she were a broken-hearted mother, feigning not to notice the anger that disfigured the King's unhandsome countenance.

"It is a lie," he thundered, when she finished her recital; "it is a foul trick to deceive me."

"I do not understand, sir," she faltered in seeming bewilderment.

Then as the King tramped heavily back and forth, frowning blackly, she added in a voice broken with tears: "It is a punishment meted out to me by the gods for having loved thee so dearly as to cause me to desert my own child."

"It is long since thou hast seen her; thou mayst have mistaken some slave for thy daughter," he suggested at length.

"Would that thou might be right," she sighed untruthfully, "but a mother's eyes, however unworthy, can never be deceived."

"Why dost thou tell me this?" he demanded suspiciously.

"Whom else should I tell but thee to whom my position is known?" she questioned wonderingly, meeting his searching gaze with great calmness.

"What wouldst thou have me do?" he growled, convinced that she knew nothing of what her daughter meant to him.

"Speak to Lucarius, tell him of what is happening," she pleaded earnestly.

"If this thing be true he will kill her," warned Ruipi.

Deseré covered her face with her hands, and so the King did not see the triumphant gleam that lighted her eyes.

"It would be better she should die rather than live as the mistress of a slave," she groaned.

Thus it was that Lucarius was disturbed as he sat late that night over a banquet he was giving in the house of one Thalia, famed for her jewels and her figure, rather than for her chastity.

The urgent summons he received to attend the King brooked of no delay. Reluctantly he departed, to learn that a King, be he ever so regal, looks, acts, speaks, thinks, like an ordinary mortal; suffers jealousies, and falls into such rages as the lowest of his subjects, and to recollect that a King was born a man before men made him King.

As to the story told him of Rhoea, that he laughed to scorn, and recognizing that scorn and disbelief as genuine, the King regained some of his calm and took heart.

CHAPTER X

Lucarius drove straight and swift from the Royal Palace to his own establishment, striding up the steps, through the echoing passages and into his daughter's apartment.

Holding back the silken curtains that fell before her door he paused, and the sight that met his eyes caused his fierce expression to soften, and a gentle smile wreathed his mouth, for there on her couch lay Rhoea asleep.

A fat wick burning in a shallow bowl of sweet-scented oil, revealed to him a touching picture, one that might well have been used as a model for the adorning of a precious vase made in honour of the goddess Hestia.

A silken coverlet revealed rather than concealed the slender form, golden red hair fell in wavy masses over a white shoulder, one little hand tucked under the cheek that nestled on its downy cushion, long lashes seeming darker than they were from their contrast with the delicate skin, the mouth had fallen slightly open, and the sleeper breathed evenly and sweetly like a tired child.

For many minutes Lucarius stood drinking in his daughter's beauty, then, turning, went silently away, convinced that there was no truth in the hideous story that had been told him.

The following morning when Rhoea came as usual to bring her father the day's greetings, he told her of his interview with the King.

Her lids drooped and her cheeks grew pale.

With quiet reproach she denied the truth of what he had heard, and Lucarius needed no further proof of his daughter's innocence.

The tears which fell from her eyes he took to be shed from wounded pride; in reality Rhoea wept, knowing that her passion-lit hour had fled, for never again must she risk a visit to the garden within the amber wall, and so she felt pettishly aggrieved.

Exultantly Lucarius went to the King, for this hated marriage was infinitely to be preferred to having one of his name branded as the mistress of a slave.

What he told his monarch caused Ruipi to hasten to the side of his beloved, bringing with him slaves loaded with rich gifts, which Rhoea, sweetly pathetic at the great wrong suspected of her, graciously accepted, lifting her Royal suitor to great bliss by acceding to his impatient request that their marriage should take place immediately.

A sullen rage beset the King against the woman who had caused him so uneasy a night.

With a mournful countenance and a bitter heart Deseré heard what he had to say.

"Thou speakest thus out of the kindness of thy heart to save me grief," she protested.

And from this cunning attitude, which placed the King in a most awkward position, she refused to be moved.

Her insistency revived Ruipi's qualms, and he left her, promising to inquire further into the matter. This he did by sending spies to the garden of which Deseré had told him, from which source he learned that the gracious Lady Rhoea had, indeed, ordered the unshackling of a slave. This information caused him such uneasiness that he questioned his affianced bride on the subject.

"I may have given such an order," she admitted easily. "I cannot bear that birds should be caged, or even base slaves chained."

And Ruipi embraced her tenderly, loudly praising her gentle nature.

But the interview left Rhoea with a growing fear, and when the monarch departed she called Dimidia. The "gentle nature" for which she had just been lauded, did not stand in the way of using the heart of this little slave, who adored her, and loved Ugiso.

"When sleep evaded me, and I have wandered forth at night to walk in the cool of the garden, I spoke with a slave," she informed Dimidia.

"Yes, Mistress."

"Ah, thou knowest?"

"Yes, Mistress."

Rhoea's eyes and mouth grew cruel.

"Thou knowest the slave?"

Again Dimidia's voice uttered the monosyllable, her eyes fixed on the ground so that she should not witness the shame her Mistress must feel on knowing that her great condescension was no secret from her, a slave.

"Go," Rhoea commanded, "await an opportunity to speak alone with Ugiso. Tell him we have been spied upon—that I cannot come again just yet. Warn him that he may be questioned, in which event he is to deny all knowledge of me, even though he be flayed alive. Remind him that he swore to die for me if needs be, and that his words may be put to the test. Ask him if our hours together are not worthy of great payment. Give him this crimson rose from me. Take great care that thou be not overheard. Go."

Silently the slave departed, her face as white as a cloud, her eyes like dew diamonds in a shroud.

Left alone Rhoea fell a prey to a guilty imagination. Supposing her own personal slaves were questioned?

The only one who knew anything of her adventure was Dimidia, of that she was sure, but could she trust her, the puny little thing was so strangely truthful, and again, Dimidia loved Ugiso.

It was late ere Dimidia returned.

"I saw him, and delivered thy message, Mistress," she said, falling on her knees.

"What said he?"

"That he understood, and would die a thousand deaths before betraying thee."

"That is well." Rhoea smiled happily.

"He thanked thee for the flower, which he bade me tell thee he kissed, and will ever cherish even after death!"

"And thee, what of thee, shouldst any inquire if thou knoweth aught?" questioned Rhoea.

"I shall say nothing."

"Means may be found to loosen thy tongue," the patrician reminded her.

"No torture could do that." An undercurrent of strength lay in the quiet voice.

"But if thou spoke at all it would be to tell the truth?"

"If I spoke at all, I would not lie." The eyes of the kneeling maiden looked up into the hard blue ones of her mistress. What she saw there caused her to shudder. A vision of the camel driver whom she had seen crushed to death floated before her.

She felt the satiny soft fingers of her adored lady on her throat, felt them grow hard as dead bones, felt her tongue protrude, her eyes bulge out, gave a convulsive gasp for life's breath, then one long shudder, and rolling over she lay very still.

Rhoea sighed relievedly ere she concealed the body, until night should shield her as she carried it into the open, to leave it where it would be found, and the strangling attributed to a robber. To heighten this impression, she stripped the ornaments from the pale slight form of what a few minutes since had been her devoted slave, and as she gently laid it beneath mournful, dark green laurels, she whispered softly:

"Farewell, thou strange slave, and yet no longer art thou a slave, for were I to command thee thou wouldst not obey, and thy mistress carries thee here in her own arms. Therefore, now that thou art dead, thou art as great as the greatest. Let that thought console thee. Again farewell."

With quite a tinge of sadness in her heart Rhoea crept back to her room, and before she fell asleep, she pondered on this strange thing called love, which caused these two Syrians to so faithfully serve her.

"Then if love maketh a lover servile I swear by all the gods never shall it possess me, but rather shall I cause all to fall into that state for me, then will I do with these foolish love-stricken ones what best pleaseth me." After which comforting reflection, she fell into a dreamless sleep.

Rhoea was most distressed at the loss of the Syrian maid, and now being robed and decked on her wedding morning, she longed for the light hand to dress her hair and arrange the soft folds of her white drapes. No one could do these things with the cleverness and skill of Dimidia; really she felt she had just cause to be annoyed, Dimidia had been so deft-handed; her substitutes suffered dearly.

The whole of Crete was decked for the festival that accompanied the King's marriage. The houses were gay with flowers and drapings, the streets thronged with merry, jostling crowds, composed of respectable citizens with their wives and families. The matrons for the most part were clad in the simple, gracefully draped garments, like those adopted by the Spartans, but the maidens wore the flounced petticoats pinched in at the waist in imitation of the aristocrats or the courtesans. The low cut bodices with tiny sleeveless jackets, shamelessly displaying white chests and shapely busts.

Those who wore hats had their hair dressed high, on top of which perched tiny rose-covered headgear with brims up-turned, or tiny flat affairs with streamers of ribbons floating gaily in the breeze.

Many feet had discarded the easy sensible sandals for tight leather affairs with uncomfortably high heels, for at all costs these sufferers must follow fashion! Courtesans, peasants and slaves, who for this memorable occasion were granted a holi-day, all issued forth to gaze on the King and his bride.

Two hearts alone were sad.

One beat in the breast of the tall young slave, who since early morning had stood on the steps of the temple wherein the wed-ding ceremony was to be performed, mourning with great ten-derness over the fate into which he imagined his poor little love was being forced.

The other unhappy being was Deseré, who found her plot-ting of no avail, for Ruipi sternly refused to further listen to any stories that sought to detract from the virtue of the young creature with whom he was so fascinated. Well nigh crazed with rage and grief, Deseré silently vowed that Rhoea should never enter the palace as its Queen while her mother lived.

With no plan formed in her mind, she donned cloak and face covering, and boldly joined the happy throngs in the streets, forcing her way to the temple steps; there she sat and waited.

At last the sounds of the flutes, harps, and syrinx heralded the coming of the wedding party; excitement grew intense, and along the flower-strewn scarlet carpet, which covered the short distance from the palace of Lucarius to the temple, there appeared a regiment of helots in full panoply of bronze armour, the plumes and crests nodding gaily from their helmets, greaves on their legs and studded belts round their waists; in their hands they carried long iron swords and iron-tipped spears.

Then flute players, clothed in short tunics of royal purple, wearing garlands on their heads, followed by a hundred harpists and a like number of those who were skilled in the playing of the syrinx, marched proudly before the Hestian virgins in their flowing white robes, scattering flowers for the bride to tread upon.

And such a bride!

No wonder the crowds cheered themselves hoarse to do her homage, as tall and slender she walked slowly alongside her father beneath the square of silk, purple in colour and fringed with gold, borne aloft by huge slaves, whose oiled bodies glistened in the sun like polished ebony. Close behind, came her maidens-in-waiting, who joined their voices to the choir of those chosen to sing the wedding song.

A new note was sounded by the shouting of the runners, who raced before the golden chariot, drawn by six white horses.

"Make way—way for the King!" they cried, as they appeared in sight coming from the opposite direction to that followed by the bride and her train.

With great ceremony the King alighted, and gaining the uppermost step of the temple turned to await the coming of his bride, with regal condescension descending to meet her as she drew near.

Pride gleamed in Ruipi's eyes as he took the slender hand in his; then a voice sharp and shrill rang out, causing all to halt and fall into a great silence.

"See," shrieked Deseré, "the King would mate with a harlot; see, there stands her concubine." Her long, bony hand shot out, pointing directly at Ugiso, who by some queer happening, or so it seemed, stood alone in the midst of the dense mass that surged and swayed on the steps of the temple, his great figure occupying a spot apart from all others.

For a fraction of a second there was a breathless pause, then: "Kill the witch! Kill the lying witch," screamed a voice.

Only too willingly the mob fell on Deseré.

"He told me so himself. I saw them. He told me. I, who am her mother," shrilled Deseré.

The crowd paused and for a black moment Rhoea felt that they doubted. Was this to be the end of her almost achieved ambition?

She felt the King's hand that held her own loosen. Desperation seized her; the situation called for drastic methods. With a swift movement she snatched a short, sharp dagger from a near-by helot's belt, and raising it high brought it down swift and sure with all her strength on Ugiso's bare breast where she had so often lain.

The great eyes in which lay no reproach, only humble love, looked full at her as she struck him his death blow.

Just one hoarse gasp that turned into a sharp cry and ended in a sob, and he fell, the blood pouring from the pierced flesh.

A rolling murmur preceded the burst of wild acclamation that followed the bloody deed.

"See how great and pure is this maiden, who would kill with her own hand any that dared defame her good name," was the cry that swayed the multitude.

The dramatic figure of the young patrician maiden was one well calculated to move them, as tall and straight she stood in her long white robe. Her head high held, and the sun shining on her wonderful hair made it appear almost of a colour with her scarlet lips and the reddened dagger, from which dropped blood of the slave, as for a moment Rhoea held it aloft before letting it fall from her hand.

With hoarse roars the people fell on Deseré, furious at the part she had played in this iniquitous scandal.

And Ruipi, for whom the besieged creature had abandoned her husband—that husband who had sold her—and the child she had borne, looked on and made no move to save her.

Slowly and proudly Rhoea entered the temple, her slender hand, which had just struck down a heart that loved her, firm and unshaking, white and soft as the breast of a dove.

The red lights in the ring she wore darted and writhed, as though the evil in them was nourished on such sights as all had witnessed, of innocent blood spilled to purchase a triumph of gilt and tinsel.

When to the sound of the joyous song and loud music the Queen of Crete issued from the temple, the body of the dead slave lay still and prone on its back, for none had been commanded to remove it, and in the half-closed hand the newly-made Queen saw the petals of a crimson rose, and the scent of the bruised flower rose thick to greet her.

Third Journey

Beneath the whorl of the silvery deodar the Yogi sat in dust that had grown heaped to his thighs. His uncombed hair, too, was thickly greyed with powdered fine earth, and he said "Om" seven thousand times. Then paused to reflect on what he had uttered, disregarding the shadow that fell athwart his holiness, and failing to hear the voice that addressed him. Many coming to do obeisance at his shrine had gone on their way without eliciting response to their humble speech, for this was a great, a good Yogi, so pious that the very gods stirred uneasily lest, when his soul should shed the flesh that held it, in death that is called life, and return through that state termed death which leads to unshackled life, he would rival their own sanctity.

This daring one who sought to distract the thoughts of the Holy Man was of a different calibre to any other that had passed this way.

"Oh, Yogi, I am loth to disturb thee at thy devotions, but surely it will be counted to thy favour if thou wilt deign to come out of the silence, and give ear to one who commands all within this fair land of Kashmir."

The young mocking voice was so persistent that ultimately some of his utterings penetrated the Yogi's auricular nerve.

"—and so I tell thee if thou wilt maintain this obstinate silence, I will pick thee up from where I sit, and dash thy frail body against the strong wood of thy sheltering tree."

These were the words that entered the Yogi's ears, and filled him with a wonderment as to who this daring one could be, who feared not to threaten a Holy Man, and he thought to himself:

"If I do not answer, this bold one will surely do as he says, and break my skull, then, indeed, will he be my benefactor, for it is weary waiting for the soul to fly free from the hampering flesh."

But so self-analytical had he become through his many years of silent meditation, that he could not disguise from himself that if he obeyed his stronger impulse and refused to answer, he would be pleasing "self," and so would be sinning. In a voice weak and trembling from long disuse he inquired what it was that was required of him.

"Ah, I thought thou wouldst come to thy senses," cried the laughing voice. "Look up, I, Rhea, the Maharajah of the greatest city in the world, command it."

Slowly the Yogi turned dim eyes on his tormentor; the dazzling whiteness of the horse, with its trapppings of silver and blue, no less than the young man in his royal attire, caused the old eyes to blink.

"What would Rhea the great Maharajah of me?" he questioned patiently.

"Thou hast heard of me?"

"No."

"Oh, come, good Yogi, thou art piqued, for surely even here, in thy dense fastness, the glory and splendour of my great palace, placed on the rolling plain of Martand, must have come to thy knowledge."

"No."

"It is the greatest dwelling of which humanity could hope to hear," bragged the Maharajah.

"Yet doubtless it is supported on pillars," mused the Yogi in his thin, high voice.

"Surely. Perhaps thou canst tell me of any abode which does not need support," laughed the youth.

"Heaven needs no pillars," stated the Holy Man simply.

"Thou art indeed a religious one," sneered the King.

"Hast thou heard of Heaven?" in his turn the old man questioned.

"I am a true Brahmin, and follow the teachings of Brahma," was the frowning answer.

"With thy heart or with thy head?" queried the plaintive voice.

"It was not with the purpose of answering questions, but asking them, that I drew rein," reminded the autocrat sharply. "No doubt thou thinkest that thine is the only way to gain Paradise."

"There are many roads that lead to Heaven."

"What thinkest thou of my chance?"

"To those whom the gods wish to punish, they give earthly power."

"It was not for aphorisms I asked, but criticism."

"How can I criticize one of whose very existence I was ignorant until a short moment since."

"Now, having seen, tell me what thou thinkest of me?" and involuntarily the handsome youth, long accustomed to hear only flattery, drew himself proudly erect, waiting for the honeyed words on which he feasted, to fall from the withered lips.

"When we reflect on what we think of others, it is unwise to ask of others their secret thoughts concerning ourselves," warned the sage.

"Has thy long sojourn here taught thee but to string empty words together?" cried the disappointed horseman.

"It may be so, but such is not my endeavour."

"And what is thy endeavour?"

"To mortify the flesh in order to learn my soul."

"Before thou becamest a Yogi, wert thou very sinful?" questioned the King curiously.

"The poor flesh in which our true entity is shrouded is infirmly porous. Sin enters all too easily."

"What was thy besetting sin?"

"I cannot say. It may have been that I was a drunken babbler, who cared only for the flesh."

"And is thy conceit so great that thou thinkest in this incarnation to learn thy soul, of which it is written that it must travel to knowledge through thousands of births?" scoffed the Maharajah.

"Even Brahma was a seed before he became a golden egg."

"Tell me, old man, how many births hast thou passed through."

"Doubtless many, but my recollection is of few."

"Why is that?"

"Why is it that we fail to recall all the garments that have covered our bodies since our birth on this earth?" the Yogi answered by asking.

"I can remember some of my apparel."

"And I some of my former births, faintly, as thou might recall a portion of thy clothing."

"Why is that?"

"God alone knows," said the ascetic piously; "it may be that the existences we dimly recall are the ones wherein we did the greatest harm, or the most good."

"Would we not be more likely to create good, if we could clearly retain the memory of our former mistakes?"

"No, experience only aids us to make the same mistakes in a different way. Wouldst thou have the hawk which perches on thy wrist remember the mother bird that fed her? No, rather have her dwell in the present, and be that which thou desirest."

"Then is it right that God should punish we poor blinded mortals, for the errors into which our ignorance leads us?"

"God does not punish mortals, it is mortals who punish themselves, and not themselves alone, but the whole of humanity, for those who loosen that which is impure know not what they do; for such a disaster, be it of thought or deed, circles ever and ever through space, like a pungent, cleaving odour, insidiously attacking those with whom it comes in contact."

"Ho, Yogi, where is thy justice, for thou art telling me that the pure must suffer for the impure?"

"The spirit that is purged free of sin is not cursed with an envelope of flesh."

"Still, my envelope of flesh does not relish being attacked by another's wrongfulness," objected the Maharajah.

"Thou speakest as the wild fowl thinks, when she runs affrightedly clucking under the very horses' hooves she fears, vainly thinking that those hooves, which are ignorant of her being, come solely in an endeavour to do her harm."

"Must we not flee from harm then?"

"First be very sure, that which affrights thee is harm."

"But that, which is wrong for one to do, may be counted right in another."

"Each heart must answer to itself."

"And to come to an understanding of the heart, is it necessary to practise such asceticism as thine?"

"To learn thy heart, rest alone and turn thine eyes inward, cleanse it as thou wouldst thy body, as a good housewife cleans her home, a gardener his land; uprooting weeds that choke, ruthlessly tearing out all that is impure and impedes upward progress."

"Do we owe nothing to this human body of ours?" queried the Maharajah restlessly.

"A body to be healthy must not carry with it a diseased mind. Think back, my son, on the greatest pleasures thou hast experienced, have they been aught but of the barest moment?"

"Of the barest moment," conceded the youth.

"Then why strive after that which is transitory, when within thyself thou hast that which is everlasting."

"But if our past deeds make us what we now are, then surely I must have striven for power, and having gained what I doubtless sought, am I to throw it aside, and retire into a silence which might lead to everlasting joy for my soul, but would surely prove disastrous for my kingdom, and my subjects?"

"Give one hour for thy soul, the rest for thy people."

"And in what way could I employ that hour?"

"Many to advantage, but none more than I have told thee. When evening falls, go alone to thy chamber, think back on what thou hast done through the day, and see if thy deeds have been fruitful of good or evil. Take one thought, which thou hast carelessly released on its neverending journey, and tracing its results, thou wilt be verily amazed, and if thou art wise thou wilt guard thy thoughts with even greater care than thou wilt thy actions."

"I am the most powerful Maharajah living, I would be also the greatest."

"Then order thy days and thy thoughts as thou wouldst have them, letting no weak impulse cause thee to swerve."

"If actions were as simple as words, we would all be gods," laughed the young man.

"Attempt the end and never doubt," advised the Yogi.

"That necessitates faith, which is a subjective hallucination, and not to be acquired as one would foot-gear or a sword."

"A soul is the Divine spark with which God has endowed us, faith is the sublime acceptance of that which our limited intelligence cannot explain. To have faith bespeaks true modesty, an acknowledgment of some power greater than ourselves, whose inscrutable workings are not meant to be understood by we, the tiny cogs in a great machine."

"I like not the thought; for, believing thus, thou wouldst place me on the same footing as the lowest of my coolies."

"I spoke of souls, not human rank," gently corrected the Yogi, "and indeed, neither the highest nor the lowest placed among us realize the power we exercise for good or evil; a thought emanating from thy coolie is as powerful in its influence as one that issues from thyself, and will cause many rings to circle through the unseen ether. A common pebble thrown in a lake will disturb the water as surely as will a diamond of great price."

"Dost think we meet again those with whom our fate has been linked in past lives?" asked the Maharajah.

"Thou art young, not more than twenty years, I should hazard, but even so thou must surely know from experience that that which thou asketh, is so."

"But vaguely," admitted the King.

"Before the day is ended thou wilt know more," prophesied the Yogi.

"What, dost thou think I shall meet soon with one whom I have known in former times?" asked the younger man, with an unbelieving smile.

"I know it," calmly answered the ascetic.

"How shall I prove to myself that thy prediction is true?"

"When thou meetest with these of whom I speak thou wilt need no other proof than the beating of thy heart."

"Oh, then, Yogi, I shall cheat thee, for I shall turn my horse's head, and ride in the opposite direction to that on which I was set," and the laughing dark blue eyes looked down on the old man from beneath the red gold hair that showed from under the gay turban.

"He who runs from his fate meets it," warned the Yogi, "and from thy words and light bearing, I know that the greatest and oldest of all human emotions has not yet come thy way."

"What meanest thou?"

"Love!"

Rhea laughed scornfully at the word.

"Nay, Karma with his spicy bow has failed to make of me a victim," he scoffed.

"Very soon thou shalt meet love, and it shall be denied thee; I read a sad life for thee, one in which thou shalt long for that affection which now thou derideth, but it will never be thine."

"I could marry whom I please," boasted Rhea.

"Doubtless, but neither marriage nor all thy riches and power can bring thee love," and then, being greatly fatigued from his unwonted exertion, the Yogi fell once more into silence, letting pass from his mind the interruption that had disturbed his peace.

True to his word, the Maharajah set silver spurs in the sides of his white steed, and rode off far into the forest, so deeply engrossed in thought, aroused by the Yogi, that he forgot the object with which he had ridden forth, namely, that of enjoying a little fowling.

It was for this purpose he carried on his wrist the long-winged hawk, her bright eyes hooded, though no leash or jess restrained her leg. The bird was a favourite of the King's, her intelligence, even when flying at hack, having been remarkable, and now she sat waiting on, for the moment when she should be unhooded, to fly high, sight her quarry, and stoop swiftly with closed sails, never failing to kill, then leaving the pelt, she needed no calling, but returned obediently to wrist or cadge, a good bird and a clever one.

On, on he rode, deeper into the forest of great chenar trees, until the stumbling of his spirited horse brought him to a realization of the fact that he had ridden further than he had intended; drawing rein he looked about him, noting the fact that no path was visible, and that here, beneath the deodar and fir, it was growing so dusk that only his ears told him the shuffling and squabbling overhead betokened a tribe of monkeys.

A little further on he saw patches of fur, which his hunting knowledge correctly interpreted as souvenirs left by fighting stags, and those nibbled leaf, bud and bark on the hazel trees, also pointed to evidence of lately passed stag.

In a vain endeavour to retrace his steps, he plunged deeper and deeper into the forest.

Then, bethinking him of his hawk, who had not been fed at her usual time, he unhooded her, for though she was well grown, he feared hunger-traces might cut the webs of her feathers, and so render her useless for further hunting. Dismounting, he drew his knife and cutting the flesh from the hare she had killed, fed the bird, after which he walked, leading his jaded steed, seeking his way out from the now seemingly impenetrable forest.

At length he stood still, and was determining to make the best of his unfortunate situation, by sleeping the night through here, and making a further essay in the morning, when a boar shuffled across his path, and went grunting on its way, to be followed later by a lolloping bear, going clumsily to the drinking-place; the sight of these beasts heralded the roar of lion, snarl of tiger, and yelping of hyena, all making ready to hunt their evening meal. To sleep here would be foolish, but what to do?

It was while he stood in sad perplexity that he heard a sound, and saw a form faintly outlined in the fading light, that caused him a queer sensation of suppressed excitement, almost of fear, a feeling he had never before experienced.

With strangely beating heart he stood still and waited.

CHAPTER XII

Straight through the forest came the form, and when within a half a dozen yards of the Maharajah it stood and looked.

He had not known what he expected, but the sight of the slim, boyish figure, clad in a coarse white ohoty, brought him inexpressible relief; the youth, with a brass lotah poised on his turbaned head, was the first to break the silence.

"Salaams, Huzzoor," he said, and on hearing the low, musical voice the Maharajah's heart leapt curiously in his bosom.

"I have ridden far, and lost my way," explained the King, and in his voice was none of the haughtiness with which he addressed his subjects.

"From whence comest thou?" asked the boy.

"From Martand."

On hearing the name, the boy gave vent to a cry of astonishment:

"Martand! I have heard of it; it is far from here."

"Thou canst point me the way?"

"Yes, Huzzoor, but it would not be wise to return through

the forest, for thou wouldst surely be slain by wild beasts, or seized by evil spirits."

"A like fate would befall me were I to remain here," said the Maharajah.

"Truly thou sayest."

"Then what ———?" The King was becoming impatient.

"If thou wilt be so gracious as to accompany me, I will lead thee to a shelter where, poor though it be, thou canst at least lie in peace."

There seeming nothing else to be done, and being by now greatly fatigued, the Maharajah followed the youth, who, walking in front, showed the way.

"'Tis doubtless to thy parents' home we go?" hazarded the King.

"Not so, Huzzoor, for I have no parents, being left an orphan long since."

"To whose dwelling, then?"

"To that of Ruipi, the wood-cutter."

"Ruipi! I know that name." The Maharajah spoke his thoughts aloud.

"Surely, all the world has heard of him," the youth spoke proudly.

"In what way does his claim to fame lie?"

"Ruipi was a prince, the only son of the great and powerful Maharajah who ruled over the state of Avantipur. Now Ruipi was proud and self-willed, a great warrior, and the god with the flowery bow not claiming him as a victim, he flew like a great black bee, rifling all flowers of their honey, until the wise men in the city spoke gravely to the King.

"'Oh, King,' they said, 'there is great murmuring among thy subjects against Prince Ruipi, in that he steals the hearts of maidens, using them for his pleasure before casting them aside;

it would be well if he would marry, for marriage is a great soberer.'

"Thus, and more to the point they spoke, and the King, knowing that he listened to wisdom, sent for his son, and bade him fulfil that for which he was born, to marry and beget a son.

"Ruipi laughed, and declining to obey his father, who was sad and filled with wrath, went on his careless round of pleasure, until he met with one whom he instantly loved. The magic of his passion for this maiden, who was named Deseré, made him desirous of doing that very thing which but lately he had refused his father.

"Hearing of his wish, the King laughed with joy, and sending for the wise men, bade them ascertain if the stars were propitious towards this alliance.

"Great was his happiness, and that of his son, when, after consulting together, the learned ones announced it as pleasing to the gods for the Prince to marry this maiden, who, being of high caste and great virtues, was well fitted to become the wife of even so great a Prince as Ruipi.

"But alas! the maiden refused him, and no pleading on his part, nor that of his father, combined with threats, could cause her to alter her way of thinking. So Ruipi fell into a state of great despondency, neither eating nor drinking, nor would he open his mouth to speak, but lay like one whose soul had already departed.

"Not the fairest maidens, whom they brought to tempt him from his sad plight, could win so much as a glance from him.

"Then the King, placing dust upon his head, went himself to the temple where Deseré, with other maidens, tended the sacred fire, and speaking sorrowfully to her, interceded for his son.

"And she, being kind of heart, wept with him, but would not consent to this marriage.

"'But consider,' cried the King, 'my son is consumed with the fire of passion for thee, and is he not worthy of any maiden, even were she a Princess as he is a Prince, for he is young and strong and beautiful to look upon.'

"'Go back to thy son, oh King,' commanded Deseré, 'and bear him this message from me. Tell him that long ere I reached my present age of fifteen years, I knew that this would happen, and though I love him even as he does me, yet I will not marry him or any other, for oft times when I slept a loud voice warned me that I had committed great sins in a former birth, that the evil I had done would need many incarnations of self-abasement and denial ere I could hope for forgiveness. To this end, then, have I consecrated my life, and whatever the cost, I must faithfully pursue it.'

"'But what of my son,' cried the King in despair; 'what of my kingdom? Must many suffer for thy former sins, for so long as thou art here, the Prince will marry no other maiden, and so he will not give me the grandson my heart so ardently desires.'

"'Then I shall go far from here, and thus he may forget me, and find some other more worthy than I, and give thee that for which thou longest,' replied Deseré.

"True to her word, Deseré left the city by stealth, telling none of her going, carrying with her a babe, who wept bitterly and clung so to her that her heart was touched; the parents of the little Ugisa consented ——"

"Ugisa!" echoed the Maharajah, for the name struck him like a blow.

"Yes, for that is how the babe was named," continued the youth, "and going deep into the forest, Deseré entered a deserted hut that was situated near that wherein dwelt my father (who was a charcoal-burner) and myself; we two alone, for my mother had left her body soon after giving me birth."

"But didst thou not tell me it was to the dwelling of Ruipi we would go?" demanded Rhea.

"Even so, for when he heard that the maiden he loved had gone, none knew whither, he raged furiously, then wept bitterly, and rising, went forth and rested not until he had found her, and on finding that not all his pleadings or tears could move her from her determination, he refused to return to Avantipur, and dwelt humbly in my father's poor hut, in order to remain near Deseré, for though the sight of her rends him with grief, he prefers this suffering to that which consumes him when he is far from her."

"It is a strange story," mused Rhea.

"Strange indeed, Huzzoor; I was but a toddling babe when these two came to dwell in the forest, and now I am a grown man," the youth swaggered proudly, "and am ever filled with wonder at the saintliness of their lives. And now that the gods have beckoned my father, Ruipi, who is a prince, follows my parent's trade of charcoal burning, and so makes a poor living for us both. His suffering is great, and even when he sleeps he moans and cries out with longing for Deseré, and now, Huzzoor, see, we stand on the roof of my home."

Looking down, the Maharajah discerned, by the light of the blazing stars, a saffron coloured plateau, beneath which was the charcoal burner's hut.

"Here is a path down which thou canst lead thy steed," pointed the youth. With a strange feeling of unreality, as though he was dreaming, King Rhea followed after his escort, then there came a sound that set his heart madly beating.

"Is it thee, Dimidia?" called a low, sweet voice.

"It is I, Ugisa," replied the youth.

"We have been uneasy at thy long absence," and Rhea's pulses leapt as he saw coming nearer the figure of a maiden.

When within a few feet from them Ugisa stopped suddenly. "Thou art not alone?" she queried, and something of fear rang through the words.

"I bring with me a stranger who had lost his way," explained Dimidia. "I will take thy steed and care for him, also I must inform Ruipi that we are to have a guest," he added, relieving Rhea of the horses' bridle, and walking rapidly away.

"No, no, do not leave me," cried Ugisa, after the swiftly vanishing form; but Dimidia did not hear her, for he continued on his way.

CHAPTER XIII

With a very storm of emotions stirring within him, Rhea stood still, gazing at this figure which he felt would mean so much to him; at first he could decipher nothing but a dim outline, then he became conscious of a pair of large, frightened eyes, peering at him from a pale oval face, crowned with a wealth of dark hair. He knew that she was trembling, and wondered why.

"Why dost thou tremble?" and he noted with amazement that his own voice shook.

"I am afraid," she whispered.

"Of me?"

"Yes."

"I would not harm thee."

He saw her crouch further from him, as her hands flew to her breast, and he knew that, had her limbs obeyed her wish, she would have left him.

"Doubtless it is the sight of an unaccustomed stranger that unnerves thee," he said gently.

"No."

"Then rather than cause thee distress I will go," he volunteered.

"It—is—too—late," she breathed.

"I, too, feel that Fate has brought about this meeting, with what purpose I know not, but this I swear, that I would sooner plunge this knife of mine deep in my heart than cause thee suffering," vowed Rhea deeply.

"What is to be, is to be," and such a wealth of sadness underlay the fatalistic words that the King felt tears of sympathy rush to his eyes.

Suddenly the memory of the Yogi's utterances recurred to him, that he would need no telling, other than the beating of his heart, when he met those whom he had encountered in a former birth.

"We have crossed one another's paths in a former life," he said.

"It may be so," she admitted.

"I am sure of it, as I am sure that thou hast a crimson rose concealed in thy dress," he announced triumphantly.

The effect of his words startled him, for she cried out in fear, and her body swayed so that he feared she would fall.

"I have no rose," she told him.

"But the scent of one filled my nostrils at thy coming," Rhea assured her.

"Thou art the only one who has detected that which haunts me since my birth," she spoke wonderingly.

"But surely so delicious a perfume is no hardship to carry?" the Maharajah smiled.

"Though I love beauty, I fear flowers; to me they speak of prison walls, and hardships and cruelty, and most of all I fear crimson roses, and yet it is strange that I am greatly skilled in the knowledge of plants."

"And thou art a blossom thyself. Why dost thou fear flowers?"

"I know not."

"Perhaps in thy former birth the flowers were jealous of thy beauty, or else, loving thee too dearly, smothered thee with kisses so ardent that they crushed the life from thy body," hazarded King Rhea.

Very earnestly she gazed at him. "No, that is not the way I left my body," she answered seriously.

At her words the Maharajah shivered, and for some reason which he did not pause to analyse, nor could have explained had he done so, he felt a thrill of fear in case she should recall anything of this life of which they spoke.

"But surely thou canst not recall anything that happened in thy other existences?" he asked uneasily.

She did not answer readily, and the King felt a sharp relief when she spoke.

"No," she said hesitatingly, "no, and yet, with thy coming I felt nearer to knowing than ever before."

"Ah, then we have met before," he cried triumphantly.

"Yes." There was no doubt in her mind that such was the case.

"We may have been dear friends," he suggested.

"No."

"Then perhaps brother or sister?"

"Never."

"Then what?"

"I do not care to say."

Desperately his will was battling with hers, trying to gloze her dimly stirring memories, to cause her thoughts to contradict her stronger instinct, to make her believe this unformed, unuttered thing was not so, for he knew that the truth, of which he had no recollection, would not be to his advantage.

"Thou canst not persuade me that we were ever enemies," he laughed.

"Neither do I think that," she agreed, "and yet all this day I have felt a growing apprehension that danger approached. Through the long last night I tossed uneasily, unable to close my eyes, for the scent of crimson roses assailed me closely, causing my heart such piteous agony that I feared it would break, and I moaned in pain."

"Thou wouldst not be so cruel as to have me think that I am the unwitting cause of thy restlessness?" he pleaded.

"Thou hast come, and never hath the dreaded perfume of roses been so strong," she spoke simply.

"Oh, maiden, the potent of thy words gives me great unhappiness, for, and I do not speak lightly, never hath my heart been so stirred as now."

"Who art thou?"

"I am Rhea of Martand," the humble tone in which he spoke was very different to the arrogance with which earlier in the day he had addressed the Yogi.

"I am Ugisa, my parents were of high caste but poor, and being so, the more willingly listened to the plea of the saintly Deseré, that I should be to her as her own child."

"What care I who, or what thy parents? All I care about is thee."

"Ah, thy words make me know truly that thou art indeed the gay Maharajah of Martand, of whom even we, in this desolate spot, have heard."

"Doubtless what came to thine ears was true," Rhea stated bluntly, "for I have been as a ship riding without an anchor, a wild hawk carelessly killing the prey that deliberately came his way."

"So said the wind-borne whisperings," admitted Ugisa.

"And wouldst thou blame the silver brook because in its mad rush it played with golden sands over which it passed? Or the merry breeze because it dallied with the leaves that sought to tangle and hold it fast?"

He saw her head move slowly from side to side.

"Then hold not my past years in reproach against me, for I have been as that ship, that brook, that breeze, following blind impulse. It is only now since I have met thee that I know my life has been wanton and foolish."

"Who am I that should reproach thee?" asked Ugisa softly.

"Thou art all my world."

"Then indeed thy world is small and foolish."

In his delight at hearing the lighter touch, Rhea laughed aloud.

"Ah, see, already thy first fear of me has flown," he cried delightedly; "soon thou wilt have forgotten it ever existed."

"And why should a King care what one so lowly placed as myself remembers?" she asked.

"If thou shouldst seek to disparage thyself, then indeed canst thou look for a return of thy fear, for such a thing I will not brook," he threatened gently.

"Better than that thou shouldst depart, for I must ever speak as I feel."

"And that will I never do, until at least, I am assured that thou wilt welcome my return," he told her earnestly.

"It may be, if thou meanest what thou sayest, that thou wilt dwell here for ever."

"Willingly, here or any other place, where thou art, for having found thee, I shall never let thee go, nor must any come between us."

Even as he spoke, his voice deep and low with sincerity, a shadow, followed by the form of Dimidia, cut Ugisa from his vision, and Rhea, who, during the long march through the forest, had with difficulty restrained a strong inclination to pick this slight youth up in his arms and place him on his horse, in order to save the bare brown feet and legs from sharp stones and tearing brambles, now grit his teeth, and losing the protective

sense he had experienced towards Dimidia, mentally con-
signed him to a deep, dark dungeon, for his interruption.
"I crave thy pardon for my lengthy absence," apologized the
innocent youth. "I remained to feed thy bird and thy horse, ere
informing Ruipi of thy coming, upon which he bade me beg of
Deseré a little rice and dal for thy supper."

"I am loath to cause so much trouble," remarked Rhea,
noticing with a jealous frown, as he walked beside his young
rescuer, towards the door of the hut, that Dimidia took Ugisa
by the hand to lead her over the dark path, and then his heart
thrilled, for Ugisa laughed, a delicious low ripple of mirth.

"Ugisa laughs at thy words," explained Dimidia, "for Ruipi
is overjoyed at thy coming, as indeed he would be at any happening that would lend itself as an excuse for bringing Deseré
into his presence."

"She whom I call mother, is the light of Ruipi's soul," explained Ugisa.

"As thou art mine," muttered Rhea, but it is doubtful whether
Ugisa heard the words, more like they reached Dimidia, who
walked nearest him.

There was no further time for talk, for now they had reached
the entrance of the charcoal-burner's hut.

CHAPTER XIV

Coming from the starlight into the hut, the glow from the
small lamp shone like a gleaming lantern.

Before looking at his host, Rhea turned his eyes on Ugisa,
and caught hers fixed directly on him.

For one wild moment he longed to pick her up in his arms
and take her far into the forest, where not even the stars could
see, her beauty was so pure, so exquisite, and withal her lovely
face, with its straight little nose, mouth like a pomegranate

bud, and great sombre eyes, held such tragic sadness, that his heart contracted with pain that it should be so.

Then Ruipi addressed him, and he turned to answer, seeing the ex-King a swarthy, clumsy man, no longer young, with a countenance lined with sorrow.

The intense dislike the young Maharajah felt towards Ruipi was instantaneous; so deep was his feeling, that he hesitated whether he should enter the hut, or turn and plunge into the forest once again.

Only the thought of Ugisa forced him to restrain his actions, and conceal his antipathy, which Ruipi did not seem to share, for he greeted King Rhea with great courtesy, and kindly welcome, watching the while with nervous excitement for the coming of Deseré.

Ugisa had departed to assist in the bringing of supper, and Rhea joined his anxiety to that of Ruipi, but each watched for the coming of a different woman.

In a short time the simple meal of *ghi, dal* curry, and bowls of rice was brought. It disturbed Rhea to find that his dislike of Deseré, whom Ugisa loved, was almost as great as that which he felt for Ruipi, and he found time to give a passing thought of wonder, at what it was any man could find in this plain, heavily built, middle-aged woman to love so ardently, as Ruipi very evidently did, for his eyes never left her, and he hung on her every expression.

As Rhea made a pretence of eating his supper, for which he felt no hunger, he marvelled at the grace of Ugisa's little blue-clad figure, flitting lightly about the hut, turning it into a palace of delight for the infatuated King. The tink and chink of bracelets on her soft round arms and slim ankles, sounded like music played on gold strings by peris from Paradise, and her tiny, henna-stained feet and slender hands enraptured him beyond expression.

When the women had departed, and the men lay on coarse mats which protected them from the earthen floor, Rhea remained with wide-open eyes, dreaming of this sudden miracle that had come to pass. He was enjoying the happy torture of those newly in love.

His jealousy of the soundly sleeping Dimidia grew, and he felt he no longer cared to live unless Ugisa would return his love.

Even had thoughts of his adored one not kept him awake, Ruipi's ceaseless moanings of the woman, for whom he had forsaken parents, friends and kingdom, would have effectually kept sleep from visiting Rhea, and much as he disliked his host, he experienced a great and growing pity for him, and he shuddered to think what a dreadful thing it would be if Ugisa condemned him to a like fate.

Again the Yogi's predictions disturbed him, and he almost cried aloud, as he recalled the fateful words:

"Very soon thou shalt meet love, and it shall be denied thee; I read a sad life for thee, one in which thou shalt long for that affection which now thou derideth, but it will never be thine."

Clearly he remembered every word the Yogi had spoken but a few short hours ago.

Rising softly, Rhea stole outside, and wandered restlessly beneath the stars, which hung low and red, as though the hot sun still lingered behind them, over the snowy hills.

The creeper-clad hut was situated in a valley, between two great towering mountains, proud and vain in their regal adornment of deodar, chenar and chestnut trees, the perfume of a thousand flowers played in the night air, but above all, the tuberoses, the "Flower that Scents the Night," rose strongest.

He strolled into the forest, throwing himself down by the side of a deep clear pool, and so still did he lie, that a markhor came fearlessly to the brink and drank, only darting off at the approach of the never-to-be-trusted snow-leopard; the black rosettes on this beast's pale greyish fur stood out vividly as he stooped to drink, swaying his bushy tail, whilst warily eyeing the panther, who with his mate, had come on the same quest. Great shaggy bears; then tigers, stags and their families, and yellow mountain lions, their eyes shining like phosphorus, all came for their night drink, and departed again, unaware of the silent form, lying so still and close.

Rhea shuddered as he watched these beasts prowling so near to the home of the maiden who filled his thoughts; it was not safe for her, he must take her away where he could guard her from all harm.

"But what if she refuses to go?" a disconcerting inward voice questioned.

"Then I shall take her." He spoke the words aloud, startling to swift spring and rush, a tiny black and white goval who had been happily bathing its feet, and drinking daintily from the pool.

Yes, that is what he would do, he decided; she must be his, and even if he took her against her will, he would love her so, load her with such kindnesses, that in time she would, she *must* come to care for him.

Silently he swore that Ruipi's fate should never be his, and cursing the old Yogi for his malevolent prediction, Rhea fell into a sound slumber.

When he opened his eyes a pink and white dawn had wiped away the stars and their dark setting, a rosy sun peeped through ridge of silver birches that stood knee deep in snow, high up like a crown on the mountain top, and round the bend of the pool, where a clump of willows had secluded her bathing-place, came Ugisa; the garment she wore twisted round her waist and over her head was as blue as the lotus that floated on the clear water.

Looking at her, fresh and beautiful as the morning, Rhea felt the love madness which had disturbed his night, swell and increase until his heart well-nigh burst, and a fierce jealousy of everything and everyone, of Dimidia, of Deseré, Ruipi, the birds, grasses, trees and the very pool in which she had just bathed, assailed him.

He would have picked her up now, and carried her back to Martand, only a reluctance to startle her restrained him; but if no other way of possessing her was possible, then he would steal her, carrying her back to his kingdom himself, the kingdom over which she must reign with him, as his queen.

All unconscious that she was being observed, Ugisa came slowly towards the spot where the King lay concealed, moving as gracefully as a young antelope.

Fearing she would pass from his sight, and that he might not again see her for some hours, Rhea stood up, and came towards her.

"Fear not, it is only I," he soothed, as she started, and the look of last night's terror returned to her eyes, and drew the pink tint from her creamy cheeks.

"Thou art an early riser," she said.

"I have lain here all night," Rhea told her.

"Ruipi will feel regret, that his best was too poor for thee," Ugisa remarked.

"Paradise itself would be poor to me, if thou wert not there."

"Didst thou have no fear of the beasts, that come here to drink?" she asked, ignoring his words.

"The only fear I can ever know, will be that I might not find favour in thy eyes. All night long I have thought of thee, oh wonderful maiden."

"To what conclusion did thy thoughts bring thee?" she questioned curiously.

"Many, but tell me, hast thou lost thy unwarranted fear of me?" he asked.

"No, that I will never do."

"And yet thou art not afraid to speak with me here alone," he said, deeply hurt at her answer.

"I, too, have been kept awake all night by my thoughts," she told him.

"Would it be too great a boldness to hope that I held some small part of those thoughts?" he asked wistfully.

"It was mainly of thee I thought," she answered, "of the strangeness of thy coming, of my apprehension, and culminating fear, of why thou shouldst so quickly detect the scent of crimson roses, of what this coming of thine boded."

"Let me interpret that last," he interrupted eagerly; "my coming can only bring thee happiness. That which frightened thee was the sudden coming of thy fate, for that I am thy true mate I am convinced, and so, too, art thou, then like a timid bird who fears a hand, be it ever so gentle, thou wert agitated, but not truly afraid."

"There is truth in thy words, for I, too, am sure that thy coming was no accident, but was brought about by fate; and yet thou art not wholly right, for indeed it was terror that clutched me when I met thee. And now, when I hear thee speak, before the words leave thy lips, I know what thou art about to say, and it seems as though we stand in some false position to one another." Ugisa paused perplexedly, as if she searched for her own meaning.

"It must be that we are part of one another, for I, too, seem to know thy every thought, thy every feeling. And now to answer thy former question, as to where my night thoughts brought me. They told me that I could not live without thee, that I loved thee with every fibre of my being. That even shouldst thou struggle against it, I must have thee for my Queen."

"Even though I do not love thee?"

"Thou wilt," declared Rhea emphatically. "I shall spend my whole life at thy feet, until from very pity thy heart will soften toward me."

"Pity is not love."

"Love is lying asleep in thy heart, I will waken it," declared the King.

She shrank from him and her voice was cold. "No, that I am very sure thou wilt never do," she said clearly.

"Am I, then, too late; dost thou love some other?" he demanded angrily.

"At whatever time thou hadst come, thou wouldst never have gained my love."

"If it be this youth Dimidia who has stolen thy heart before my coming, I will kill him, then, crushing thee close in my arms, will kiss away all memory of him from thy brain," cried Rhea fiercely.

"Is this what thou deemest love?" and her voice was icy cool; "this thing, thinking only of itself, would bruise the heart which it declareth affection for."

The scorn combined with the bitter knowledge that her words were justified, drove the Maharajah into a paroxysm of wrath.

"Ha," he cried, "then it is true; thou dost love Dimidia!"

"That, sir, is a matter that concerneth myself and Dimidia," she answered with quiet dignity, and turning, left him standing there, a prey to bitter feelings. The perfume of crimson roses floated heavily on the morning air.

Moodily Rhea returned to the hut, where, refusing food, he curtly thanked Ruipi for his hospitality, and mounting his horse, rode off, deliberately ignoring the wondering Dimidia.

Through the forest he galloped, crushing the scarlet lilies, the geraniums and wild fuchsias, the salvias and other flowers unfortunate enough to come before him, with a savage delight; for Ugisa did not care for them; it was this feeling that made him tear down trails of jessamine, honeysuckle, and rose.

To stop, for the purpose of breaking off large, innocent buds of lemon-scented magnolia, and branches of hybiscus, which he cast from him and left to die in his mad trail.

Arriving in Martand, weary and heart-sick, he found the perfume of crimson roses as strong in his nostrils as it had been when Ugisa stood before him.

CHAPTER XV

Again, and yet again Rhea rode through the forest to where he had found his heart.

Sometimes the fates were propitious, and he saw and spoke with Ugisa; it was on one of these, to him, fortunate occasions, that, finding her alone, seated near the pool, he had once pleaded with her to become his wife, and again she had refused.

"How long wilt thou continue to fly in the face of thy fate?" he asked her in despair; "for, as thou hast thyself admitted, we have met for some set purpose, and my heart tells me, as must thine, what that purpose is."

"I have told thee ever since our first meeting, that I feared, and could never love thee," was Ugisa's only reply.

"Thy fear is unjustified and cruel; I could soon drive all such feeling from thee, if thou wouldst grant my request. I would delight in finding new ways to make thee love me; the fairest silks that are spun in Kashmir would clothe thee, and jewels would load thy limbs; I would give thee slaves to wait upon thy barest murmur, and I, myself, would glory in being the chiefest and humblest of those slaves. My kingdom and I would be thine to rule as best pleased thee, and never another wife would

I take but thee. Oh, my little love, thou canst not listen un-moved to my prayer." The Maharajah's voice shook with the earnestness of his desire.

Ugisa shook her head sadly. "I grieve much to cause thee pain, but my answer must ever be the same."

"If thy regret is sincere, the remedy is within thine own hands, and thou canst quickly remove the deadly pain from which I suffer. And listen, cold blue lotus blossom, for such thou art, floating in the deep lake of icy remoteness with which thou hast surrounded thyself; dost thou not fear the anger of the gods, for that which thou makest another to suffer will surely recoil on thine own head, in this, or some future life!"

"That is true, and yet by coming with thee, I would not re-move suffering, but add to it."

"That could not be," the King rejoiced, for now he thought he had found a means of persuading her to his will.

"Yes, for then I would cause many to be unhappy, to relieve one," she explained.

"Who?"

"Myself for one."

"Then, my beloved, thou art committing a sin in selfishly monopolizing thy own beauty," he chided gently; "and who else?" He had an argument ready against the next reply, which he anticipated would be her pleading for the loneliness her leaving would cause Deseré, but he was wrong.

"Dimidia," was the name she mentioned.

On hearing the name of another man on her lips, all his old jealousy returned and broke from him like a torrent, saying those things which men are wont to say when moved by that strange twin-brother of love.

Pale as a white cloud, Ugisa rose to depart; she had already turned away, when Rhea, mad with despairing love, jealousy and rage, swooped down upon her, and picking her up as though she had indeed been the flower he had likened her to, he mounted his horse, and placing her before him rode swiftly away; nor did he draw rein until he reached the gates of his own palace in Martand.

During that wild ride through the forest, Ugisa lay still and pale, like a body from which the spirit has already departed, while ever and ever again Rhea would bend to press passionate kisses on the closed eyes and ashy lips lying so near to his own.

"Mine, mine," he would cry triumphantly, too intoxicated at the closeness of the precious body, for compassion, or any feeling except one of exultation, to move him.

Arriving at the palace, he carried her still form in his own arms to a luxurious apartment he had caused to be prepared for Ugisa after his first meeting with her. Placing her gently on the couch of silken cushions, and summoning the women who were to wait on her, he ordered them to treat her as their regal mistress; then with joy in his heart at having her under his roof at last, departed, leaving word that he was to be notified when she was prepared to see him.

Hour after hour he waited in an antechamber for the desired message, pacing up and down like a young lion, and presently it came, but in a manner he least expected, for on turning, he saw at the far end of the marble-paved apartment, the delicate figure of Ugisa herself, standing very still, and clad in the blue *saree* which she had been wearing when he carried her from her forest home.

"Ah, my dear one, thou art better?" he cried, going swiftly towards her.

"Come," he said gently, taking her hand, and finding it icy cold, "rest here, and I shall listen like a penitent at thy feet, and thou shalt call me harsh names, and heap abuse on my head, for having so roughly stolen thee away." Though his words were humble, his tone was triumphant.

Still, as a picture painted on a wall, she stood, the rose perfume thick about her.

"I have come to ask thee what it is thou art minded to do with me?" she asked.

"Love thee, make thee my queen, cause thee to love me," Rhea replied quickly.

"Love," she laughed contemptuously, "who art thou to speak that word? For love would flee from one like thyself, who knowest only desire."

"True, I am consumed with desire for thee, a desire which springs from love," he admitted pleadingly.

"Love is kind, and would not harm the one on whom it was bestowed; it would rather sacrifice self, and is self abasing?"

"And am I not ready and willing to abase myself, to place myself at thy feet for a footstool? Ah, do not be so unkind, my beloved."

"What right hast thou to sue for kindness from me, whom thy great strength alone hath brought here? Wouldst thou look for kindness from a lion thou hadst captured and placed in a cage, or expect gratitude from it because the bars of that cage were formed of gold?" Ugisa asked scornfully.

"Thou art not a lion, but a timid maiden, and when thou hast overcome thy shyness, and the strangeness of this, thy new home, thou wilt learn to love it, and me." Rhea spoke with assurance.

"That will I never do," she answered quickly.

"Wouldst thou keep me for ever burning like incense on the altar of thy vanity, as Deseré doth with the poor foolish Ruipi, cursed be her name? For I verily believe it is only in emulation of her madness that maketh thee so persistently cruel to me."

"Not so, thou conceited one. I tell thee solemnly that had I for thee the merest shadow of the love which lies in Deseré's heart for Ruipi, I would not be so abjectly unhappy as thy presence makes me."

"And thou, who swore love was kind, how canst thou explain Deseré's cruelty to this man who hath deserted all, to dwell near her?" asked Rhea triumphantly.

"Because she is a saint, and remembering something of her former life, liveth now as her conscience dictates, not to gain forgiveness for her own past sins alone, but in order to help the man she loves to find happiness in the future, as well."

"Doth this same feeling drive thee to deny me?" asked Rhea.

"No, for I am no saint, but filled with faults of the flesh, and fear that my soul would suffer if it came in conflict with the body," Ugisa admitted contritely.

"Out of thy own mouth hast thou exonerated me, and I delight in proclaiming myself, even as thou hast declared thy dear self to be, filled with faults, and willing to pay any price the unknown future might demand of me for loving thee, if indeed such an inevitable happening should be deemed a fault."

"Thy every word brands thee as selfish, for thou braggest of thy disdain at any punishment to be meted out to thee, caring not if I too am to suffer some of that chastisement," Ugisa pointed out coldly.

"The gods are just, and would not punish thee for my faults," the King assured her.

"And my crime would be doubly that of thine, were I to consent to thy wish and stay with thee as thy wife, for there is no greater sin than to marry without love, that would indeed be to enter purgatory with open eyes."

"But dost thou then hate me?" the man cried despairingly.

"I do not like thee," she told him truthfully.

"Surely I can win thy kindness. Thou canst not look un-moved on all the luxuries I have prepared for thee, the fine silks, the rich jewels, the horde of attendants, thy chamber set with lapis-lazuli, onyx, jade and precious stones, thy couch of sandal-wood and silver, without a tinge of gratitude touching thy heart."

"Sir, I do not doubt that one-half this splendour would purchase for thee many poor creatures who sell; I am not one of these," and no amount of pleading or argument would move her from her attitude.

CHAPTER XVI

Weeks passed, every hour of which Rhea thought only of Ugisa and his feeling for her, to the utter neglect of his kingdom.

Each day, and many times a day, he visited her, always meeting with the same cold scorn, and crushed and soiled though the blue *saree* became, Ugisa clung to it, refusing the lure of soft finely-woven garments, with their wonderful embroideries.

One night when Rhea was absent from the palace, and all her attendants slept, Ugisa crept softly out, and gaining the street without having been seen, ran swiftly, not knowing in what direction her flight led her, her intention being to make for the forest, and return to Deseré and Dimidia.

Veiling her face with a portion of the blue robe, she hurried on; then the sound of music caught her ear, and she paused to detect from whence came the tinkling of the stringed *sarangi,* and the beat of the *tablas.* The noise drew her to the spot, and she stood, her eyes shining and her heart throbbing, watching the clumsy gyrations of the great bear and trained monkey obeying the active stick and cruel cords of their squatting master.

Her ears gleaning more delight from the music than her eyes from the sight, unconsciously her feet kept time to the rhythm which so pleased her, that she followed the man and his animals from spot to spot, until at last he noticed her, and approaching, asked for payment of his performance.

Having no money, Ugisa stripped her arms of their bracelets and tendered them, pleased when the rascal gleefully accepted so rich a reward.

Like a child with a new toy, forgetting everything but the music, Ugisa stayed on, and it was thus Rhea, catching sight of the blue *saree* he knew so well, stopped his carriage, and, descending, found his beloved lady wandering like a veritable *abhisarika** in the open streets.

Raging at the careless attendants who had slept when on duty, he took Ugisa back to the palace.

She made little protest at his action, seeming more to resent being taken from the music, than returning to her prison.

The Maharajah noticing her curious elation and learning the cause, promised her all the music and amusements of that sort she cared to have, and late as it was when they entered the palace, she demanded of him to keep his promise.

Immediately the household was roused, and the palace soon blazed with lights and resounded with music. Bears, monkeys, goats, birds, every sort of performing animal and bird was brought to amuse this maiden, whom the King was delighted to have at last roused to an interest in something other than her forest home. He laughed amusedly at her generous bestowal of gifts on those who performed for her pleasure.

Now began a new era in the annals of the court of Martand; every day, and far into the night, there rang out the sound of mirth and music, in the palace and also in the bejewelled pavilion, a veritable fairy-abode with its delicately fretted walls of

*Abhisarika—shameless woman.

pure marble, set in the centre of an ornamental lake, on which floated lotus flowers and proud white swans.

Ugisa, reclining on the silken cushions which bestrewed the carpet of cloth of gold, chewed *bhetel,* and drank iced sherbet served her by slave girls, or partook of some of the luscious fruits the eunuchs held in costly golden salvers, whilst she listened to the music, or watched the performance of plays or, what delighted her most, apart from the instruments, the graceful dances of Nautch girls.

Quickly discovering the power money possessed to infuse a zest in those who served her, Ugisa gave lavishly, dealing out handfuls of silver or gold from the sacks which the King ordered to be placed beside her. Smilingly he watched the dispensation of gifts, as though it was a huge jest, encouraging her munificence, ever seeking for new amusements with which to attract her. New plays and players were sent for, even from India, when those of Kashmir became wearisome to the increasingly capricious Ugisa; fresh dancers were searched out, great fêtes held, and Martand became one continual round of revelry.

While accepting all his tributes, Ugisa still treated Rhea with coolness and disdain; but she had begun to look on him with a different eye, and finding that by decking herself in fine clothes and jewels, she could please and inspire him to even greater efforts to find her amusement, she was not slow in taking advantage of this discovery, and spent much time in adorning herself with the beautiful things he provided for her use.

The infatuation of the young Maharajah was spoken about in every home and bazaar throughout Kashmir, and even gossiped of in remote parts of India.

At first his subjects laughed, pleased that their King should amuse himself; but when the object of his devotion became increasingly extravagant they began to murmur.

"Every bee must sip honey," they admitted, "but it is not right that he should become drunk and forget his duties. And if this present state of things continues the city will be ruined and our King become a bankrupt. Furthermore, this woman refuses to marry him, and as he hath sworn to marry no other, then Martand will have no prince to reign when he goeth to his gods."

These whisperings, growing to loud talk, soon reached the ears of the Maharajah, who spoke to Ugisa of what he had heard, and as she listened her brows frowned and her lips pouted.

"Then if thou art to be ruled by thy people, whom till now I thought thou governed, it is better I should join them, and command thee," she said haughtily.

"That hast thou, and no other, ever done, my beloved, and now tell me thy latest whim that I may hasten to obey it," begged the King.

"Send me back to my forest home," and as she spoke, Ugisa looked close into his eyes, using her own to contradict her words, for she no longer wished to leave this life that Rhea had taught her to love.

"Anything but that, my pearl," he cried. "But surely, now thou art not so averse to marrying me, and will consent to be my wife, and thus make me the happiest mortal on earth, and at the same time satisfy my people."

"I will never marry thee," she informed him, playing with his latest gift, a rope of emeralds interspersed with carved squares of gold, that hung round her neck.

"That I will not believe," he protested, "for thou hast changed so, loving the things that once were despised of thee, as, in time, I live on the hope that thou wilt change towards me."

"As thou sayest I have changed, or no, rather do I think that much that lay dormant in me before thy coming, has been roused to activity, strange feelings have assailed me since I lay in thy arms on that journey through the forest."

"Tell me of thy emotions," he begged, hoping to read an awakening of her affection for him in her words.

"The great strength of thy arms, seemed even less than a force I possessed within me, one which until thy coming I had half wittingly tried to conquer. A longing to know life, to live it, to travel unveiled where I would, and take that which came my way for pleasure. A feeling that never would I be happy bound to one person, loved by one man alone."

"But thou art a maiden, and such ways would not be right for thee," explained Rhea, a little disturbed at Ugisa's confidences.

"Knowing that, I fought against myself, but thou hast changed me, I would be as thou art, free; so that my comings and goings, whatever I chose to do, would go unnoticed, as Dimidia could be if he wished, but he is a gentle youth, and cares nothing for those things which please most men."

"Thou art a woman, my Ugisa, and formed to be cared for and protected," explained Rhea.

"Mm! The thought of such a life irks me. I would not be chosen by man, rather would I choose any with whom I cared to mate, free as a bird, or a man," she cried impatiently.

"If I am thy choice, then thy whimsical outlook on life will meet with my approval," he said smilingly.

"What care I for thy approval, with or without it I shall yet gain my way," she informed him carelessly.

"And I would have thee remember thy promise," she added cunningly.

"What promise have I made thee that I have failed to fulfill?" he asked.

"That I should rule here, over all, even thee," she reminded him, looking softly into his eyes.

CHAPTER XVII

So madly did the King desire this woman, who played with him, giving no thought for the ruin she was working, that he could refuse her nothing, and the city of Martand was rapidly declining in power, for the major portion of his subjects readily followed their King's lead, and gave themselves up entirely to pleasure, and Ugisa's growing improvidence was emptying the royal coffers in wanton extravagance.

Her innocent joy at the paroxysm of delight into which a Nautch girl and her accompanying musicians fell, when they were presented with a *crore* of rupees apiece, supplemented by a necklace of matchless pearls, which Ugisa, taking from round her own neck, placed over the head of the dancer who had particularly pleased her, was so infectious, that Rhea joined in the applause that followed the munificent rewards.

The Maharajah had begun to fear his lady's temper, for she did not hesitate to severely punish any who displeased her.

She was, indeed, taking him at his word, and ruling as a veritable despot, and while great wrongs could go unrighted, terrible crimes unpunished for aught she cared, if any incurred her displeasure, or failed to gratify her slightest whim, the poor unfortunate would quickly learn that her frown was to be more greatly feared, than even that of the King himself.

It was after one eventful evening that Rhea in despair sent for Dimidia to come to Martand in order to speak with Ugisa, and beg of her to curb her extravagant conduct.

The evening in question was one on which Rhea had been forced to entertain many notable Rajahs from adjoining cities, who, visiting Martand for purposes of state, must be entertained as befitted their rank.

Very reluctantly Rhea had torn himself from the side of his adored Ugisa, to be present at the banquet held in their honour, and to remain afterwards in the superb hall for which his palace was famous, there being none other like it throughout the land.

The four pillared walls were of ebony. Negroes wearing black and white-hooded skull-caps stood in the sixty concaved spaces, holding silver rods, from which hung lamps of sweet-scented oil. A hundred slave girls, draped in scanty coverings of silver and scarlet, knelt with trays of ebony and silver bearing rare fruits, sweetmeats and cooling drinks.

The floor was composed of ebony blocks, joined together with smoothly beaten silver bars, kept tight with turquoise-studded pegs. The lofty ceiling was of massive burnished silver, the cupola shaped centre bore cleverly worked designs depicting famous gods, whose eyes of turquoise or great emeralds shone down with weird lifelike effect, which the gaping mouths filled with ivory teeth helped to heighten.

It was here, entertainments were provided for the amusement of the guests. As the night grew late, and the feeling of happiness and well-being increased, that men of every age, and all ages, will experience after a hearty meal, they indulged in such pleasures as befitted Eastern potentates.

Heavy eyelids fell over languorous eyes, and they gave scant attention to the musicians or dancers, until suddenly they were stirred to tense wakefulness. For there floated into the centre of the hall a new-comer. Her tiny henna-stained feet almost lost in a maze of jewelled coverings, her pinked fingers and round arms were also laden with gold and precious stones, the golden *chuddar,* that half clothed the upper part of her body, showed

dimly through the rows upon rows of hanging chains of precious stones which bent her slender neck by their weight.

Between the end of the *chuddar* and the golden *saree,* into
which had been worked curious designs with sparkling stones
of great value, the slim waist showed bare.

Across her face she held the drooping end of the *saree.*

With her came many musicians and singers, and to the seductive drone of the *sarangis,* accompanied by frantic beating
of *tablas,* the mysterious stranger began a dance that fired every
man present, and roused the gloating audience to a frenzy of
enthusiasm.

As the music became wilder, and the singers more flowery and
passionate in their songs, the dancer swayed on and on, in such
movements as the oldest and most experienced Rajah present
had never beheld.

Rhea felt his blood run cold, it did not need the choking perfume of crimson roses which had entered with the new-comer
to tell him who she was. For the first time since he had known
her a feeling of rage against Ugisa assailed him, for very shame
he could not rise and carry her from the hall as he longed to do;
but sitting like a marble statue, he suffered the torture of seeing the maiden whom he wished to make his Queen dancing
like a common Nautch girl, or an independent *abhisarika,* a
mere shameless woman, disporting herself for the amusement
of his guests.

At last in sheer weariness Ugisa ceased dancing, falling like
a graceful bird on the cushions which bespread the rich carpet.

Tumults of applause went up from the throats of the guests,
the only voice that remained silent being that of the Maharajah
of Martand.

Jewels were torn from fingers or great dark necks, and cast
at her feet; showers of gold and silver coins fell about her;

flowers were torn from massive jars, and flung to eulogize the seductive dancer. Ugisa's heart beat wildly, she was intoxicated with this adulation. Well aware of the unprecedented act, which followed her already discreditable conduct, yet heedless of Rhea's wrath, she rose from the floor, and facing the ring of eager spectators, slowly drew the golden veil from before her face. The sudden hush that fell, only made the deafening roar of approbation that resounded through the great hall, all the more marked, and gratified even her greed for admiration.

"I will give my kingdom for this Golden Rosebud," impulsively proclaimed one Rajah.

Immediately a competition arose for possession of this beauteous maiden, who, with gleaming eyes, and demurely smiling, scarlet lips, stood like a queen among them.

Then in a very arrogance of abandonment she let slip from her head and shoulders the golden veil, the more fully to display her charms.

With a queer contraction of his heart, Rhea saw a tiny scar just below the left shoulder, and he wondered he had never noticed it before; the sight of it made him mad to kiss it, until it disappeared, leaving the fair skin (of which Ugisa was so proud) clear and unblemished. But now he could not have moved, had he desired to do so; he was held firmly like one who had been hypnotized.

As in a trance, he beheld the handsome young Rajah of Kanauj, whose extravagances and excesses were already famous in story and song, approach the bewildering beauty, and taking her hand, place upon it a ring from his own finger. The blood-red rays of the stone set in the golden circle winked wickedly, and involuntarily Rhea closed his eyes, but only for a moment, and when he next looked, Ugisa was smiling delightedly, holding her hand up, the better to admire her latest gift, looking alternately at it, and its bestower.

Then, as suddenly as she had come she departed.

At the first available opportunity Rhea left his guests, and went in search of Ugisa, but though he looked for her throughout the palace, he could not find her; for she lay in the arms of the Rajah of Kanauj, who had won her with the milky stone containing the red fires.

It was then Rhea sent for Dimidia, who came at the bidding, clothed in his coarse white *dhoty* and a turban of like material on his dark, youthful head. In silence he listened to what the Maharajah had to say, and then he was ushered into the presence of her, with whom he had played when they were children in the forest.

Ugisa greeted him kindly, but with no enthusiasm.

"Deseré sent thee greeting, little sister," Dimidia said, after he had embraced her as a young brother might have done.

"And doth she still deny Ruipi?" inquired Ugisa smilingly.

Dimidia's eyes opened in amazement, for Ugisa's words and tone, like herself, were greatly changed.

"But yes," she admitted carelessly when he told her how altered he had found her, "that is true, and thou, too, wilt change after thou hast dwelt here with me," she assured the startled youth.

"No, no, I cannot stay with thee, Ugisa," he cried in alarm.

"But thou must; why shouldst thou not?" she demanded pettishly.

"I must return to Ruipi, to the forest."

"The forest, to Ruipi," she scoffed. "What have they to offer thee? No, my Dimidia, thou shalt stay with thy Ugisa, for she hath great need of thee," she finished with a sigh.

"Thou art unhappy here. I will take thee back to the great

cool forest, and again we will all four be happy together, as we once were before thou left us," he cried eagerly.

"Not so. Thou shalt remain here, and I will teach thee what thou hast never yet known," coaxed Ugisa.

"What is that?" he asked wonderingly.

"True happiness, little Dimidia," she laughed. "I will teach thee how to live. Thou shalt have fine clothes and jewels, and great wealth, and many slaves to wait on thee; thou shalt learn life, as I have done."

"No, no! Ugisa, I am afraid," he demurred timidly.

"Dost thou no longer care for me?" she asked sorrowfully.

"Thou knowest that I love thee dearly," he assured her quickly.

"Then stay and comfort me; I need thee so, little brother. If thou refuseth, thy Ugisa will leave her body from grief." Tears came to her eyes as she spoke, and she continued to plead and cajole, until the youth reluctantly consented to remain.

"It is because she hath been lonely that she hath done these wild things of which the Maharajah spoke," Dimidia assured himself. "I will speak gently to her, and she will weep and repent."

He soon learned that Ugisa would not brook the criticism which, in his horror at the life she was leading, he attempted, nor would she permit him to depart, although at first he made frequent attempts to leave Martand.

Gradually the idle luxury in which he dwelt overcame his scruples, and the pleasures in which Ugisa insisted on his indulging, dulled his finer nature, until he came to care for naught else, even in time learning to laugh with Ugisa at her numerous lovers.

"Come, rest thy head on my knee, and tell me what thou hast been doing," she commanded one morning.

Dimidia, clothed in lavishly embroidered pale blue garments, with a turban of the same hue in which shone a rich ruby, the glittering stone matching in colour his outer coat of velvet, soft shoes of the same material and tint adorning his feet, obeyed the autocrat; and seating himself on a cushion, took her ring-laden hand, but instead of speaking he listened amusedly, whilst he tried to purloin a blood-red ruby from her finger, which he considered would look well on his own.

Ugisa gleefully confiding to him her adventures of the previous night, when she had been beset by three importunate lovers:

"—therefore leaving those two to quarrel between themselves as to which had the prior claim to my favour, I slipped away and joined Kanauj; he, being the wickedest of the three, pleaseth me most," she finished her story exultantly.

And Dimidia, having succeeded in extracting the ruby ring and placing it on his own finger, laughed with her, and agreed that she was indeed clever thus to play with the hearts of men, and chiefly they gloated over the astuteness with which she maintained her power over Rhea, from whom she took all and gave nothing.

And the red fires in the moon-coloured stone which she always wore, laughed with them.

CHAPTER XVIII

"Oh, Yogi, who hast so long remained here on my land resting undisturbed through my clemency, I, Maharajah of all Martand, beg of thee to be my *guru*. I will be as thy servant, and beg for thee from door to door. All I ask in return is, that thou shalt teach me to be even as thou art, a man who is no longer a man, a being who has the power to disregard all responsibilities, to crush all human emotion."

At long last, Rhea succeeded in waking the Yogi to a sense of his presence.

Looking up with dim and rheumy eyes, the ascetic blinked at this intruder.

At length he spoke. As a sharp wind whistling through a reed, his voice sounded as though coming from a far distance . . . "Thou hast come to tell me thou art weary of the world," he shrilled.

"Even as thou sayest, wise one."

"Then thou liest."

"Thou art not courteous," Rhea frowned.

"And thus speaking, thou art convicted of the lack of truth, for if thou wert truly done with the world, then wouldst thou look for truth rather than courtesy," said the Yogi bitingly.

"Be not harsh with one who cometh humbly to beg of thy assistance, good Yogi," pleaded Rhea.

"Thou art arrogant in proclaiming a humbleness that thy every thought disclaims."

The cobwebs spun by spiders round this form, which for so long a time had remained silent as the trunk of a tree, trembled as the Yogi spoke; fine dust fell in little showers round him.

"Thou art enraged against me, in that I have disturbed thy pious meditation," sneered the Maharajah.

"I have waited thy return, for it is written that twice should I be interrupted by thee."

"That being so, thou wilt need no words of mine to tell thee why I have come." The King spoke dispiritedly, a fact which the Yogi was not slow in remarking.

"Thou hast stained thy soul with the purple in which thy body was born, for thou art aggrieved that I am not confused with joy at a Maharajah condescending to become my *chela.*"

"Truly I am aggrieved at thy coolness in receiving me," admitted the King. "But what can it matter to plastic clay how a potter moulds it?"

"Thou must be thy own potter," stated the Yogi dryly.

"What! Dost thou refuse to take me as thy pupil?" cried the King in astonishment.

"A pupil comes to a teacher to learn."

"That is my desire."

"Thou must first unlearn."

"And wilt thou not teach me to do so?"

"The only master for that, is thyself."

"How can I, whom thou truly sayest hath learned much that is not wise, ever hope to come by right knowledge unless guided thereto?" asked the Maharajah in exasperation.

"Every eye must see for itself, every heart must choose for itself, every soul must learn for itself."

"Wilt thou not give me that help which I crave?" demanded the King wrathfully.

"Thou didst not come for help but for sympathy, of which thou art not deserving, for I read thy life, and know it is because thou hast been baulked of carnal pleasures that thou wouldst play at being my *chela*."

"If thou dost truly know my life, thou wilt know that I have ruined myself and my kingdom by my own generosity, that I have given all to a woman, who, dispensing my gifts to others, flouts me," Rhea explained bitterly.

"Say rather that thou hast put evil in her soul, which she is ever passing on, as though thou hadst carelessly dropped a lighted spark on a blade of grass in a dry forest, which smoulders until, bursting into flames, it goeth like a raging lion, destroying all with which it cometh in contact."

"Can it be that thou art accusing me, whose only fault hath

been over-generosity, of being the cause of her weakness—I, who have given all, receiving nothing in return? Oh, Yogi, thou hast, indeed, a wrong outlook on life."

"Is it true thou desired this woman?" asked the ascetic.

"Greatly, but in honourable marriage," the Maharajah pointed out virtuously.

"She hath refused thee?"

"Yes."

"Why?"

"She does not love me—I, who worship her." The King struck his hands together in despair.

"Not so; it is thyself thou worshippeth. She is right in refusing thy love if she hath none to give thee in return."

"But she is my Fate."

"An illimitable Fate is a goddess created by incompetent grumblers," nodded the Yogi.

"I can but faintly remember my former lives; all that I retain is a strong conviction that my soul has inhabited flesh, and that each time this woman was my mate," asserted the Maharajah stubbornly.

"Then no doubt it was for some sin committed against her that caused thy first fall, for thou must often have passed through births without ever encountering her; but if she is, indeed, thy other half, when ye two (who should be one) did not meet, that existence would leave no impression on thy soul."

"Ha! then thou thyself have admitted that she is rightly mine," cried Rhea delightedly.

"If thou canst rightly win her," corrected the Yogi.

"I have lived for nothing else but to gain kindness from her."

"So, tearing her body which thou wished to enjoy, forgetting the soul that went with it, thou lavished gifts of gold, jewels, and fine raiment on it, all for thyself, to the one end, that she might succumb to thy selfish generosity. Thou are rightly punished that she hath refused thee."

"That I have been punished, and beyond my deserts, is indeed true," groaned Rhea.

"Not so; for it will take many births for thee to wash out, not only the faults thou hast been guilty of, but also those which she, and through her, others have committed," corrected the Yogi.

"Art thou condemning me to a million births of suffering?" cried the King in despair.

"Not I, but thyself."

"Then I would begin my reparation now by abandoning my life of ease and grandeur, and becoming a lowly ascetic such as thyself," determined Rhea.

"If thou art in earnest, and would truly begin to make amends, thou must not desert this woman whom thou hast corrupted; but rather, returning to her, will endeavour by every means in thy power to right the wrongs which together thou hast committed, and if thou hast one tinge of true love in thy heart for her, thou wilt never cease striving to kill the evil thou hast wakened, and fostered, and set uppermost against the goodness, which was there ere she met thee, else must she too suffer in the lives through which she must pass."

"Now, oh, Yogi, thou art going against thy own teaching, for but a moment ago when I pleaded with thee to help me, thou replied that none could help me, save myself; how then am I to help another?"

"By force of thy example alone. Thou hast kindled this fire; be it thy task to quench it, not by sitting here brooding over thy imaginary sorrows, but by living up to the best that is in thee, for more than that, not even Brahma the divine Essence could do."

Moodily the Maharajah returned to his palace, and going to Ugisa, told her what his intention had been, and she, fearful of losing the main supplier of her luxuries, looked at him sideways from beneath her lashes and pouted.

"What manner of affection dost thou call thine that would desert me, to sit with a withered Yogi, until thine own beautiful skin, which is fairer than my own, should become burned with the sun, and shrivelled with old age?" she asked softly.

"My skin is not to be compared to the satiny softness of thy delicious one, oh Heart's Delight," he cried; but he smiled, well pleased at her praise of his splendid firm white flesh, of which he was exceedingly proud.

Then forgetting the Yogi and his warnings, Rhea willingly allowed himself to be seduced by Ugisa into following the life which she had come to love.

The Yogi, for all his harsh words, gave vent to a sigh of pity, as once more falling into silence, he saw into a future, where the Maharajah of Martand and this woman for whom he craved, were old before their time from excesses and debauchery. The once glorious city falling in ruins about them, apes swinging and chattering in the ebony hall, sheep browsing in the pleasure gardens and cattle herding in the pagoda on the lake, while weeds grew unheeded in the very entrance hall of the palace itself.

The most decayed things in the midst of all this ruin and desolation, being the souls of Rhea and Ugisa, so black-stained that only a pitying God would not turn shuddering from them.

"Excuse, Lord. Your unworthy wife is filled with bitter sorrow."

Teh-Hur looked down at the recumbent form of Teh-Kong-Hsi, and wondered what it was this painful thorn of his had been doing, and why she lay still in his presence.

Teh-Hur followed the honourable profession of his forefathers, that of a towing coolie, with its poor pay, but fine pickings, one-fourteenth of a cent per junk, so that, working hard, eighteen hours a day, he earned almost two dollars a year.

But there were the wrecks, and that was why towing coolies formed themselves into a close corporation, and were envied by other coolies; that was why Teh-Hur was able to drink brick tea, and eat number six rice.

Now, he had just returned after several days' absence, for it was the good stormy month. Wrecks on the Pearl river had been plentiful, and many junks had foundered; therefore, Teh-Hur, with the fellows of his guild, had reaped a rich harvest. The satisfaction he had felt, as, tired and hungry, he hastened through the foul-smelling, narrow streets of Sui-Hing, with their teeming, shouting crowds, towards his home, died.

Teh-Hur's home itself was merely pieced together fragments of an old junk, welded closely in between other similar habitations. This one had been converted into two rooms by means of discarded pieces of packing cases, their trade marks and labels conveying to those who could read, something of these deal boards' chequered careers.

Patches of decayed matting, helped out with clay, straw and mud, formed the walls, and odd tiles, broken pottery and straw, kept in place by the cunning use of mud, made a flat roof that was at least watertight.

The entrance of Teh-Hur's house was the kitchen and living room; in it smouldered a fire on a home-made brick receptacle, over which steamed an earthenware saucepan, containing rotten cabbage stalks, a handful of grey rice, and a small portion of putrid fish, a savoury dish that was being prepared by his mother-in-law, who, together with her husband (old, blind and useless), a small cock, two thin, almost featherless hens, and a lean pig, inhabited this section of their son-in-law's home, he being parentless.

Beyond a few earthen pots and vessels, and some tiny saucers and handleless cups, the apartment, even for a Chinese dwelling, was bare, which, in the circumstances, was fortunate; otherwise the old couple could not have enjoyed the cramped comfort which was theirs at night, when their ancient mats were spread, to keep them from the mud floor, in the few places where mat, not ragged holes, remained, for their sleeping outfit.

Impending disaster had struck at Teh-Hur as he passed through the living room, for his mother-in-law, abandoning her task of stirring the mess over the fire beside which she was squatting, threw herself face downward on the floor, groaning and crying out words of woe.

The toothless, blind old man had immediately taken up his wife's moaning, and shrilly denounced all women.

That was all right, Teh-Hur knew, not so much from personal observation, but from the wise sayings of Confucius, which had been told him (for he could not read), that all women were woodenheads; but he had not yet grasped the reason of "the creature of the back room's" abasement.

Then from the far corner of the conjugal chamber, which the small and antique, cane sleeping mat completely furnished, he heard a low gurgle, like that a puppy might make. His slant eyes wandered from his wife's face to the direction from whence issued this curious noise, and fell on a tiny bundle of rags that moved feebly.

"On the accursed seventh day of this miserable month at the seventh hour I disgraced your honourable ancestors by producing a degraded daughter," confessed Teh-Kong-Hsi mournfully.

"Hi Yah."

This was very bad. Women were indeed mud-worms, and never to be trusted. Teh-Hur was righteously indignant; that this abased creature, whom he rather liked, should have committed such a crime in his absence, fell as a bitter blow. He had depended on her to give him a son necessary to carry on the towing work, up and down the yellow Kiang, when he himself should have gone to join his ancestors, and the desired son was needed to worship his own memory. Every man must have a son.

A daughter! Of what use could such a thing be?

Apart from being a superfluous extravagance, Teh-Kong-Hsi had perpetrated the double crime of giving birth to this unwelcome child on an unlucky day, and, furthermore, had not rectified her error by drowning it directly she had realized her guiltiness; but, judging from the puppy-like squeak, and the movement of the bundle, had permitted the scandalous thing to live.

Teh-Hur was most annoyed. He stood looking at the trembling Teh-Kong-Hsi, not knowing what to do, for it was only permitted to drown such disgraceful appendages if the act was committed immediately on birth; but the seventh day was three days ago. No wonder Teh-Hur felt wrathful.

Then, although he was tired and wanted his supper, the newly-made father turned, and passing by the still groaning couple, who had waited the death cries of their careless daughter for her wicked act, Teh-Hur made his way back to the Pearl river, through the streets of this important suburb of Canton.

There he invested a whole *"cash"* in the purchase of a paper boat, with its accompanying small bundle of straw; an extravagance to be sure, for a cash is the tenth part of a precious farthing. Still, Teh-Hur was a reckless man at the moment, and must ascertain how the gods felt about his wife's evil deed.

He did not set the boat alight, as some careless, hard-hearted men might have done, but gave it an added chance of sailing safely away, by merely setting it on the turbulent stream. This act he performed with great care and solemnity, squatting on his haunches to watch with intense interest its fate. If the boat foundered, or came back to the shore, then Teh-Hur would be forced to punish Teh-Kong-Hsi severely; if it sailed safely away, that would denote Fung-Sui (the gods of wind and rain) were not overwrought with anger.

The fragile pink and blue thing, with its bands of scarlet, dipped, and as Teh-Hur leant forward with eager eyes, the fateful toy was caught lightly by a gust of wind, and blown deliberately back into the affronted father's face.

"Ho! ho! This must be a very devil female baby, to thus impudently treat her parent."

Teh-Hur's indignation against mother and child increased. Still, he was just, as witness this journey, when a less patient man would have immediately strangled the guilty ones, before enjoying his supper and falling soundly asleep, to be in readiness for the next day's work.

Taking the limp boat, Teh-Hur spoke seriously to it, ere again setting it on the swollen yellow waters; without a second's hesitation the impertinent thing collapsed, and was rapidly sucked beneath the angry stream.

The gods had decided.

With justifiable rage, Teh-Hur left the banks of the Pearl river, and began his journey back, towards that "gourd full of evil," and her girl baby.

The town of Sui-Hing was now lighted up, and the crowds in the streets were merry. Teh-Hur was caught in a procession in the shape of a huge dragon lantern; back and forth swayed the grotesque lighted paper image, the men, whose heads and upper parts were inside the dragon-lantern, turned and whirled, giving vent to the shrieks and groans which they fondly believed were excellent imitations of live dragon voices, to the great delight of screaming urchins, and a general rout of rag-tag and bobtail loafers.

Teh-Hur was carried along some distance by the dragon bearers, then, the paper catching fire, the loudly yelling "dragon legs" deserted their burden to burn itself out, and repaired to a street café for tea, and perhaps a pipe of opium.

Although it was not his usual custom, means not allowing, the sorely afflicted husband and parent threw himself wearily on to a bunk-like couch, slung in the back of the café, and lying beside the tiny lamp, accepted the long, slender stem, with its apple-shaped bowl, in which a hole had been scooped. Taking the knitting-needle pin, and spearing up a pill of opium from the box brought him, he roasted it over the flame of the lamp, kneading the ball against the outer portion of the bowl, wherein he then placed the heated stuff. As he held the bowl against the lamp, Teh-Hur sighed with self-pity, and inhaling a deep whiff, swallowed slowly, then another, and another. His eyes half closed, he lay back, and cleared the bowl ready for a fresh pellet.

Ah! this was better; he felt soothed. Then if one little pill could bring this good feeling, he would try more. He smiled sadly at his afflictions. The things he could visualize clearest were the wriggling bundle near Teh-Kong-Hsi; the faded blue trousers of his mother-in-law, as she lay flat on her stomach and yowled beside the smouldering fire, and the toothless, blind old man in blue and yellow rags, with his straggly grey beard, and wispy *queue,* into which fragments of black horsehair had been interwoven with the ancient one's own sparse locks; a droll figure, sucking at the broken pipe with nothing in it. Teh-Hur smiled amusedly.

Women were weak, silly, undependable creatures. Confucius was wise; he had said: "God places souls in women's bodies to punish them."

Poor souls!

Teh-Hur likened woman to a crazy junk on a stormy sea; none knew the trouble either gave until he had tried to steer one.

"That bundle——!"

Teh-Hur slept.

CHAPTER XX

"This 'bitter stone' has killed her father," Teh-Kong-Hsi announced to her parents, when days passed and Teh-Hur did not return.

And the "bitter stone" smiled up at the low ceiling, chirruping conversationally to it.

"And what else could you expect, worthless daughter, if you

would have your mud-turtle child born under the Tiger?" demanded Teh-Hur's mother-in-law acrimoniously.

"It was a disastrous act," sighed the blind man, "when you recall that you and your master were born under the Goat, and tigers make meals off goats."

"Aré-ya," gurgled the Tiger-born one happily.

"Aré-ya, aré-ya," snapped the disconsolate grass widow. "You cry out that all the time. I will give you a dose of *muktong;* that will poison you, you frog's-chin. What have you done with your honourable father, eh?"

"Poooooof! Aré-ya," giggled the abused *Sho-sho* to its only confidante, the ceiling.

No amount of neglect appeared to weaken Aré-Ya, as she seemed to have named herself, for she thrived in body and spirit, the strongest and merriest child in that overcrowded spot. From the moment of her birth she had never cried, but lying on her back, crooned and chuckled, seeming to find life a rare joke, which she shared with her best friend the ceiling, or the lean pig and featherless hens; of her kin she took not the slightest notice.

"Ah, unnatural sorrow-spume, you laugh because you have eaten your father. Come, I will give you to the devil who sent you to be a bad thorn in my side." And picking little Aré-Ya up in her arms, Teh-Kong-Hsi toddled swiftly down to the banks of the Pearl river, which, now that the storm had ceased, flowed smooth and yellow as buttercup petals.

Aré-Ya tried to swallow her fist, chortling with joy, and when her grief-ridden mother placed her on the water, that seemed to be the crowning jest of all, and, gurgling and smiling, Aré-Ya on the little mat which her mother had generously provided for her to lie on, floated happily out of sight and so out of her parents' lives.

Then Teh-Kong-Hsi went in search of her missing lord, and told him that the venom-blot had gone.

Upon which good hearing he was graciously pleased to return to his home, and as her next effort produced the longed-for son, she was accorded the forgiveness due to a truly contrite wife, and lived happily with Teh-Hur, forgetting Aré-Ya, who was picked up by Ai-Hsiu, a wrinkled hag employed in the rice fields that skirted the Pearl river.

In a very few years Aré-Ya was also working in the rice fields, and Ai-Hsiu saw to it that she did not neglect her task; even when the tiny fingers bled from the making of bamboo rakes, her foster-mother would allow no rest.

As Aré-Ya continued her task, taking the bamboo pole, splitting and bending the end, into which she inserted a small scrap of plaited grass in order to spread out the prongs, fan-shaped, she crowed and laughed to herself.

When Ai-Hsiu cut her feet, pinched or bit her by way of punishment, and she did not cry, the old woman marvelled, and wondered if, after all, she had been wise in courting disaster, by rescuing this weird thing from the water, and becoming a little afraid of the devil-child, ceased to punish her so often, and the soles of Aré-Ya's feet, which were a mass of cuts from the beatings by cane that had been inflicted, healed, and her arms and body being left unpinched lost their bruised patches.

Aré-Ya felt no animosity towards the crone for these castigations, neither did she experience gratitude at the respite.

From daybreak to sunset, the unwanted infant worked in the rice swamp, thinking her own thoughts, gaily chattering to herself, listening to the continual croaking of frogs, or catching grasshoppers, when her guardian's back was turned.

This last, she discovered to be a source of income, for one

happy day Ai-Hsiu groaned with a gripping cramp, and Aré-Ya was sent alone to the field, where, instead of working, she spent most of her day watching the gaily-coloured junks, with their queer, square-topped, red sails, drifting down the Kiang.

The sailors, amused at the small figure, cried words of bantering good-nature, to which she replied with streams of virulent abuse that she had learned from her guardian.

To her unqualified joy, one junk, with a delightfully malevolent face painted on its prow, was forced to stop for some necessary repair, anchoring close to the bank on Aré-Ya's side of the river.

One of the sailors, noticing a grasshopper held tight in her hand, begged it from her, for he was a connoisseur in sporting crickets; in return, he presented her with a small portion of sugar-cane.

Darting off, Aré-Ya soon returned with several more crickets, and earned two *cash* and a bamboo flute, for her wares, the first payment she had ever received in her life. Her satisfaction was intense.

The rest of the day she spent in producing weird sounds from the instrument, which became her treasured god, and was carefully hidden from the jealous eyes of Ai-Hsiu, who would certainly have deprived her of it had she known of its existence.

The first kindness she met with was from a monk, who lived alone, in charge of the Temple of Heaven.

The rice field in which she and Ai-Hsiu toiled, was situated at the foot of the hundred and fifty sugar-loaf summits topping the tortuous gorges, that wound down the steep valleys, on to the plain of the Seven Stars, named thus from the seven high raised masses of white marble, that were dotted about at irregular intervals.

In the centre of this plain stood the Temple of Heaven.

On pillars of pale green jade, were three tiers of lapis-lazuli, with a small dome of gold on the summit, standing out clear against the sky.

This gloriously coloured thing had long ago attracted Aré-Ya's eye, and the faint sound of drum, and tinkling bell, which rose above the croak of frogs, she felt sure must emanate from this mysterious blue, green and gold monster.

One clear moonlight night she crept from the bedside of Ai-Hsiu.

With fleet feet, on which no proud parent had bent the toes to make lily-shaped, she ran through the sodden rice fields, past the Seven Stars until she reached the ancient, treeless park that surrounded the Temple.

Creeping past the simple doorway, and up the avenue of acacias, she was met with a heavy iron gate, through which she peered curiously.

Finding the gate locked, thus baulked of entry into the building that had so attracted her, perhaps she would have returned, had not the sound of a gong, followed by the clanging of the Temple bell, fallen on her ears.

She caught her breath, and thrilled to the sound.

Then she had been right in her surmise that the fascinating noise issued from this thing.

It was the first feeling she had ever experienced, excepting those of hunger, thirst and weariness.

With all her might, her tiny, work-stained hands clung to the iron bars of the gate, her face, too, was pressed close to the metal, her dark, slant eyes glittered, and she waited until the booming and tinkling ceased, then—

"Again, again," she shrieked, rattling the gate with all her baby might.

Silence reigned, and lifting up her shrill treble voice, Aré-Ya rained down curses on this thing that did not obey her.

"The curse of all the gods rest on you, and your children, and their children's children," she screamed, "you tongue of an evil serpent, you diseased leg of a rat! May the poison of your voice follow your ancestors to their resting-place, and drip misery on their heads. May their feet bleed and swell with festering wounds, so that their long journey may be torture and their faces turn black with pain."

"What evil is this I hear a small tongue crying?" interrupted a thick, harsh voice, and there issued from the Temple a tall figure.

Aré-Ya's voice died, her hands fell from the gate, and she looked at the monk, who, wearing a bright orange robe, showed clearly, as he stood on the uppermost of the last tier of wide marble steps.

Slowly he descended, and leaned against the sacrificial altar at the foot of the stairway.

"Who spoke?" he asked.

"This insignificant one, Lord," piped Aré-Ya.

"A child's voice," he marvelled aloud, and as he came towards her, Aré-Ya could see in the bright moonlight that his shaven head was branded with many marks of sainthood, burned in by means of red-hot pieces of metal, and the sticks of incense adhering to his head by means of resin, stood erect like stiff twists of hair; a very saintly monk was this.

"I want the noise again," stated Aré-Ya, as he approached the gate where she stood.

The monk looked down in wonderment on the tiny figure, kow-towing gravely, with its head of untidy, unplaited hair, one bony shoulder issuing from the soiled jacket which she was wearing with a pair of ragged black trousers, bound from ankle to knees by coarse green grass.

"Who are you?" he asked.

"The contemptible Aré-Ya, spawn of the devil and a mud-turtle, honourable one," recited the treble voice faithfully. Ai-Hsui had so often told her of her origin that she knew it quite well; again she kow-towed.

"And what want ye here?" inquired the monk.

"To hear again the *'bhoberry'* that the gracious one's lordly hut cries," explained the maiden concisely.

"The bell of worship," mused the monk, slowly unlocking the gate, through which the mite quickly slipped.

Together, these two queerly contrasting figures moved towards the Temple steps, where Aré-Ya, being tired from her journey, calmly seated herself, and placing two skinny elbows on her knees, cupped her chin, and looked up with shining, beady eyes at the monk.

Soon he drew from her as much as he could tell him of her eight years of life; then it being the hour appointed, he left her seated in solitude, while he re-entered the Temple to beat the drum and ring the chimes.

When he returned, his self-invited guest prostrated herself on her face before him, lying flat on the marble steps.

"Oh, heavenly one, your *bhoberry* comforts my vile belly, and brings this evil one great happiness," she sighed contentedly; then rising, she produced her one treasure, and placing it to her lips, blew, watching him with great pride, eager to see the effect her magic reed would have on this "Wonder Worker."

In pitiful silence the monk listened to the crude squeaking, then taking the flute gently from her, he set it to his lips, and Aré-Ya heard her flute played by an artist.

Sitting on the step, he showed her where to place her fingers, and how to play the roughly fashioned instrument. For an hour he let her stay, then escorting her to the gate, sent her back to Ai-Hsiu.

"This unworthy Chinese-sorrow will come again, even though it be but for a moment, to hear the *bhoberry,* and see the honourable one," Aré-Ya promised, kow-towing politely.

"A few minutes is long if you use every second," replied the monk.

"The wise one's words shall be remembered, and this vile piece of mud feels like a dumb man, who has swallowed a tooth; he can say nothing, but it is all inside him." After which quaint way of expressing her gratitude, Aré-Ya departed.

CHAPTER XXI

A new life had opened for her; two or three times a week, whenever she could creep away unobserved, whilst Ai-Hsiu slept, the child ran to the Temple of Heaven, and the "Lordly One" always welcomed her kindly, teaching her to play her flute, and telling her of the good in life.

The monk, whose name had been Lui-Peh, had chosen this vocation, in preference to obeying his parents' demand that he should marry, and beget a son, for he felt a strange disinclination towards matrimony, never having met anyone to whom he felt attracted, and declining to wed from a sense of duty.

Poor Lui-Peh, the blessing of sons was not to be his, for he would never marry. He could not know that his objection to matrimony was shared by another—a maiden of ancient lineage, and no beauty, who dwelt in far-off Venice.

Her lack of good looks was a sore trial to the parents of Deseré (for such was the maiden's name), and they greatly rejoiced on finding a wealthy, though elderly, gentleman of equally good pedigree, backed by the riches that they lacked, who looked on their plain daughter with amorous eyes.

With a sore heart, and eyes rendered red and swollen with weeping, Deseré was led to the altar, and made an unhappy wife.

She, too, was naturally ignorant of the celibate in distant China; neither would it have interested her to hear of him, and yet——!

Lui-Peh felt strangely drawn to the little Aré-Ya, and taught her all that her short visits allowed him to do. Nightly visits, which he came to look forward to as eagerly as the child herself.

"This monstrous villain will stay for ever with the 'Lordly One,'" Aré-Ya announced on one of these occasions, and Lui-Peh smiled.

"No, small spirit; you must return and do your obedient duty to Ai-Hsiu," he told her.

"Ai-Hsiu is a slit-eyed, evil cow," she informed him calmly.

"She saved your little carcase from the water," he reminded her.

"Hi-yah! That was the old, black, stealing crow's luck," was Aré-Ya's response. "This small meek one would eat her, and *chin-chin* to the *joss* of tooth-worship after the meal; only the tough, bad one would turn my trivial belly sour," she added thoughtfully.

"If the small, meek one, lets such thoughts dwell in her mind, she will become evil, even as she terms this poor, ancient Ai-Hsiu," warned the monk. "It must be that my fierce small one was born beneath the Tiger."

"Even so, that thought is pleasing," Aré-Ya nodded gravely; then: "But the Lordly One need not fear; this savage beast will not eat him," she hastened to assure the tall, lean man.

"The powerful one is kind," thanked the monk just as gravely. "It would be well if she would be as generous to Ai-Hsiu."

"A kind one receives kindness, and wicked one evil," stated Aré-Ya firmly.

"Not so," corrected Lui-Peh. "If any are not kind to us, we must not pass that hurtful quality on, but in the strength of one born under the great Tiger, that unhappiness must be killed by a gentle deed, for it needs a powerful one to be tender under bruises. In this way, small one, strength becomes greater."

"The Lordly One is wise, and should know," she sighed unbelievingly; adding after a moment's thought: "Then shall this impure Tiger cub strive to follow this good teaching, for it would be pleasant to grow big, and muscular enough to beat the revolting Ai-Hsiu until her bones cracked."

Distressed, but not discouraged, Lui-Peh sought painstakingly to inculcate love and charity in the child's heart.

As she rose to go, she pulled out one of her precious *cash,* and presenting it to him with a magnificent air, said grandiloquently: "Here, Lordly One, take payment for your teachings, and observe that the Small One is charitable."

"Ah," he smiled, "listen to the tale of the begging monk and the lion, who met in a great forest. The monk being afraid, clashed his attracting-cymbals at the lion, then threw them in its face. The beast swallowed the cymbals and came growling towards the frightened monk, who had nothing left in his hand but his small collecting book, that he hurled too, and the lion ran quickly away. When he reached his den, he lay down contented. 'For,' he pondered, licking his chops, 'even though empty, I am a lucky lion, to have escaped from the begging monk without paying anything.'"

The story amused Aré-Ya, and she turned the *cash* to its hiding-place, relieved, yet a little hurt at Lui-Peh's gentle refusal of it.

"Ha! This despicable offering, like the unworthy giver, is too small," she commented.

"No, no," he hastened to assure her. "But if the generous one wishes to make payment, let it be as the ox told the toad."

"Will the Lordly One explain what that was to these waiting ears?" she asked.

"A small Toad lived in a pool, to which a great Ox came to bathe and drink.

"'Ah,' sighed the Toad, 'if I could build a house worthy of this magnificent bulk, he would stay here for ever, and I would swell with happiness,' for she loved the Ox.

"Then she set about trying to cut down a large willow tree in order to build a palace for the Ox, who watched her efforts with surprise.

"'Tell me, small Toad,' he asked her one day, when many months had passed, and despite her efforts she had not succeeded in making even a mark on the tough tree, 'what are you trying to accomplish this foolish task for?'

"'To make for you an honourable dwelling, so that you may always remain near me,' she confessed meekly.

"'Ho! ho!' said the Ox. 'If you wish to be kind to me, jump on my back and keep away the flies that pester so.'

"'That is so small a thing, and a task I would not like,' she protested.

"'But, well-thinking Toad, if you really desire to serve my clumsy self, let it be in the way that will best please me, and that will be by doing this little kindness to any tormented like my provoked self,' begged the Ox.

"So the small Toad did as he requested her, and by giving great relief to the teased Ox, became happy in this menial service; for she knew that distasteful as the work was, it delighted her beloved Ox.

"—and if my small Toad will do any little kindness that comes her way, that will be a great and generous payment to her humble teacher, and also she will find her own soul," finished the monk.

"Anything that this unfortunate Toad finds, the grasping Ai-Hsiu seizes for herself," said Aré-Ya acridly.

"Not Ai-Hsiu, or any other, can seize a soul; that, little Bitterness, belongs to each human and is his alone to make good or evil," Lui-Peh explained.

"Yi! Oh! It would be amusing to have something tucked away from her old prying crook-claws. How, then, can this lurking mystery be discovered?"

"One day, small Toad of great resentfulness, your soul will stir to activity. When that time comes, you will suffer, for it is through anguish alone that the soul is wakened."

"My corrupt body does not wish to be tormented," pondered Aré-Ya pensively; "still, it would be cheerful to anger the tainted hag."

"When my little unfortunate one gives birth to her soul, the pain through which she must first pass will cause her to be gentle, even to those who have done her most harm." Lui-Peh spoke as he hoped.

"Will my indisposed body be torn as is that of a bitch when she gives birth to puppies?" inquired Aré-Ya uneasily.

"The torment through which one passes at such a birth is not visible to naked eye, but none the less surely is the body wracked, little Toad."

"And to which medicine *joss* must *chin-chins* be made to relieve the base pain, oh, Lordly One?"

"A soul does not waken idly; it, alone, will show the way to a healing, and when that time comes my paltry words will be remembered," he prophesied.

"The Lordly One is wise, but his disquieting words make my contemptible backbone quiver," confessed Aré-Ya, as she rose to go. "May a myriad years be given to one who has a heart of such kindness, and a tongue of such piety," she gave as benediction, kow-towing her farewell; then a rush of gratitude for the refused *cash* caused her to pause, and call over her shoulder an addition to her blessing—:

"—and may a thousand sons be born to the Heavenly one!" Then breaking into a rapid trot she disappeared down the hill.

Then Lui-Peh lost his small visitor, and though he grieved over her non-appearance, and often speculated as to what had become of her, he never again heard of, or saw her.

Aré-Ya had run away.

Ai-Hsiu coming suddenly and unexpectedly on the waif, had discovered her hidden among the tender green of the rice plants, playing softly, as Lui-Peh had taught her, on the flute.

Enraged at this flagrant waste of time, the old crone had fallen on the child and beaten her severely. That, Aré-Ya did not resent, it was quite bearable, and only right, but when her instrument had been seized, she fought for it like a crazed monkey; but Ai-Hsiu proving too strong for her, the treasure was spitefully smashed into a hundred splinters.

In a white heat of rage, Aré-Ya called down curses on the head of the cruel old hag, at whom she sprang, in a blind fury, and seizing her tormentor's *queue,* lifted her short, sharp knife which she used in her daily work, and cut the appendage off close to the roots of the ancient one's head, then, turning, fled far from her, paying no heed to the shrieking threats of what would befall her on her return.

That night she secreted herself on a stationary junk, and crouched under a ragged sail, one throb of agony, not from the bruised body, but for the loss of her god, and perhaps also because her eyes were, as ever, tearless.

Lying beneath the sail, Aré-Ya slept.

CHAPTER XXII

Towards dawn, when Aré-Ya wakened, she found that the junk was no longer still, but moving swiftly down the Pearl river.

Peeping cautiously out from beneath her covering, she saw a strange land; from over the sides of the junk, she caught vistas of neat, gaily-coloured houses, surrounded by picturesque gardens, interspersed with miniature lakes, and fascinatingly crooked paths.

"Hi Yi, this is good," she chuckled to herself; "now will the tainted cow who destroyed my music-giver cry uselessly for my return, and she may *chin-chin* to her *joss* in vain, for I have her tail, and without it, she can never be drawn up to Heaven. May she live to be imprisoned in a brick wall and die of thirst, and when she returns to earth she shall come back as a vile rat, and I shall be the cat to catch her." This was a nice picture, and Aré-Ya liked to dwell on it.

"I shall await the stopping of this devil-junk and slip away," she decided.

What she was to do then she never thought, nor was she in the least afraid, the future could not be worse than the past, therefore let it come.

But the "devil-junk" did not stop, and during the morning she was discovered and dragged from her unsavoury nest by a sailor, to whom, despite his questionings, she gave no satisfaction, therefore he took her before Yu-Cho, the merchant owner of the vessel, who seated in his own tiny cabin, going through accounts, was not pleased at the interruption.

"Oh, Son of Heaven, this unworthy dog found yonder crab's-claw hidden beneath a sail," explained the sailor, falling on his knees, his head on the ground, his heels in the air.

The stout merchant looked through his tortoise-shell rimmed glasses, his writing brush suspended in the air, and saw a tattered girl-child, staring at him unafraid, as she politely kow-towed.

"How did this grain of rice come aboard my vessel?" inquired Yu-Cho.

The coolie, loath to confess ignorance, gave many explanations, one being that the cormorants, which were kept for the purpose of catching fish, having been unloosened and given the word of command, dived overboard, when they were drawn back by the cord, which tied round the neck serves the double purpose of retrieving the bird, and at the same time prevents his swallowing his prey; with great volubility the coolie explained that as he held the cormorant over a basket, and drew down the lower mandible, so that the fish would pop out, instead of a finny creature, this devil-girl issued from the bird's neck.

Upon hearing which, Yu-Cho gave it as his positive opinion that the coolie was lying, and ordered him to be beaten with the three-piece cane.

The coolie retired protesting and howling, for he dreaded the two little canes, which used rapidly in a masterly fashion, soon broke the tissues underlying the flesh, which the larger cane merely bruised.

The coolie liar disposed of, Yu-Cho turned his attention to Aré-Ya.

"Where do you come from, small frog's chin?" he asked.

"The field of the King of Hell, oh Big Belly," replied Aré-Ya.

This polite form of address pleased Yu-Cho, for, like all his sex, he loved flattery.

Aré-Ya's shrewd, slant eyes told her that she had pleased this mighty one, whose finely-embroidered robe, with the multitude of useful and ornamental appendages dangling from the button of lapis-lazuli, affixed to the breast of his robe, fascinated her.

There was a curious crystal ball, a jade fish to keep away the evil eye, a slender ivory scoop for his ears, and a fine comb of bone, a toothpick of the same material, and many other wonderful things made of various compositions.

All this her sharp eyes noted, as well as the long finger nails, carefully bound in silk to prevent their breaking, which told her that he was a great man, as also did his close-fitting, black cap, with its scarlet band, and distinguished button, coloured blue, in mourning for his wife.

To all his questioning Aré-Ya lied calmly, even backing up the coolie's statement that she had been brought aboard by a cormorant.

When Yu-Cho threatened to throw her back into the *kiang,* she looked at him fearlessly.

"Very well, Son of Heaven, commit this foul-mouthed one to the insignificant waters, if such is your honourable will," she told him.

Yu-Cho was secretly amused, and being at a loss what to do with his stowaway, placed her in the care of his *chwanjoo,* and this captain, being a family man, and one with a kindly heart, took the child under his own especial care, giving her, her first blissful taste of pork.

From which time, her one idea of Heaven became a place where she could have as much of the succulent pig as she wanted, listen to musical *bhoberry,* have a flute of her own, and in her spare moments torture Ai-Hsiu.

Whenever the junk stopped, in order to take in, or unload merchandise, Aré-Ya hid until they once more set sail, in case the Heavenly, Big-Bellied one should cause her to be set ashore, for she was thoroughly happy in her life on board this boat, where every man, from Yu-Cho down to the lowest coolie, petted and played with her; indeed it was the great merchant himself who, discovering her longing for such a plaything, presented her with a small jade flute, and so earned her undying gratitude.

Aré-Ya's life of peace and affluence bred in her an overwhelming contempt for the coolie women whom she saw working, and to some of these toil-wracked things, who bent and panted hoarsely under the weight of huge, overhead loads, or others, hardly to be distinguished from the men whom they and their children worked beside, treading creaking waterwheels to propel heavy river junks, she would cry jeering words of scorn, encouraged thereto by the applause of the coolies on Yu-Cho's boat.

"Oh ho, pig-eyes, base-born slaves," she would pipe derisively, clinging to the mast that held the scarlet sail upright, "work and sweat like dishonourable barbarians, or you will be beaten as vile oxen, or slain as foul rats, and thrown aside like the stinking refuse that pollutes my Heaven-bred nostrils. Look well at me, the beautiful and favoured Aré-Ya, who am born to adorn the world, and must never work, but grow the long finger nails, and eat pork."

If the creatures whom she taunted were goaded into pelting stones or mud in her direction, she would scream with joy, and sliding from her vantage point, crouch near the vessel's side, until well out of range of her attackers.

A merry life was Aré-Ya's.

Slipping ashore at one of the ports, she crept into a teahouse, attracted by the music, and there the wonderful sight of dancing girls delighted her.

On her return to the junk, like a clever monkey she faithfully imitated the swaying movements of the dancers, and, finding her efforts met with uproarious applause, worked incessantly to perfect herself in this new talent.

So, with flute playing, dancing, and learning all the *Chwanjoo,* or his sailors could teach her, of both good and evil, Aré-Ya passed the days sailing down the Pearl river very agreeably; only once did she earn the displeasure of the crew, that was when she inadvertently seated herself on the bow of the junk, to be immediately and unceremoniously jerked up by the coolie who stood nearest.

On it being explained to her that the bow was sacred to the sailors' guardian-deity, she kow-towed apologetically, and never afterwards omitted to perform a deep obeisance to the sacred bow, or to burn a stick of incense before it, when such a thing was given her.

Fair or ill weather was all the same to her, or whether the country through which they passed was flat and uncultivated, or teeming with orderly, brightly-coloured bamboo huts, the inhabitants gay and cleanly dressed.

She believed that the otters really caught the fish they ate, with their paws, as the coolies sincerely thought, and buffalo cows with their calves that swam alongside the junk bellowing for food, amused her.

Then to her two joys of music and dancing was added a third, for she learned to gamble.

Chi-mooe, where one guessed how many fingers would extend, when the hand was suddenly flung forward, was all very well; but shuttlecock played with the soles of one's feet was better, and *pu-chee,* or cards, were amusing, but best of all was a cricket match; this sport Aré-Ya loved whole-heartedly.

The arena of the fight was a flat-bottomed bowl, in which

two combatant crickets would be placed by their proud owners, and incited to fight one another by being tickled on their backs with a rat's bristle inserted in the split end of a stick.

Yu-Cho himself never failed to be present at one of these contests, and did not disdain to yell and shriek with excitement, urging on the cricket he had backed, with prayers, curses and wise sayings.

To the clamorous howlings of the interested spectators, for every coolie risked money on his favourite cricket, Aré-Ya's shrill treble piped clear and loud.

"I put a *cash* on Tong," she yelled, dancing up and down in wild excitement. Her bet was taken by a backer of the rival cricket, Ling, and when the latter turned tail, Aré-Ya's enthusiasm was hysterical, for Tong had won.

And so to her original two *cash,* which she had always kept carefully hidden away tied up in a rag inside her black trousers, she added another coin, and became a confirmed gambler.

One beautiful sunshiny morning, as the junk sailed slowly past gay orchards of fruit trees in pink and white blossom, growing round tiny toy-like houses with bamboo sides which were covered by clusters of wistaria, the delicate fragrance of the purple flowers melting into that of the orange-tree blossoms; then, dipping her rusty sails to float under a bridge of twisted creepers, the rolling boat moved by blue lakes, on which floated scarlet lotus and blue water-lilies, forests of great cryptomaria trees, where the mellow note of the thrush known as the Yellow-eyebrow mingled with the cry of high-flying Bean goose and the trill of the lark, Aré-Ya noticed without much interest a small island towards which they were steering; it was set in the middle of a deep swamp, and on it there appeared to be little vegetation apart from a dreary rice-paddy.

Now the beautiful forests and lakes were left behind, there

was an intense stillness, even the coolies had ceased jabbering, and no note of wild-bird disturbed the air.

As they drew nearer to the mournful island, Aré-Ya descried some hundred or so squat, white-washed shacks.

Suddenly there arose a cry, it came from the land, and seemed to be a signal of some sort, for immediately from fields and shacks there swarmed in view the inhabitants, who came running and crawling towards the edge of the island. Aré-Ya watched in petrified silence the shrieking, moaning, whispering scraps of humanity, some with faces eaten completely away, others with legs and arms hanging rotten from their diseased bodies; many of them had nothing remaining but a trunk and a piece of revolting head, only a few of the lepers wore clothing, the rest were naked and shone dazzling white, like blocks of salt.

A groan came from the child's throat, all her flesh crept, and she sank to the bottom of the junk, her face pressed close to the deck.

Closing her eyes tightly, she placed her hands over her ears, so that she should not hear the harrowing cries of the piteous wretches.

The *Chwan-joo* bade the coolies hasten to place the bales and boxes of necessities they had brought for the lepers, on the fringe of the island.

Then as the junk began to turn, the flapping sails aided by a long oar on each side, worked by six men a-piece, ten coolies remaining inside the boat, whilst one either side dropped over the rail, to stand on narrow planks the better to help their fellows; Aré-Ya, whose never-failing policy was to be up and doing, sprang from her recumbent position, and flinging herself on the long handled *yuloo,* added every ounce of her puny strength to aid the chanting sailor men hasten the boat away from the plague-stricken spot.

Above the coolies' howl and song, her voice rang out, urging them with profane curses and dire threats to hurry away from the hideous island of Kowloon, where these slowly rotting creatures dwelt, hating one another and cursing God. The horror of it bit deep into Aré-Ya's very being; so long as she lived she always looked back with a shudder on her glimpse of Kowloon.

CHAPTER XXIII

Yu-Cho watched Aré-Ya dancing for the amusement of the coolies, accompanying herself on the jade flute he had given her, and decided she would prove an attraction to one of his tea-houses in Canton, and on arrival at the port he determined to hand her over to the matronly Ah-Foo, who had charge of the girls in one of his elegant places of entertainment.

Calling a coolie with a barrow, shaped like a miniature jaunting-car, the portly merchant, with large scarlet umbrella upheld, occupied one side, and swelling with pride, Aré-Ya sat like one born to such luxury (which she was experiencing for the first time) on the other, reclining lengthways, her feet on the seat.

She felt very distinguished and wealthy, for now she owned forty-four *cash,* gained by luck at gambling with the junk coolies, and several precious articles of clothing tied up in a blue cloth, and securely fastened to a tiny cane pole, so that she might the more easily carry her worldly possessions over her shoulder. Her hair was well oiled, and on her head she wore a jade green cap, on the summit of which was jauntily stuck the rakish scarlet and golden-brown feather she had wrenched from the tail of a protesting bantam cock, whose foolish crowing had attracted her attention to where he was tied to the side of a *sampan* lying near Yu-Cho's junk.

Glancing down at her apparel, she nodded pleasedly; for were not her black cotton trousers new, as was her Nankeen blue shirt, and joy of joys, this garment was well braided, and fastened with a black cord-loop and button. Her white-soled shoes, with black and blue tops, fitted nicely over spotlessly clean cotton socks. She experienced the superiority natural to every female who knows she is well dressed and in the height of fashion.

The loud squeaking of the unoiled barrow-wheels, seemed to scream for all to stop and gaze at this fashionably dressed lady out for an airing with a wealthy Chinaman friend; jolting and bumping over the unevenly cobbled streets, which were always wet from the leakage of skins carried by water coolies.

After leaving his charge with Ah-Foo, Yu-Cho drove relievedly off to his own son.

He had but one child, whom he adored, and the ten-year-old Yu-Chi-Soh, had never made a request of his father in vain.

During the following eight years, little Chi-Soh became big Chi-Soh, and his proud father rejoiced at the successes achieved by this idol of his heart, at the great colleges to where the boy had been sent.

Now Chi-Soh's schooling days were over, and Yu-Cho made a great feast, to celebrate the entry of his child into the respected business house, which in future was to be known as Yu-Cho and Son.

Chi-Soh was a merry young Chinaman, and his lightness of heart delighted his indulgent parent, especially when he found that the boy seemed likely to become a serious man of business.

Yu-Cho being an exemplary father had already prepared a wife for his son; this was a fair flower, one Me-Dyah, the daughter of his good old friend Wang-Thsu, and though the latter was well aware of the respected Yu-Cho's wish, and heartily concurred, still above all things etiquette must be observed, therefore no word had yet been deliberately spoken, though over many a quiet game of draughts, the two venerable ones hinted at the desired alliance, drinking fine green tea out of delicate china vessels, kow-towing to one another whilst paying subtle compliments, each to the other's ancestry.

Yu-Cho bland, and of great and beautiful fatness; Wang-Thsu equally bland, but with a body small and frail.

In the meantime, Chi-Soh worked well in the business which his father had so carefully built up, and played heartily in his leisure hours, while his prospective bride, little Me-Dyah, as fragile in appearance as her father, remained like a dutiful daughter attending to her embroideries, and learned the duties that would be hers, when her parents gave her to be a wife.

Yu-Cho's prognostication that Aré-Ya would prove an attraction to this tea-house of his, known as "The Scented Blossom," had been more than fulfilled, for as she grew to maturity, she became exceedingly good to look upon; her skin, of which she was justly proud, was so fair that she might have been the offspring of one of those foreign devils, who came from far, far away across the great ocean, and who (so the knowledgeable Ah-Foo declared) licked their babies, as cats do, in order to make their skins soft and white.

Aré-Ya's great talents, those of dancing, singing, and playing the flute, to some degree compensated for her feet, which, though small and slender, were not lily-shaped like those of other Chinese girls, whose parents had loved well enough to painstakingly bend the toe-joints and bind their feet tightly, when they were babies.

In a very short time Aré-Ya had many admirers, and entered into the life of a tea-house girl with every expression of approval, her strong will and fearlessness making her a leader among the other butterfly occupants of the "Scented Blossom."

To dance, sing, play and be admired, that was all she lived for, and although her quick temper and inclination to domineer led to some sharp bouts with Ah-Foo, still on the whole her life passed happily enough.

Before she had reached the age of fourteen, two Mandarins and several wealthy merchants had desired to purchase her, and within the next year or so, many offers of honourable marriage had been refused by her, or by Ah-Foo on her behalf.

"The Scented Blossom" had a valuable property in Aré-Ya, and Yu-Cho nodded approvingly when Ah-Foo confided in him that the waif, he had so charitably rescued from the river, showed no inclination to desert the tea-house in order to marry; he marked his appreciation of her attitude by supplying her with still finer clothing, and costly fans, combs, and other ornaments.

"The Scented Blossom" being a well-conducted, very excellent tea-house, was patronized by the noble and wealthy ones of Canton, and as they sipped tea they talked, and the talk of their patrons was the chatter of the "Blossoms" who listened, therefore they knew much of the inner family life of the Cantonese.

They twittered like starlings and chattered like magpies over the return to Canton of their master's esteemed son, and they knew before he did that an alliance was to be formed between him and the Twining Flower, Me-Dyah. Aré-Ya took but little part in this gossip.

Anything that did not immediately concern her, she passed by without concern; even when the betrothal of Chi-Soh with Me-Dyah (after the stars having been consulted and proving propitious) was announced, she showed but languid interest.

However, on the day the marriage ceremony was to be performed, she dressed herself with great care, for many would see her in the streets, and accompanied Ah-Foo, who was escorting any of the "Blossoms" who wished to see the procession, with its bands and lanterns, paper dragons, and fireworks, which would surely be on a lavish scale, for the two well-to-do young participants. Seated in their wheel-barrows and jinrikshas, the "Blossoms" gossiped of the five hundred coolies who had been employed in order to carry the bride's contribution to her husband's home, and of the husband's seven hundred men, some on horseback, some marching on foot, who had gone with him to take presents to his bride and her parents and distribute *kumshaw* to beggars, street urchins, or any with whom they came in contact.

"Hi, Yi, they must be of great wealth," sighed Aré-Ya, and becoming weary of the seemingly endless procession of lanterns, which were shaped like boats, houses, shoes, tigers, flowers, men, women, articles of furniture or clothing of every conceivable size and colour, and of the hordes of fairies, gnomes, giants and buffoons generally who danced and postured to the music of flutes, fiddles, bells and gongs of every tone, and medley of time, she wished she had stayed quietly at the "Scented Blossom."

Then the bridal chair appeared, elaborately carved and decorated, scarlet inside and out, with wonderful pictures burnt into the lacquer, and further ornamented with kingfisher feathers which had been gummed on, giving the effect of enamel work.

The satin curtains, which hung either side, hiding the bride from view, were plucked at by inquisitive members of the crowd, and this act taking place near where Aré-Ya sat in her rickshaw, she glimpsed the bride, seated like a lifeless doll in her heavily-brocaded robe of scarlet, a huge open-worked collar of red, gold, and pearls standing stiffly behind her head, which was draped over with a thin veil kept in place round her high-coiffure by rows of pearls.

Aré-Ya had even time to notice with quick eyes the tiny lily feet and long, reddened finger nails.

Then the bride passed, leaving a new-born envy in Aré-Ya's heart, why or of what, she could not say.

She watched the bridegroom approach on his gaily caparisoned coal-black charger, whose tail swept the streets, and as he drew near, she idly noticed his gorgeous apparel, worthy of a Mandarin, and then her eyes went to Chi-Soh's face.

Now there was no lack of interest, and the long moment during which he rode slowly past, seemed an eternity and a lightning second all in one to the tea-house girl.

That night Aré-Ya did not sleep, the handsome face of the young bridegroom occupied all her thoughts; her envious feeling of Me-Dyah grew. Ever after the day of the wedding she listened avidly to all gossip of Chi-Soh and Me-Dyah.

She lost some of her joy in playing and dancing, and even the zest of her beloved gambling games, which she had taught her sister "Blossoms," could not make her forget for one instant the son of her master.

A year later she heard of the birth of a son, which made Yu-Cho a happy grandfather, and with conflicting feelings she went with Ah-Foo to witness the extravagant display of fireworks with which the event was celebrated.

Some months later, during the hot season, when the air hung heavy and still, calling for the continual use of fans and punkahs, Aré-Ya, tiring of her own miniature apartment, sauntered forth to the rock-garden that surrounded the tea-house, and wandering idly along the cunningly constructed narrow paths, came to the flower-draped pagoda where many patrons preferred to sit and drink their tea.

As she drew near to the fairylike erection, she heard the tinkle of laughter and the chirruping of girls mingling with a man's voice, and although she had never before heard him speak, she knew the deeper tone belonged to Chi-Soh.

For a moment she paused, a sudden excitement took possession of her, her almond eyes glittered, and above her ribs something beat a strange tattoo. Raising the jade flute to her lips, she began to play softly, moving in time to the music towards the pagoda.

Up the low wide steps she swayed, with demurely downcast eyes, and into the pavilion, round and round she danced, posturing gracefully, playing sweetly, never raising her eyes, appearing oblivious to any occupant other than herself.

At her coming, the laughter and chattering ceased; in and out among the kneeling "Blossoms" moved Aré-Ya, and then, whether on purpose or accidentally, she herself could not truthfully have said, the skirt of her knee-length coat caught Chi-Soh's lightly-held tea-cup, brushing it from his hand and breaking it into a thousand fragments at his feet.

"Hi! Yai!" cried Aré-Ya, ceasing her dancing and piping, and falling on her knees beside the broken china and, incidentally, close to Chi-Soh, to whom she raised her eyes in plaintive distress.

Like a flock of twittering sparrows, the "Blossoms" fluttered round, picking up the pieces, squeaking out expressions of regret for the accident. Slowly Aré-Ya's head touched the floor, her feet raised high in the air.

"Will the lordly son of Heaven deign to forgive his base-born slave's carelessness?" she pleaded.

"It is for the rough earth to beg forgiveness of the fairy blossom, because he was there when she floated near," Chi-Soh said gently.

"Then the exalted one is not angry with his insignificant servant?" asked Aré-Ya with every appearance of relieved apprehension, raising her head, and with flute clasped between two upheld hands, she looked full into his eyes.

"I am deeply in the debt of the graceful summer cloud, for sending my heart dreaming like a bubble on a cool lake, and my ears laughing with joy as though they had been touched with golden petals," he assured her.

By this time the busy little "Blossoms" had cleared away the broken china, and presenting the son of their master with a fresh cup of tea, ran, giggling and fluttering their fans, from the pagoda, leaving Aré-Ya to make humble apologies.

"Tee hee hee," she tinkled delightedly, looking at him archly over the top of her outspread fan, "then the gracious one is generously pleased with his vile servant's poor dancing?" she queried coquettishly.

"As pleased as any lowly mortal could be, whose eyes have been well-nigh blinded by the sudden vision of a fairy," he said.

"And this miserable flute?" she asked, insatiable of praise.

"Miserable flute indeed, now that it has been taken from the puckered rosebud that caused it to sing like a blossom-bell whispering of budding love," he replied earnestly.

"Then if the Son of the Sun is pleased, this vagabond heart is content," she sighed, dropping the petal of a golden tea-rose lightly into the cup he held.

"It is sad that I have never before come to this Gate of Heaven," he remarked.

"No doubt the noble lord is honourably occupied with worthy affairs."

"No affairs could be honourable that kept me from knowing the Flower of China," he spoke earnestly.

"To some, with less graciously inclined eyes, the flower is a rank weed," she told him sadly.

"Such ones had better quickly become engaged in dying, for their sight, which must have been cursed by a bad joss, may lead them to swallow their wives in mistake for rice grains," was his entirely satisfactory reply.

"How can this evil slave express the gratitude that the Perfection of Happiness rouses in her tantalized heart by his indulgent words?" she cooed.

"If the little Summer Breeze will stay to gladden my unworthy eyes, and give joy to my longing ears, she will transport me with her kind unkindness, for the load of debt I will owe her for so doing, will for ever bow my degraded head to the earth."

"If my master is pleased to listen, it is his odious servant who will be overburdened with his claim on her gratitude."

Picking up a two-stringed fiddle with its attached bow, Aré-Ya drew an accompaniment from the instrument as she softly sang an improvised song.

> *Old Wisdom murmured to*
> *Young Love in far Loo Choo,*
> *"Cease thy sportive play,*
> *Glean knowledge day by day,*
> *Learn Duty. Ope thy eyes,*
> *Grasp things that all men prize,*
> *Gain rank and riches rare,*
> *Life passes quick. Beware!"*

> *Young Love laughed loud and long*
> *And raised his voice in song —*
> *"Oh foolish one, my play*

Is Heart of Life alway.
The thing that wise men prize
Is true love in maid's eyes.
Gain that, and thou shalt be
As wise as foolish me."

"True love! True love!" breathed Chi-Soh, when the song ended, his hand clenched on his knee, his eyes roving over the nodding plum tree that sheltered the steps of the pagoda, "True love——!"

"The exalted one has it in abundance?" questioned Aré-Ya.

"No, Bird Voice, but my foolish heart will seek for the treasure you speak of."

"And how will the Commanding One find the path if he has no map to guide his exalted feet?" she asked earnestly.

"The only map that can help me, must hang on the wall of my heart," he answered slowly.

"Does the powerful lord know where he can become possessed of the map that is ordained to be so happily placed?" she questioned.

And leaning close down, he looked steadily into the eyes so near to his own:

"I think I do, I hope I do," he said earnestly.

CHAPTER XXIV

Aré-Ya no longer graced the "Scented Blossom," she inhabited instead a flower-boat, moored in a delightful backwater of the same Pearl river whereon she had been placed by her sorely-tried mother nearly twenty years ago.

It was Aré-Ya's wish to have a flower-boat to live on, and the infatuated Chi-Soh readily acceded as he did to almost every desire she expressed. He had suggested that Aré-Ya should inhabit his own palatial mansion, which stood within its high red walls in the fashionable east side of Canton; that he should "suggest" instead of "commanding" obviously showed the state of subjugation to which the tea-house girl had brought him.

She had pointed out that such a thing could not be, for as she could not be his *kit-fat,* Me-Dyah holding this honoured position of first wife, she would not submit to hold any secondary position in his household.

"No, Gladness of Day, do not take your Thorn of Woe to your distinguished palace, for I would pollute your reverend hearth, and unless you killed the Fragile-One, there would arise a tangle of trouble that would vex your serene heart," she told him.

"Then what does the Delight of my Soul suggest?" asked Chi-Soh, who did not feel inclined to murder his *kit-fat,* the delicate Me-Dyah, whom he respected as the mother of his son, and loved in a fashion different to his feelings for Aré-Ya.

"A flowery-boat, in a corner of the Pearl river, if my adored lord will permit," Aré-Ya was not slow in answering, for to possess just such an abode had long been her ambition.

Now Aré-Ya had her flower-boat, named by Chi-Soh *Ai-Sin,* Heart of Love, after the little song she had sung him on the first day of their meeting.

The *Ai-Sin* was coloured scarlet, with quaint lacquerings in black and bright blue, depicting scenes from the lives of Chi-Soh and Aré-Ya, interspersed with representations of terrible dragons with many tongues, who were to warn Chi-Soh if his lady-love was unfaithful to him, and also to keep away robbers. And storks put there to continually whisper his love words in her ear during his enforced absences.

In this delightful backwater of the Pearl river Aré-Ya dwelt very happily with an ancient *amah* to keep her company, do her bidding, and see that the couple of coolies whom Chi-Soh detailed to care for the *Ai-Sin* and the small bricked-in garden to which it was moored, attended to their tasks.

On the upper deck of the *Ai-Sin,* Aré-Ya would sit for hours, playing, singing, dancing, or entertaining the girls who came to visit her from the "Scented Blossom," proud to show them all the beautiful things her honourable lord showered upon her.

Chi-Soh's Canton, gossiped about the liaison, and Me-Dyah heard of it very quickly; her pride in the unusual faithfulness of her husband received a severe blow, for she had bragged everlastingly to less lucky wives, that her lord would have no other wife or wives, for which eccentricity Chi-Soh was looked upon as peculiar; and this particular oddness on the part of her spouse made Me-Dyah greatly envied by other Cantonese ladies, whose husbands indulged in a plurality of wives.

The little *kit-fat* did not dare to openly upbraid her lord, but he soon discovered, from her tears and sulks, that she knew of Aré-Ya, and disapproved.

Thereupon, man-like, he evaded his doleful spouse, and spent more and more time with the fascinating being on the *Ai-Sin.*

Sometimes old Yu-Cho accompanied his son on these visits and, being very wise, held his peace, although many things happened on the *Ai-Sin* that distressed, and gave him grave thoughts about Chi-Soh's future welfare.

Happenings, that the elderly Chinaman noticed unknown to Aré-Ya, as he sat in seeming peace and happiness on the vine-draped upper deck, or in the tiny pagoda, built in the small, flower-laden garden at the rear of the boat.

Delicately sipping his green tea, his eyes gazing far away across the old red wall, to where the five-storied bronze temple, standing tall above the little hills, shone brown, scarlet, and green, Yu-Cho listened but made no comment on what he heard.

At his son's own house, he maintained the same wise peace, although he silently sympathized with Me-Dyah, whose growing jealousy of Aré-Ya led her to form many crooked plots in an attempt to wean him from this tea-house girl, even going to the length of suggesting other wives to her husband.

This was a crafty move, because she, being the *kit-fat,* would have power to treat any other wives of her lord as she pleased, their very children would belong to her; their real mother would be merely their "black aunt."

If Chi-Soh had great attractions in his own home (*her* own home) his visits to the hated *Ai-Sin* would surely cease, but alas for Me-Dyah, her master turned a deaf ear to all her cunningly baited plans, and the wife burned incense to her joss, with great chin-chins, and procuring an image from a Witch-woman to represent Aré-Ya, stuck pins in it, and forming a hump on its back, solemnly assured the cardboard thing, that such an affliction would surely befall her, for stealing away the love of Chi-Soh.

The only satisfaction Me-Dyah had, was that so far, her hated rival had no children; this terrible disgrace pleased the wifely heart.

This "terrible disgrace" also pleased Aré-Ya.

"No, beloved lord, this lazy one does not want children," she told Chi-Soh when he confessed to her what a delight he would take in a child of theirs, "for they are a left-handed joy, they make the back to break when they are little, and the heart to ache when they are big. Your unworthy Aré-Ya would live alone for her offensive self, and her sagacious lord. We are happy without biting cares, and it is better to be free, than burdened, even with a load of scented cherry blossoms."

Indeed Aré-Ya would have been exasperated had she a child, or any care on her shoulders, for her whole time was spent in following any whimsical way to enjoy herself, that entered her wilful head.

Delightful as the *Ai-Sin* and its garden was, the petted occupant began to weary of the monotony after the gay tea-house life, and unbeknownst to Chi-Soh, would slip away in her sampan, the experience she had gained among the coolies on Yu-Cho's junk many years ago made the manipulating of the small boat an easy matter, and in the toy-like thing, which resembled a flower-basket, she would paddle away through the water-gates to the foot of a long steep street where, leaving her conveyance in charge of a water coolie, she would hail a barrow or "rickshaw," and drive rapidly into the heart of the busy town of Canton.

Dismissing her vehicle, she would wander serenely through the narrow twisting streets, her small nose delightedly sniffing the malodorous atmosphere in which she had been born.

Pausing to watch artisans at their work of making earthenware vessels, beating metals into quaint shapes, painting rice paper pictures, or busy at the intricate inlaying of silver with the beautiful blue kingfisher feathers.

Buying incense, she would trot off to light it in front of her particular joss, or purchasing a lark in its picturesque cage, would saunter idly along, feeling a very plutocrat in carrying a bird as the wealthy aristocrats loved to do.

The theatres greatly attracted her, with the wailing actors. The men who impersonated women by wearing little blocks on their feet in order to appear lily-footed, always moved her to mirth, and the accompanying music of tom-toms, drums and horns thrilled her, while she shuddered delightedly at the villain of the piece, whom she recognized at once from his blackened face and whitened nose.

On the whole theatres were her greatest diversions, until she chanced on a gambling parlour.

With fascinated eyes she watched the proprietor hand a bag to one of the players seated round a long low table. Putting his hand in the bag, the player pulled out a fist full of discs, and placed them on the table. Each disc bore a painted character corresponding to hundreds imprinted on the table round which the gamblers were seated.

Eager heads bent over to watch the sorting of the discs, and each one who had placed money on a figure on the table, that corresponded with a drawn-out disc, won back twice his stake.

"Hi-Yah! This is a good game," cried Aré-Ya, and digging deep into her loose sleeve, she pulled out a small silk money-bag, and placing a square, silver *tael* on the figure of a tiger, held her breath whilst the bag was well shaken, and another player was invited to produce a handful of discs.

Her face was wreathed in smiles, as three silver *tael* were placed before her, for she proved to be one of the lucky ones.

This was the beginning of her gambling in Canton, the fever of it gripped her anew, as it had done on board the junk, when she had risked one of her two precious *cash,* for though she had enjoyed many a quiet game in the "Scented Blossom," Ah-Foo's disapproval, and the girls themselves being disinclined to risk their small stores of wealth, Aré-Ya never really had an opportunity for "big" gambling until now, and with all her heart she seized it.

She soon learned to despise the poor parlour situated in the densely populated street called "The Weary Mile," and found a more sumptuous abode, where she played with increasing recklessness, and, as is the way with gamblers, the greater her losses, the higher and more wildly placed were her stakes.

Chi-Soh was puzzled at her insistent demands for money. Questioning her on the sudden need, she lied, fearful of his putting a stop to her pleasure.

Money being necessary, she took some of her trinkets to the *Yamen* in his square-towered building, for this high placed official was a bland pawnbroker in his spare time. Her secret method of raising money came to Chi-Soh's ears through her pawning of a small, bronze, open-mouthed dragon, at whose feet squatted a jade frog who always appeared to be just about to leap down the yawning throat.

Aré-Ya had not been able to redeem this treasure, which had been a gift from Chi-Soh, therefore the *Yamen* had sold it, unfortunately for Aré-Ya, to one of Chi-Soh's friends, in whose house he saw it proudly reposing.

He would have recognized the unique thing even without its distinguishing hall-mark, which read:

"Made in Studios of Fragrant Peace."

"I purchased the ignoble thing, that is happy in pleasing your illustrious eyes, from the *Yamen,* who told me a gambling woman had pledged it with him in order to pay her debts," his friend explained to Chi-Soh's question as to how he had obtained the work of art.

That night there was a stormy scene on board the *Ai-Sin,* and peace reigned once more, only when Aré-Ya promised to give up gambling.

A promise which she kept for two whole days.

During the next few months Aré-Ya changed her gods very often, but none of them seemed inclined to bring fortune to smile on her luck, chin-chin she ever so devoutly, abusively, coaxingly or threateningly, for she lost steadily at whatever game of chance she essayed.

"My noxious skin is an evil bladder, favoured only by the Evil one, who uses it but to hold his punishing burden of soured luck," she exclaimed irritably, after a long afternoon of losses.

"The god of luck is ever ready to smile favourably on compassionate new moons, who are pleased to bestow bounteous kindnesses on him," a man's voice said in her ear.

Turning her head, Aré-Ya saw a slant-eyed young Chinaman, bowing obsequiously to her.

Her shrewd eyes noticed his outward display of wealth, his rich apparel, the many gew-gaws hanging from his jade button, the long oiled *queue* amplified with false bits and twined round with scented grass-ribbons ending in a gay tassel; the sticks of his fan were carved ivory, and in his hand he held a gold bird-cage containing a singing lark. The purple cloth cap banded with gold was set rakishly on the back of his head, but it was the gem on his longnailed finger that caught her attention; in the gold circle was set a milky stone, in the depth of which shone red fires; they seemed to be claiming her as an old acquaintance.

She stood up, and kow-towed politely.

"If the gracious son of Heaven would compassionately tell this imbecile servant how to win such an endless blessing, he would earn her undying gratitude," she told him.

Young Wong-Chu, well pleased at the promise of an amorous adventure, begged permission to escort her to her abode.

"Ha! this puppy-faced one with a head like a *lychee* and ears like a fish's tail is rich," Aré-Ya decided, noting the three coolies, one pulling front and the two others pushing behind the double ricksha, which, accepting his offer, she entered.

Instead of going direct to the *Ai-Sin,* Wong-Chu persuaded the willing lady to partake of food on board one of the numerous boat-restaurants, where he ordered a dainty meal, beginning with green tea, spiced with salt and ground ginger; then dessert of many fruits, candied walnuts and delicious apricot kernels, which had been preserved in oil.

Aré-Ya ate with relish the toothsome bamboo sprouts, and sea slugs, accepting with gratification the complimentary offering he proffered her with his own chop-sticks, of a succulent morsel of deer's sinews, returning, with her chop-sticks, a like piece of shark's fin, then, when they finished the last course of birds' nest soup, Wong-Chu called for dry native wine, which Aré-Ya sipped like a connoisseur from the small cup in which it was served.

By this time they were on very excellent terms, and the gallant young Chinaman was rapidly becoming enamoured of this bewitching damsel, who was beautiful, witty and charming, and possessed such elegant manners, her long and loud eructations after eating, proving her to have been accustomed to the best society.

Aré-Ya did not return to the *Ai-Sin* until very late, making ingenious excuses to Chi-Soh, who, with his father, had been awaiting her return to the flower-boat.

He accepted her voluble explanations because he loved her, and did not wish to hurt her with his anger, but deep in his heart he knew she was lying, and the knowledge made him unhappy and restive.

On the journey back to his own home, his father, who had offered no opinion on Aré-Ya's absence, or the story she related on her return, told his son a little fable.

"My son," he said, "it is well to remember the story of the tiger cub, who left parentless, was adopted by a charitable sheep."

"What was the story, my precious father?" inquired Chi-Soh.

"It is an old tale, I will tell it to you," and as the sampan in which the merchant and his son reclined, was deftly manoeuvred through the myriad of lantern-lighted boats, to the tinkle of the little bells attached to the prow of junks and sampans, Yu-Cho recited the following:

"Aing! Aing!" whined Tiger Cub, unto a kind bland Sheep,
"May I come in your field, to eat and drink and sleep.
I have no honoured kin, may Mild Lamb be my brother,
Oh, condescending Sheep, and will you be my mother?"
"Come in, sad wailing Cub," kind-hearted old Sheep baa'd;
"Big World for soft and young, is very, very hard."
The thin one entered swift, and Mother Sheep was thrilled,
With pity and with love, her mother-heart was filled.

Together, frisking Lamb, and growing Cublet played,
Ate, drank and slept beneath, an oak tree's generous shade.
Then one amazing day, toothsome Lamb had disappeared,
Not one white wool was found. He was lost, his mother feared.
She cried and fretted much, and ate the luscious grass,
"My mysterious Lamb has died," she moaned, "alas, alas!"
She looked at Tiger Cub, so sleek and fat, and sighed—
"My heart for this lone one, is filled with love and pride."

As day passed after day, and Cub increased in size,
The Sheep observed his girth, with content-filled, sheepish eyes.
But, hearken unto this, no Sheep remained one morn,
And placid Cub was left, in field, alone, forlorn.
He did not search for her. He dropped a yellow tear,
'Twas stomach, not his heart, that caused him grief, I fear.
He smiled at his fat sides, in pool, then went to sleep.
This sleek young Cub was filled, with pride and also sheep.

"An amusing parable, respected parent," commented Chi-Soh, when Yu-Cho finished, "but this dense one does not see——"

"You will," dryly interrupted the wise old merchant.

CHAPTER XXV

The peace that had once reigned on the *Ai-Sin* had vanished, for Chi-Soh had not been able to close his eyes and ears to Aré-Ya's reckless gambling, and her loose acceptance of new friends, whom she discovered were useful as young Wong-Chu had been, to extract money from, for these games of chance.

Apart from the fact that Chi-Soh appealed to her more than any other being, Aré-Ya did not want to lose his valuable protection, and as she could no longer disguise from him the fact that she still gambled, a passion which she emphatically refused to subdue, she sought by cunning means to keep him in her power.

She dressed, painted her face, danced, sang and coquetted, in order to gain her own ends.

Instead of supplying him with tea to drink when he visited her, she replaced it with wine, persuading him to accept it with honeyed phrases and arch looks, for wine made him less inclined to object to her doings; opium too, was a good soother, and he soon grew to love the pills the crafty, beautiful one rolled for him.

"This dejected admirer is always loth to leave your enchanting loveliness," Chi-Soh said one day, when he regretfully rose from the couch on which he had reclined while he smoked the long-stemmed pipe, and watched her dance, or listened to her singing to him.

"Then why does not my powerful lord remain always with

his insignificant slave?" she asked softly, for if he was ever with her, she had faith in her power to extract all she wanted from him.

"My miserable heart is desolate that the bewitching divinity's tempting suggestion cannot be fulfilled," he sighed.

"Does my adored master not care enough for his afflicted servant then?" she questioned wistfully.

"Leaving my apple blossom, I am like a cherry without a stalk, and my growling heart turns surly, but I have the bemoaning mother of my son to think of," and at his mention of Me-Dyah, Aré-Ya frowned.

"Does my compassionate lord love this happily placed woman more than he cares for this despised one?"

"A pearl in a ring has its own beauty, the stone is not despised because the gold band is admired," was his cryptic way of telling her that both she and Me-Dyah appealed to him, in their several ways.

"A proud ring, and a happy stone to encircle so soft and firm a finger," she cooed.

The words touched some hidden chord in Chi-Soh's memory, he opened his sleepy eyes quickly.

"Ah, those words, they seem as though they should have issued from my rude lips," he said slowly.

Puckering his brow he thought deeply, and by so doing lost a chance he may have had of remembering times and words of long ago.

The deadening hamper of logic, overweighted faint, stirring memory.

Aré-Ya's lures influenced Chi-Soh to such an extent that Me-Dyah's wish was partially granted, and her husband now had several wives, and the *Ai-Sin* did not see him so often.

This neglect did not affect Aré-Ya to any overwhelming

grief, for, despite her wine and opium, she and Chi-Soh quarrelled increasingly.

One day on leaving a gambling establishment with Wong-Chu, she was about to enter his ricksha, when Chi-Soh, who was passing at the moment, stopped her. There being nothing for it but to obey his imperative command, she left Wong-Chu, and returned with Chi-Soh to the *Ai-Sin*, where mutual recriminations were freely indulged in.

Bitter words were said, and when Aré-Ya loosened her naturally uncontrolled tongue, her early training with Ai-Hsiu, and among the junk coolies stood her in such stead, that Chi-Soh could only listen in amazed silence.

After a tirade of foul abuse, during which she expressed the wish that he would be seized with violent pains, and die a painful death, she wound up by taunting him with being an opium-sodden "outside countryman."

Insult could go no further than this, he turned and left her, and for a long, long time she did not see him.

The cessation of his visits to the *Ai-Sin* left Chi-Soh restless and discontented, therefore he sought distraction in some curious haunts peculiar to Canton.

Despite her lord's new profligacy Me-Dyah rejoiced, and her sister-wives chirruped cheerfully in chorus with the powerful *kit-fat,* on whom their happiness depended, far more than on their husband.

With great ceremony Me-Dyah took all Chi-Soh's wives to do a big chin-chin at the temple known as the "Hall of Perfection."

Underneath the orange and green tiles, they devoutly kowtowed, to the gaudily-painted figure of red copper, then, in case the god should be sleeping, Me-Dyah struck a drum to call attention to her generosity, before ceremoniously setting a light to her richest costume, which she had brought for the purpose.

In the fire of her sacrifice, she and her companions burned the carefully thought out prayers, they had written on long rolls of rice paper.

Gathering up the ashes, which they placed in a box brought for them so that they might be taken home and used as medicine, they told the god he had done well in listening to their request, that Chi-Soh should abandon Aré-Ya, but if he would do still more and strike the base tea-house girl with a pestilential disease, his reward would be still greater.

The two divining rods which lay before the gods, for the use of generous worshippers, were deftly thrown in the air, and squeals of delight went up when the sun-dried bamboo sticks (which, having been split in two, were rounded one side and flat the other) came down propitiously, one round, and one flat, lying uppermost.

Me-Dyah was glad she had sacrificed her treasured costume, otherwise the rods might have come down both on corresponding sides, then she would have wept.

After tying paper images representing Chi-Soh, upside down, to a pillar of the "Hall of Perfection," with accompanying incantations which would assuredly bring the erring husband back to the fold, the ladies, resting on the steps of the temple, chattering like linnets, ate oranges and flat green peaches, cleaned out their ears, and returned home well satisfied with their morning's pilgrimage.

And the gods to whom these intoned orders were given remained thoughtfully stolid, and unbending, while God, who made the hands that formed them, sighed. Parents sigh pityingly when their foolish babes turn and beat them furiously, because tiny hands are suffering from burns through touching forbidden but tempting looking red fire.

On the journey home, Me-Dyah, noticing a small ill-clad

boy weeping by the roadside, stayed her ricksha to inquire the cause of his tears.

His parents being dead (he told her), he had been taken by a man and his wife who worked him very hard, and treated him cruelly.

Me-Dyah, feeling at peace with all the world for the god's kindnesses, and her belief that still more beneficent gifts would be hers after her great sacrifice of an hour ago, spoke tenderly to the boy, presenting him with fruit, and a few *cash,* and promising if her husband would permit, to take him into her own service, drove on, leaving the boy smiling through his tears, as he greedily sucked the orange she had given him.

And the Infinite smiled as a mother smiles, when her child atones to some extent for a fault.

CHAPTER XXVI

One rainy night when Aré-Ya could not sleep, she roused her *amah,* and bade her call a coolie from the mat-hut that stood on its bamboo poles in the water, alongside the flower-boat, in order to take a message to Chi-Soh, for she was possessed with a great longing to see him once more.

Interviewing the coolie herself, Aré-Ya promised him good *kumshaw* if he found, and delivered the message speedily to Chi-Soh, and a severe beating if he did not.

The coolie gained his *kumshaw.*

The summons was at once obeyed, not only because Chi-Soh still retained his affection for Aré-Ya, but in these days any diversion appealed to him.

He had long noted with apathetic dismay that he was losing his power of enjoying life, due, no doubt, as he candidly admitted to himself, to the years of dissipation in which he had indulged.

He was pleased to be once more back on the *Ai-Sin,* and this evening, he promised the still fascinating Aré-Ya, should mark the renewal of their happy, bygone days.

The gladness she experienced at the return of her lover, was overclouded by the consternation she felt at the change, time had wrought in him; the handsome youth looked double his age, his fine, clear skin was wrinkled and blotched, his voice too had altered, it was no longer so smooth and musical as she remembered it.

"Time must mark all," she thought, and showing no signs of the distress with which his transformation filled her, she smiled, happy to have her lover once more beside her.

At least his rich costume was pleasing. Chi-Soh had always been inclined to foppishness where his apparel was concerned.

As they sat and talked, he put out his palm for her to place her hand within it; then he paused, and drawing it swiftly back, held it rigidly in front of his eyes, looking, looking, ever looking fixedly at what he saw.

His jaws fell open, fear and horror brought a glint of the old fire back into his eyes, for the tips of his fingers were white, like dazzling crystals of salt.

"What is it that disturbs my benevolent protector?" asked Aré-Ya, bewildered by the sudden change that overcame him.

With no word of explanation or excuse, the leper stumbled to his feet, and reeling like one who has drunk too much wine, disappeared from her sight, leaving her a prey to amazement, and rising anger.

Filled with blind horror, Chi-Soh regained the city of Canton. With eyes that saw nothing but these hideous white spots on his finger tips, he passed through the still crowded streets. The lights, cries, laughter, quarrelling, did not enter his senses.

On and on he went, across the city, until, reaching a little tributary of the river called "Chinese Sorrow," he bade a coolie row him across.

Where he was going, what he was to do, he could not think; only one thought was clear, he must get away by himself, where no stern official should pounce down and drag him off to the island set apart for such as he.

Gaining the further side of the river, he threw the stolid coolie a fist of *cash*.

With hands held behind him, so that he should not see the dreaded taint, he toiled onward and upward, until, scaling a low wall that barred his way, he dropped shivering and exhausted, panting and moaning in short, sharp gasps.

Prone on the rain-soaked earth he lay in the "City of the Dead," as this vast cemetery to which he had inadvertently come, was termed.

He was dazed, and for a long time he could not think clearly, but rested there. The smell of gunpowder which still hung thick in the air, from a recently celebrated funeral, was stifling.

"I am a leper! I am a leper! Unclean! Unclean!" he groaned aloud.

Why could he not have died a natural death?

Why should the gods punish him in this way?

To die honourably was one thing, that had no terrors for him; but to live on, with his body slowly, but visibly falling from him in diseased shreds!

Chi-Soh bit into the earth and writhed.

Now he understood the lassitude, accompanied by loss of appetite, and fits of great depression to which for some time he had been subjected, and the tenderness of his skin, the thickness that had attacked his mouth and throat, causing his voice to be little more than a hoarse whisper, the incurable ulcerous sores, that had formed from the small irritating lumps, which he had noticed with a certain amount of indifference, on his body; all should have warned him that the nauseating malady was creeping on like a poisonous stream of slimy loathsomeness, polluting his whole system.

He shuddered deeply.

Recalling lepers he had seen in distant parts of China where they were not incarcerated, but allowed to wander free, rotting slowly, as they crept about the country in the grey robe which marked them for what they were, striking the warning clackers, so long as they had hands to carry them, croaking hoarsely: "Unclean! Unclean!"

As the miserable, polluted bits of flesh dragged themselves along, all who heard the cautionary sound, went hastily in an opposite direction.

Now he, too, must proclaim himself as "Unclean." Here in Canton he would quickly be taken to the leper-island, to be herded with the other putrefying bits of flesh, to watch those rotting hulks, and see his own body, of which he had been so proud, decaying and dropping to pieces.

Writhing in a torture blacker than that of death, the miserable wretch choked dryly.

He had money, he would spend it all in effecting a cure; but even as this thought came it died, he knew that the disease had gone too far to be arrested.

All night long he stayed in the "City of the Dead," suffering grim torture.

Towards morning, numbed and mud-stained, he rose and went slowly towards the city; so far as lay in his power he avoided meeting any human creature, his tell-tale hands hidden in his sleeves.

His plans were made, for though his wealth could not kill

the devil that had taken hold of him, still it could buy a solitary prison, where none should ever know of his affliction.

He confided his hideous secret to the one being whom he knew would not divulge it, his distracted father.

It was Yu-Cho who quickly bought a small, solitary island, far away from town or village; in the middle of the island stood a lone house, and it was here Chi-Soh buried himself.

Only the grief-stricken Yu-Cho knew of his son's whereabouts, and the old merchant came himself once a month to leave provisions on the fringe of the island, just as he used to do in the prosecution of his merchant's vocation, for the lazar island of Kowloon.

Here on the "Dow-Hee" (Black Island, as this spot was appropriately named) the leper existed in solitary misery, until he could stand his state of lonely abandonment no longer, and in a voice that scarce rose above a raucous whisper, he conveyed this fact to his father, when the old man appeared alone in the sampan which he rowed himself from the junk, for not even a coolie must know the pitiable truth.

Placing the boxes full of every luxury his loving heart could suggest for the alleviation of his cherished son's misery, Yu-Cho, after listening to Chi-Soh's statement, offered, nay begged, to be allowed to come and share the "Dow-Hee," but to this heroic suggestion Chi-Soh would not listen, and not all his father's pleadings, his pointing out that he was old, and in any case could not expect to live much longer, would move his son from his determination, nor could he be brought to consent for Me-Dyah to be told of her lord's illness.

Then Yu-Cho suggested Aré-Ya.

Chi-Soh, his short burst of energy exhausted, languidly expressed a wish to see the tea-house girl again, and with glazed eyes watched his father row away in the sampan, leaving him to his demon of desolation.

CHAPTER XXVII

When Chi-Soh had gone from her so suddenly on the *Ai-Sin,* leaving no word or sign to elucidate his mysterious conduct, Aré-Ya fell into a rage of resentment at his disdainful conduct, vowing irefully never to speak with him again.

Searching for a reason to explain the quick change that had come over him, her hand fell on the little ring with its stone of milky-blue, with blood-red spots that Wong-Chu had given her, and which she always wore suspended by a cord round her neck.

It was the sight of this red-eyed treasure given her by another man which, moving him to jealousy, had made him leave her, she decided.

As months passed, and she neither saw nor heard from him, she became unhappy and beat the coolies whom she sent with messages bidding, or pleading with him to come to her.

With joyous elation she received Yu-Cho, and when he told her that Chi-Soh had gone to live on an island, and wished her to go to him, she expressed willing assent.

Yu-Cho took her himself, and as he listened to her laughing and chattering gaily during the voyage on the junk, he excused himself for what he was doing on the plea that this girl belonged to him, for he could have drowned her years ago, when, like a fearless frog, she had come unbidden, on board his vessel.

Entering the sampan, she merrily took the paddle from the old merchant's hand, and herself conveyed the tiny boat towards the island, while he pointed the way.

She shook her head disapprovingly after asking the name of the island.

"No, Portly one, 'Black Island' is not pretty; my gracious lord will change it to 'Dawn,' for 'Lee-Ming' is more beautiful than 'Dow-Hee,'" she decided.

When they reached the "Dow-Hee" she skipped lightly ashore, kow-towing in scarce concealed impatience to the departing Yu-Cho, who, thinking it better to leave Chi-Soh to make his explanations alone, rapidly paddled back to the junk, and without delay returned to Canton.

Smilingly Aré-Ya turned her face towards the house which she descried between the trees, and as no one appeared to welcome her, she slung her fiddle over her back, and producing her flute, walked slowly over the grass, a roguish gleam dancing in her eyes, as she softly played her mellow instrument, watching eagerly for Chi-Soh to appear running delightedly to meet her; then, as not even a coolie came to light, she ceased playing, and creeping close to the house, she swept her fiddle round her body, and twanging the strings sang the little song of "True Love," which had so enraptured him on their first meeting, when the sun was warm, and the old plum tree guarded the entrance to the pagoda in the garden surrounding the "Scented Blossom." Still a deathly silence pervaded the place, and a thrill of apprehension struck at her.

True to her childhood's attitude of fearless action, she approached the silent mansion, noticing with surprise its neglected appearance, and the ruins in which the surrounding grounds lay.

Her thick-soled shoes made a dull pad, pad, on the floor of the wooden verandah, as she stole across it to the closed window.

Leaning forward, she peered through the thin horn pane. For a moment she thought the room into which she looked was deserted; then she descried a figure sitting alone in the far corner. Closer and closer she leaned.

Her heart began to beat in a most extraordinary fashion, and she felt the flesh on her bones creep. She continued to gaze at the still form, there in the dim room.

"Gracious lord, are you within?" she cried, her voice ringing queerly in her ears.

Then as the figure moved, rising heavily, an icy fear shook her heart.

"The door stands ever open for so Heavenly a visitor."

The thick, whispering voice clutched at her throat; she gave a frightened little cry, and then, with a return of her old dauntless spirit, she essayed a laugh, which ended in a rasping gurgle.

Something propelled her feet towards the door, and, telling herself that there was no cause for this despicable terror, she ran through the large room into which she first came, and entered the one she had seen through the window.

The figure was now standing.

Her tripping steps stopped, and, pausing on her toes, she felt her whole body stiffen as she looked at the rapidly decomposing clay that faced her.

Its nose had disappeared, leaving two holes where the nostrils had been; gone was one of its arms up to the elbow, no ears remained, and only dull sockets for its eyes.

Her half outstretched arms crooked, as did her fingers, her eyes wrinkled up, her mouth fell open.

"Ah! Ah! Ah!" she breathed from her throat in long, rasping gasps.

"The gods will repay the charitable one, who has come thus to dwell with this polluted wretch," whispered the leper.

"No, no," and, to her hideous alarm, she found that she too was whispering hoarsely, as did this terrifying apparition: "No, no, do not come near. Do not touch. I will kill. I will kill. I will kill. Spawn of evil! Wicked barbarian! I go, I go," but her limbs were powerless to move.

For the first time in her life she was afraid.

"Was not the truth told the generous one?" croaked the almost sightless thing.

"No. No. Ah! False black speck! But never shall this clean one stay with a leper. Coolie, Coolie," she shrieked hysterically, and suddenly recovering the power of her limbs, she fled from the room, and left the house.

Down to the edge of the island she sped, calling wildly, but there was none to hear except the rotting hulk in its silent tomb.

Round and round the small island she tore like a crazed person, seeking for some means of escape.

It was not until two days later that, as she sat in a corner of the grounds, she wept.

Never before had tears fallen from her eyes, and now she cried as though she could not stop; great sobs shook her slight form.

At length, exhausted by her unusual outburst, she lay almost unconscious from grief, helped out by the fact that she had not tasted food or drink since landing here.

Crouching against the trunk of a whispering-willow tree, Aré-Ya felt a great throb of pity for the unfortunate creature caged in its prison.

"Poor, poor thing! Poor, poor thing," she repeated in little whimpering cries.

Deep, long shudders shook her frame, until her head quivered, her eyes closed and she breathed in short, hard gasps through tight-clenched teeth.

Still, rather than remain here she would drown herself. It was iniquitous of him to have sent for her. It was monstrous of that sly merchant to have brought her.

No sign of living soul had passed the island during the long hours she had spent there, and there was no way of escaping; then she must either die of starvation, or else go back to that house.

"No, no," she shrieked wildly. "It will be better to drown cleanly."

Then again:

"Poor, poor thing. Ah, poor, poor thing."

"—We must not pass hurtful things on, but in the strength of one born under the Tiger, that unhappiness must be killed by gentleness."

Who had said that?

Aré-Ya sat erect and opened her eyes, then:

"—Do any little kindness like the small Toad did for the great Ox."

Yes, of course, it was the Saintly Monk who had spoken these words long ago.

But this would not be a little thing. This was something that even a Tiger-born one was not strong enough to do; it needed more power than she felt herself possessed of, to conquer the loathing any would feel for that decomposing apparition.

"—The awakening of your soul will give you much pain; it will come through a great suffering, and will cause you to be gentle even to those who have ill-treated you."

She remembered her teacher's words, even as he had told her she would, and she recalled also that he had warned her, that only she herself could cure her suffering.

This throbbing, hurt inside her; this pity for her one-time lover, that racked and bit like a living thing. Was this, then, her "soul"?

If a soul was something that only hurt, of what use was it?

Why should she be cursed with such a thing? She had been happy enough all these years before this undesired entity leaped to life.

How could she send it to sleep once more?

Pitiable little mortal, she was to learn that a soul once roused could never again lie dormant.

What had she done to deserve such suffering?

For hours she sat and thought over her every deed, her every thought.

She recalled many wrong things: had she not shrieked, in a moment of ungovernable rage, this very curse that had befallen him?

There alone, with the vision of that horror in the house, she sat thinking. She looked at the yellow water, and turned from it, trembling as though with an ague.

The necessary courage to walk into the cold, muddy, sombre river was not there, it would give the physical discomfort she always sought to avoid, and spoil her beautiful body.

And yet if she remained here in juxtaposition with this diseased one——

"Poor, poor thing." Involuntarily that phrase rose to her lips.

She beat at her bosom, scratching the flesh, trying to claw out the tormenting pain.

The monk had lied; the soul was not noble, it was her body that was good. Why should she be the one chosen to come in contact with foulness, she would catch it, as surely as a ratchet would the cogs of a wheel, against which it was placed.

Then who would come to her?

To whom could she turn for consolation?

Yes, she loved her spotless body, yet strange that this burning "soul" inside this very body, should not think alone of the fair form which held it, but turned ever and more pityingly towards the afflicted inmate of the silent house.

Then the monk had not lied, the stirring soul was compassionate! That being so, perhaps his other words had been wise, and she must look inside herself for the medicine to cure its agony.

How?

The Toad, the Ox, the Flies.

She! Chi-Soh! Leprosy!

"She could not cure him!"

"But she could stay with him, be kind to him, forget self," ran an internal argument.

A dull rumbling in her stomach reminded her, that though the thought of food nauseated her, she needed nourishment.

If she could but control her stomach, she could wait night and day for weeks, until a stray boat should hove within call. But she could not.

Then if she could control her soul, so that it did not urge her to stay with Chi-Soh! But she could not.

Aré-Ya did not know that if she could control stomach and soul she would have been superhuman.

"Poor, poor thing!"

No, not that; she must think of herself and how to get away.

And leave the man whom she had loved and given herself to, who had been so good and generous to her, alone?

But if she did not go, then she would rot and fall to pieces. A picture of the lepers on the lazar island of Kowloon, whom she had seen years ago, came vividly before her.

Towards early morning of the third day, a junk rounded the corner.

For a moment she could scarcely believe her eyes, swaying unsteadily to her feet, a revulsion of feeling at the sight of so god-sent a means of escape, made her dizzy.

With hands tight clutching her breast, Aré-Ya waited for it to come near. Watched the rusty-red sails dipping low to catch the little breezes.

Slowly, oh, so slowly, the clumsy boat tacked crookedly back and forth. Now, ah, now it was near enough.

Why did she not cry out? Why would her voice not obey her wish, and call loudly?

Why? why?

Then, as in its clumsy gyrations it almost touched the island, she quivered with excitement, not because it was so near, but in case it should stop.

Her nervous hands unconsciously clenching the little cord on which hung the milky stone, gave a nervous twitch, the cord broke; for an instant she gazed in puzzled wonderment at the gem lying in her hands; then, with all her might she flung it far from her, into the river.

With a sob of relief she saw the junk laboriously disappear round the bend.

On tottering feet she ran towards the house. A crooked smile parted her dry lips as she noticed a pile of food reposing well outside the house.

The leper must have crept forth at night to leave it for her. Passing it by, she went in through the door, and with a face white as a shroud, her lips stiff and her brows contracted, she entered the room where the stricken remains of the man sat huddled in his corner.

"This unworthy slave has come to stay with her lord," she said; her strength had not been great enough to keep her eyes directed on him; her lids dropped, but she did not move from the room.

"No, no, the sacrifice of the Merciful Blossom must not be," he whispered, shrinking further back against the wall.

"I stay," she decided.

Then, fearing the hideous sobs that broke from his dry throat would drive her to hysterical madness, she turned, and went in search of utensils with which to prepare him some rice.

When she entered the cook-house, she was pleased to notice brooms, pans and clean dusters.

Fifth Journey

CHAPTER XXVIII

The quiet of the peaceful Sabbath morning was broken by the simultaneous entry from the opposite ends of the Rue du Bac, of two equally magnificent carriages.

With great rattle and clatter over the cobbled street, the vehicles drew up, so close to one another, that the heads of Madame de Guyon's bay horses actually touched the grey ones which drew the equipage of Madame d'Elbrai.

The cessation of noise caused by the wheels did not make for peace, for now the air was rent with shrill screams from the aristocratic occupants, who rained abuse on one another's houses, ancestry, and personal characters, each demanding right of way, and citing their own claims to precedence, a recital in which the rival coachmen and footmen joined vociferously, while their fair mistresses shrieked orders for their several servants to hasten into the tiny shop they had entered the Rue du Bac to visit, and in front of which they were both stationed, and demand their separate fans of Monsieur Denys, the blind Irishman, the greatest exponent in Paris of these dainty articles.

The black and scarlet livery that denoted the house of Guyon, jostled with the canary and buff of Elbrai, as the two rival lackeys, tumbling from their perches on the carriages, scrambled speedily, but with distressing lack of dignity, to be first to ask for the desired fans.

"The fan of Madame d'Elbrai," bawled Canary-and-buff.

"Madame de Guyon requires her fan," panted Black-and-scarlet.

Both heads were thrust through the small shop door, and the two voices made their requests at the self-same moment; anxious for the precedence of their mistress, the irate men-servants turned sharply to glare at one another, which action causing their heads to bump, led to fresh abuses, and louder quarrelling between the opposite factions.

Vivacious little Madame d'Elbrai, fearing that the hated house of Guyon would be first served, sprang lightly from her seat, and tripped quickly, skirts high upheld in front, displaying claret-coloured silk stockings, kept in place below her knees with elaborate blue ribbons, to demand, in person, her fan.

Seeing which, Madame de Guyon, not to be easily outdone, climbed with amazing alacrity for one so fat, to the ground, and disregarding her trailing skirts, ambled in the more sprightly lady's wake.

By this time the whole neighbourhood was in an uproar, a laughing, jeering crowd had sprung from nowhere, windows were flung open, men and women in night attire, unwashed or unshaven, some half clad, all wigless, leaned watching the fray, crying advice or laying wagers as to which lady would win.

Behind his shop counter stood the great figure of the fan-maker, his fine, old, smooth face rather pinker than usual from this unusual uproar on his doorstep, his white hair neatly brushed straight back, and falling unbound on his shoulders, his sightless blue eyes wide open, while in his hand he held the gold sticks of the delicately fretted fan-handle belonging to Madame d'Elbrai; on the counter in front of him, lay the exquisite ivory toy which Madame de Guyon had come to claim.

At Monsieur Denys' elbow stood his fourteen-year-old granddaughter; her dark blue eyes a-glitter with excitement, her translucent skin showing dazzlingly white beneath the mop of disorderly scarlet hair, Rhoea watched with intense interest the race between the two aristocrats.

A burst of jovial cheering greeted the advent of Madame d'Elbrai, who was the first to reappear in the street, her fan proudly held aloft.

Pompous Madame de Guyon, puffing at the victor's heels, with tears of rage flowing freely adown her fat cheeks, stayed but an instant to cuff Canary-and-yellow, who had come to blows with her own Scarlet-and-black, before she took one long and agile step in order to place her heavy foot on her rival's train, which, now that the race was ended, swept the street in flaunting disarray.

Rrrrrip!

She of the proud house of Elbrai felt herself pulled backwards by the sudden weight of the large foot, and heard the gathers being torn from her waist. She gave a cry of wounded indignation, for how now could she continue on her way to show herself before His Majesty Louis XIV., at church, and incidentally say her prayers, with a torn garment! Her skinny little hand stretched out, and pulled at the fat lady's chignon of curls, and a roar of laughter, as the draggle-skirted, small, dark lady held up a bunch of golden curls which she had snatched from the plump one's head, made the street ring joyful.

The merry Parisians watched the ensuing fray with uproarious mirth, as both ladies, forgetting dignity, smacked and scratched one another's faces, whilst pouring forth virulent abuse, containing strictly personal allusions.

Madame de Guyon was the first to enter her carriage; d'Elbrai regained her own vehicle, barely in time to prevent the enemy driving off in triumph.

The street itself being too narrow to allow of two vehicles passing abreast, and neither consenting to give way, both coachmen lashed their horses, and jolting dangerously over the curbed footpath, smashing the shop windows, the two aristocrats drove off to hastily refurbish their toilettes, before appearing in the sacred edifice of Notre Dame.

"Such are the manners of great ladies," sighed Monsieur Denys, when once more peace fell on the Rue du Bac.

"Neither of them paid for their fans," Rhoea spoke indignantly, as she settled down to her work of affixing the brins in between the two stout outer guards, before confining the end of the whole with the stout pin that acted as a pivot, on which the fan opened and closed.

"Now look at that," ejaculated the blind man. "Sure, now, ye must go and remind them."

"That I will, but it will mean the loss of a whole day's work, and moreover, they do not pay easily," she complained.

"Ah, there ye go now, abusin' the poor things; they will pay, and it is fine money they give," chuckled old Denys.

"And for why should they not?" bristled Rhoea.

"Whist, whist, now," soothed her grandfather. "Ye are named Rhoea, it being the Latin word for 'poppy,' which was what your small red head reminded your father of when you were born; but it would seem as though your temper is growing as fiery as your hair, my lassie."

"It is as well one of us has an eye to the accounts, else would you do your beautiful work for naught," his granddaughter told him.

"Ay, ay, a good lassie, but a hasty one. Sure, your poor old grandfather would be lost without you," he sighed.

"Dear granddaddie," smiled Rhoea. "'Tis happy I am to live with you, though betimes I long to see my own father, and wonder greatly if my little half-sister at all resembles me."

"You know I have never seen her," said the old man.

"Tell me about my father."

"Your father was a wild lad, and on the death of your mother, he left France, and went to become acquainted with Ireland."

"My father was born there, was he not?" asked Rhoea, coaxing the old man on to speak of bygone days, for she loved to hear of them.

"Yes, Shan—that is, your father, was a bit of a boy when I left the old country to come to France. Happy enough, and steady too, he was, with your mother, but when he lost her, the wildness came back to him. Then he married an Irish colleen, and it is little I hear of him or your half-sister, my lass."

"I will warrant she could not help in the making of fans as I can," bragged Rhoea.

"Like not," the sensitive fingers busy with the delicate carving of fine gold frond.

"Denys fans are the vogue; none other are to be compared with ours," stated Rhoea, proudly. "Myself, I do not think you place a sufficiently high price on them," she told him, and he smiled.

"A very little suffices me for my wants," he replied.

"A very great deal would be more to my liking," she said, with some asperity.

"How now! What then would you do with wealth?" Monsieur Denys questioned curiously.

"There are times when I do not want wealth, but feel content to go on working beside you. There are other moments when a desire comes over me to possess all the money in the world," confided Rhoea, then her busy fingers stopped working, she looked dreamily into space.

"Granddad," she spoke very seriously, "a part of me cries for riches so that I might help all who needed assistance. I want to give and give and give; money if I had it, or if not, then sympathy and care for the sad, and sick, poor ones."

"That is my good little lass," praised Monsieur Denys.

"But the other side of me is different," confessed Rhoea.

"So! And what says it?" inquired her grandfather smilingly.

"I would have many serving-wenches, and varlets in uniform to wait upon me; my dresses would be of the richest and my hose of silk; I would marry only one high-born, whose position would warrant my giving place to none, except Royalty. I would not deign to know the affairs of my own household, nor the cost of living, even though my servants paid as much as two sous a kilo for onions, nor would I inquire as to what use they made of candle ends, or fats."

"How now, you aspire to become an aristocrat," chuckled the old fan-maker, "and what then would become of me?"

"I would take you with me, granddad."

"Now that would be kind of ye. Your talk is only that of a little, young thing."

"Not so young, grandfather; many maidens are already wives at my age," Rhoea reminded him.

"True, I am forgetful of your fourteen years," he nodded assentingly.

"Not that I am wishful to wed, unless it be for such a purpose as that of which I spoke, for it would irk me to marry a man who would seek to restrain me, for that I could not abide," she spoke determinately.

"It is your mixture of French and Irish blood that causes you to speak so wildly. Now, my lass, we will go for our Sunday promenade in the Place Maubert, before eating a fine meal at a restaurant," he decided.

This was their weekly treat, to dress in their best and parade with the other artisans in their haunt of fashion, listening to scandal, and exchanging greetings with neighbours.

As Rhoea walked by the side of her grandfather, his hand on her shoulder for guidance, she talked over one of her ambitions, which was to make enough money to buy a titled husband, pointing out to the amused old man, that many of their acquaintances having done likewise, she saw no reason why she should not succeed in becoming a great lady.

"Our fans are selling well, and we have no one to consider but ourselves, grandfather; then for why should I not plan that which will please me best?" she asked, and the old man nodded careless assent to his beloved grandchild's speech.

The next day, donning her best gown, a full ankle-length skirt of good grey cloth, with its adornment of scarlet braid, a basqued bodice, the large puffed sleeves and square-cut neck finished off with embroidered muslin cuffs and collar freshly laundered; round her red hair, she dared so far ape the fashion of modish ladies, by wearing a *chaperon* of scarlet velvet; frowning as she pulled on her red woollen hose, one day, she vowed, she would wear only silk; her thick-soled, flat-heeled shoes, too, did not please her. Then, with a frown of annoyance at the worldliness of her own thoughts, Rhoea went quickly to a corner of her poorly furnished little chamber, and falling on her knees before the figure of the Virgin Mary and the Baby Jesus, she begged for forgiveness of her sinful longings, and prayed fervently for pardon.

After which Rhoea set forth, walking smartly along the Rue

du Bac towards the Pont Neuf, and so on to the fashionable Rue Vaugirard, where both the debtors lived. It was to the house of Elbrai she first went, where her request to see Madame was scarce even listened to by the haughty varlet who had charge of the door, and perhaps Rhoea would have been forced to put her spoken determination, of waiting all day if needs be until the lady appeared, into execution, but for the intervention of Monsignor Tullia di Masino, who was honouring the house by his presence at breakfast, finding that his prison fare was poor, coarse, and not to his liking.

The whole of Paris had heard the history of this Italian, who thirty-five years ago had come from his home in Piedmont and been promptly arrested and thrown into prison, for what reason no one could remember, nor were any sufficiently interested to inquire; he was released as suddenly and mysteriously as he had been arrested.

"What, now that I'm an old man of sixty or there-abouts, am I to be cast forth from the only house I know, into the unknown streets of Paris, or driven back to an Italy that has forgotten me! No, no, this prison has been my home for thirty-five years; my home it must remain until I die!" di Masino had cried, when his janitors had told him he was free.

No objections being made, he remained in his cell, but now he was free to come and go as he pleased, and also to sell the paintings which he had learned to execute so delightfully during his incarceration.

His story amused Paris, and he became a lion in society, his presence giving a cachet to every house that he consented to accept entertainment from.

Madame d'Elbrai considered she had scored a great triumph in having persuaded di Masino to superintend the artistic attempts of her only son, a youth of seventeen, who caused his mother great annoyance because of his curious outlook on life, for young Ugiso d'Elbrai took no interest in the fashionable life with which he was surrounded, refusing to join in the festivities and gaieties which made up the entire existence of his lady parent and her set. His addiction to strong wines and drugs did not distress her in the least, but his declining to appear at any rout or amusement, even a Court ball, drove her to the verge of despair, his painting being the only thing in which he showed any interest.

Signor di Masino was clad in the skin-tight jacket, which he had worn on landing in France so many years ago, plum-coloured then, a faded nondescript colour now; the fur lining to his long sleeve points, once a rich ermine, looked more like the pelt of a rat, to which stray portions of decayed fur still clung; the buckle that had used to catch his leathern belt, having long since been bartered for food, was now replaced by an iron stud; the silk tights which had encased his legs when, as a youth, he had left sunny Piedmont, had fallen to shreds, so now he wore tightly fitting nankeen breeches of a bright yellow hue, purple silk stockings fastened below his knees with red braid; his head was covered with a peaked hood of black cloth, the same coloured material forming the long cape that was attached to the quaint head-dress, while many strange characters were embroidered in various colours on the lining of the voluminous cloak.

"What have we here?" inquired this queerly apparelled being, whose extraordinarily large and brilliant black eyes, overhung by iron-grey, bushy brows, burned like fires in his skull-like face.

"I come for the money which is owing to my grandfather, Monsignor," spoke up Rhoea quickly, before the servingman could answer the question.

"You do not speak like a demoiselle of Paris," he commented.

Rhoea blushed with pride at being thus termed.

"My grandfather is a noble, but poor gentleman of Ireland, who is reduced to earning a livelihood by the fashioning of fans, the best in Paris," she assured him, proudly.

"This little Tête-Rouge will entertain Madame," decided Monsignor, and with no further ado Rhoea was allowed to follow the favoured Italian into the presence which she had come to seek.

CHAPTER XXIX

"Ha, Masino, you find me desolate and like to die," greeted Madame d'Elbrai, yawning widely. She was attired solely in a not too clean night-shift, greatly bedecked with lace, which, falling from her shoulders, exposed much of the lady's thin person. Seated on the edge of her tumbled bed, dangling her bare limbs, her hair falling in lank disorder about her face, which still retained blotches of the paint applied the day before, she did not present a pleasing picture.

Heavy damask curtains shielded the carefully closed windows, preventing any daylight from entering, but many candles, burning in elaborate silver sconces, illuminated the room.

Rhoea's eyes went from the dishevelled figure on the bed to the two bustling tire-women, who were preparing Madame's toilette; then to the foppishly attired young man, whose large, feathered hat, which he retained on his head, did not hide the powdered wig of great dimensions, nor the weak, fair face, and bored, blue eyes which he scarcely raised from the little dog he was playing with to glance at the new-comers; this was Monsieur Gilles Rallecourt, one of Madame's many admirers.

"It is Ugiso," explained the lady, in answer to Masino's question as to what troubled her, "a pest on him; he made me a fine scene when I insisted on his attending the fête to be held at Versailles this very day, and swore he would not so much as accompany me to the gate; not a step will he come, although I have made a rendezvous for him with the daughter of the wealthy de Bryère. A fine match that would be, the de Bryère is no beauty, to be sure, being over fat and lacking in intelligence; but what of that, it is only as a wife, not as a mistress I would have him take her, and the good God alone knows I am in sad need of money; is that not so, Gilles?" she appealed to the languid one.

"What! Ah, yes, money!" he sighed heavily, "'tis the plague of my existence, the plague, I tell you," he roused himself sufficiently to say, before falling back listlessly, to again tease the poodle.

"It may be that Ugiso will relent, and accompany you. I shall speak with him," consoled Masino.

"Speak with him," screamed the aggrieved mother; "by the blood of the Saints, if speech could avail he would be already married these two years. Seeing I was determined to take him to-day, what must the unclean animal do but put his foot in the fire and hold it there until he made himself incapable of walking. A pretty son, truly, for me to be afflicted with."

"Give her snuff," drawled the young fop, as Madame seemed likely to become hysterical.

"How now, Masino, what is this you have brought with you; I thought your prison had killed all desire for our sex," d'Elbrai said, on catching sight of Rhoea, after she had been soothed with a draught of scented water and wine.

"Am I to be pestered by such *canaille* here, in my own apartment?" she demanded, when Masino had explained the errand on which Rhoea had come.

"As Madame gained the victory over the fat one yesterday, I

thought it would be only courteous to come here first, for payment, before going on to Madame de Guyon," Rhoea cunningly interpolated.

"By Our Lady, a sly minx," smiled the well-pleased Madame; "it was amusing that episode, when I held up her wig, was it not?" she queried.

"That it was, it put me in much pain with laughter," answered Rhoea.

"Go you, Masino, and speak with that unnatural son of mine; I will entertain me well with this amusing one," commanded d'Elbrai.

Then while the great lady had her hands washed, and her body attired, she spoke with Rhoea; the bored Rallecourt in the corner taking but little interest in the dressing of his hostess, although he exerted himself sufficiently to hold a candle while her hair was dressed, and her face repainted; with an effort he made a momentous decision as to the exact spot whereon patches should be placed; agreeing with Rhoea that they would look better near Madame's flashing eyes, than lower down, close to her mouth.

It was Rhoea's suggestion also, that the dark beauty should wear a filet of tiny golden leaves on her unpowdered hair, instead of a velvet *chaperon*.

Altogether, the little "Tête Rouge" so pleased Madame d'Elbrai, that she was paid without demur for the fan, and bidden to come again on the following day.

"Your son is desirous of speaking with the fan-maker's granddaughter," Masino entered to say.

"By my faith, what next!" ejaculated the lady.

"He is set on painting a satin to be formed into a fan," explained Masino.

"Go, child, humour the wicked one. Masino, you accompany her and remain there, although I do not think even this Tête Rouge will move his sluggish blood," she added despairingly. "Return here ere you depart," she commanded Rhoea.

Led by Masino, Rhoea entered a handsome apartment. The sun streamed through uncurtained windows on to a narrow couch, where reclined a sombre-faced youth, his jet-black hair falling squarely about his shoulders, his olive-tinted face pale from the suffering he had endured through the burning of his foot; in his dark eyes shone brooding discontent, and a peevishness and weakness marked his handsome, sensitive mouth.

"I pray you will pardon my not rising," he begged Rhoea, as she entered.

"It is not for Monsieur to rise for such as I," she deprecated, sweeping him a curtsy.

"It is not possible for me to move, for I am dead," Monsieur Ugiso d'Elbrai informed his startled guest.

"But how can one be dead and converse?" she asked him, completely mystified.

"It is my spirit that speaks, I am no more; regard my shroud," he bade her, indicating the white garments with which he was swathed.

"Then how can you paint these satins?" inquired Rhoea.

"I can paint, and my spirit speaks, but I cannot eat or move; therefore I am dead," he insisted.

"Since when?"

"Since countless centuries, but it was only this morning that I finally gave up the ghost. I shall be laid out with many candles, and white flowers this evening. So now I would dispose of these paintings, in order to gain money for my burial; it is only so grave an affair has caused me to see you, for I do not like strangers," Ugiso informed her seriously.

"Perhaps I can cure you," offered Rhoea, after a startled

glance at Masino, who nodded and signed to her to humour the spoiled youth.

"A dead man cannot be cured," he replied irritably.

"I have healing powers for which I am well known; the neighbours send for me in all their ailments; even the most virulent plagues have I cured, and it seems as though I possessed some charm, for fevers and other ills do not touch me," she bragged.

"Ah, well, you can do naught for me except purchase my paintings," he sighed.

"This one is gay," she commented, picking up a fragment of satin on which he had amusingly depicted two tiny mice clutching the tail of a large black cat, "and this one, of the small sweep peering from the chimney at the lady and her lover—oh, but yes, they have much *chic* and originality," she praised. "I am sure my grandfather would be willing to pay you for them," and at this assurance the "corpse" smiled.

As the young people chatted, a diversion was created by the entrance of two footmen bearing their master's luncheon on gold salvers.

Falling into a paroxysm of rage, Ugiso hurled the dishes of food at the terrified varlets' heads, bidding them begone, and to learn better than to mock a dead man by bringing him nourishment.

"But had you not better eat so that you may keep your spirit alive until to-morrow, when I shall return to let you know what my grandfather has to say with regard to these satins?" suggested Rhoea.

"My spirit will hear you, and you may come to-morrow. I, who dislike strangers, do not feel that you are one," he informed her with a lordly air.

When Rhoea returned to Madame's apartment, she found it

overflowing with company. Her red hair and general appearance was freely commented on by the fashionable, mannerless throng, and nothing loth, she complied with d'Elbrai's command to give her version of the vanquishing of Madame de Guyon in the Rue du Bac.

Peals of laughter greeted her spirited recital, which she sadly exaggerated and gave with much gesticulation.

"By the blood, I shall reward you for that," cried a young nobleman, one Count Filippe de Maureaux, wiping tears of mirth from his eyes, and stooping his monstrously bewigged and hatted head, he kissed Rhoea full on the lips.

"Sacred name of a dog, take that," she flashed, and with all her might she smote his painted cheek with her open palm, her face scarlet, and her eyes blazing with outraged dignity.

In bewildered amazement, de Maureaux's hand felt his stinging cheek, as he gazed at the infuriated damsel, who had inflicted this punishment on him, merely for conferring the favour of a caress on her plebeian mouth. He felt that here was something unique, for his kisses were sought after by the very proudest of Court beauties.

"I am sorry, I am sorry," cried Rhoea, immediately her hand had left the smitten cheek; "not," she added quickly, "in that I struck you, monsieur, but to lose my temper was a sin, and I shall tell it in my confession, so that I shall be made to do a great penance."

When the roars of mirth which Rhoea's action had caused, died down, she informed Madame of her interview with Monsieur Ugiso.

"*Morbleu!* That was to be expected of him, for the wicked one would go to any length to plague me, and he well knows I depend on him to make a marriage that will replenish my fortune; it was only last week that he conceived the atrocious idea of paying all his debts. That, well-nigh broke my heart," wailed the much-tried mother.

"I think, beauteous lady, that your son may come to life in his interest over these fan paintings," consoled Masino.

Whereupon Rhoea was bidden to attend, without fail, the house d'Elbrai on the morrow, in order to revivify the "corpse."

Making her farewell curtsy, and kissing her hostess's hand, Rhoea departed, but her day of eventful happenings was not yet to end, for as she gained the street, the overdressed Filippe de Maureaux joined her.

"Do not fear, demoiselle, I have not come to do you harm," he consoled, as she shrank from him.

"I am not afraid, but what is it you want of me?" she asked, standing still and looking at him defiantly.

"Not to punish you for the blow you dealt me," he smiled.

"I' faith, my punishment came before I raised my hand," she answered quickly, and de Maureaux laughed.

"It is the first time my caresses have been unwelcome," he boasted.

"You will find it will not be the last time if you lavish them on me," Rhoea assured him heartily.

"By my soul, you pique my interest; may I humbly crave the pleasure of your society?" he asked.

"Whither?"

"Your way shall be my way, strange one," he answered, bowing low.

Rhoea's heart thrilled with pride, the youth himself held no interest for her, but she secretly rejoiced at the rich dress and graceful air of her aristocratic escort, as she condescendingly accorded him the desired permission to walk beside her on her homeward path.

Faithfully mimicking the little mincing steps of the grand

ladies who visited her grandfather's shop, she walked the long length of the Rue de Vaugirard, and so on to the Rue du Bac, chatting gaily to her delighted, and delightful, companion, who was secretly amused at her frank speech, delivered with more than a suspicion of Irish brogue.

So unused was the young Comte de Maureaux to walking, that he begged permission to enter, and rest for a moment on reaching the fan shop, where old Monsieur Denys received him courteously, and listened interestedly to his account of the punishment meted out to him by Rhoea.

"—And well I deserved the blow," Filippe finished his story by confessing naïvely.

"My little granddaughter is a self-respecting lass, but a hasty one," commented old Denys.

"Pity it is there are not more like her, say I," complimented Filippe.

"Like who, my little Comte?" inquired a fresh voice, at sound of which Rhoea frowned, for the wealthy and beautiful Widow Valeron was no favourite of hers, although she was one of the best customers the fan shop knew.

"Ah, Madame, as beautiful as ever," Filippe flattered, neither rising nor removing his hat.

"What brings you here, Filippe?" asked the widow.

"A desire to surprise you by the purchase of a fan for the fête this afternoon," he invented as an excuse.

"That is not what you told me," corrected Rhoea quickly.

"Ah ha, little Comte, so it's the Tête Rouge that attracts, eh?" the widow smiled languidly.

"And, furthermore, Madame Valeron does not attend the King's fête," Rhoea put in mischievously, for in the gossip that came to her sharp ears, she well knew that for all her large and buxom beauty, and the wealth her deceased husband, a velvet merchant of Lyons, had left her, Deseré Valeron could not obtain an entry into the Court circle, which fact fretted the poor lady exceedingly.

"Then if Madame's presence is to be denied the festivities, I am willing to wager that many will be sad, and none more so than myself, and Marquis Saint Ruipi," courteously declared the young Comte, designating Ruipi du Buisson by the title by which the very virtuous Marquis loved to be known.

"La! la! that man!" deprecated Madame Valeron, self-consciously, a pleased smile curling her lips, for she dearly liked to be twitted on the constancy of this admirer de Maureaux mentioned, of whom it was said, that if he could but find a way of serving both God and Mammon, he would marry the handsome widow. Nothing would have pleased her better than to change the plebeian name of Valeron to the aristocratic one of du Buisson, and, moreover, becoming a marquise, enter the ardently desired Court circle; but the Marquis exhibited no greater signs now than he had done all the years she had known him, of becoming anything more than an admirer; his well-deserved reputation for sanctity having become an obsession with him, he could not bring himself to lose it by marrying. So torn betwixt love of Deseré Valeron, and an aspiration to increase his fame as a saint, the Marquis Ruipi du Buisson spent his time equally between prayers and good works, and sighing at the feet of his inamorata, to the great glee of gossiping Paris.

"Oh, hard-hearted, alluring one, I pray of you, at the cost of my own lacerated feelings, to be kinder to Saint Ruipi," bantered Filippe, who well knew the widow's ambitions, and the quandary into which the Marquis had fallen.

"Ha! ha!" Rhoea's raucous laugh was that of a little *gamine*. "In the country of my grandfather, Monsieur le Marquis would be termed 'le flirt,'" she said bluntly.

"Hush, hush, lass," chided the old man gently, and the widow, tossing her head and sniffing disdainfully, departed, carrying Filippe with her.

"I do not like that one," exploded Rhoea, as Madame Valeron disappeared.

"So it would seem from your acerbic remarks, my fiery child; but why is it you do not like the good lady?" old Denys asked.

"For no reason," admitted Rhoea. "For all her wealth she is avaricious, yet that is not why I mislike her; she is desirous of becoming a great personage, as am I myself. Indeed, grandfather, I know not what it is in her that causes me to feel such a scratch-cat."

In silence the two worked diligently at the fashioning of fans. Rhoea's thoughts ran to wondering if ever she could earn a large enough *dot* to induce even such a one as the Comte de Maureaux to bestow upon her his hand and title, thoughts for which later that day she repented, and spent hours on her knees before her adored figure of the Virgin, pleading for Divine help to overcome her baser self.

CHAPTER XXX

Early the following morning whilst Rhoea was dressing to sally forth, in order to collect the money due from Madame de Guyon, before going on to tell young Monsieur d'Elbrai that her grandfather had consented to purchase his painted satins, the Italian, Tullia di Masino, presented himself at the fan shop to beg of his little friend with the tête rouge, to come quickly to the house where he had met her on the previous day.

Ugiso d'Elbrai, it appeared, had persisted in adhering to his delusion that he was dead, and any attempts to persuade him to eat, only threw him into an uncontrollable rage, so that servants feared to approach him, and physicians had departed in despair.

The very lively corpse was insisting on Rhoea's return, so that he might dispose of his paintings, for, he declared, that having paid his debts he was now a pauper, and must gain money for a Christian burial.

"Ah, dilatory one," the freshly-bathed "corpse," in his clean shroud, greeted Rhoea as she entered his chamber with Masino, "my spirit might have departed, unlighted, and un-shriven, had you delayed much longer."

"Here are four *écus* to purchase three paintings," proffered Rhoea, handing him the equivalent of a *louis*, which he eagerly grasped; "but as to your death that does not concern me, I am too well accustomed to much more lifeless ones than yourself."

"Such a statement cannot be true," he blazed, hurt at this be-littling of his state.

"I have no time for the whims of idle ones, and, moreover, if you are discourteous, *Monsieur le Cadavre*, I will neither purchase your satins, nor visit you again," Rhoea stated impatiently, whereupon he burst into a flood of bitter weeping, which was so vehement and lasted so long, that Masino, becoming alarmed, whisperingly begged Rhoea to humour and conciliate the poor youth, who had become so enfeebled by wines and drugs, that he could not be held responsible for his eccentric spasm.

"Never before have I seen a dead person weep," Rhoea told Ugiso forcefully.

His sobbing grew less, and he pondered over her words.

"Also, all my lifeless ones eat," she added as an afterthought.

Now his interest was well wakened, to the inexpressible re-lief of Tullia di Masino, who had grown sincerely attached to this poor young scion of nobility, who had been alternately ne-glected and spoiled when a babe, spoiled and hurled into dissi-pated surroundings while still a delicate child, by a mother who cared for nothing on earth but her own pleasures.

"Perhaps it would be as well for you to join these others who are in a like state to yourself," suggested Masino.

"That will I do, after my lying in state to-night," Ugiso decided.

Though the Italian feared the boy's life would in reality be endangered from his lack of nourishment, with this ultimatum he was forced to rest content, and busy himself with the arrangement of candles, flowers, and catafalque for the night's ceremonies, as ordered by the son and heir of Elbrai.

Late that same evening, Masino once more visited the fan shop, this time with an urgent message from Madame d'Elbrai, who begged and commanded, all in one breath, that the Italian should arrange for her son to be humoured on the morrow into taking some nourishment when he put his plan of visiting Rhoea's home into effect, in order to see the dead feasting.

"I pray of you, Monsieur Denys, to permit the little Tête Rouge to assist us, otherwise the poor deluded boy will in reality die," pleaded Masino, his extraordinary eyes blazing like living coals, in his anxiety for the health of his erstwhile pupil.

"What say you, granddaughter?" queried the fan-maker, after listening to Masino's curious request.

"I have seen this young Monsieur, and feel a great pity for him; it is a plaguing affair, but I fear me we must consent," sighed Rhoea, not at all pleased at this interruption of work, and yet a curious feeling that she was bound to help this half-crazed youth if it lay in her power to do so, possessed her.

Tullia di Masino it was, who arranged for the easily persuaded Parisians to come, clad in shrouds impersonating corpses, so that their capricious-minded friend, d'Elbrai, seeing them thus attired and seated at table, might join them in their feasting.

Filippe de Maureaux and other idle *flâneurs,* nothing loth, entered into the affair as a huge jest, and surely never was seen so grimly humorous a party, as the one that met in the Rue du Bac, in the living room behind the fan-maker's shop.

The drive through the air from the Rue de Vaugirard having given Ugiso an appetite, he ate with his fellow corpses, but the trouble came when, it being time for them to depart, he refused to go, and no amount of persuasion could bring him to stir.

Back and forth went the buff-and-canary liveried servants, carrying messages to and from Madame d'Elbrai, until at length the lady herself appeared, but the sight of her caused her son to fly into so violent a temper, that she begged of Monsieur Denys to permit her troublesome son to spend the night beneath his humble roof.

"It is Rhoea who must decide," the old fan-maker informed her, "for it is on the child's shoulders the burthen will fall, and truly, Madame, she is over young to be inflicted with a greater responsibility than my own blinded self," he sighed.

To the little Tête Rouge the distressed lady turned, and with the calmness of despair, Rhoea consented to accept this added load to the household, whereupon Madame d'Elbrai, much relieved at the disposition of her son, departed for the festivities on which she throve, leaving Rhoea busily preparing one of the several vacant rooms above the shop, for Ugiso's reception.

It was thus Monsieur d'Elbrai came to live in the Denys *ménage*, for even when he outgrew his delusion that his life was extinct, he was so happy, sitting all day helping the blind man and Rhoea at their work, that he refused to quit, and in time came to be as much part of the household as either his host or hostess, whom he called respectively "grandfather" and "Rhoea" (or "Tête Rouge"), while insisting that they should abandon ceremony, and address him as "Ugiso."

The news soon flew about Paris, and the Rue du Bac became thronged with sensation-loving, fashionable crowds, a-visiting their friend to see him employed on his plebeian task, and while Rhoea enjoyed the notoriety thus gained, the new order of affairs caused her a great deal of disturbance. Not only were her household tasks increased but she resented these grand people because she was not one of them; still, she aped their talk and manners, and every available sum was hoarded away for the *dot* that was ordained to purchase an aristocratic husband, or to be given in charity, when she had quite decided for which purpose she most desired wealth.

Madame d'Elbrai, finding that her son resolutely refused to marry any of the rich damsels whom she selected, abandoned him altogether after some spirited interviews, at the last of which, Ugiso assigned to her all his patrimony on condition that she left him in peace, a stipulation the gay mother readily acceded to.

"I do not wish for money for my paintings, grandfather, if you and little Tête Rouge will give me bed and meat," Ugiso explained to easy-going Monsieur Denys.

"That, you are welcome to, young sir, if Rhoea has no objection," he told Ugiso.

"Well, Tête Rouge, do you agree?" d'Elbrai inquired.

"It seems I must, else you will return to your deathbed," was her ungracious reply, as the three of them sat busily working on the perfecting of fans.

Rhoea, with an apronful of brins and outer guards, into which she was attaching pivots, was seated on a low stool between the two benches; over one, the old grey-haired man leaned, carving ivory or golden sticks, whilst Ugiso's dark head bent over parchments and satins, busy with his paint brush.

Two of their most constant visitors were Comte de Maureaux and Tullia di Misano; scarce a day passed without their spending much time in the Rue du Bac, where they delighted to loiter, chatting with the toilers.

Madame Valeron, too, came often to the shop, sometimes alone, or more frequently accompanied by Saint Ruipi, his sad, snuff-coloured garments, with no embellishment of ribbon or jewel, making him a marked figure in contrast to the gay attire of other young gallants who paid court at the shrine of the wealthy widow, who encouraged their attentions, in a vain endeavour to win a proposal of marriage from the ascetic Marquis du Buisson, who, at the age of twenty, had suddenly become acquainted with Deseré Valeron, just as he was on the point of taking the vows necessary to becoming a monk; the strong attraction he had instantly felt for her, had caused him to abandon his cenobitic intention, and for ten years now his indecision had tortured him.

Was he to secede his saintship, or abjure the lady?

Poor Saint Ruipi, he abased his flesh with scarification, chafing, coarse under-garments; scapular, fasting and other dire penance, until he had grown lean and haggard, a mere shadow of his former, handsome self. He considered his love for the fascinating widow, a dire sin, and yet, alas for the weakness of human nature, he could not bring himself to remain long from her side.

Rhoea and Saint Ruipi were the firmest of friends, and to him she spoke quite frankly of her projects for the future, and also, was not at all reticent in speaking to him of his own affairs.

"It is foolish to allow one's mind to hesitate," Rhoea stated in the course of an idle discussion which had arisen one morning as she worked beside her grandparent and Ugiso in the shop, where the emaciated Marquis was sitting, half hoping, half fearful that Deseré Valeron would appear. "For then, one's life would be wasted," she finished decisively.

"The Tête Rouge is strong-minded," laughed Ugiso, who was growing as young as his years under the simple régime of the artisan's household.

"I am," she admitted candidly.

"But as your ambitions, of which you have told me, are juxtaposed to other, equally strong desires, what then? " inquired Saint Ruipi.

"In life it must be the head or the heart that rules, and me, I shall be guided by my head; it is saner," she asserted.

"Nevertheless, it is your great heart that will guide you," her grandfather contradicted.

"Of that, I, too, am sure," agreed Comte de Maureaux, who had entered in time to hear Rhoea's statement, and Monsieur Denys' reply.

"Be not too sure, Monsieur le Comte," Rhoea warned. "True it is that my heart and head are not always in agreement, but with the aid of the saints I shall conquer one or the other, and realize my ambition, whatever it may be," she finished triumphantly.

"And having realized it, you will cry aloud against Fate for treating you so cruelly as to permit you to have had a choice in the making of your life, thus are frail humans constituted," commented di Masino, who was bending over Ugiso's shoulder, criticizing his pupil's painting.

"A husband may interfere with her ambitions," bantered de Maureaux, who was in ignorance of those aspirations.

"The husband I will take must help, not hinder my plans," Rhoea answered quickly.

"My soul is melting with curiosity to hear what Mam'selle considers essential in he, who is to be so blessed as to become her husband," and beneath the light jocularity of his tone, de Maureaux instilled a conscionable degree of earnestness, which Rhoea's ear was quick enough to catch.

"For one thing, I would not have him wear the badge of the people," she retorted slyly. Filippe joined the laughter which this remark caused at his expense, for attached to his coat was a wisp of straw, a conceit much affected by noble dilettante, who pretended to socialistic views, and so wore this symbol of the people, but while he laughed, he detached the offending straw, and leaning across the counter, dropped it gracefully at the little fan-maker's feet.

"Ah, ha," her astute mind gloated; "perhaps it might even be that I shall in time become Madame la Comtesse de Maureaux, and attend the Court of His Majesty King Louis. The Valeron would not like that," she chuckled inwardly.

During the year that followed Ugiso's entry into shop life, Rhoea was very happy, despite the extra duties his presence entailed, for while she worked hard, trade was increasing, and prices soaring, so that already she had nearly two hundred silver *écus* hidden away, and the store was increasing daily, so Rhoea sang at her tasks, while she coquetted with Filippe, who showed every sign of becoming enamoured of her, and, indeed, this was so, for the Tête Rouge was such a complete change from the vitiated circle in which he spent his life, that this fact alone would have attracted him to her. Still, he had spoken no direct word of love as yet, but Rhoea was in no hurry, she waited contentedly, tending her grandfather, and watching over Ugiso as though he were in reality her brother, rejoicing at his mending health, chiefly due to his discontinuance of strong wines and drugs, against the taking of which, Rhoea had resolutely set her face.

"See how much better you are, how much greater is your

appetite," she pointed out joyfully to Ugiso one day, after he had partaken heartily of his simple meal.

"That is true," he agreed smilingly.

"Then knowing how much better you are without your harmful drugs, why do you try to take them?"

"They had become a habit."

"A bad habit," she reprimanded. "You should try to cure yourself, instead of depending on me to restrain you."

"It is so much easier to lean on your strong will," he explained lazily.

"In that way, your own will, will never grow strong," scolded Rhoea.

"That is true," he admitted. "Indeed, I make good resolutions, but when temptation comes I grow weak, and look to you to help me."

Ugiso sighed.

Although Rhoea frowned, his words pleased her, she liked the thought that she was strong, that this youth was weak enough to lean on her.

During one sultry June morning, when Rhoea was about to abandon her work in the shop in order to set about preparing the midday meal, a small maiden, whose black clothing made her white face appear more pallid by contrast, entered the shop.

Her clear blue eyes, and fair curly hair barely topped the counter.

"Is this where Mister Denys be livin'?" she demanded, in English, with a strong Irish brogue.

"Yes," answered Rhoea, for it was in this tongue she and her grandfather often conversed, therefore, she spoke English almost as well as she did French.

"The Saints be praised," ejaculated the child, dropping the clumsy bundle she carried beneath her arm, heavily to the floor, and turning, she walked to the door.

As Rhoea watched the self-possessed, diminutive figure, her heart sank strangely.

"It do be all right; ye can go," she shouted to some invisible person or persons. "It was Molly O'Ryan, her it was fetched me across to me gran'dad."

"What name is yours?" asked Rhoea, while Monsieur Denys dropped his stick of ivory and stood up to listen.

"Sure, I am Dimidia Denys," announced the owner of that name.

"My son Shan's other lassie," cried the old man, holding out his arms.

"My little sister," exclaimed Rhoea simultaneously, running round the counter to embrace the new-comer.

"Thin you are Rhoea," remarked Dimidia, eyeing her half-sister curiously, whilst she straightened her black bonnet, which the ardent caress had knocked awry.

"Yes, come round to grandfather," invited the excited Tête Rouge, taking the child's hand.

"Me father told me ye're hair was red, and sure 'twas no lie," commented Dimidia, allowing herself to be kissed by the old fan-maker.

"And how is your father, my dear?" tremulously asked her grandparent.

"He is dead, may his soul rist in peace," the orphan crossed herself cursorily.

"My Shan, my boy, dead!"

"Ah, my poor father, and you, my poor little one," cried Rhoea, bursting into sobs, while two big tears coursed down the old man's cheeks.

Dimidia's white forehead wrinkled, and her eyes opened wide, as she looked from one to the other of her sorrowing relatives.

"'Tis better off he is in Hivin," she consoled philosophically.

"While he lived, me mother would not hear of me comin' to Paris," she added, as an afterthought.

"The poor soul, she is heart-broken, no doubt," mourned the grandfather.

"Not so heart-broken as she moight have been, but for Black Michael O'Grady," smiled the child knowingly.

"Ah, well, she will need the consolations of her friends," sighed Monsieur Denys.

"Black Michael is no friend," scoffed Dimidia.

"No?" her grandfather was puzzled.

"No; he is her husband," was the astounding announcement that fell on her listeners' ears.

"Me father has been dead these three months now," volunteered the damsel, "and me mother has been married to Michael O'Grady for nigh onto a month, so she said I had best go to me gran'dad and let him have the keepin' of me," she ended her amazing story.

"You poor wee thing," petted the "gran'dad;" and Rhoea's arms crept pityingly round the orphan's slender shoulders, and——

"Who is he?" asked Dimidia, pointing to Ugiso, whom she eyed through her long, curling lashes.

CHAPTER XXXI

Dainty little Dimidia was accorded the position of petted plaything in her grandfather's establishment; she graciously accepted the best everyone could give, as her just due, and although only two years younger than her half-sister, her tiny stature made her appear much less than her thirteen years. Her small white hands did not seem as though formed for work, which by the way she made no pretence of attempting. The coarse black dress in which she arrived, was quickly cast aside, in favour of gaily coloured clothing, and much of the money which Rhoea would have added to her hoard, went in payment of finery for the fairy-like creature, and very attractive she looked in the pretty costumes on which she expended so much time and care.

This fresh occupant in the Rue du Bac, left Rhoea very little time to work in the shop, for Dimidea's ruffles, cuffs, collars, and chemisettes were worn every day, instead of being kept, as Rhoea did her own, for Sunday wear, and the burden of washing and ironing them fell on Téte Rouge. Ugiso, too, came under the child's spell, and spent much time in painting pieces of satin for her golden hair.

"Gran'dad, I saw a string of fine blue beads on a stall by the *Palais de Justice,* that would well finish my new costume," she coaxed, and the old man, who could refuse her nothing, would hand her out the money for which he worked so hard.

She was so fragile, and ailing, and fell into such storms of weeping if anything was refused her, that she generally gained her way with but little trouble. The fashionable customers who visited the shop made a great fuss of the pretty child, her quaint brogue and broken French delighting them, and none more than the young Comte de Maureaux, indeed, he became her chief escort in her rambles abroad, and many a fine present she wheedled from the generous youth.

"It is noble of you to come walking with me, who am so poorly clad," she touched his chivalrous nature by sighing, pausing to gaze at some fine, buckled shoes.

"*Au contraire,* it is you who are kind to accept my company; as for your costume, it is so *chic,* and fine as that of a Court lady," he replied gallantly.

"You say that without having remarked my great, clumsy shoes," she pouted, holding out a small foot to display their neat, flat-heeled gear; "it is happy I would be to have such a pair as those," pointing to the scarlet shoes that had attracted her attention.

"Ah, now, I shall appear as tall as Rhoea," she cried delightedly, as she limped home on the monstrous-heeled, red things; "it is wearisome being of such a small size that even when I was a babe my father, who studied the Latin language, named me Dimidia, which he said meant 'half;' for one so small as I, appeared to be but a portion of a child."

Filippe laughed as he looked admiringly at the fair piece of vanity beside him, while he made some complimentary remark about little fairies.

"I have brought Tête Rouge a small present, as well," de Maureaux remarked, after the Denys household had well admired the new red shoes.

"That is very kind of you," exclaimed Rhoea, turning eagerly to look at the tiny packet he produced from his pocket.

"There, I hope it may please you," he said, holding up a beautifully carved, broad gold band, in which had been set a single stone.

"Oh no, oh no, please not. Oh no," and to the amusement of Filippe and Dimidia, Rhoea turned shuddering from the gemmed gift.

"But why, do you not like it?" he asked.

"I—I do not know why, but for some reason an opal affrights me," she told him, her white face and terrified eyes bearing out her statement.

"Me, I adore such stones," broke in Dimidia, eyeing the milky bauble in which red fires flashed, with a longing not to be denied.

"Then you had best accept it, and I must look for some other thing that may chance to please Tête Rouge," laughed Filippe, presenting the delighted Dimidia with the ring that he had ordained for her sister.

Thinking the outing would do her good, Rhoea took her sister to Versailles, where she had to journey in order to deliver a fan, for no less a personage than the famous Madame de Maintenon.

The beauty of the palace grounds caused the eyes of the two girls to glitter, for hundreds of fountains were playing on the groups of gods and goddesses which the genius of sculptors had erected on rocky mounds in the centre of marble basins; the shady grottoes and stately walks, as well as the wonderfully picturesque gardens, designed by the famous Mansard himself, delighted them. In the palace was such luxury and splendour, curiously intermingled with discomfort, that at one moment they would be over-awed at the magnificence of pictures, tapestries, rich hangings and lavishly decorated furniture, and in the next, would wonder how the inhabitants could exist without fires, or see by the aid of the one poor tallow candle allowed them.

Madame de Maintenon commanded the girls to be brought to her in her own apartment, where they found her seated near the window at her spinning-wheel, her legs encased in bags filled with straw, in order to keep warm, for not even this great lady was permitted more than a very meagre allowance of firewood.

She received her humble visitors with the great kindness for which she was famous, her own childhood having been so harsh that she was ever ready to speak gently to children; praising the beautifully carved gold fan, with its exquisitely painted satin leaves, and paying the price with some extra *sous* for the bearers, and spending some minutes in questioning them as to their lives; then, as she was about to dismiss them, there arose great excitement and commotion, and in walked King Louis himself.

Rising from their curtsies, the girls would have departed, but His Majesty stayed them, while he interrogated Madame de Maintenon regarding her visitors.

"So you make fans?" he smilingly asked, turning to Rhoea and Dimidia.

"Yes, Monsieur," Rhoea answered.

"And you, little fairy, what is it you find in me to make you stare so?" he smilingly demanded of Dimidia, whose blue eyes were gazing wonderingly at the immense wig the king was wearing.

"Sure I am thinkin' if that hair is your own, it must pain you to untangle it," she replied, quite unabashed. Nor was she at all overcome by the laughter her pert answer produced, prattling gaily half in French, half in English with the royal gentleman.

"This must surely be the Tête Rouge of whom Saint Ruipi has spoken," commented Louis, regarding Rhoea.

"Yes, for it was from Marquis du Buisson I learned of the fan shop," agreed Madame de Maintenon.

"Alas, it is not only my head that is fiery, but my grandfather says my temper, too, is that way inclined," Rhoea confessed.

"A pretty trial your poor grandparent must have to be inflicted with two such maidens," and as the King spoke his eyes rested first on one and then on the other slim figure before him, while Madame de Maintenon, noting his interest, grew uneasy. "You must tell him that should he desire to be relieved of his responsibility, this palace is large, and can well-accommodate any who are interesting or amusing," quoth His Majesty.

"I would like fine to live here," cried Dimidia quickly.

And all the way home she spoke to Rhoea of nothing else, and now her discontent with the small shop and its apartments increased daily. From that period she began to scheme as to how she could enter the palace as an equal. To this end she devoted much time to questioning Ugiso, and when she learned that he remained away from the magic Court circle from choice, she never ceased pestering him to abandon his self-inflicted toil and take his proper place in life, and his refusal to do so, led to quarrels. The acrimonious abuse she heaped on the sensitive youth's head, caused him to fall into such a state of despondency that he became more like his former weak self, and the whole household suffered accordingly.

"Ugiso, why are you so feeble, why do you allow Dimidia to plague you?" demanded Rhoea impatiently, on one occasion, after Dimidia had teased the youth until he had become fretful and ill-tempered.

"I am not feeble," he protested; I could be strong-willed an it pleased me."

"By my faith, I wish it would please you, then," cried Rhoea.

"It may some day, but I mislike the exertion it would cause me," then he became peevishly obstinate, and demanded to be left in peace.

All this trouble, with the extra work entailed by Rhoea's inability to apply herself to helping in making the fans, which her arduous housekeeping tasks prevented, enfeebled Monsieur Denys, and his health caused Rhoea grave concern; many days the blind man was unable to leave his bed, and work fell in arrears, and so naturally, money became more scarce.

This last deprivation vexed Dimidia exceedingly, and she eternally sulked, wept, or grumbled.

Tullia di Masino and Saint Ruipi were not favourites of Dimidia's, neither did they care for her; on the contrary, she and Madame Valeron became very excellent friends, and nothing delighted her more than to go driving with the widow in her luxurious carriage, very often accompanied by the Comte de Maureaux, or other young gallants who considered it legitimate sport to make fatuous love to the vain little *bourgeoisie,* who tossed her golden curls delightedly at their inane compliments.

"Rhoea, the good Madame Valeron is taking me to the theatre to see Madame de Caylus in the play of *Esther;* you would not have me go in this shabby gown, and disgrace you, now would you?" coaxed Dimidia one morning, and Rhoea, who was worked to a shadow, her nerves at a tension from trying to keep out of debt, and yet supply her ailing grandfather with luxuries, while she nursed him and soothed the fretful Ugiso, told her half-sister curtly that she must be content with the clothes she already had.

" 'Tis jealous you are, because Filippe prefers my company to yours," taunted the disappointed damsel, playing pointedly with her opal ring.

There is nothing annoys like the truth, and the jibe contained some degree of veracity, for Rhoea had long noticed that Comte de Maureaux seemed to find more delight in the society of this butterfly than he did in hers.

"That is a wicked thing to say," she blazed quickly.

"Well I know that you hoped to marry him, but that he will never do," jeered Dimidia.

Like a flash Rhoea's hand descended on the pink and white cheek of her tormentor.

"Oh!" cried the assaulted one, and again, "Oh! you cruel, ugly virago."

"Dimidia, little sister, forgive me; I am sorry, please, please forgive me," begged Rhoea, her hasty display of temper over.

"That I will not, and you will see I shall have my revenge," panted the offended maiden, backing away from Rhoea's proffered embrace. With great show of wounded pride, she turned and walked into the street.

Late that evening Saint Ruipi came to tell Rhoea, who had been fretting at her sister's absence, that Dimidia was spending the night beneath the roof of Deseré Valeron.

"The poor little thing, I struck her," confessed Rhoea, whose eyes were red from weeping.

"So she said," admitted the Marquis dryly, "and doubtless, well she deserved it," he added consolingly.

"No, I should not have done such a thing; please tell her how sorry I am, Monsieur," begged Rhoea.

The following noon, Dimidia drove up to the shop in Madame Valeron's carriage, not to stay, but merely to collect a few things before returning to the more luxurious dwelling, which pleased her better than the shop.

Before departing, she smiled at Rhoea, which Tête Rouge took as a sign of forgiveness, and was greatly relieved.

During the next week, the shop was not visited by Dimidia, and, as now Monsieur Denys was unable to leave his bed at all, Rhoea was rather glad than otherwise of her frivolous sister's absence.

One day, requiring money for something her grandfather needed, she reluctantly approached her hidden treasure, to which she had been unable to add anything for many months; to her bewilderment the corner where her money had been concealed was empty, and search as she might, not one single *sou* could she find.

Ugiso was sitting in the shop with Tullia di Masino when, in despair, Rhoea entered to tell him of her loss.

"That explains where the little monkey obtained her wealth from," exclaimed di Masino.

"Of whom do you speak?" asked Rhoea, her heart sinking heavily, for at his words, she knew at once Dimidia must have been the thief, on the day after she had been struck.

"Mam'selle Dimidia," he spoke the name she expected, yet dreaded to hear; "she purchased for herself a most ravishing gown, and a gold comb worthy of a Court lady. Being conversant with her affairs, and well knowing that the handsome widow is not over-generous with her money, I wondered on seeing her so gaily adorned," di Masino acknowledged.

Rhoea covered her face with her hands and groaned, she felt life was very hard.

"How now, what ails Tête Rouge?" queried the Marquis du Buisson, entering at that moment.

"Many of us were struck with the richness of her dress at the theatre," he said, after Tullia had told him of Rhoea's loss, and the cause of it.

"It is most unjust," she protested indignantly.

"That, my poor Tête Rouge, is not for us to say," gently reminded Saint Ruipi.

"But why should I have all this trouble to bear?" fretted Rhoea.

"Ah, why?" di Masino shrugged his shoulders, and spread out his hands expressively.

"Who can tell why these trials are sent; it must be the good God, whose ways are just but inscrutable, deems them right for us," Saint Ruipi spoke thoughtfully.

"But is it right that Monsignor di Masino should spend the best years of his life in prison for no crime? Is it right that I, who love life, and the good things in it, should be forced to toil and strive with no relaxation, or pleasure, while others go gaily on their way, freed of all responsibilities?" cried Rhoea resentfully.

"We know so little, Tête Rouge, we know so little," sighed the Marquis du Buisson. "I would beg of you, whose young life is filled with heavy burdens, which you have ever borne so nobly, to bear up bravely now, so that the good you have done shall not be undone," he counselled.

"Why should I not abandon all responsibilities and go, too, to enjoy myself?" demanded Rhoea; "and never, no, never, shall I welcome that wicked one back here," she declared vehemently.

"So that the good you have done may not be undone," musingly, di Masino repeated Saint Ruipi's words. "Yes," he continued thoughtfully, "those are wise words, and the good our little friend here has accomplished in her humble way may have vast bearings on many lives, far more than she will ever know of."

"How can any little thing that I do affect other people?" asked Rhoea curiously.

"A poet who lived and died long, long ago in my beloved Italy, wrote:

'The perfumed gardens are thrown open wide.'

and also I mind me of these lines:

'In curious fountains plays the water clear,
Throws its fair streams, and glistens far and near.'

Beautiful thoughts are these; for a garden that has been well tended and cultivated with care, not only delights the owner, but the soft and soothing odours which he permits to float out through the open gates, must give joy to many, as must the glistening waters playing in the fountain. Flowers and fair streams, ah, yes, they are as refreshing and far-reaching as good deeds, pure thoughts. Then, my Tête Rouge, if you will permit, there are still more of this same poet's words I would quote:

'A woman sitteth to spin at the window,
She stayeth her hand, and tangled the thread.
Spoiled is the thing which she had begun.'

Sad, that, do you not think?"

"Ah, yes, poor woman," agreed Rhoea.

"Dimidia is very young and thoughtless," commented Ugiso.

"Tell my little sister her chamber is kept ready for her, when she cares to return to it," Rhoea whispered to Saint Ruipi, ere he departed, and, raising his hat, he reverently kissed her toil-worn hand.

CHAPTER XXXII

But Dimidia never did return to reside at the fan shop in the Rue du Bac. To be sure she paid Rhoea a visit on the death of her grandfather; curt and very brief was her stay, for she had married the Comte de Maureaux, and developed into a fashionable lady, becoming such a stickler for her rights, that on one occasion, rather than permit some truly great lady to precede her at a ball given by Louis at Versailles, she lay abed for two whole days, feigning an illness in excuse for not obeying the Royal command to present herself at the affair.

All Paris laughed at the vagaries of the sixteen-year-old Comtesse de Maureaux.

Following the lead of their King, the courtiers petted and spoiled Dimidia, encouraging her in her impertinences, and extravagances.

Her fashion of hairdressing, which suited her piquante face, that of parting it in the centre and wearing it in bunches of curls over either ear, became the mode, and it was the little Comtesse who named the round black patches of black silk or velvet "Assassins," while those worn near the nose she called the "Brazen," and near the mouth the "Kisser."

"And what might that one be termed which reposes so happily by your lower lip?" asked Louis one day.

"That, Sire, is the 'Discreet,' and this one near my dimple shall be known as the 'Sprightly,' but if your Majesty were to wear one on your forehead, it would well become you, and would ever be known as the 'Majestic,'" she informed him pertly.

"You have taken quickly to Court life and its ways," he commented amusedly.

"It is the only one I care to live; I adore it," Dimidia said enthusiastically.

"And your sister with the wonderful hair, what of her?"

"I have no sister, Sire, only a distant connection by marriage, whose ways were not mine, whose life I could not lead," she spoke sadly.

"Poor child," the King laid his hand sympathetically on her golden head.

"I am to be envied rather than condoled with, in having so generous a friend as yourself, whose kindness emboldens me to crave of you a favour," she said cunningly, always quick to take advantage of the moment.

"What is it you desire?" he asked.

"No less a thing than your Majesty's presence at my masquerade," she informed him.

The Comtesse de Maureaux held her head still higher, and became more arrogant than heretofore, on the King agreeing to become her guest at the magnificent masquerade which she had planned to begin at six in the evening, and was to be on a most lavish scale, the fireworks alone, costing a fortune, and the illuminations on the lake, where Dimidia had planned a midnight regatta, coming to such a sum, that Filippe frowned thoughtfully on hearing the price.

Invitations to festivals given by "Madame du Toupet" (which name she had well earned by her impertinences) were eagerly sought after, for one was sure to be well amused by any entertainment engineered by the Irish lady, who was never at a loss for ideas, which, with the vim and exuberance of youth, she carried through to a successful conclusion; as, for instance the incident which occurred during the early hours of one morning, when a ball she had given was nearing its end, and yawning guests who had fatigued themselves with dancing, were about to depart, she suddenly conceived the notion of stopping the peasants who were driving their cows in to be milked, and instituted a milking competition, into which the magnificently arrayed guests in their paint, powder and patches entered heartily.

Another of her daring escapades had taken place at six o'clock one summer's morning when, in order to rouse her jaded guests, she suggested a race, in which the ladies, mounting the boxes with cavaliers beside them, placed the coachmen and lackeys inside the carriages, and drove at break-neck speed through the startled Paris streets to an allocated destination. A merry race that, the upsetting of milk cans and vegetable barrows, which the slow-moving peasants had not been able to place safely out of the way, adding to the fun of the thoughtless aristocrats.

Ah yes, the fair Comtesse de Maureaux could always be relied on to amuse. Her sharp speeches, to which her soft Irish brogue added charm, were repeated far and wide, gaining for her, reputation as a wit.

She chafed incessantly under any restraint that kept her from taking precedence of even Royalty. Madame de Maintenon was a thorn in her side, for, as the King's favourite, the great and gentle lady came before Dimidia, and the chagrined Comtesse could not drop her out of her invitations as she had done poor Madame Valeron, for the latter was no longer considered aristocratic enough for "Madame du Toupet" to associate with.

"'Tis a pretty thing that I should be taken to task for refusing to admit the plebeian widow of a common velvet merchant," she sneered disdainfully to her husband, on his interceding for Deseré Valeron, who had called at the palatial residence where her one-time protégée now dwelt in regal state, and been refused admittance by order of Madame la Comtesse. "It is suffi-ciently galling for me to be forced to countenance la Scarron, whom the King has named de Maintenon, for it was a friend of the Aubignés herself, who recounted to me how Françoise de Maintenon, before Paul Scarron took pity on, and married her, was no more than a minder of turkeys in a farm-yard; a fine thing truly, that this one who wore wooden shoes and a mask over her face to guard her complexion, whose only sceptre was a wooden rod to drive the fowls, should now take precedence of me."

And Filippe, remembering the humble origin of his wife, laughed amusedly at her scornful words.

However, although she invited Madame de Maintenon to her masquerade, she scored a victory by obtaining secret per-mission from Louis, to enjoy the distinguished privilege of wearing the same colours in her costume on that occasion, as he himself sported, and furthermore, had the supreme satisfaction of seeing Madame de Maintenon's fair cheeks flush painfully when she noted this significant fact of Royal favour.

Rhoea heard of her half-sister's doings from Saint Ruipi, and other courtiers who visited the shop where she toiled inces-santly, with the aid of a hired assistant, in order to pay off the debts she had been forced to incur during her grandfather's illness.

When Monsieur Denys died, there had arisen a discussion as to the propriety of Ugiso remaining on under the same roof with so young a girl as Rhoea; but the mere suggestion of de-parting had caused him such suffering, and thrown him into so high a fever, that all talk of his departure had been dropped, and he remained on, immersed in his painting.

"I cannot live like this for ever," Rhoea said one day, when her two faithful friends, Saint Ruipi and di Masino, had come as usual to sit and chat with her, and Ugiso in the shop. "I shall continue my fan-making until all debts are paid, and then, leaving Ugiso in charge of the business, shall make another life for myself."

"In what manner will you employ yourself, Tête Rouge?" inquired di Masino.

"I shall become an actress," she announced decidedly.

"A *métier* for which your voice and figure make you admirably suited," the Italian agreed.

"The work would be hard, and the life not one I would care to see you associated with," Saint Ruipi demurred.

"At the Hôtel de Bourgogne a countryman of mine is producing plays, I could speak to him of you," offered di Masino.

"No, it would be better, if Rhoea is bent on this project, that she should become attached to the Illustre Théâtre," Ugiso pronounced as his opinion, "for Molière is a great artist, and would help her well."

With this end in view Rhoea worked industriously, and might have achieved her latest ambition, only for an event which occurred just about the time she was deciding that, all debts paid, she could abandon the shop, and take up her new career.

With some excitement, she heard from Ruipi of the birth of a son to her half-sister.

"What happiness for her; how wonderful!" she cried delightedly.

With great eagerness she questioned the Marquis du Buisson, but he could tell her very little beyond the mere fact that the birth of the child had taken place.

For the first time since Dimidia had married, Rhoea called at the great house of de Maureaux, but the Comtesse refused to see her, and with tears in her eyes Rhoea returned to the

Rue du Bac, her heart hungry to kiss and embrace her new nephew.

Some weeks later, towards dusk, when Rhoea was seated alone in the shop, which she had completed arrangements to leave, for the Illustre Théâtre, where the great Molière, on Ugiso's intervention, had promised to receive her, a closed carriage stopped at the door, and from it descended a soberly-clad little figure, heavily veiled, and carrying in her arms a bundle.

"Yes, Madame?" questioned Rhoea.

"My sister, do you not know me?" asked Dimidia, for it was the Comtesse de Maureaux who had entered.

"Dimidia, oh, how good of you!" Rhoea cried joyfully, then, as she embraced the small form—"surely—oh, is that the baby you have with you?" she asked, almost breathless with excitement.

"Yes, take it," and as though pleased to be rid of a burden, which she was holding for the first time, she placed the babe in Rhoea's only too willing arms; the opal stone in the ring on her ungloved hand catching a portion of the child's fragile clothing, tore a spiteful rent in the tiny garment, and Dimidia, disregarding the rent garment, looked quickly to see that the thread had not loosened the red-gleaming jewel.

"The dear, tiny thing, how you most love him!" said Rhoea wistfully, as she raised the covering that lay over the infant's face, in order to kiss the morsel of humanity.

"Children are a great trial, and cause one much suffering," complained Dimidia.

"Poor little mother," soothed Rhoea, her eyes never leaving the face of the sleeping babe, "but any pain must be worth going through for such a treasure as this," and again she softly kissed the wrinkled face.

"You do not know what you are talking about, for you have never brought a child into the world," Dimidia spoke pettishly.

"True, but I could conceive no greater joy than having a child of my own," said Rhoea softly.

"I have not found it so," and Dimidia's voice was contrastingly harsh.

"But——do you not love your son?" asked Rhoea wonderingly.

"I hate the brat!" Rhoea shuddered at the unkind words, no less than at the tone in which they were uttered.

"Dimidia!" she gasped.

"It is true; here do I put myself to all the inconvenience and pain of bearing a child, so that the de Maureaux name and title may be perpetuated, and what arrives, but a wretched deformity. It is cruel, cruel, I tell you; I wish it had never lived," she finished bitterly.

"A deformity, this poor mite——"

"Yes, that poor mite," mimicked the exasperated mother. "I could strangle it, only that I am a good Catholic, and besides, too many know it lives," she asserted coolly.

"How can you talk thus; it is not the babe's fault," admonished Rhoea. "In what way is he deformed?" she asked, after a moment's silence.

"It is malformed, with a crooked back, plague take it!"

"Oh, the poor little thing; how terribly sad; but surely that should only make you love him the more," rebuked Rhoea, holding the tiny bundle still more tenderly, while a softer light suffused her eyes.

"Love it! I hate it, I tell you; I could scarce bear to hold it on the journey hither," she admitted, with a hard laugh.

"And what does your husband say?" inquired Rhoea.

"Filippe is doubtless as disgusted as myself, but men do not see these things as we sensitive women do. He is inclined to be sorrowful about the thing, rather than offended. I have let him know very plainly that he cannot expect me to keep it beside me; my faith no! that would be a pretty disgrace, and a constant source of annoyance," Dimidia spoke fretfully.

"Then what do you intend doing with the pitiful babe?" asked Rhoea.

"Letting it die, for aught I care," the callous mother answered coldly.

"You could not be so wicked." Rhoea was horrified.

"If you would save me from such a sin, keep the brat out of my sight for a short time, until I may become reconciled to the infliction of a hunchbacked child," suggested Dimidea.

"You cannot be serious!" gasped Rhoea.

"Indeed I am that; it was only the thought of your softheartedness, upon which I depended to take pity on me, that gave me courage to carry the thing here this evening," the self-absorbed Comtesse admitted bluntly.

"But what could I do with a child?" asked Rhoea, bewildered.

"Much more than I could. After all, you are older than myself, and will be better able to deal with it than I," it was truly Madame du Toupet who spoke.

"Your husband, what would he say to such an arrangement?"

"He has faith in you, and will consent, of that I am very sure. I wished to send the thing into the country, where I need never have seen it again, but he exhibited such unreasonable stubborness; even though I endangered my health by screaming like one demented, and weeping a veritable river of tears, still he would not agree to the brat being hidden in the country. You must consent, Rhoea, for after all it was because of your cruel blow that I left here, and so married Filippe, and now have this infliction, and if you do not help me, you may have the sin of its death on your soul," she warned cunningly.

It was only some hours later, when Rhoea had ensconced the abandoned babe in a hastily manipulated cot, where it slept peacefully, that it dawned on her that this fresh care would necessitate the postponement of her prospective change of plans.

Then, as the infant stirred and wailed feebly, Rhoea bent crooning over it, her heart welling over with tenderness for the deformed and despised mite.

CHAPTER XXXIII

The "short time" which Dimidia had suggested Rhoea's keeping her child grew into weeks, then months, for every time there was any talk of the mother retaking her offspring, she begged for just a little longer respite, and out of pity for the tiny hunchback Rhoea consented to retain the burden.

But the Comtesse de Maureaux had not the faintest intention of ever again receiving back her son; she was far too busy to be troubled with such an undesirable responsibility, which she sought to forget in a continual round of gaieties. Her passion for card- playing caused Filippe grave uneasiness, for she lost heavily, especially at a game called *lansquenet*, of which she was particularly fond.

Many people were cajoled into paying her debts, Louis himself on more than one occasion settling the score for her, and at one period even Madame de Maintenon, taking pity on the fragile-looking Comtesse de Maureaux, found the money of which she wept she was so sadly in need, on her promising never again to gamble, a promise which, needless to say, she did not keep.

This obsession of hers drove her once more to the Rue du Bac, where she arrived after dark.

"No, I have not come to see that thing," she quickly replied, in answer to Rhoea's question as to whether she wished to see her son; "in fact, Rhoea, I have come to question you on a matter which has ofttimes been in my thoughts, regarding our grandfather's affairs."

"What of them?" asked Rhoea.

"As I remember, he made quite a satisfactory sum from his fans. Now surely I, who was equally his granddaughter with you, am entitled to my share of what he left," was the brazen suggestion that met the astounded ears of Rhoea and Ugiso, who was present at this interview.

"Our poor grandfather left nothing but debts," Rhoea informed her curtly.

"Oh, come, come, Rhoea, if I insisted on my rights and had this matter thrown into equity, I could not be put off with such an answer, for there is the stock he left, as well as the goodwill of the flourishing business he built up by his own efforts," protested Dimidia.

"Assisted by Rhoea," Ugiso reminded her.

"Of course, Rhoea worked well, so did I, before she drove me away by her harsh treatment. Believe me, I am reluctant to speak in this manner, but right is right, and I am sadly in need of money," she sighed.

"Filippe has plenty," Ugiso remarked brusquely.

"He may have, for all the good I get from it; he has developed an incredible niggardliness, and refuses to allow me enough to cover my daily needs," complained the spendthrift Comtesse.

"The sale of the whole of this shop and its contents, would not supply you with one of your ordinary day's expenses," commented Ugiso.

"Still it should be mine," insisted Dimidia.

"So should the expenses of your child," he told her bluntly.

"By my faith, this is a pretty thing!" fumed the Comtesse, "when my own sister not only refuses to give me my just dues, but grudges the trifle it takes for the upkeep of a helpless babe."

"No, that I do not, but if you fulfil your threat and have this place divided, how, and where am I to keep the child?" asked Rhoea desperately.

"La! la! Do not plague me with such details," fretted the grand lady; then Rhoea ran to comfort the babe, who, newly awakened, was wailing loudly, leaving her sister alone with Ugiso.

"You think I am very hard, Ugiso," she said, leaning across his work-table and stroking his face with her delicately white hand, "but in truth you do not know to what straits I am pushed for money," she said softly.

"Curtail your expenses," advised Ugiso, disregarding the gentle caress.

"Oh, cruel," she pouted, "a lady of fashion has great calls upon her purse, that neither you nor Rhoea can know of. But stay" (she added as an afterthought), "you must have some knowledge of what expenses I am put to, for I had forgotten you were one of us in your youth," Madame du Toupet patronized, and Ugiso laughed.

"Do you assist me, Ugiso," she coaxed.

"I have no money now," he told her gruffly.

"Your mother has wealth; much of it is yours, so I have heard," and she continued to caress his ear and cheek, watching him narrowly.

At length, in order to save Rhoea from being further importuned, he reluctantly promised to visit his mother, and see what he could do for the greedy Comtesse de Maureaux.

Madame d'Elbrai, who had aged very rapidly, and now spent her time in churches at confession, and playing at being a *religieuse,* welcomed her son with open arms.

"You come in answer to my prayers," she told him sanctimoniously, "for I had been on the point of sending for you. Your Uncle Pierre, whom you know is a recluse, and moreover possessed of great wealth, is ailing and like to die; then, my beloved son, you will once more have the riches that will aid you to restore our shattered fortune," and even as she spoke, Madame d'Elbrai decided that there was no immediate need to prepare her soul for death, that after all, with fresh opulence, the world had still some claim upon her.

However, Ugiso would not comply with her entreaty, but after raising a few hundred *louis* for Dimidia, he returned to his painting at the shop.

But his mother did not despair of ultimately persuading him to return and share his coming legacy with her, and to prepare against a return to her fashionable world, the poor lady took a bath, and died.

"My poor Ugiso," soothed Dimidia, on calling to condole with him on the loss of his parent, "it is very sad for you, but your mother should not have been so indiscreet. I cannot think what induced her to do so dangerous a thing, for she was not ill," and indeed, all the Court circle marvelled as to what could have possessed Madame d'Elbrai to commit such a crazy act as to take a bath.

Very soon after his mother's sad demise, the recluse uncle died, and Ugiso fell heir to a very great fortune, and Dimidia pestered him incessantly to leave the shop and return to his proper station in life. Only in part did he yield, for the major part of his time he still remained over the work that pleased him best.

Gradually, the Comtesse de Maureaux enticed him more and more into her life.

All talk of the babe being taken back to its parents' home had ceased, and Rhoea, who had become sincerely attached to the little weakling, nursing it through its childish ailments, and tending it as nurse and mother in one, had abandoned all thought of doing more with her life than looking after her half-sister's child; all fears for its health she bore alone, for on several occasions when the sickly infant was attacked by childish maladies, and Rhoea had sent post haste for one or other of its parents, Dimidia had refused point blank to obey the summons, and Filippe had presented himself tardily, if he happened to be in Paris, but as he spent most of his time hunting in the forests, he seldom heard of his son's illnesses until they had passed.

One night when the little boy had arrived in his second year, he was seized with so choking a croup that Rhoea was concerned for his life; unavailingly she tried every simple remedy known to her.

She was alone in the place, Ugiso having been carried off by Dimidia to attend a banquet and *bal-masqué* that was to follow it, therefore, there being no one whom she could send to summon aid, she wrapped the suffering child warmly in her long black cloak, and carried it swiftly to a physician.

The good man employed all his skill in aiding her to relieve the choking child, but he proved powerless to save it, and an hour before midnight the little hunchback lay rigid and breathless, its short life lived out.

Well nigh crazed with grief, Rhoea, wrapping the meagre figure in her cloak, fled with it to its mother's mansion.

The hour was late, and the festivities were in full swing. All was magnificence and illumination, when Rhoea, narrowly missing being overrun by crashing coach wheels and confused by the torches and shouts of lackeys, dashed into the entrance-hall among her sister's guests.

Flowers, lights, brocades, music, dancing, a perfect whirlwind of gaiety and excitement greeted her.

The large cloak she wore caused her to pass unnoticed, for many of the masquers were clad in like attire; in the crush, the poorness of her own going unremarked. Oblivious to everything excepting the little corpse she held out of sight, she went wildly from room to room searching for the dead babe's mother.

Many a gay guest sought to detain her with quip and jest, some even laid hands on her, but she pulled away, and went on her mad search.

She gained the great, glittering, flower-decked ballroom just at the hour of midnight, which was the stated time for all to unmask.

Laughter, and cries of merriment resounded as masks were torn from flushed faces. Looking wildly round, Rhoea spied a slim figure in the blue satin suit of a page, standing in the centre of the room; it was the Comtesse de Maureaux, and so well had she maintained her disguise as a pretty boy, that now her surprised and delighted guests thronged round her crying their congratulations.

Through the gay assemblage Rhoea pushed, and reaching her sister, threw wide her cloak, and before Dimidia realized what was happening she held in her arms the corpse of her hunchback son.

It was some moments before the merry, wine-soaked revellers realized that this was no jest, but a grim tragedy.

The laughter and cries died, an uneasy stillness descended.

Then Dimidia spoke.

"It is a poor crazed soul whom I have assisted," she said, betraying no trace of emotion, her clear treble voice quite calm. "She has been enamoured of some naughty man, with this result. The 'people' will ever ape their more discreet betters," she sighed, and laying the dead babe on the floor, she turned with a shrug of her shoulders to take the arm of her cavalier, at the same time calling a lackey, and ordering him to see the poor woman safely off the premises.

"Be gentle with the mad-woman," she warned, and these considerate words were counted as great kindness of heart in the gay little butterfly.

Dumbly, Rhoea picked up the inanimate form, and stumbled out into the night with it in her arms.

Before she left the room, the band struck up a lively air, and Dimidia, the gayest of all that gay concourse, floated away in a merry dance, laughing and jesting, causing the unfortunate incident to be forgotten.

CHAPTER XXXIV

The following day, while the Comtesse de Maureaux slept off her weariness pursuant on her night of tiring gaiety, Rhoea followed, as solitary mourner the funeral of the hunchback babe, and waiting until the earth covered the small coffin, laid a posy of white rosebuds on the diminutive grave before returning to the solitary shop in the Rue du Bac.

The death of the child left her feeling very old and lonely, for now Ugiso had practically deserted her, Dimidia having inveigled him into becoming her constant attendant, his money was useful to her, and under her sway he gradually sank back into the weakness of his early youth, spending most of his life in bed, under the influence of wines with which the Comtesse kept him generously supplied, paying for them from his own pocket; his freakish whims, from which Rhoea had rescued him, being retailed by Dimidia to her gay circle as jests of surpassing merriment.

The Widow Valeron, despairing of bringing the Marquis du Buisson to the point of a proposal, had accepted the hand and heart of a decrepit miser, whose wealth, added to her own, was her only solace in life.

So Saint Ruipi's mind was made up for him, and with a sigh of relief he entered an order of saintly brotherhood and became a holy monk, well pleased with his own piety.

At first, Rhoea told herself that she could not bear her solitary condition.

"I am so alone, so loveless," she complained to di Masino, who continued to come to the little fan shop as he had been used to doing when old Monsieur Denys was alive, and Ugiso worked there.

Rhoea made him this confidence, as she sat working over the fashioning of a fan, and he looked gravely and kindly at her with his great dark eyes that age did not seem to dim.

"Loveless," he echoed questioningly, "ah no, not that, my friend; you are beloved by the whole neighbourhood, they come to you in all their joys and griefs."

"It is true they all come here," admitted Rhoea; "they are very good to me," she added.

"And you are good to them, you are the trusted friend of a multitude, and mother to all the babies in Paris."

"Not quite all," laughed Rhoea. "I love little children, and the mothers credit me with great healing powers, so they run to me with their ailing babies as though I were a magician."

"You love them, and love is magic."

For a while Rhoea worked in silence, then——

"I become weary of this dullness," she burst forth, hurling the fan on which she was working far from her, "when I think of my ambitions, my life generally, of my dreams of greatness, I resent what I have become."

"And what have you become, my Tête Rouge?" asked Masino gently, employing the name he had given her so many years ago.

"A dull spinster, whom no one loves, but on whom every one calls when they need sympathy."

"Any who have calls on their hearts, cannot complain that they are not loved. You remember our talk of long ago, of the perfumed garden, and fair streams that gave delight to so many; you are like those beautiful things, and so, are as blessed as they."

"I want to receive, not to give. I want life as others know it. Why should Dimidia have all the good things in life, and I, nothing. Why should Ugiso desert me, who care for him as though he were in reality my brother, I, who alone sorrow over his weaknesses, and would help him overcome them. Why should I have had the care and grief of Dimidia's babe. In fine, why should I bear other people's burdens?" demanded Rhoea heatedly.

"How know you that these are other people's burdens, and not of your own making?"

"Mine!" Rhoea was more amazed than indignant at the suggestion.

"Yes, yours."

"To have those troubles placed on my shoulders is as unjust as was your imprisonment to you."

"How know you that our trials are unjust?" asked Masino gently.

"Are they not?" demanded Rhoea.

"God is just."

At Masino's remark, Rhoea gave an impatient exclamation, rising she recovered the discarded fan, then reseating herself worked feverishly. For a few moments there was a silence, which Masino broke, talking slowly and quietly.

"While I lay solitary in prison, having none with whom I could converse, I learned my soul; it was an interesting study; I was as a man who, having lived all his life in a small village, suddenly became a great traveller, learning other cities. The first few years of my incarceration, being young and head-strong, I cursed God, then I denied Him altogether. For (I asked of myself the question you have even now put to me) if there be a God, and a just God, why should I, who have harmed none, suffer for no fault of my own.

"Imprisoned there in that dark cell, I began to realize that stored up within me was a force. Put there by whom, for what purpose, were the questions I asked myself. Then I called on that force to help me, for I needed help, needed it desperately. Christ knows how I wanted help, and Christ gave it to me.

"He gave it in His own way, not in mine. Gradually it was borne in on me that this so transient life is given us in which to work out some great purpose of our Maker's. We are apprenticed to life as a father articles his son to an artisan.

"If the little work boy commits a fault, his master punishes him. But (I asked myself) what fault have I committed that the whole of my life should be ruined? 'The whole of my life.' That sentence haunted me. I fretted exceedingly as I dwelt on the brevity of this life. This turned my thoughts to the world-old worship of some Divine Being, for there has never been an æon in which humans did not worship a God.

"But, I argued, if there be a God, and we are part of Him, why is life so finite? Then it seemed as though the wax in the ears of my understanding had come away, so that I heard aright for the first time. The 'I' that is I is not this poor carcase that withers and rots, but an essence that will live for ever, that is part of the Divine Creator. Then, it was not God on whom I should turn and rail, but on myself, for I alone was the culprit, for no doubt remained in my mind but that this essence had existed before, and perhaps sinned deeply.

"Having committed sins, I must atone for them. In some past I had made my present, as now in this present state I am creating my future. It was all so simple, so glorious, that I shouted aloud with laughter, until my jailers, hearing the unusual noise, came running in haste to my cell. Ah well"—Masino rose slowly and picked up his hat—"it grows late. I must return to that cell, which I have learned to love."

Rhoea rose too, her eyes, which had never left Masino's face as he spoke, were shining, to her cheeks had come a flush of excitement.

"If, oh, if you are right," she breathed.

"In my mind there remains no doubt," smiled Masino.

"Then it may be the good God is letting me work out my own punishment for crimes of which in some forgotten period I have been guilty of; it might even be that I had harmed Dimidia and Ugiso——" she paused, her whole soul shone in her eyes, as she looked questioningly at the Italian.

"It may be even so, we can but conjecture, it is only God who knows."

"Yes—only—God."

Sixth Journey

CHAPTER XXXV

Listen, I will tell you the truth.

It will be hard to speak it all. Hard for you to listen in silence; to have patience with me, for I am an old man, and, God forgive me, not over blessed with patience. I never was, even when I was a young man, but that is a digression, it was not of myself I would speak, but rather of him, of my *poverino. Ohimè!* my poor boy. God rest his soul.

Again my recital will be rendered difficult from my accursed pride, for I like it not to tell of the things in my heart, but I shall do so. Again I beg of you to bear patiently with me, and to remember, when that patience is being sorely tried, that I, who have the pride of a Sicilian, and moreover that of my family, for, as you know, I am of the great and nobly born Torretta, which makes it doubly difficult for me to lay bare my heart before you, but this shall I do, nor spare myself in the telling. At the finish of my story I promise you a big surprise, so stay until the end, and Allessandro and Pico shall serve the little glasses of yellow Rosolio for you to sip, or, for those who prefer it, the sweet wine of Lipari—my own wine, made from the vineyards which my father left me.

Lipari wine! It is like bottled sunshine; drink, and tell me if I am not right.

And, as you drink, let a prayer go up from your hearts to the good God who has taken to Himself my boy. Yes, *my* boy. I defy any to deny me the right to call him mine.

You, *Sor* Michelo, and you, *Sor* Giulimo, have many years to your count, as have I myself, and you remember the things that happened long ago, and you others have heard the talk of what occurred in the grand family of the Torretta.

Per Bacco, you start with surprise to hear me, Ruipi, Baron Torretta, speak aloud in such a way, for you know that heretofore it meant death to any babbler who was indiscreet enough to let the idle sayings of his tongue come to my ears.

Although my heart is heavy, my eyes are undimmed with tears, and I remarked, as we rode through the castle gates, that many of you looked curiously at the clump of cypresses; you have heard, that is the spot where many unshriven souls lie, having gone to a hasty death dealt them by my hand, for their careless daring in speaking of that which disgraced the Torretta, my sister's shame.

I invited you into my castle to listen to the story of the boy whose funeral we have just attended, but to tell all, I am constrained to speak of his mother, my sister.

Has it occurred to you, my friends, that it is a strange thing so many of you best respected, and wealthiest citizens of the country, should have put aside your daily tasks to follow to his last resting place the body of an unnamed boy, a misshapen little fellow, who all his short life toiled as a *caruso* in the sulphur mines?

For that is all the little Ugiso was, a *caruso* among hundreds of other small ones, who are beaten back and forth, down into the black gulf, a sad, dark procession, who under the cruel whip of the *picconiere,* fill their sacks with sulphur, then, staggering under the great weight, they are forced to labour up the steps, their tiny backs bent, their naked breasts streaming with perspiration, their breath coming from their baby throats in whistling moans, up to the top, into God's sunshine.

You have seen them, how they must run to empty their sacks, then, not even pausing to look up, to rest for a breath of pure air, they must run swiftly back through Hell's gate, down into the foul pit that swallows up their young lives, deforms their puny bodies.

They do not know what it is to laugh, to play, to be gay.

And I, God help me, have battened and grown increasingly rich from the toil of these babes. I, who have fed well, have ridden down at my ease to pass the heavy moments in watching this inferno, watching it with the eyes of my head, not of my heart, feeling no remorse, no pity, not though I have seen these small workers fall exhausted, to die gasping in agony for a breath.

I cover my eyes with shame when I think of the deformed limbs, narrowed chests, twisted bodies, tortured eyes——

Then I have come back here, into this very room where you are seated now, to enjoy the cooling breezes that blow from over the plains, breezes heavily laden with the sweet perfume of citron and orange flowers, to sip my wine from the delicate glasses which you are honouring by using, to be waited upon by many servants, to listen to soothing music, to eat dainty foods, to bow my knee with smug sanctity before the altar of our Lord.

Gentle spirit of my soul, would that I could recall a space, however brief, of that time gone by.

Ben bene, we speak now of Ugiso, not of my remorse.

You have all heard talk of my sister, my only sister; much younger than myself was Dimidia, and so beautiful, like an angel she was with her white soft skin that made one think of the petal of a camellia, her great dark eyes. When first she opened those eyes on the world, she wished to rule; she made as though the universe was her plaything. My father, my mother, the peasants, everyone had delight in spoiling the lovely child, she did what she pleased; always laughing was that one, just as Ugiso, her son, might . . . but that part comes later.

Dimidia had the pride that is born in all Sicilians, but in her case was added that of the Torrettas, and we gloried in the fact that she was so proud.

Recollect yourselves, how enraged she grew on hearing that the Christ the priest of Montedoro had prepared for the crucifixion at Easter time, was made of cardboard.

"Per Dio," she cried, "this is a pretty thing, if we of Montedoro must needs put up with a Christ of cardboard, while the very peasants of Campofraveo have a wooden Christ that does not melt in the rain. We, too, must have an image that will please the Blessed Virgin, otherwise great harm will befall us from the wrath of Mary the Mother. Truly, I would cover my face for shame, when I went to the church to pray to our Blessed Lady if we could do no better than this for Her Son."

And I, who had a leaning towards entering the Church as a holy man, I, *per Bacco,* applauded the little one's protest, and upheld her demand for a wooden Christ.

Perdone, I wax long-tongued, suffice it to say that my sister was a true Torretta, or so we thought, with all the fierce pride of our race. Then came a day . . .

My friends, I am weak, I cannot tell all that happened, of my sister's shame, nor does it concern you. Only this, my father drove her from Torretta Castle when he found she had disgraced his name, drove her out through the gates with curses and harsh words, nor did he care where she, and her unborn child were to seek shelter.

I, in my self-applauded holiness, deemed my father right. I felt that my own sanctity had been smirched by the sin of my sister, therefore, I too, turned from her, shaking her off, bidding her go, and never more to count me brother.

With scornful looks, and bitter speeches I bade her begone out of my sight. Then I sought my chamber, and sinking on my knees, called on God to forgive sinners.

Thinking, blind imbecile that I was, that the good God and his saints must surely listen to so pious an one as I deemed myself to be.

It was harvest time when all this happened, I remember it well, for, as I rose from my knees and looked out through the window, I could see the reapers, with their long scythes in their hands, their scarlet head-handkerchiefs showing well against the waving, yellow corn, singing as they laid low the ripe ears.

Then came clearly to my ears the words they sang:

Look out, comrades, for God is passing, and when He passes
He passes for all.
Look out, comrades, and prepare harmony, for the Lord is passing
*   me just now.*
Look out, reapers, the Lord is passing, and when He passes,
He leaves us His grace.
Come quickly, comrades, do not delay, for He wants to forgive thee.
Evviva; Evviva;
Praise God.

The scene pleased me. Away to the east stood the great, snow-topped Etna mountains, whilst below spread the plains of half Sicily, nearer to my vision lay the white, peaceful houses of Montedoro.

From the garden below my window the scent of thyme and

rosemary came to soothe my senses, mingled with the perfume of pale tea-roses and wild carnations.

Yes, the scene pleased me well.

Allessandro entered to inform me that supper was served, and speaking with that freedom which his lifetime of service to my family permits, said:

"The profile of your Excellency as you stand against the window, is as beautiful as a cameo."

And I smiled, with never a sigh of pity for my little sister. I smiled, I, who had deemed myself worthy to serve Christ . . . . *Perdone,* my friends. Allessandro, Pico, the wine of Lipari, the Rosolio. Replenish the glasses. So!

CHAPTER XXXVI

Although I refused to allow anyone to speak to me of my sister, refused fiercely, and, as you know, violently, still there drifted to my ears news of her, of how on leaving this Castle, none would give her shelter; partly, no doubt, fearing the wrath of my father and myself, and partly, knowing her condition, they deemed her a shameless woman.

A woman, *per Dio,* and the little Dimidia but sixteen years of age. It was the old witch Marietta, who gave her refuge in a forest hut. It was in this hut that she gave birth to a son.

The years went by, and I carefully suppressed any longing my heart inclined to, for news of my sister.

Still, whispers reached me of her.

When I heard she had still lower laid the Torretta pride, by marrying a peasant, my wrath against her blazed anew, and I killed any who dared mention her name in my presence. Yes, beneath that clump of cypresses lie the unshriven . . . ah well.

My father died, God rest his soul, soon after my sister left the Castle.

It was about this period that I became enamoured of the Contessa di Racalmuto.

You all know her, or of her. Her family is as ancient as my own, her beauty is the pride of Sicily.

I crave your indulgence, while I speak still of my affairs instead of that which I promised you, of Ugiso.

My nephew Ugiso.

You look with wonderment at one another when I speak thus, I, who am not worthy to claim the boy as a kinsman.

This talk of my affair with the Contessa must be told; it bears, as you will see, on what I have to tell you.

I visited Racalmuto, and became the very slave of my lady.

When I begged of her to bless me with her hand in marriage, she refused. She was rich, and growing richer, she lived for her money, and, telling me so with wonderful frankness, confessed she would marry no one whose fortune did not equal, or overshadow her own. I will pass over the time of doubt and suffering that came to me on hearing my beloved lady speak thus.

My love for her grew, until I became obsessed with the one thought, of how to rapidly increase my already large fortune, and so win the Contessa.

It was with this object I visited my sulphur mines.

Greater, and greater became my demands, until my overseers were driven well nigh crazed, until they in turn harried and shouted at their underlings; night and day we worked the mines, increasing the hours, and decreasing the pay, until the miners complained and became threatening, so that they were beaten, or turned away to starve. If any worker broke down, I grew fretful, not at his illness or death, excepting that it affected the output of the mines.

My life was now devoted to amassing money.

Money, and the thought of the Contessa di Racalmuto engrossed my every thought.

I would stand for hours and watch the *carusi,* those little boys, panting up from the mines with the loads that bent their young spines into permanent crooked backs, grinding my teeth impatiently if they faltered, or fell from physical exhaustion, calling on the *picconiere* to use his whip to egg his *carusi* on to greater efforts.

The few minutes allowed for the gangs of *carusi* to eat their morsel of black bread was grudged, so anxious was I to see the sulphur mounds grow big, to watch the ore being separated and moistened, to be made up into loaves.

I would bend over these loaves until the sun hardened them, and disregarding the law that forbids the burning of sulphur before the first of July, in order that the almonds and corn may not wither from the smoke, I would command the burners to melt the yellow stuff, that was to bring me in more, and still more money.

How I gloated over these pale yellow blocks, adding up in my mind how much more they were each day bringing to my pocket.

Then came the feast day of Saint Joseph, and no threats of mine, nor whips of my overseers, could keep the miners from attending the *festa* of their Saint, so the mines were left strangely silent, like a large city on the Sabbath.

Like a lost spirit I was wandering disconsolate among the mounds of drying sulphur, fretting at the waste of time, when I stumbled over a prone figure.

I snarl out a malediction, and look down.

It is a small boy, one of the *carusi.*

All of the *carusi* are small, it is the heavy loads on their backs that keep them stunted, and makes them grow misshapen, that gives them diseases, and weak chests.

They are small, yes, but this one that I knock my foot against is of the size of a little child not yet come to ten years, his face is of a yellow colour, much like the sulphur, his hair is black like a true Sicilian, but it is his eyes that I remember best, it was his eyes that I looked into as he lay in the dust.

A dirty young one, with a chemise that is torn and open, some pieces of cotton stuff round his legs.

Ah, well, all *carusi* are poor and have no clothes, but never a one of them had the eyes of this one. I learned afterwards that his eyes were blue, not a common colour among our people.

But at first I did not know the colour of his eyes, all I saw was—well, just those great eyes, with a something at the back of them.

"Ha, you stay back from the *festa* to steal, eh?" I call out at him. I had an evil mood, and wished to frighten, to hurt, to make suffering.

"No, Excellence, I do not steal." He give the answer most politely, and rising himself up, he makes the motion of kissing my hand, but with so dignified an air that I frown.

"No, then what do you, lying there?" I ask more loudly.

Still his eyes regard me with calmness, he has no fear, that little ragged one, and I knit my brows together at him. Now he is standing, and I see he has one crooked leg, like as though it had been broken some time, his shoulders too, are not straight, he would make one unhappy to look at him, but his eyes——

By the Holy Virgin I swear to you they make me, Ruipi di Torretta, feel as naught; he look right up at me.

"I make pictures," he tell me.

"Pictures! Of what?" but I am curious, and I look while we talk.

"Of my friend," he say quietly.

I see some markings on the dry slab of sulphur where he had been lying. I bend down, and for a long time I study that slab; I forget that little *caruso,* I forget there is a *festa* and my work is stayed, I forget my money, and, yes, I forget my beautiful Deseré, *perdone,* the Contessa di Racalmuto, whose baptism name is Deseré.

I look, and look, and I am lost in bewilderment, for the picture was so wonderful.

See now, I will tell you of it.

One figure floated in the air, it was the figure of Christ, but such a Christ, *per Dio,* the love and kindliness, it made my heart move, I shut my teeth hard, I cannot look away from that figure; it had great strength in the drawing too.

This Christ carried on his back a great cruel cross, His eyes were full of pity for the toiling figures of men and women who staggered along, weighted down by little, small crosses.

"This," I marvel to myself, "is all accomplished with a sharp piece of flint." *Davvero!* It is a miracle.

"Which is your friend?" I ask after a long time.

"Christ," he say, putting his finger so soft on the hovering figure.

"And you speak of the great Christ as your friend?" I say to him with contempt, and he laugh.

Now I will tell you the truth, I am pleased when I hear that laugh, for I am in an evil temper, and wishful to have something to vent it on.

"You dirty little boy, you misshapen one," I cry; "show reverence when you speak of the Son of God," I tell him.

"*Perdone,* Excellence," he say with much gravity, "I wish it not to appear I have no reverence."

"Then why make a laugh?" I ask with anger.

"Christ is my brother. He has said His Father is my Father. If your Excellence had a small brother or sister, you would like it that they are happy when they say your name, that would show they loved you, and were not afraid. I laugh when you say I am a dirty one, and am crooked, these things will cause Christ Jesu to love me the more." I say nothing, but look again at that picture.

"See," he say, kneeling down and pointing, "these poor ones, who struggle and groan under the little light weight of their troubles, while the Christ, with His heavy cross to bear, can still find it in His heart to grieve for them, although, well He knows that their burdens are as nothing. Me, I was one of those silly complaining ones when I was little," he added thoughtfully.

"You are none so large to-day," I remind him.

"I have fourteen years, Excellence," he told me proudly.

"Since how long a time have you worked?" I confess it, I was interested in this dirty, ragged one, with such eyes. Spirit of my soul, they held me like in a tight grip, I could not look away.

"Since six years now, Excellence."

I came quick away.

Dear Saints in Heaven, that *piccolino* had been toiling for a few *soldi* since six years.

Yes, I swear to you, I hastened away, back to my Castle, to eat the good food, to listen to the beautiful music, to gaze at my great pictures, to walk in my perfumed garden in order to divert my vexed thoughts.

All that night I tossed restlessly. Anger grew in my heart against this impertinent boy who had dared obtrude himself on my notice by lying under my feet.

His eyes haunted me.

Per Bacco! I was enraged against him.

CHAPTER XXXVII

After that *festa* day of Saint Joseph, when I go to the mines, I look for that *caruso,* and I watch to see if he work well.

"Ha, ha," I tell myself, "I will catch him wasting my time making his pictures again maybe, then I will send him away, for he will have proven himself a rascal."

But no, never can I catch him idle; hop, hop, he hurry along, his one leg being much more short than the other, still he keep up with the speed of his fellow *carusi,* his eyes are not looking to one side or the other.

At first I wished to trap him at some tricks, then I find myself possessed of a great longing to see those eyes again, and I watch and watch, until I see the *picconiere* speak among themselves, and regard me with strange looks, which makes me much more enraged against this little *caruso.*

Then one day I speak with the *picconiere* who is in charge of this gang of *carusi.*

"Why do you keep that very small, lame *caruso?*" I ask, and he look at me very funny——

"He works well, Excellence," he tell me.

"You speak for him, it may be he is your son." I make the remark to draw from that miner who the boy is.

He look hard into my face for a moment, then he give a strange smile——

"No, he is no son of mine, Excellence."

"Who then are his parents?" I was forced to put the straight question.

"His mother is the wife of Ludovico, there are many children, and Ludovico has a dry throat, and a thirst that is endless, his legs become unsteady before he can quench his thirst." The *picconiere* shrug his shoulders.

"Then this boy must work for his father," I suggest.

"For his mother, and her children. Ludovico is not the father of this one." I detected much meaning beneath the words, and moved away, as though I had no further interest in the *caruso* and his antecedents.

Later, I notice this *picconiere,* to whom I had spoken, whispering to his fellows, and laughing as at some great jest, and I knew they spoke of me.

After that, I avoided that part of the mine, but a strange thing had happened to me, I could not rid myself of thought regarding that one with his big, dark blue eyes.

Then an accident happened, it was nothing much, merely a boy had slipped on the steps as he was coming up from the mine, and the others, following, had fallen on him and crushed him badly; it often happens, and the work is delayed until they carry the hurt one out.

Thus it was I came on he who had occupied so much of my thought; he leaned, panting and coughing against the side of a mound; I stood and looked at him.

"I watch to catch you wasting time to make more pictures," I growl.

He look at me and smile, and, when he can speak for his cough, he say:

"No, Excellence, not since the day of the *festa.*"

"How acquired you the art of drawing?" I demanded.

"I do not know, Excellence. Always I have wished to make pictures." He looked fatigued, and the sweat poured down his narrow chest.

"Some one has given you teaching how to design?" I insisted.

"No. Ah, if I could have had lessons," and he sighed.

"You would like to be an artist?" I asked, and the tired seemed to vanish away, to his small face there came a great light.

"An artist," he breathed, "an artist, me! Oh, yes, Excellence."

"But you must work for your bread. Eh?"

The light went from his face, and in its place came an expression of great strength.

"It is good that I am strong, and can work," he declared stoutly.

"*Per Bacco;* your words are bigger than your body." I laugh.

"Indeed I am not a large size," he regretted, "but I have great strength," he added with confidence.

"You give all your earnings to your family?" I was curious.

"All except one *soldo.*"

A long time afterwards, I find out that this one *soldo* he put in the box for the Virgin Mary.

"Your mother is good to you?" I ask.

"My mother is an angel."

"Your papa, he drink too much wine, I hear."

He look at me very steady, and his face get red under the yellow skin . . .

"Piedro Ludovico is not my father," he tell me very grave.

"Your own papa is dead then?"

"I do not know, Excellence," and all the red departed from his face.

"What name was your mother's before she marry with Ludovico?" Something make me ask the question.

"Dimidia di Torretta," he say very slow.

Dear Mother of Christ! I know not how I felt when he say that name.

Every emotion rush through my being, I am dazed as though I would fall in a faint, I am amazed, and yet it was as though I had known that this *caruso* with the blue eyes of my sister must be her son. I am enraged that he should stand there so small and daring, and say aloud the forbidden name of Dimidia di Torretta.

Later on I grow surprised that this one boy out of all the hundreds of *carusi* should have come so strangely under my notice.

Now, when I get my breath, all I say to him in a voice of thunder:

"By what name do you call yourself?" My clenched fist was raised high, and I swear to you that had he answered "di Torretta," I would have felled him to the earth, the saints forgive me for my intention.

"Ugiso," he informed me.

"Ugiso what?" I insisted.

"Naught else, Excellence," and again the red blood flushed his face, although he did not lower his head, and his wonderful eyes did not leave my face.

I turned, I came quick away, nor did I visit the mines for three days.

Now I understand why the *picconiere* had looked at me so strangely, why he smile, what it was he found so amusing to tell his comrades.

He knew that it was my own nephew about whom I questioned him.

Madre di Dio, how I suffered during those three days. How I cursed my sister, and cried maledictions on the head of Ugiso.

Those days of agony! I gave no thought either to my beautiful Contessa nor to my wealth; only of my wounded pride, of my sister who had disgraced my name, of that boy.

No, no, my friends, do not go, I pray of you be seated. I but jumped up and struck my forehead, in that I suddenly perceived that I spoke too much of me, of my feelings, of my suffering.

See, I am calm once more, I crave your pardon. You are good to bear with me, to stay so silent.

I will endeavour to cut short my story, to tell you why I am boring you with my affairs. You will see. So.

The eyes of Ugiso drew me back, I returned to the mines, and walked swift and steady to where he worked.

"Come here," I bade him, and when he came I spoke long with him.

I passed through many months of torture. Sometimes I would stay away from the mines for weeks at a time. I would make myself come to the point of galloping down and turning him away, and forbidding him to ever again dare near my estates.

Yet always would the thought of him draw me to where he so bravely toiled, the sight of his thin body, the ribs! (one could count the ribs as they showed through the ragged chemise), the reedy arms, the limping leg, would tear my heart, the courage in his eyes would abash me.

Little by little I learned of his life; some of his story I heard from his own lips, other pieces from conjecture, or from those who were best acquainted with him.

With never a murmur of complaint, never a cry against his fate, he toiled diligently for the few *soldi* that he could earn, to help his mother, and her little children.

I tell you, the angels must have rejoiced in Heaven this day in receiving such a saint among them as was the little Ugiso.

We say no mass for the repose of his soul, ah, no, he does not need our prayers.

CHAPTER XXXVIII

It has already been told how my sister found a resting place with old Marietta of the forest, a good heart that ancient one must have carried in her decrepit body, but she was poor, and my sister had not been brought up to work, and Marietta could not afford to feed an idle mouth, and soon there was yet another one to be fed.

I will pass over the struggle the poor little despised mother had in trying to obtain work among the peasants. They all knew her shame, and closed their doors against her, neither did she have money to take herself and her *bambino* away from Montedoro, so it came to pass that she married Piedro Ludovico.

He was not a bad chap, this Ludovico, and knowing all, forgave his wife her past; he cared very much for her, and truly, I believe for her sake he tried to overcome the aversion he had conceived for her son, but this he was unable to do, more especially after his own children were born; it was then he spoke out, and demanded that Ugiso should be sent far away.

To this request my sister turned a deaf ear, she loved her firstborn, and would not part from him.

Then Ludovico took to drinking too much wine, and became extremely jealous of his wife's affection for the child that was not his.

The little Ugiso spent his time for ever making pictures, he was meant to be a great artist, that one.

He would lie for hours making marks on a discarded piece of paper with a morsel of charcoal, or on a stone, or bark of a tree with a piece of flint, anything would serve his purpose.

Ludovico seized upon this trick of the child's, on which to vent his anger, and he would destroy any pictures he found of Ugiso's, and would beat him if he discovered him so amusing himself.

There were three other children now, and Ludovico made a poor mouth at the expense he was put to of keeping another man's child.

At last it culminated in his taking the boy and putting him to work as a *caruso* in my sulphur mines; this he did with a purpose.

"For," he said, "let his grand-gentleman uncle pay for his hire."

It seemed a pretty jest to his drunken wit.

Dimidia wept bitterly at the putting of this tender son of hers to such arduous toil, and he having barely eight years to his count.

It was Ugiso himself who gave her consolation, he stroked her tear-wet face, and bade her not to weep, that he, her big son, would work well, and buy much bread for his adored mother and her children.

It was thus he spoke to her with a smile on his baby lips, which all his brave words could not keep from trembling, indeed his whole body shook with fear of the sulphur works, which, he has since told me, he dreaded with every fibre of his being.

He was highly strung, and of a sensitiveness incredible. I have gone deep into those early days of his, and he must have suffered veritable torture, and all his pain must be borne alone, for these two, the mother and son, found that her sympathy roused the drunken Ludovico to a pitch of brutality if he perceived so much as a look of sympathy in her eyes for her breadwinner on his return to the miserable abode he called home.

It does not seem possible that the few *soldi* the boy earned could mean so much, and yet such was the case, for more children came to Dimidia, and Ludovico drank increasingly; their poverty was great.

There was a young girl, the Virgin Mary reward her, who looked with pitying eyes on the son of my sister; she is the daughter of the Serrafia, Leco Serrafia is, as you all know a prosperous farmer, a good man, but narrow in his views.

This *signorina* would watch for Ugiso to pass by her father's fields, to give him a cheery word or a smile, and to press into his little palm a few olives, or an onion, or perhaps it might be a fig.

These acts of kindness sank deep into the boy's heart, they meant much to him.

Rhoea, for that was the name of the *signorina,* knew well of his passion for making pictures, and she procured for him a block of paper and a red coloured pencil.

Such treasures! The day he received them, he went on to the abhorred sulphur mines on dream wings; what pictures he could now make, how he clasped the precious things to his breast.

Alas, they brought him great misery.

The way of it was this.

The *picconiere* under whom this gang worked was a harsh man, and becoming enraged with the boys, accused them of neglecting their duties.

This was due to my having complained that he was not getting enough work out of his underlings, for it was at this period I had become engrossed in making great wealth for my beautiful Contessa.

I would go to her every evening and she would say: "How much?"

And if I was able to tell her that our output of sulphur was greater than the day before, her lovely eyes would shine with pleasure, and she would be very charming to me.

The *picconiere* on discovering the block of paper and red coloured pencil on Ugiso, became very wrath, and taking them from him, raised his heavily booted foot, and kicked the small boy as he stood at the door of the mine, which kick caused him to fall backwards down the steep steps, and thus it was his leg was broken, and he became a cripple.

The affair created no trouble, for who was there in this world to care, for the broken leg of a stray poor boy.

The father of the *Signorinia* Rhoea came to hear of his daughter's generosity, and he talked with sternness to her, forbidding her to speak with so terrible a person as this fatherless one.

"Tell me, Ugiso," I asked him when I came to know him well, as I did in the course of time, "did it not fret you that the help, the sympathy of *Signorina* Rhoea was taken away?"

"I had a pain in my heart at first," he confided gravely, "for I had come to depend greatly on her kind words, and smile. I will tell you the truth, Excellence, I was so young, so weak, that when it came night time, and no one could see, the tears would run down my cheeks. It was when I lay waiting for my leg to mend, and I had much time for thought."

"Tell me of those thoughts," I requested.

"The big thing in my life arrived to my mind one night. I saw how feeble I had been, how ready to dream and make the grand pictures, to eat the bread that I had not earned. I did not wish to work as a *caruso*. The good God saw this, and He must have said: 'Ha, this wicked idler must learn, he must be made to become strong.'

"Then, as I lay there I found much in my heart to make me content, therefore I cried no more. I must cure my own weaknesses, I must dry my own tears."

It was thus my nephew ever talked. No word of complaint ever passed his lips.

I do not change easily, but gradually I found that I looked on many things with a new vision. I went still to see my adored Contessa, but I no longer desired great wealth in order to win her.

Do not mistake me, *signores,* I loved her no less, *per Dio,* no!

So much did I love her, that I dared risk losing her by telling her the truth, rather than bask in smiles falsely won.

I told her that my zest for wealth had vanished. I writhed beneath her cold scorn. Her displeasure was hard to bear, and when she found I was not to be moved from my decision, that my whole life was not to be spent in amassing wealth, she refused any longer to receive me.

Ah, well, you are my countrymen, and have all loved in your time . . . .

Slowly I made many drastic changes in my mines, the hours were lessened, the pay greater.

My greatest reward came when I saw a look of pleasure in the eyes of my nephew on my approach.

At last I braced myself up for the great effort and visited my sister.

Blessed saints! how changed, how frail, how aged from the bearing and caring of her family. It gave me pleasure that, though she loved her children, Ugiso was the adored of her heart.

Despite her poverty, she was not altogether unhappy, she had found a true friend in the *signorina* of whom I have told you, Rhoea, the daughter of the farmer Serrafia.

Serrafia had allowed himself to become hot with the young girl, because she had refused to accept any man whom he chose as a husband for her. Her great desire had been to enter the Church, but to this her father would not give his consent, therefore she spent her life in the doing of charitable works. Nursing the sick, and tending to the needy. She loved Dimidia as though they were blood sisters.

Dimidia was merciful enough to forgive me for the harsh treatment of her, and was gracious enough to permit that I should lighten her load in various small ways. But for all my pleading she would not return to this castle, for her husband, who is never sober, refused to accompany her, and said that if she went she went alone, and her mother heart would not let her be taken from her family.

I begged leave to take Ugiso to live with me as my own son, and I put it to him, telling him of the advantages such a position would give him, for then he could follow his longing to become an artist. Big as was the temptation, Ugiso refused. Refused with courtesy, and gentleness, yes, but none the less he refused. He must remain with his mother, so he told me, and I, perforce, must bow my head to his decision, still I counted myself happy in having gained his friendship.

All the changes I wrought in the mines were rightly credited to the influence of Ugiso, and the workers called his name blessed.

It came so that the whole countryside heard of the crippled saint, who worked as a *caruso*. You yourselves, *signores*, have learned to love and respect him.

The angels in Heaven must rejoice at his coming to them, I said. Nay, the Blessed Mary and Her Son Jesu themselves will cry out with joy to see him among them.

One more word, and I have finished.

The cough, Ugiso had contracted through spending his childhood days breathing the fumes of sulphur, grew worse, his chest, his lungs were so affected, that at length he could no longer work.

As you, who came to visit him, know, I was never absent from his bedside.

Then one day a miracle happened, for there entered the poor abode where he lay so patient, so cheerful, no less a person than my beautiful Contessa.

How good, and gentle she was with my boy! *Ma che!* but how adorable she was; truly I had never loved her as I did then.

The evening of that day she sent for me, and on my obeying the summons, she told me that the avarice had gone from her soul. That my example, *my* example, note you, I who . . . ah, well I must refrain, and hasten to a finish.

Deseré . . . the Contessa di Racamulto, had fought with the demon of greed that had possessed her, and had conquered.

She wished for my aid to spend her money, every *soldo* of her great fortune, on those who were in need.

Holy Apostles, such a miracle.

Signores, I wish to tell you, that, although you will ever be welcome here at the Castle di Torretta, it is no longer merely the home of this selfish old man. No, indeed, it is to be kept open to receive any who are destitute. I would have it known throughout Sicily, that every poor boy will be welcome here as an honoured guest. If he has a longing to become an artist with the pencil or the brush, or to have training for singing, or a profession, then he shall have his desire.

It will be the coming here of any *carusi,* that will rejoice me most.

My boy, my Ugiso has departed. His body we have laid to rest in the earth, his soul is with God, his spirit he has left with us.

Signores, I have finished. I thank you for your kindly attention. See, the light breaks in through the East.

Signores, addio.

Seventh Journey

CHAPTER XXXIX

Doctor Amersham had a comfortable little practice in Appledore, he also had a managing wife and two daughters.

Lillian, the elder of these two daughters, lay asleep in her little chintz-hung bedroom, her pretty fair face was flushed, and her golden hair lay in becoming disarray over the pillow.

The night before, a most wonderful thing had happened to Lillian: Sir Peter MacLaughton had proposed, and she had accepted him.

The excitement of the episode had prevented sleep from visiting Lillian until the small hours of the morning, and now at six o'clock on this chilly November day she lay in dreamless slumber.

The bedroom door creaking open, did not disturb the sleeper.

Wider and wider opened the door, and the tiny, pink-pyjamad figure of Doctor Amersham's other daughter entered.

The little bare feet pattered across the room, and coming close to the bed, she remained silently gazing at her big, much loved sister.

Seven years ago, when Lillian had been a big girl of fifteen, the Amershams' other child had been born, and Lillian, with her parents had worshipped at the babe's cradle.

"Lillyun, Lillyun," whispered the little girl, then, as her voice did not cause the closed eyes to open, she lifted her hand, and patted the sleeper's cheek.

With a start, Lillian awakened.

The pale sun peeping through the window, lent the mop of curly hair as pink a glow as the pyjamas in which the diminutive figure was clad.

"You naughty pink baby," scolded Lillyun gently, her arms extended, "you will catch your death of cold."

"I am cold, I am shivering," piped the mite, with a cunning bid for sympathy.

"Climb in, and cuddle up and get warm." The expected invitation had been scarcely waited for.

"Were you asleep, Lillyun?" questioned the visitor, as she snuggled down under the blankets, enfolded warmly in a soft embrace.

"You know I was, you naughty imp," smiled Miss Amersham.

"Were you dreaming?"

"No," the answer was given drowsily.

"Had you gone on a journey?" the eager interrogation continued.

"No, I was just sleeping."

"Oh," a deep sigh accompanied this ejaculation, "I go on journeys," she confided.

"Do you?" Lillian was half asleep again; "tell me about them," she suggested, and while the child prattled, she dozed.

"Soon as Nannie puts out the light, I shut my eyes, and something inside me creeps out, and goes floating off; I go quicker and quicker until I do not feel I am flying, but I just get there."

"Where?" asked Lillian; her half somnolent mind was dwelling on the sweet things Peter had said to her last evening.

"Wherever I go to. Sometimes it is to a garden, and, oh, Lillyun, the flowers are so lovely. Sometimes I go and play with a lot of children, they have all creeped out like me," giggled the traveller.

"Naughty children," smiled Lillian absently.

"We are not really naughty," championed the little girl, "because you see our daddies and mummies have not told our flying away part to stay in bed; we are not naughty, are we, Lillyun?" the imperative earnestness of the question was accompanied by a little shake.

"No, baby, of course not," was the hastily given assurance.

"You see all this part of us" (rubbing her hand over her pink pyjamas) "stays in bed, so if anyone comes in they see us lying there, and do not know that part of us has gone. Then we come creeping back, and no one sees us coming." A shriek of delight drove all hope of further sleep from Miss Amersham; she smiled down at her small companion.

"But supposing you were late coming back," she asked, entering into the spirit of the tale.

"Sometimes I am, but Nannie never sees me getting back."

"Are you not afraid to go out at night by yourself?" was the spoken question, while inwardly she wondered if there would be a letter from Peter during the morning.

"I never go by myself," triumphantly.

"Do the fairies call for you?"

"I suppose it must be fairies that help us fly about."

"How lovely." Lillian was trying to decide which dress she would wear. Peter was coming to Saffron House to lunch with her father and mother, and of course with her. The brown velveteen suited her, but perhaps her new coat and skirt. . . .

"I will tell you a secret," generously offered the small maiden, "a little boy always waits for me."

"Good gracious, how exciting; is he a nice little boy?"

"Mm!" the curly head nodded a vigorous assent; "he is bigger than me," she sighed.

"Then he can look after you."

"Oh, he does," with great emphasis.

"Splendid. What is his name?"

"I cannot exackerly remember," the baby brow was puckered in effort.

"Never mind, we will call him Tommy," consoled the grown-up.

"But that is not his name," with swift decisiveness.

"Then Jimmy."

"No."

"Perhaps it is Billy or Jack."

"No. I know it when I meet him, then I forget when I come back here." The big blue eyes were very troubled.

"You must ask the fairies to help you to remember ."

The great eyes became very solemn, a quick suspicion that this beloved sister of hers did not really truly believe, made the little heart heavy. She curled down under the bedclothes, and lay very still.

Lillian decided after all she had better wear her brown velveteen, it certainly suited her fair beauty. Peter had said he liked her in brown.

"Dear Peter," Lillian smiled, and in a sudden access of tenderness bent over and kissed the solemn baby beside her.

CHAPTER XL

Mrs. Amersham was distinctly pleased with her elder daughter.

Lillian had been married to Sir Peter for twelve years now, the marriage had turned out a very happy one, and the Doctor and his wife were well content.

Their younger daughter . . . well, of course she was a sweet child, and they loved her devotedly . . . "she is just as great a dreamer" (was how her mother was writing of her "baby" to Lady MacLaughton) "and as merry and happy as a child, but really, my dear Lillian, she is nineteen, and it is quite time she began to think of marrying and settling down; not that your father or I contemplate losing her with any pleasure, we would miss her terribly, but for her own sake she should marry. We found Peter's cousin quite charming, and he plainly showed his infatuation for the child, it would have been such a nice match for her, but no, although admitting that she liked him very much, she definitely refused to marry him.

"She is still most anxious to become a nurse, I think that is mainly due to the villagers, who declare their cures are owing to her (such a slight on your poor father), although I do not know, I must admit her very touch takes away my dreadful headaches. But a nurse! and she is so pretty, it would be a wicked shame.

"When she comes to stay with you in London, you must speak seriously to her."

This, and much more, Mrs. Amersham had written to her married daughter.

Lillian had read the letter just after she had dressed to attend a dinner party, prior to looking in at Mr. Lynruth's studio, for this was Monday, the evening of which day he reserved for his friends.

These friends! They were gleaned from every class of society; to some this was a most deplorable fact.

Mrs. Ellis . . . her pardon, Mrs. Brendon-Ellis, spoke gravely of . . . "that charming Mr. Lynruth's lack of sense of proportion."

That was after this particular Monday evening; for when

Lady MacLaughton arrived at the beautiful studio in Regent's Park, among the guests, she met Mrs. Brendon-Ellis, the latter was paying her first visit here, and . . .

"Really, oh really," she ejaculated many times during the evening. "I had heard such praise of Mr. Lynruth," she confided to Lady MacLaughton, in a tone that betokened lost faith in the frail word of humanity, "then his picture in the Academy was so sweet, that old Italian nobleman and his wife, 'Mates,' he called it, *so* quaint. Then I met him at Lord Challon's, so thought he must be quite nice, and now . . . well really."

"How has he disappointed you?" asked Lillian amusedly.

"Such queer people. You must not think that I am not broad-minded; my husband and I always attend our servants' balls, and I go quite regularly to talk to my girls at their club in the East End, but to invite such persons into one's own drawing-room, it just is not done."

"It is here," asserted Lillian bluntly.

"Why the man must be a socialist." Mrs. Brendon-Ellis made this announcement in the same tone she would have used had she proclaimed him a pickpocket.

"Rather an individualist, I think," her companion corrected.

This conveyed nothing to the offended lady; by the way, Mrs. Brendon-Ellis could never be mistaken for anything but a lady, even though the fact that her husband was *the* Thomas Brendon-Ellis, frozen-meat millionaire was not known. To see her without the backing of a luxurious motor car, or carriage, to meet her and be unaware that her town address was Park Lane, still one would have instantly recognized her as a "lady." The term "gentlewoman" would have been incorrect. Briefly, she always travelled first class, she could not afford to go third.

"Do you know I have just recognized my own carpenter

here." She leaned forward and conveyed this awful intelligence in a shocked whisper to Lady MacLaughton.

"You mean Mr. Pcal; yes, he is here with his wife; they are perfect dears; have you met them?"

That is actually what Lady MacLaughton said.

Mrs. Brendon-Ellis did the only thing that a lady could do in the circumstances, she held herself erect, raised her brows, pursed up her lips and drew in her chin.

What was society coming to! Of course everyone knew that Lady MacLaughton had been the daughter of a mere country doctor, still as the wife of a baronet, she should know better, indeed she owed it to her husband to learn.

"Poor Sir Peter!" Mrs. Brendon-Ellis sighed at the pathos of it all.

Her own father was an auctioneer, and still lived in Upper Tooting in the house where Mrs. Brendon-Ellis had been born, and married from, when Mr. Brendon-Ellis was still plain Tom Ellis; but these were things best forgotten, the lady herself seemed to have had no difficulty in obliterating her early life completely from her mind, not only these facts, but her widowed father as well had been dropped out of her life.

It was very sad, but necessary, at least to Mrs. Brendon-Ellis, she had sighed when she decided to sacrifice her father, and hyphen on the "Brendon."

The tense silence that reigned between Lady MacLaughton and Mrs. Brendon-Ellis was broken by their host.

"Mrs. Ellis has just recognized your models for 'Mates,'" Lillian informed Mr. Lynruth, smiling mischievously.

"Old Ruipi Peal and his wife Deseré, it was a great pleasure to me to paint them," the artist asserted, glancing affectionately in the direction where the couple alluded to, sat, surrounded by an interested group of (what Mrs. Brendon-Ellis would have termed) "quite nice people."

"I actually thought when I saw your picture, that you had secured the real things." Mrs. Brendon-Ellis was plaintively reproachful.

Mr. Lynruth looked puzzled. . . . "But they are," he said, "if ever there existed a couple truly mated, it is Ruipi and his wife; I hoped I had got the very spirit of them into 'Mates'."

"Oh, dear Mr. Lynruth, your picture is too sweet," Mrs. Brendon-Ellis made haste to console the artist, "only stupid little me, I thought from the clothes you dressed them in, their slender hands and noble bearing, that you had procured genuine Italian aristocrats."

"You were quite right, they are aristocrats in the truest sense of the word," and Lady MacLaughton was wicked enough to laugh aloud in genuine amusement, at the marked disdain that expressed itself in the face of the lady on hearing such a statement.

"Why the man is a mere carpenter. . . ."

Lillian, feeling her patience drawing to an end, turned away quickly, and greeted a small individual, his olive complexion, jet black eyes and hair proclaiming him for the foreigner he very evidently was. Beneath his arm he carried a violin, in his hand the bow.

"Are you going to play, Monsieur Ramon?"

"But yes."

"How splendid."

"But I wish to spik wit' Monsieur Lynrut', for one little word."

"What is it, Ramon?" asked the artist.

Then, while the musician and his host conversed, Mrs. Brendon-Ellis questioned Lady MacLaughton.

"Who is he?"

"The most wonderful violinist in London."

"A professional?"

"He will never accept money for his playing."

"Really! introduce him," for if the Frenchman could provide cheap entertainment, he was worthy of cultivation.

Again the mischief lights danced in Lillian's eyes as she performed the desired introduction.

"I have heard such praise of your music, Monsieur Ramon, you must come and play at my house." Mrs. Brendon-Ellis was the personification of smiling graciousness as she spoke.

"It is mos' kin' of you, Madame." The Frenchman, showed his white teeth in a pleased smile, as he bowed with a sharp click of his heels.

"Then next Thursday afternoon. . . ." began the delighted lady, for on that day she was entertaining.

"Ah, I regret Madame, but in the day time I am much occupied wit' my work."

"Your work?" the lady was puzzled.

"Monsieur Ramon is a hairdresser," and oh, but Lillian looked demure, all excepting her eyes.

"A . . ." Mrs. Brendon-Ellis appeared as though she might faint.

"But yes, I 'ave so nice a shop in the King's Road," said the Frenchman proudly to the lady, whose geniality died a sudden death; her eyes went cold and hard beneath half closed lids, the violinist no longer existed for her.

With a forced smile she rose, and murmuring something about wishing to speak to Lady Chane, moved across the room.

"Madame is displease' wit' me. Yes?" queried Monsieur Ramon in distressed bewilderment.

"Madame is wearing her soul in tight shoes and they are pinching her."

Lady MacLaughton spoke with considerable vim.

"Go and play, we need soothing," Mr. Lynruth smiled kindly at the Frenchman, who obediently trotted off to obey his host.

"*I* need soothing, you mean," corrected Lillian.

"Yes," admitted the artist candidly.

"I am sorry, Ugiso, but that woman is so narrow-minded."

"So are you."

"I am not, I am the broadest-minded person in the world." Lillian was most indignant.

"If you were, you would be tolerant of everyone's views, and that, you certainly are not."

"You make me cross, Ugiso. I was remarking to Peter, the one fault I have to find with you is that you are too saintly to live." Lady MacLaughton spoke quite crossly.

Ugiso Lynruth gave vent to a hearty roar of laughter.

"By Jove, that is a sweeping condemnation," he complained amusedly.

"Peter and I think you are the dearest thing we know, and for your sake I shall be an angel to Mrs. Brendon-Ellis for the rest of the evening."

Lillian smiled as she made the promise.

But Mrs. Brendon-Ellis was no longer in the studio. As she crossed the room to speak to Lady Chane, she had received a most appalling shock.

"Hullo, Milly," a boisterous voice greeted her, and a heavy hand descended on her haughty shoulder. "Well this is a bit of all right; how are you, my dear?"

Mrs. Brendon-Ellis felt her flesh creep, her blood went cold, she drew herself from the detaining hand, and looking at her father with an unrecognizing stare, left the studio with as much haste as dignity would permit.

Lady MacLaughton and Mr. Lynruth were calmly chatting

on various subjects, totally unware of the terrible tragedy that had befallen poor Mrs. Brendon-Ellis.

"Which do you consider your best picture, Ugiso?"

"One I have never shown."

"What is the subject?"

"A girl on the threshold of an open door," he explained briefly.

"What is beyond the door?"

"I do not know."

"Oh, but surely . . ." she began protestingly.

"No, really, I have not the slightest idea, in fact, I have been quite curious myself, as to what it is she sees that makes her so radiantly happy," he spoke very seriously.

"What have you called it?"

"On the threshold."

"On the threshold of what?" demanded Lillian.

"I do not know," he admitted, "I have tried to puzzle out whether it is peace, joy, love, knowledge . . . yes, knowledge," his brow cleared, and he smiled, "of course, she is standing on the threshold of knowledge," he exclaimed, as though he was glad to have freed his mind of some great problem.

"My dear Ugiso, does knowledge make for happiness, for you told me the girl in your picture expressed untold rapture," she argued.

"She does, indeed she does," he protested quickly, then . . . "she appears to me as a little child might, who has overcome the onerous task of learning her letters, so that in the future she will be able to read easily, and learn her lessons with ease," he explained slowly.

"Who was your model?" she asked curiously.

"A dream lady."

"No one you have ever met?" Lady MacLaughton eyed him keenly.

"Not in my waking moments," he assured her.

"You . . . you incorrigible artist," she scolded goodnaturedly. Then . . . "Peter wants to know if you will play golf with him on Wednesday," she said.

"With pleasure," Ugiso Lynruth spoke enthusiastically, "by Jove, a day on the links will do me no end of good; we are about even there, but I can lick old Peter hollow at tennis," he bragged.

Then, as Monsieur Ramon began to play, they fell silent.

No one stirred or spoke until the plaintive melody was finished.

CHAPTER XLI

Mindful of the appeal in her mother's letter, Lady MacLaughton intended speaking seriously to her sister on the grave question of marriage; but a whole week had passed since Miss Amersham's arrival in London, without the desired opportunity presenting itself.

Now as she stood at the door of her own ball-room watching the informal gathering of young people, among whom her radiant sister danced incessantly, she turned to her husband, who loitered near.

"I do wish she would marry your cousin Clifford," she sighed.

"There is lots of time, she is happy as she is, best leave her alone," advised Sir Peter.

"Happy," echoed his wife, "she is the happiest being I know, and she has the blessed gift of conveying that feeling to everyone with whom she comes in contact; the children adore her, the very servants worship her."

"A jolly good-looking girl," commented the man, gazing admiringly at his slim sister-in-law, who passing them at that moment in the arms of as excellent a dancer as herself, sent them a smile full of the joy of living.

"I shall speak to her to-night." Lady MacLaughton nodded her head determinedly.

It was well after midnight when she put this resolve into execution. Clad in a dressing-gown, she knocked at her young relative's door.

"Oh, Lillian, how nice of you; come in and let us have a long yarn," was the way Lady MacLaughton was greeted.

"Are you enjoying yourself?" she asked her guest, sinking into a chair before the fire, and looking admiringly at the picture before her, that of a slender girl clad in a white, fur-trimmed dressing-gown, thick masses of red gold hair waving free to well below her waist, a skin of transparent whiteness, and great dark blue eyes in which shone the very soul of happiness.

"I am having a wonderful time, thanks to you and Peter," declared the girl, sinking on to a stool at her elder sister's feet.

Then they fell to discussing Appledore and the people of the village. The talk drifted to many subjects, that night's dance was touched on. Then . . .

"I noticed you dancing with Clifford this evening," remarked Lady MacLaughton.

"Yes, he dances divinely."

"He is such a dear, Peter and I are very fond of him," was the matron's next, wily remark.

"So am I," was the enthusiastic agreement, "he is charming."

"He apparently finds you something more than charming." This was said with much significance.

"Has he told you?" quickly.

"That he wants to marry you? Yes."

"Poor Clifford." The dark blue eyes looked pensively into the fire.

"But if you like him . . ."

"I could never marry him," swiftly, convincingly the girl interrupted.

"You admit you like him," pleaded Lady MacLaughton.

"Like, yes."

"He has such sterling qualities, you would grow to love him in time."

"One does not grow to love anybody, not in that way, Lillian dearest; love is either there, or not there, and no amount of trying will make it come."

"How do you know?"

"I just know," with complete disdain of logic.

"But you must marry some day."

"Perhaps."

With praiseworthy insistence Lady MacLaughton pleaded the cause of her husband's cousin.

"You are an obstinate monkey, and I am going to bed," at last she declared, rising to her feet, "Good-night, sleep well."

"Good-night, Lillian; I am sorry about Clifford, you are not cross, are you," and two slender arms crept round the elder woman's neck.

"No, you darling, I never could be really cross with you. Do you remember when you were a tiny mite, and used to creep into my bed, and tell me wonderful tales of your fairy journeys?"

"Yes, indeed, but they were not fairy journeys."

"What were they then?"

"I do not know, but I love them."

"You have surely outgrown all that childish nonsense, you silly little thing?" queried Lillian laughingly.

"Indeed I have not."

"What, do you still go careering off away from your body after you have gone to bed?"

A nod of assent answered her.

"And the little boy whose name you could never remember?"

"I still cannot remember it, but he is grown up now."

"What an imagination you have," and both sisters laughed, as they kissed one another an affectionate goodnight.

"I have done my best, Peter," Lady MacLaughton confided later to her husband, "but I am afraid poor Clifford's case is hopeless. I must try and marry her to someone though."

With this end in view, her Ladyship became indefatigable in both attending, and giving entertainments, into which her guest entered with whole-hearted enjoyment.

It was about this time that Mr. Lynruth received a visitor.

"Miss Amersham," announced the servant.

Turning quickly, the artist looked at the girl who stood in the open doorway.

The servant disappeared noiselessly, leaving these two alone.

The second that elapsed before either spoke might have been eternity.

The soundless messages that rushed from one to the other were untranslatable.

Then he advanced, and taking her hand in greeting, drew her into the studios, and closed the door.

It may have been, conventional words passed between them. She may have explained that she had come to meet her sister there.

They spoke very little. Then . . .

"Come and I will show you my picture," he invited.

She followed him to a corner of the long room. Going to an easel on which stood a large canvas, Mr. Lynruth pulled back the velvet curtain that covered it.

The smile in the girl's eyes deepened, as she gazed long and searchingly at the picture.

"On the threshold," lowly, slowly, she read the inscription below it.

"Is that the way you saw me?" she asked.

"Yes. What is it you see through that door that makes you so happy?" he inquired.

"Another door, I think," and they both laughed aloud.

"Tell me, what *is* your name?" There came a little puzzled frown to her brow, as though she should have known the answer without need of a question.

"Ugiso," he told her.

"Of course. I never could remember," and again they laughed.

"You are? . . ." he paused.

"Rhoea," she supplied quickly.

"Rhoea," he echoed; "yes, that is right. Come and sit down, I have so much to say to you," he added.

"I knew I would meet you some day." She extended her hand impulsively as she spoke.

His own hands covered hers warmly.

"Yes, we had to meet," he agreed very gravely; "people who truly love always do," and looking into one another's eyes they smiled happily, understandingly.

THE END

THIS EXCLUSIVE EDITION
has been typeset for The Reincarnation Library
in Garamond #3,
and printed by offset lithography
on archival quality paper at
Cushing-Malloy, Inc.

The text and end-papers are acid-free and meet
or surpass all guidelines established by
the Council of Library Resources
and the American National
Standards Institute™.

Design by Jerry Kelly.